THAT SHIP HAS A PHAT ASS

THAT SHIP HAS A PHAT ASS

UNLIKELY BOUNTYHUNTERS™ BOOK 3

MICHAEL TODD

DISRUPTIVE IMAGINATION®

LMBPN Publishing
PMB 196, 2540 South Maryland Pkwy
Las Vegas, NV 89109

Version 1.00, July 2021
eBook ISBN: 978-1-64971-876-1
Print ISBN: 978-1-64971-877-8

THE THAT SHIP HAS A PHAT ASS TEAM

Thanks to our Beta Team:
John Ashmore, Kelly O'Donnell, Rachel Beckford

JIT Readers

Deb Mader
Jackey Hankard-Brodie
Dorothy Lloyd
Debi Sateren
Zacc Pelter
Peter Manis
Paul Westman

Editor
Skyhunter Editing Team

DEDICATION

To Family, Friends and
Those Who Love
to Read.
May We All Enjoy Grace
to Live the Life We Are
Called.

— Michael

CHAPTER ONE

"'Let's make a little more money,' she said. 'Come out and spend Christmas in L.A.,' she said. Two Johns listening to two women making such innocent-sounding requests."

"What are you babbling on about?" Hix grabbed his arm and slid them both around a corner, throwing both of their aims off as they fired behind them.

"Just philosophizing about how guys will do anything a cute chick asks them to."

Jo dropped a dead battery out of his pistol and into a pocket, then jacked in a fresh one as Hix took in the compliment.

"So I've been upgraded from a blue chick to a cute chick?" She kissed his cheek for luck and Jo almost passed out from the pheromones when her breasts made contact the same time her lips did.

"Kiss me or kill me. Either way, I'm gonna be dead in a minute if we can't put together an exit strategy."

Hix pulled a second gun from one of her thigh holsters,

and they both returned fire at the dozen men chasing after them.

"Okay, so I was wrong. I thought this would be an easy-in, easy-out job."

"Apology accepted. It's not like this is our first bounty hunting gig that went sideways."

John and Meehix. The NutBusters bounty-hunting duo was back in action as Jo and Hix, and neither one of them was having anything resembling a good time at the moment.

"How many did you count?"

"A dozen, give or take one or ten," Hix pulled a smoke-em grenade from part of her arsenal pack and looked across the small indoor courtyard. "I see two hallways. Do we go straight or to the right?"

"The right seems easiest. We can follow the wall."

Hix tossed the smoke-em around the corner back toward their pursuers, then both closed their eyes and made a run for it. The smoke-em didn't cause any breathing problems, but it stung like hell if you weren't wearing goggles. Keeping to the right and feeling their way along the wall, they made the hallway and wiped any residue off their faces.

Eyes now open, they had about ten seconds until the smoke cleared behind them. Sometimes you needed to stand and fight. Sometimes you needed to run like hell. They ran.

The Freeland Corporate Office building was a huge monstrosity of an architectural disaster. Hix and Jo, just chilling as Meehix and John, didn't know it when they'd taken the job. Even their partner, the notorious Chuckie N, hadn't researched it very thoroughly.

The three of them had been sitting around their home base office, counting up the money they'd made from their last job, one that had ended up being *very* profitable. They were trying to decide if they ever needed to work another day in their lives or should they buy a small cozy moon and chill out.

Just chilling out was in none of their DNA, so when Meehix had found a Crec Alert for an easy bounty hunting gig that paid way more than it should have, she brought it to her partners' attention.

Their last job was to rescue a demon's succubus niece who'd been kidnapped, crated, and shipped to an undisclosed location.

This job was simply to go to the Freeland Corporate Office and bring in an accountant who'd *mismanaged* some money from his last employer. The accountant still had to earn a living while giving the funds a chance to cool down, so he'd hired into Freeland for a few months.

The Crec Alert had his name as Olee McDeal and even gave his office location on the third floor of the Freeland building

"C'mon guys," Meehix had said on that lazy afternoon. "Look at the pay to bring in an accountant in hiding."

John and Chuckie looked over her shoulder as she brought up the details. Being too rich for words did lend itself to a certain amount of boredom, and this job looked like a nice cure for an itch they all felt but couldn't scratch.

The money looked so easy that they didn't dig any deeper. If they *had* dug a little deeper, they would have learned that Freeland Corp. was one of Victor Vikrellion's enterprises and it was a setup.

Victor knew that two bounty hunters had killed his little brother. One of them was a tall Kdackan male. The other was a blue chick. He also suspected they were the same duo who'd invaded his home and set off a whole chain of events that he was still dealing with. He wanted them more than he'd ever wanted anything.

There was no accountant named Olee McDeal, but there was such a high bounty placed on his head that any bounty hunter who saw the Crec Alert wouldn't be able to resist going after him. Victor had laid his trap.

There was only one entrance to the Freeland building. He had security keeping a close eye out and intercepting any bounty hunters who weren't a tall Kdackan male or a bluesy from entering. Victor had his team stationed inside, ready to bring the two back to him and the justice he had prepared for them.

Jo and Hix were running again. *Easy-in, easy-out* meant they hadn't come fully weaponed-up.

Other than the first shootout, when it was only them and the give or take a dozen, no one was shooting because there were too many day-to-day workers doing their jobs. That didn't mean that they weren't still under attack. They elbowed open a door and discovered they were running through a cafeteria.

It was lunchtime, and the building's various workers were sitting at the tables as Jo and Hix crashed in.

"Duck and cover!" Jo shouted and upended any table within his reach.

Hix slapped the loaded trays of those waiting in line

to pay.

Chaos and distraction were what they were going for to slow their pursuers.

Jo slipped on a pile of what looked like blue mashed potatoes and cursed.

"Those are frimlies, dimpwad," Hix shouted at him.

Jo scooped up a handful and stuffed them in his mouth. He loved frimlies. He just didn't recognize them scattered on a floor.

They burst through the kitchen doors and yelled apologies to the cooks. The shouts of their pursuers rang out behind them as they exited out the back door and raced down another hallway. They pounded up a flight of stairs, but not before Jo wiped some frimlies from his mouth and tossed them toward the walls heading down, hoping to throw off those who were after them and buy a little time.

One floor up, they emerged on the office level and ran to a nondescript room where they could hide while figuring out their next move.

Five minutes of silence later, Hix heard Jo utter, "No fucking way."

"Will you please keep your fucking voice down?"

Jo was sitting at a desk, pulling up files on a computer. He motioned for Hix to join him, which she did, both of them keeping guns on the door.

"There's no accountant named Olee McDeal on the payroll." He tried to keep his voice down.

"We were set up?"

"That's my guess."

"By who?"

"Not important." Jo pulled up another screen. "I don't

know what else Freeland Corp. does, but tell me what that looks like in the basement."

Hix took a good long look. "Prison cells."

Jo had pulled up the building's architectural design, trying to figure out the best path to freedom, but there was no way they didn't recognize the layout of a prison wing.

They'd met in one. They'd attacked another one and freed the occupants.

Jo had done some quick digging, which they had neglected to do before signing on, and pulled up another page.

"No fucking way." Hix read the name of the head of Freeland Corp. *Victor Vikrellion*. "So now we know who set us up."

"We also know," Jo scrolled back to the prison layout, "that those aren't just prisoners held down there."

"They're slaves." Hix had seen enough. They both knew what they had to do next. Jo scrolled through more of the building's design plans as they tried to figure out the best way to make it to the basement.

"We should have come better armed. How much charge you got left, Jo?"

"Enough to last through lunch, as long as we don't linger over dessert."

"Scroll back," Hix commanded. "There! That's a chemical lab."

"Gotta have a lot of weird shit in it, right?"

"Time to improvise." She double-checked her remaining charge "Lab first. Prison second."

They peeked out the door. Either their pursuers had given up or had gotten lost. They made a break for it and headed toward a different stairwell entrance on the opposite side of the large room.

Shots rang out when they were partway there, causing the workers in cubicles to duck as the two strangers ran through. Their pursuers had found them and hadn't given up.

"Heads down! Heads down!" Jo shouted as they rushed toward the side door and made it to the flight of stairs.

The lab was one floor down. Gunshots ricocheted behind them in the stairwell as they burst into what should have been the chem lab and discovered that the floor had undergone remodeling since the architects had drawn the original designs.

The room they entered seemed to be some kind of animal research lab. Cages lined the walls, and several sat on a long table in the center. Jo had seen and met many aliens since he first rescued Hix but had never seen any animals or pets. He tried to take in the vast assortment in the cages and make sense of what they were, but a tour would have to wait for another time.

"Where's the chemical lab?" Jo shouted at a three-armed white-coated technician.

Jo and Hix didn't look like they were in the mood for a long conversation so the tech pointed at a door on the other end of the room.

"Through the door and right across the hallway."

"How do you tell the workers from the animals?" Jo had to know.

"The animals are the ones in the cages."

"Are you sure?"

The gunfire had ceased, but they heard footsteps

rushing on the stairs now.

"Not the time for this discussion, Jo. Open as many cages as you can and let's get out of here."

Hix took the left side. Jo took the right, and between them, they managed to set free nearly two dozen species before they hit the door and rushed across the hallway.

The five lab-coated technicians freaked out as the room suddenly filled with *honks* and *squeaks* and *EEEOOOWAAs*. Jo could have sworn he heard a couple of *yippees* thrown in too. Every second counted, and they'd bought themselves at least thirty of them as their pursuers had to fight their way through a large recently released menagerie.

They burst into the chemical lab, found a half-dozen technicians, and pulled their guns.

"No time for questions!" Jo shouted. "What's the most dangerous chemical you have?'

"Are you terrorists?" came a terrified response from one of the techs.

"What did I say about questions!"

"No," Hix tried to calm them down because the big scary-looking dude had, indeed, scared them. "We're freedom fighters. No one is going to get hurt. Just show us the most dangerous, and we'll all be on our way."

"The orange." The technician pointed at a glass jar with a heavy seal. "It's still in its experimental stage, but its fumes are deadly to at least eighty-five species. We're trying to get it up to a hundred before we give it to the military."

Jo grabbed it and held it high as a dozen armed men came storming in after them.

"Tell them what you just told us!"

The technician obeyed.

"Guys," Jo explained as their pursuers lowered their guns. "You got us outnumbered. So Hix and I got nothing to lose by killing us all. If this jar hits the floor, everyone dies."

The guns remained lowered.

"You can feel free to follow if you want, but we're heading for the basement."

Hix led the way with Jo walking backward behind her, holding the jar out for the dozen following behind them to see. It wasn't easy to back down the steps, but Jo managed to make it.

"I don't remember. Do we turn right or left?" Hix asked when they'd reached the basement level.

"Left. I mean right. Your right, my left."

Right, they headed. Shortly, they found the guard station—a secured room with a door and a window built into the side facing the hallway. A metal gate blocked the hallway and appeared to lead to maybe twenty cells at a glance.

"Looks like a familiar setup." Jo agreed with Hix's assessment.

"Shoot the glass out in the door if they won't open it." Hix agreed with Jo's advice and held up her gun for the two guards inside to see.

From inside the station, the guards saw one blue chick with a gun, one big guy behind her facing another dozen heavily armed men, probably giving them their orders on how to attack. The door *clicked* open. Jo handed Hix the toxic jar so she could hold the pursuers back as he went inside and found the controls to open the cells.

"We're not here to hurt you," Jo informed the guards, who didn't seem like they were going to put up much of a fight. "We're here to free the slaves. Open the doors."

There were eighteen buttons. Seventeen were black, and one red. One of the guards opened the gate to the hallway.

He then hit all of the other buttons except the red one. The cell doors opened down the row, and the prisoners ran out and through anyone in the hallway, not caring whether they had guns or not. It was a prison break, and they were breaking.

Jo noticed that there was one door at the end of the cellblock that hadn't opened. *Must be someone important.* He also noticed the guard. Vranlict, he thought his badge read.

"Vranlict, why is the one door still closed and why haven't you hit the red button?"

"You don't want the last door to open. We never touch the red button."

Jo put his hand on the button. "Why is that?"

"Because bad things will happen."

The guard sounded sincere and sincerely scared. Jo decided not to push the red button and was about to take his hand off it when Hix opened the guard station door. "The slaves are running, and we gotta go."

Her bump caused him to push the button accidentally. Jo didn't have a view of the hallway, other than the chaos directly outside the guards' window where slaves tussled with their pursuers. No guards had fired shots because Hix still held the orange jar of toxicity, but that didn't mean that punches and kicks and a bite or two didn't happen.

Hix, however, *did* have a view toward the end of the

prison cells when the last door opened. She grabbed Jo's arm and jerked him into the hallway. "We *really* gotta go now."

To Jo's eyes, it looked like a horned toad from back home in New Mexico. He also knew that back home, it would technically be a lizard, not a toad, but semantics didn't seem important.

Coming down from the end of the cell row, a step here, a hop there, came a scaly green and blue lizard. Five horns stood out from its head, one of them directly in front and facing forward. Its tail seemed to have half a dozen spikes at the tip. All four of its feet sported three five-inch claws. It paused as a red tongue lashed out at nothing, then it licked its lips and yawned.

It would have looked interesting if Jo had seen one in a zoo or stumbled across one in the desert, but this one was seven feet tall, three feet wide, and when it yawned, it exposed a double-row of sharp yellow teeth.

Shots rang out. Everyone cast petty agendas aside because they all now had one common enemy. The main effect of the blasts caused it to blink rapidly and open its gaping mouth again. Three steps and one long leap later, it was at the open gate, trying to figure out which of the too-scared-to-run attackers it was going to pounce on.

Jo grabbed the toxic orange jar from Hix, shoved her down, and commanded everyone,

"FIRE AGAIN!" He hit the floor as shots rained out over his head.

The effect, again, was to cause it to blink several times as the bullets bounced off its scaly covering. Jo took that moment to unseal the jar, keeping the lid on but loose.

When the creature followed its blinks with another yawn, Jo threw the jar right into its gaping mouth.

It was a perfect throw. He could see the lid come off as it entered and nicked a tooth, shattering the glass as it ended up in its throat. The creature blinked again, swallowed, and took a short, stumbling step backward.

"Nice toss, Jo," Hix said as she and Jo regained their feet and hustled everyone back to the stairway, not caring to wait and watch the beast die a quick and probably painful death. Even its death throes, the claws and tail could still do some serious damage.

Slaves, guards, and pursuers had all made it safely into the stairwell. Hix and Jo paused at the door to take one last look back.

"You do realize," she whispered, "that without the orange goop, we're now hopelessly outnumbered and outgunned."

"I do now. Any thoughts?"

Before Hix could share her thoughts, the creature let out a painful roar, then belched, followed by a long leap forward.

"RUN!"

No one needed Jo's advice on that one as feet pounded their way up the stairs. As the beast appeared in the doorway, one of his previous attackers tossed Jo a hand grenade.

"Pin's already pulled. Five seconds!" a voice hollered down.

Jo counted to three and tossed.

CHAPTER TWO

"You're not an easy man to track down, Trexit."

"That's because my job is to be the tracker, not the trac-kee, Captain Prooshevekk. Which do you prefer to do first? Eat, or talk business?"

"I haven't had much of an appetite lately," the Blavarian captain of one of the deadliest ships in the dreadnought line replied.

"Ahh, yes. I believe the offending quote is, 'shove it up your ass and suck on a big plate of veonk spheres while a Quoteggian female busts a nut on your face and eats it, so go fuck yourself.' Do I have that correct?"

"Close enough...drinks first." The captain sighed. "Maybe you can help me regain my appetite."

"That is my intention. The food here is the best one can find on Space Station L-222, and it would be a shame for you to pass it up."

Trexit summoned their waitress and ordered two Noreliuns, warmed, not chilled. The perfect drink to take the edge off. The drinks came, and Trexit pulled a knife and threw it at a corner in the ceiling behind the captain. Everyone turned to look at the blade, still quivering high in the wall, and he took that moment to slip a fast-dissolving tablet into the captain's drink before apologizing to everyone in the room.

"Sorry, I thought I saw a splindler."

Everyone nodded their acceptance. Splindlers were the bane of many restaurants' health ratings, crawling around on the ceiling and suddenly dropping onto the plates of whatever meal the diners were trying to enjoy.

"Nasty little fucks," Captain Prooshevekk returned his attention to his drinking, and if everything went well and he regained his appetite, dinner companion.

It was a simple Noxit that Trexit had spiked the captain's drink with. Blavarians were notorious for their temper, and "just chill dude" was not a concept they were familiar with, so he'd wanted to help the edge drift a little farther into the distance so they could get down to business.

"All right, you found me." Trexit had savored his first sip of the Noreliun and was enjoying the warmth as it flowed through his body. "Not that I've been too hard to find since I've been hanging out here for the last fourteen rotations, waiting for some reinforcements to arrive."

"Tough catch you're after?" Prooshevekk thought it would be nice to hear of someone else's woes for a bit. Might make him feel better about his.

"More tricky than tough." Trexit had come to admire the pair. "They're either extremely ballsy, brave, or lucky. Here one minute, somewhere else the next. I just want enough reinforcements to cut off their next escape. I hate to admit it," he silently added, *one professional to another,* "but they've managed to stay one step ahead of me so far. I don't know where they are, but I know where they're eventually going to be, which is why I'm waiting."

"Pisses ya off, don't it?"

Everything pisses a Blavarian off, but the Notix is kicking in.

"So give me more details. All I know so far, which I have only picked up from rumors, is that a no-name piss-head told you off and got away with it."

"That's just it. A no-name got away with it. As you said, you've heard the rumors. Half the known galaxy has heard. I'm the captain of a dreadnought! I've worked hard to earn my commission and my reputation."

"Yes, you have." Trexit sipped again as the captain took a larger drink. "One of the reasons I agreed to meet with you was because of your sterling reputation."

"My reputation is now for shit! Wherever I go, do I hear, 'there goes the dreadnought captain who once took on three destroyers and left no survivors?' No. Do I hear, 'there goes the dreadnought captain who once stopped a rebellion on Lenoriana by capturing the leader and single-handedly brought him and his followers to a swift justice?' No. All I hear, although no one says it to my face, is 'there goes the dreadnought captain that a no-name grunt once told to *fuck off,* and he let the grunt get away!'"

Maybe Trexit had overestimated Blavarians' tolerance for Notix.

Prooshevekk lowered his voice and leaned closer over the table.

"I want the little fucker. I want to stick one of my dreadnought's forward laser cannons up his ass and squeeze the trigger, oh, so nice, so gently, so slowly, that anyone within fifty click-meters will run and duck for cover because they won't know if it'll be his brains, his guts, or his shit flying their way once I fire."

"Ahh. I'm beginning to understand." *I'm about to sign a new client.* "You want him, but as the captain of a dreadnought, you can't run off on a personal mission of revenge."

"As much as I'd like to, the answer is no. I can't."

Trexit now understood why the captain was, indeed, in a fix. Notix was a fast-acting medication that wore off quickly, so he knew the captain would be back to his normal not-quite-easy-going self any minute and would have the munchies, one of the side effects.

"I believe that I can help you out, Captain."

Trexit flagged down the waitress again and ordered the largest tray of munchies on the menu, two more warm Noreliuns, and a pitcher of water. The water came first. She served the Noreliuns when she brought out the food.

"What can you tell me about the little fucker?" Trexit asked after he'd placed the order.

"Not a goddam thing," the captain admitted.

"That doesn't give me much to go on now, does it?" Trexit was a professional and prided himself on not taking anyone's money to go chasing after some fool's errand.

"All I know is that while we were on another mission, we received an emergency request to intercept a ship and bring back a recent escapee."

"The escapee's first name was Meehixiheem, a Dolurulodan." The captain pulled out a well-worn photo of the transmission and set it on the table. "That's all the info I have. Tell me straight and tell me no, if you have to, and I'll pay for the meal and be on my way and thank you for your time."

Trexit looked at the photo. It didn't do the blue chick justice. He then pulled out and laid down a photo from the security cameras of the Tri-2-Beatum Casino's security cameras that he'd paid a pretty penny for.

"Do you see any resemblance?"

Captain Prooshevekk took a good long look and realized that although this wasn't *the* day he'd been dreaming of, he now had it in his sights.

"And the asshole with her?"

"Do the words *fuck you* ring any bells?" Trexit gave that a moment to sink in before continuing. "These two have been partners in crime ever since they first crossed my path, so you give me your best guess."

Prooshevekk took another close look at the pair in Trexit's photo and felt his appetite returning.

"Partners now."

"Partners then," Trexit finished the sentence for him.

"You're already on their trail?"

"That I am, already hired by a previous client. You're not the only one that these two have pissed off. I can't guarantee that you'll be the one to put an end to him, but I can assure you that you can be there to watch, and it will be a lot more painful than a cannon up his ass. Will that work for you?"

The food arrived, and they both dug in.

Dinner and dessert finished—*damn, Blavarians can eat*—Trexit charged the meal to his room's account, which was being paid for by Victor as he tracked down Frelo's killer.

Prooshevekk pulled out his M-lick. "How much?"

"It might take two days. It might take twenty. I don't know when the asshole and the bitch will return." Trexit took the last sip of his Noreliun. "Normally, I charge hourly and expenses. For you, my Blavarian friend, I'll charge a flat rate."

He wrote down the price on a napkin and passed it over.

"I'll be invited to the hopefully painful execution and death?"

Trexit nodded. Two minutes later the money showed up in his account, and they parted as two best friends.

After watching the Blavarian leave, Trexit made his way toward the door. He took the time to move a chair over and pulled his knife out of the wall high in the corner.

"Charge the repairs to my room."

When Trexit got back to his room, now having two jobs tracking down the same pair of troublemakers, he fired up his trans-comm and found a message waiting for him.

Backup not available. Subjects already set up in a trap. May not need your services after all. Expenses still being paid. Wait for further instructions.

Will wait. Trexit hit "Send."

No point in wasting extra words when he knew damn well that whatever trap Lazy Buff and Victor had set up, chances were that the duo would manage to find a way out of it and he would be waiting. Eventually, the twosome would return to L-222. Sooner or later, Lazy Buff and

Victor would learn that sending the backup he'd requested earlier would be their best option.

If they didn't, he would charge Captain Prooshevekk an extra fee to be able to fire his laser canons up the asses of both people who embarrassed him personally. Win-win, either way.

He called the concierge and requested a companion for the night. Thought better of it and asked for three. Trexit had a good day.

The concierge placed a call to the casino. An hour later, Trexit wished he had six hands because the two he *did* have were full. *What's a poor tracker to do?*

The hand grenade went off and slowed the horned-toad beast from hell down for a moment. It was a short moment. Sounds of fighting came from the stairs above as Jo's and Hix's pursuers struggled with the freed slaves to be the first ones out of the staircase and away from the beast.

Having recovered from the grenade, the beast hungrily eyed Jo and Hix and leapt, mouth wide open at the same time that one of their pursuers tumbled down over their heads and directly into its mouth.

There was a *crunching* sound and a scream. Doors slammed open up above, and no one, including Jo and Hix, felt a moment of cowardice for running like hell.

They reached the stairway door as an alarm was sounding. A panicking crowd was headed one way for the exits. Hix and Jo headed in the opposite direction. They hated crowds.

Jo hit the comm-stick that they never left home without.

"Where are you, Ship?"

"Just hovering and hanging out. Where do you want me to be, John?"

"Do you see a crowd rushing out of the building?"

"Hard to miss."

"Meet us on the opposite side and lower the ladder!"

It wasn't the first time they'd used that routine. Doors had their uses, but when chaos reigned, then bullets through windows were often the best option. They had their guns out and ran down the opposite hallway, firing at the window that had freedom and safety on the other side.

Leaping through it, they tumbled and came up running, grabbing hold of the ladder they knew would be waiting. Shippewa rose quickly enough that they left the beast who'd followed them down and out through the window snapping at the air.

"He's faster than he looks." Jo looked down at the snapping jaws.

"Shall I come lower so your new pet can join us?"

"Would you be kind enough to carry us up to the roof so we can come aboard, somewhere other than in midair?"

Ship obliged, and two minutes later they'd boarded, retracted the ladder, and headed for the cockpit. Ship was only programmed for two hours of self-pilot and was nearing the end of that allotment.

Meehix took the pilot's seat, slipped her hands into the controls, and lifted off, getting her bearings as John took the shotgun seat.

"Don't say it, John. I admit I might have been wrong about the *easy money* job."

Before you two take the time to apologize to each other and say, *no, no, it was my fault*, I need to bring your attention to the three ships coming at us. I don't believe their intentions are kind, and there's no time for me to disguise myself as an innocent cloud.

"Show 'em how to do it, partner," John buckled up.

That was all the acceptance of her apology she needed.

I'm a wild goose, and you're gonna lose this chase!

Meehix loved to fly and had more than a little chip on her shoulders that earlier in her life, no one ever trusted her at the controls. She was in full control now!

She'd had the time during their earlier adventures to learn Shippewa's weapons potential, and as she cranked Ship up into a straight, full-thrust vertical leap, she released two missile decoys that would keep them safe from incoming fire.

The ships attacking them watched as a burst of flames shortly followed.

You ain't seen nothing yet!

Meehix reversed course and headed straight down between two of the ships. They fired their heat-seeking missiles at her but missed her and hit each other's ship, with the result of them both bursting into flames and disintegrating before they had the chance to hit the ground.

Two down, one to go.

There ended up being no one to go.

The ships who'd been attacking them were simply mercenary backups, hired by Victor Vikrellion. The same mob boss and slave owner who'd set them up on this mission that hadn't quite gone according to his plan.

The mercenary in the third fighter made the wise decision to "fuck it" and booked it out of there.

Satisfied with the carnage she'd left in her wake, Meehix turned to John.

"Can we go home now?"

John yawned and closed his eyes. "Are we there yet? I have to pee. I'm hungry. Mom, he's looking at me. He started it."

"Help me out here, Ship."

"I suspect that he might have taken a vacation drive with Gage's family more than once."

"Oh."

John smiled. Meehix was behind the controls, and he dropped off to sleep, wondering how old Gage-O was doing.

Meehix used three different galactic Gates to get back home. Only two were necessary if you were flying direct, but she wanted to make sure that no one had been able to follow them. Safely back and docked in their reserved space on L-222, they both wanted to take a minute to relax before heading home to find out what kind of trouble their partner, Chuckie N, had lined up for them next.

"So. You're not mad at me for getting us into that last clusterfuck?"

John stretched. "You also got us out of it. I call that debt-even."

"Speaking of debts." Meehix had pulled out her tablet. "While we were out gallivanting, Chuckie found the highest bidder for the identity card you gave me." She smiled.

"Are you going to make me guess or torture me with suspense?"

"How does one-point-two mil sound?"

"It sounds like you're not going to be poverty-stricken anytime soon."

They'd set up a joint-access account. One under her number and one under his. They had free access to each other's, but John knew that having control over something meant a lot to someone who was recently declared a non-sentient property and had been living, technically speaking, as John's slave.

"Pushing half a mil your way."

"That's not quite a fifty-fifty split." John wasn't concerned. He was curious.

"Once we get settled back in, I'm going to do some serious shopping." There was her crooked-assed irresistible smile.

"Under whose name will it be?" John was both looking forward to and fearing her reaction when she found out.

Chuckie had been left in charge of setting up her new identity, using her card, and had clued John in to what he was going to go with before they'd set off on their fools' errand.

"We'll keep her first name," the evil genius had told him, "because no one needs to learn two names at once."

"So she'll only have to get used to her new last name?"

"Correct."

"Give me a clue."

Chuckie had smiled. "Let's just say that whatever happens in the future, and no matter how fucked up things get, she'll never be able to forget us."

Meehix hit the page and found her new identity.

"I'm now *Meehixiheem JoNorris?*"

"We wanted to make sure you'd always remember us."

As a wrestler and rugby player in high school back on earth, John had received his share of blows, but nothing had ever matched the impact to his cheek that Meehix now gave him with her lips.

"I'll go collect our bags." She headed to the cargo area before anyone could see the tears that were about to collect on her cheeks.

"Are you okay, John?" Ship asked while Meehix was busy in the back.

"Yeah, Ship. I'm fine."

"I only ask because your hand hasn't moved from your cheek. Is there pain that I am not aware of involved with kisses?"

"Define pain."

"It looked like you blacked out."

"Let's just call it an unexpected glitch, and I had to do a system reboot."

"Ahh. Been there, done that."

Meehix returned to the cockpit and tossed John his bag.

"I took the liberty of contacting the company, and your auto-driver is waiting."

"Thanks, Ship." Meehix smiled up at the screen and led the way out. John held back a moment, looked at the screen, and shrugged.

"**Women**," was Ship's only response. John hoisted his bag and followed his partner.

They rode in silence, each lost in their thoughts until the auto-driver dropped them off at the home and office they shared with Chuckie N. Reaching the front door, they discovered that the old door was no longer there.

A stylish yet intimidating metal replacement with no doorknobs had replaced it. A smooth touch-pad with no instructions alongside it had replaced the doorbell.

"Chuckie's been busy in our absence. Any suggestions?"

Meehix was tired. Instead of taking the time to contemplate and respond to John's question, she slapped her palm on the touch-pad, resulting in an AI voice asking a question from somewhere up above.

"What is the chief export of Chuck Norris?"

"This one's all yours, John." She took a step back.

"Pain," John answered with no hesitation.

Meehix shook her head. *Boys.*

"Approved," came the voice from somewhere above, as if they had gained God's approval to enter. The door swung open.

They carried their bags inside with no small amount of annoyance. It was, after all, their home too, and neither one thought they needed anyone's permission to enter.

Setting their bags down on the front office floor, they found Chuckie hustling over from the seat behind his desk to greet them both with a smile.

John swept him up and twirled him around. Chuckie was only half John's size, and being a little sensitive about his height, would have been pissed if anyone else had done that to him. John set him down, and Chuckie bowed to Meehix.

"Welcome home, Meehix."

"Don't you mean, welcome home Ms. JoNorris?"

"She noticed, did she?" Chuckie turned to John.

"Once we got back and docked, she took a moment to check the credit account and her new name."

"How'd she take to her new surname?" Chuckie scooted behind John to avoid any wrath that might be coming his way.

"I'm trying to decide between love and shooting you both."

"Everyone voting for love, raise their hands." John hoped for the best as Chuckie joined him with both hands raised high.

Meehix slowly approached Chuckie with pure menace in her eyes. Chuckie quickly lowered his hands to protect his balls. He'd seen Meehix deliver a swift kick before. She grabbed hold of the little man's head and planted a big old smooch on top of it.

Chuckie managed to stumble his way back to the seat behind his desk. *I'll never wash my hair again.*

Meehix and John took their seats to give the emotions in the room time enough to settle down.

"The job was a bust, Chuckie," John started.

"Yeah. The whole thing was a *my bad,*" Meehix admitted.

"The whole thing was a setup," John continued the story. "The building complex, and everything in it, is owned by one Victor Vikrellion."

They gave Chuckie a moment to take that in.

"So…" once Chuckie took less than a moment to put it

all together, "You're saying that he didn't take kindly to us killing his brother, invading his home, freeing his slaves, and robbing him blind, and set up the Crec Alert to draw you in?"

"A dozen mercs waited to ambush us as soon as we entered the building." John filled in one detail. "Oh, and twenty slaves and a beast from hell locked in a dungeon in the basement."

"And three other mercs in the air," Meehix added.

"I guess we've struck a nerve." Chuckie smiled.

"Or three." Meehix, exhausted, headed to her room, not sure if she wanted a hot soak in a long tub or to make sure that the batteries in her pleasure toys hadn't gone dead.

"Meehix!" Chuckie called after her in a tone of voice she'd never heard from him before and caused her to turn back.

"Yes?"

"Did any of the imprisoned slaves manage to escape?"

"I think...maybe...all of them?" was her weary reply.

"Well done!"

"Thank you, Chuckie N. Thank you, Jojacko. See both of you idiots tomorrow."

Chuckie and John watched her walk off, and for perhaps the first time, both of them knew when to keep their mouths shut.

CHAPTER THREE

"Go away."

"I'm bored," came Chuckie's voice from the other side of John's bedroom door.

"Go away."

"Okay. Got it. You're jacking off. I'll be back in five."

"I'm not jacking off."

"So let me in."

"Why?"

"Because I'm bored."

"Okay. I *am* jacking off."

"I'll wait. Let me know when you've finished."

"You're not going to go away, are you?"

"I'm bored."

"What you are is a pain in the ass."

"Tell me something I don't already know. Come on, man. Whatcha got going on in there?"

"You'll laugh."

"If I promise I won't laugh, will you let me in?"

"Why?"

"Because I'm bored. Haven't you been listening to anything I've said?"

John knew he'd regret it, but he hit the remote to turn on the lights and got up from his desk to open the door.

"I never bother you when you're in your room."

"That's because you know I'm doing something disgusting,"

Chuckie walked past him and made himself comfortable on a couple of boxes stacked in a corner. *He really is bored,* was John's first thought, followed by *Little Chuck Horner, sat in the corner.* He stopped himself before he got to *Little Miss Muffet, sat on a tuffet.*

"I give. What's up?" John returned to his desk chair.

"We never talk anymore. I'm beginning to think you don't love me."

"We've never talked, and I've never loved you."

"Oh. Well, that explains a lot," the little man said.

John couldn't help but laugh.

"Seriously, I'm bored," Chuckie went on. "You'd been spending a lot of time in here before you and Meehix went off on the last job, and I was curious what you've been working on."

John picked up a sketchpad and a point-tip from the top of his desk and handed them to Chuckie.

"Draw something."

Chuckie looked at the pad and point-tip as if they were alien creatures.

"Visual artistry is not one of my fortés."

"So keep it simple. You either draw something or leave. Your choice, Mr. I'm Bored."

Chuckie thought for a minute and envisioned a sun.

Then he drew a circle with several lines coming out of it, representing rays, and handed it over.

"Happy now? I'm awaiting your critique of my artistic skills."

John took the pad. "Not bad for a beginner. You should have seen my first effort."

They were the best coders either of them had ever met, but they both sucked at drawing anything, and they knew it.

John took the pad and set it on his desk under what looked like a small flex-arm lamp. He then hit one button to turn the lamp on and the remote to turn the lights off.

Floating in the middle of the room was a holographic spider with seven arms.

"I drew a sun with some rays coming out from it."

"Looks like a spider missing a limb to me."

John flipped on the lights and handed the pad and point-tip back to Chuckie.

"Want a do-over?"

Chuckie drew an oval, with four lines coming down, a small circle on one end, a squiggly line on the back end, and handed the pad back. He kept the point-tip.

Lamp on. Lights off.

"You drew a puppy." John smiled, as a body, a head, four feet, and a waggly tail appeared in front of their eyes.

"What the fuck is a puppy?"

"Back on Earth, they're nothing more than piss and shit buckets."

"And you let them live?"

"Look at the tail wagging. Everything gets forgiven when the tail wags." John handed the pad back.

"You've been working on building a hologram lamp?" Chuckie was impressed.

"Just tinkering with it. Never tried one before."

"Let's see how this one comes out."

Chuckie drew a box with triangles covering every inch of its inside corners, forming sharp points and two long lines coming down from the bottom two corners.

"Whoa!" John was startled when a hologram appeared that looked like a two-legged, squared-off, gaping shark's mouth ready to do some serious damage. "What the hell did you draw?"

Chuckie was pleased with the reaction.

"Have you ever wondered why you haven't run into very many Dolurulodan men?"

"They don't like space travel? I only visited Meehix's planet once, and that was a quick trip. From what I remember, it was a beautiful place, and I wouldn't have wanted to leave it if I didn't have to."

"Yeah, it's a lovely place on the surface, but dangerously volcanic if you get down toward its core. Just like its women."

"Okay, I get it." John flicked off the image. "Meehix can get a little emotional when pissed off. Who doesn't?"

"I'm not talking about her *emotional core*, Bro-Jo. I'm talking about the danger of what you'd find waiting underneath if you were ever to flip her flap."

John turned the hologram back on and stared at the sharp rows of teeth.

"You're not serious."

"Don't worry," Chuckie explained further. "The teeth don't bite off the dicks. I just didn't know how to draw something that represented the poison they inject into any penis that leaves them unsatisfied and causes it to blacken and shrivel, leaving the men with nothing more than a small, limp, piss tube."

Once again, off went the hologram. John hit the lights, not sure if Chuckie wasn't just fucking with him.

"So, are you still a virgin, or do you have a shriveled, blackened dick?"

Chuckie hopped up and headed for the door, his mission of fucking with John's head completed.

"I'm neither a virgin nor a near amputee." Chuckie grinned his most evil grin. "Remember, I said any penis that doesn't leave them completely satisfied. I always leave 'em with a smile."

"Hey," John stopped him as he reached the door. "Question?"

"Sure." John sounded earnest, despite the fear he might be feeling regarding the flipping of the flap.

"I can't get into any Kdack systems from out here, but you have a lot more workarounds and ways to track information in space."

"Don't feel too bad, sport. Until recently, you never knew there *was* any information floating around outside of Kdack. Except those silly transmissions you people keep sending out with *Hello, greetings from Planet Earth* in two hundred and forty-seven languages."

"Those do seem kind of lame, now," John admitted.

"You haven't asked your question yet."

"I was wondering if…well, is there any way to find out how much the U.S. government back on Earth paid out to be able to capture Meehix? I don't know for a fact, but I've often wondered if Daukhl had set the whole thing up in advance for a price."

"Ahh, Daukhl the Dickless." *Talk about uniting around a common enemy.* "You mean the one who managed to crash his party ship, leaving Meehix a captive, and somehow managed to skip merrily along his way back home and the next party?"

"I've wondered about that myself. Now that the NutBusters are between jobs, and I'm independently wealthy, I'll see what I can find out."

"Thanks."

Chuckie nodded and left John to his holograms. He headed back to his room, smiling, wondering if John had bought the bullshit about what was behind a Dolurulodan's flap.

Left alone, John pulled up the hologram one more time, studying it closely, still not sure if he'd been taken in again by the notorious Chuckie N, the outlaw with the sickest sense of humor.

Early that afternoon, Meehix found their joint office empty. She didn't want to intrude on Chuckie and whatever he was doing in his room—*God knows I don't want to know*—but tracked John down in the gym.

"Judging by the way you dressed, I'm guessing you're not up for some cardio?"

"Right you are. But if you're up for some weight training, you can tag along with me and carry my bags.

"Heading out for that shopping spree?" Meehix smiled and nodded. "I'm going to have to pass."

"Why? You don't have enough muscles to carry forty thousand credits' worth of clothes?"

"I don't have the patience to sit through repeatedly trying on and discarding forty thousand credits' worth of clothes."

"You're not as dumb as you look." Meehix smiled again. "They have shops here that never close. Don't wait up."

She exited and found the NutBusters' auto-driver parked out front. Although Meehix loved to drive, Chuckie was too short. John could handle himself as a pilot in space but was terrified of actual space station streets, so they'd made a mutual decision to have an auto-driver and car ready. They leased him by the month for slightly less than the payments on an actual vehicle would have cost.

They could have called for a taxi whenever anyone wanted to go somewhere, but space-cabbies were annoyingly chatty. Auto-drivers weren't programmed to speak, leaving the passengers in peace and not having to bother with tedious conversations about whether they enjoyed their stay on L-222 and making suggestions about things they should see and do.

Meehix was going to treat herself to a "me" day, or, she thought, *a Meehix day.* She had a new identity and credits to burn. Tossing her shoulder bag in, she headed for Trovian's Treasures.

Trovian's was nothing short of a rich girl's wonderland. Two hours and ten thousand credits poorer, she wore one of her new stylish-yet-practical outfits, with a new bag over her shoulder. She popped the trunk, and three

Trovian assistants loaded her recent purchases. It had been a good day for those who worked on commission.

Next stop, hair and nails!

Before Meehix had crashed and been taken captive on Earth, she'd been the daughter of one of the richest and most influential families on her home planet, Dolurulod. Having been rescued by John, Jojacko to his closest friends, she'd returned home to a not-quite-welcoming reception.

Due to her non-repentant partying ways, the family had not only disowned her, but they'd also had her galactic status changed to a non-sentient property. Leaving her with no last name and no rights… In short, she was a slave, available to the highest bidder. Thanks to their recent adventures, she was no longer a slave. She merely had to get used to a new surname.

It was a slow day at the Blast & Last Salon until Meehix walked in the door. She had smiled at the name, thinking that Blast & Last Saloon might make for a good name of a few of the roughest bars she'd visited, but it had gotten good reviews. Her new Vermleen shoulder bag gave away the fact that here was someone with money.

The owner himself, the one and only Glamorio, hurried over to greet her. Taking both of her hands, he gave her a double-cheek kiss.

"Oh, my dear, it is our pleasure to serve you. Which first, nails or hair?"

Meehix didn't think her hair needed any attention, but then again, she hadn't paid much attention to it lately and was ready to be pampered.

"Let's start with the nails. Then discuss the hair."

"Absolutely. Certainly." He led her to a chair where two

technicians were waiting. "This is Floreen. She'll take care of your hands." Floreen smiled. "This is her sister Norleen. She'll be the one pampering your feet."

Glamorio backed away and left the girls alone.

"Just call us Flo and No." Floreen smiled at her. "We're the Flo-No Twins." The technicians giggled as Meehix took her seat.

"I'm Meehix."

"Our pleasure to serve you." No sat on a short stool and slid Meehix's boots off before she placed her feet in a vat of warm bubbling oil. "Tell me if that doesn't feel like your feet just went to heaven."

To Meehix, that sounded like a rhetorical question.

Neither of the twins topped four feet tall. They were short, skinny little things with long nimble fingers. While No prepared more treatment for her feet, Flo took hold of her hands.

"Oh, these have been so mistreated lately."

She slipped them both into mittens, hit a button, and five minutes later, took the mittens off. Meehix looked at her hands that now felt five years younger and three shades of smooth prettier.

Between the three of them, they chose colors for the nails—silver for the four thumbs and neon pink for her fingers. Meehix was beginning to relax until the twins also proved themselves to be chatty.

"It's not often," Flo started, "that someone as well off as you are has hands that look like they work for a living."

"Not everyone in my position was born into wealth. In fact," *Why not? I'm a new me now. I need a new history.* "I was born the daughter of loving but poor farmers. Due to a tragedy, I ended up raised as an orphan."

"Oh, no," said No.

"It was sad." *Truly tragic.* "My parents died in a horrible accident when a meteor struck our small family farm."

"The meteor hit the house?" Flo sympathized. "Lucky you weren't in it at the time."

"No, it didn't hit the house. I was only three at the time, but the meteor hit the pasture and sent our herd of wathanors off in an absolute panic, and they trampled my parents to death. We were poor, so there was no life insurance policy or insurance for the farm. It was only three-year-old me, and there were no other relatives to take me in, so I was shipped off to an orphanage."

"That must have been horrible."

"No, no. It helped make me who I am today." She leaned forward and lowered her voice so the twins had to listen very carefully.

"Because of how rough my upbringing was, I ended up forming a bounty hunting company with two others who had hard backgrounds, and the three of us are now one of the highest-ranked hunters in the third arm."

She leaned back, satisfied with her tale so far.

"That's why I haven't had time to take care of my hands and feet lately, but we're taking a work break, and I intend to enjoy some time off."

Flo and No looked at each other, their jobs almost done.

"I say yes," said No.

"I say no," answered Flo.

"Am I missing something? Oh, my nails are perfect, great choice on the colors."

"I think everything you said is true," explained No.

"And I think," Flo laughed, "that everything you said was a way of entertaining and distracting us because you didn't want to bore us about your family and how wonderful things are, like most of our customers."

Finished and carrying her boots while wearing a complimentary pair of sandals so she didn't mess up her toenails until they'd had at least an hour to thoroughly dry, Meehix paid for the pretty hands and feet treatment and left a very generous tip.

"Well?" Flo asked as Meehix reached the door, wanting to escape before the owner came back to discuss her hair. "Which of us is right?"

"Who said either of you were wrong?"

Too late. She had her hand on the door, but Glamorio grabbed her wrist. With an arm around her back, he guided her into the hair station and sat her down.

It was the most comfortable seat she'd sat in for quite a while. *What the hell, what's the worst that can happen?*

"I love the green." The Glam-man ran his fingers through her hair. "So *au naturel!*"

It had been a long time since anyone had run his fingers through it, and since it was obvious that Glamorio was never going to make any attempt to disrupt her flap, she decided to let him play with it.

"But tsk, my dear, you've mistreated it lately."

"Actually, I haven't been treating it at all."

"Oh, poor hair." His fingers were gentle as they combed

through it. "The first step is to give it a nice rest and a Timiare treatment."

He spun her chair, hit a foot pedal, and she found herself staring up at a ceiling mirror as her head leaned back and she could watch as Glamorio soaked her hair in a warm bath.

"That feels nice," she had to admit.

"Timiare has improved tremendously since it first hit the market."

He massaged her scalp as her hair soaked. "Have you ever considered a new cut and style?"

"No." As relaxed as she felt, that was one suggestion too far. "If a pair of scissors ever gets near it, that will be the last pair of scissors you'll ever hold."

"Understood, my dear." His fingers continued their massage. "And perfectly understandable. You have a marvelous conglomeration, and I wouldn't dream of doing it any harm."

She could accept that response.

"I'll be happy to restore it to its previous glory."

She was becoming truly relaxed now.

"But may I offer a temporary change of pace? Just for fun?"

An hour later, with no scissors involved, Meehix found herself staring in the mirror at a stranger with straight hair, flatteringly curved around the contours of her face. But it was definitely a stranger she was looking at because her hair was now bright orange.

The Flo-No twins were clapping their approval. Meehix had to admit that she didn't look too shabby for a night of dancing as her *new her*.

"You shower and rinse," Glamorio assured her, "and your hair will be back to its glorious green. If, after having a night of the orange on blue, you decide that you like the look, well, you know where to find me."

He took her hands again, guided her to the door, gave another two-cheek kiss, and sent her on her way.

Meehix's next stop was a very upscale hotel, two doors down from the Galactical-Bash, or the G-B as most commonly referred to it. She intended to do more than a little drinking and dancing at the G-B, but not until she'd changed into some more appropriate clothes.

She grabbed a couple of small self-protection items from her trusty old shoulder bag, popped the trunk and carried two bags of her recent purchases into the hotel, paid cash, and headed to her room. She had no intention of staying overnight in the room, but it was nice to have space to herself where there was no worry of the testosterone twins disturbing her.

Laying several outfits out on the bed, along with three pairs of high-heeled shoes that were suitable for dancing, she stepped back and had a moment of reflection. *Dammit, I wonder which ones the boys would choose for me if I'd given them a chance?*

The thought made her smile, wondering which choices they'd make, and for a moment, just a moment, she missed them. *They'll still be there when I get home.*

Keeping the latest NutBusters' adventures in mind, she went for a combo-look. Short, tight skirt, perfect for dancing and showing off her legs. A loose-fitting, low-cut blouse, perfect for accentuating her breasts on top and out front, but loose-fitting enough around her waist to conceal the holster strapped under it that could hold one of her short-blades and a small three-shot pistol.

A flouncy, colorful sash of a belt, loosely wrapped, also helped to disguise the weapons. She compromised on the heels, going with four-inch platforms. Spiked heels were a pain in the ass to run in should the need arise.

She left her Vermleen bag. Too bulky, and she also didn't want to keep track of a small, strappy purse, especially when there were no girlfriends to keep an eye on it for her. Amongst her purchases had been a pair of matching silver-studded bracelets, three inches wide with discreet zippered pockets—enough room to hold her ID in one and credits in the other.

She checked her look in the mirror, not needing anyone's approval but hers. The orange hair was still up for debate, but she approved and headed for the G-B after tossing her bags in the trunk of the auto-driver cab.

There was already a line of a dozen people waiting to be allowed in. She took her place and spent the next ten minutes annoyed as hell listening to the four empty-headed bimbos who'd lined up behind her.

Insipid. Banal. Inane. Vapid. *Oh dear God, is that what I used to sound like?*

"ID?" the doorman asked when she finally reached him.

Meehixiheem JoNorris handed her new ID card over.

"Welcome back. I thought I'd seen you before." He returned her card.

"You thought wrong." Meehix paid the cover charge to enter, along with an extra twenty.

"I've been wrong before." He put the cover charge in the

till and deftly pocketed the tip as he pulled back the rope to let her enter.

She smiled and sashayed past him, knowing that his eyes would follow her ass the whole way before he turned back to greet the four bimbos.

Hitting the bar first, she ordered a double dibble-blink and tried to be patient while it was made and served. When it arrived, she downed it in one long gulp. "Oh, now that's a girl's best friend."

She slapped some credits on the bar, not taking the time to count, then leaned over so the bartender could hear her. "You count it up. Make sure you have twenty left for yourself and cut me off once the money runs out."

The bartender took a quick look at the credits and smiled at her. "I think you have enough here to dance until closing time and I'll still have my tip left over."

"You don't close until dawn."

"Exactly. Enjoy yourself."

Meehix eyed the scene. Sure, it was relatively early, but the four-handed DJ already had the music spinning, and the dance floor was empty. A three-deep crowd was hovering along the walls, everyone seeming to be afraid to make the first move.

What? Is everyone here reverting to being awkward twelve-year-olds afraid of asking someone to dance?

She bopped out onto the dance floor, grabbed the arms of four males of various planetary origins who were in the front row, and practically tossed them out into the middle of the floor. They stumbled, not having expected the toss, and stared at each other with idiotic "What do we do now?" looks.

She then grabbed the arms of the four bimbos who'd followed her into the club and tossed them into the center of the floor too, where they staggered and stumbled into the four dumbfounded males.

The DJ switched to another beat.

The party girl was back and started spinning with her arms raised.

"Anyone not out here dancing in the next ten seconds will be incinerated in, Ten! Nine! Eight! Seven! Six! Five!..."

The walls emptied, and the dance floor was filled, with everyone joining in on the countdown. "Three! Two! One!"

Over the next several hours, she wore her four-inch heels down to three inches.

Meehix was in the house!

CHAPTER FOUR

The only problem, as the auto-driver dropped her off back home in the middle of the night, was that Meehix couldn't get into her own damn house! She put her hand on the touchpad, and the AI voice asked, "What time is it where Chuck Norris lives?"

"How the fuck am I supposed to know?"

"Wrong answer. Who drove Chuck Norris' mom home from the hospital after he'd been born?"

"Fuck Chuck Norris!" She started banging on the door.

The door opened moments later, and John saw a Meehix he barely recognized. She was wiping tears and smeared makeup from her face with a sleeve. John had been worried about her, which was why he'd been in the front office scanning police reports when the pounding on the door started.

Her face was a mess, but her clothes were perfect, so he assumed no one had attacked her. He'd also seen her under attack before, and it was always her attackers who came out wounded. This was something else, something *other*.

"What the hell happened to your hair?"

"Nothing that a shower, shampoo, and rinse won't fix. Nice to see you too."

She shoved past him and down the hallway to where her room branched off down the right wing, and his and Chuckie's rooms branched off down the left. They reached the crux at the same time that Chuckie hustled out of his room.

"An alert came on. Someone's at the front door with no right answers!"

"That was me, you jerk-wad!"

"Who the fuck are you and what the hell happened to your hair?"

Chuckie did his worst Chuck Norris impression and scampered back into his room.

Meehix headed toward her room, but John grabbed her elbow and forced her through the kitchen, where he toe-tapped the painting before she had a chance to damage either the picture or her feet while kicking it.

The door swung open, and he led her into the gym.

"Sit!" John commanded, trying to sound stern.

"I don't want to *sit!*"

"Then what *do* you want to do?"

"I want to *hit!*"

John grabbed a pile of workout clothes she'd left in a hamper. They were sweat-stained and had smelled better, but the outfit she was wearing was a killer, and John didn't want it to get damaged.

"Then kick off your heels, change clothes, and glove-up! I'll turn my back."

John had no idea what had happened, but he knew

pent-up emotions when he saw them. Heaven knew he'd had a few of his own that he'd taken out on rugby and wrestling opponents.

His and Meehix's earlier battles with space pirates and slave owners and what-not's were simply the cost of doing business. This seemed personal, and he knew that she had to get it out because none of them would have any peace until she did.

"You can turn around now and prepare to get your ass kicked!"

John turned and fired the first shot. "Did you hire a clown to do your makeup?"

"I tried to, but you weren't available!"

That's my Meehix! John threw a roundhouse punch that she ducked.

"I did a little shopping." She hit the floor and did a slide-swipe kick that he easily jumped over.

"I saw the outfit. Did you dress in the dark?"

They stood toe-to-toe and exchanged punches that both of them blocked, ducked under, or leaned back to avoid. Sparring partners as the conversation continued. Fighting with her was easier for John than to try to count her tears, which had now dried up.

"I used to have a family."

"Yeah, yeah, but they disowned you. Poor little rich girl."

That one earned a flurry of jabs.

"But now you have a new family." John ducked and dodged. "A dick of a family for sure, but not the most dysfunctional one I've ever encountered." He dove for her waist and tossed her over his shoulder and back onto the floor.

This time, she managed to sweep his legs before he had a chance to jump.

"Truce?" John asked as they faced each other while still on the floor, sweat and running makeup now covering both of them.

"Talk to me."

John stayed on the floor and laid on his back as if he was gazing at the stars. He touched his chest, inviting Meehix to rest her head against it. She took up the invitation, and the conversation continued as they unlaced their gloves and stared up at the unseen stars.

Gloves off, with her head resting on his chest, she held up her hands.

"Four thumb matching silver nails, complementing the neon pink fingers. Nice choice."

"Thank you."

"Was your hair defenseless?"

She lowered her hands and rested them out of sight as she nestled into John's chest. The energy release in the gym was taking effect, but the dibble-blinks hadn't completely worn off yet, and she began to ramble.

"After taking the time to pamper myself properly, I hit an old party palace and was the old Meehixiheem again."

"That's good, right?" John wished that there were actual stars to see inside the gym.

"No, it wasn't good. I saw my old self reflected in everyone on the dance floor. Hollow creatures with empty eyes. I...*they* were not a pretty sight. You told me once, at least I'm pretty sure it was you, who said something like 'Don't let others judge you by what they see. Judge yourself by what you do.'" She managed to focus her eyes back on him. "That *was* you who told me that, right?"

"It sounds like something stupid enough for me to have said." He stroked her straight *orange* hair.

"I knew I'd heard it somewhere." She nestled a little farther down onto his chest. "You and me, Jojacko, we've done some pretty cool shit together, right?"

"I don't know…escaping from your captivity on Earth, rescuing dozens of slaves while robbing a crime boss blind, fighting pirates, and freeing more slaves…I guess some folks would consider that cool."

"I want to be that cool chick, not the party girl who danced tonight away." She fell silent, her head still resting on his chest.

John stayed still until he knew that she was completely exhausted and thoroughly asleep.

He then picked up his partner, who'd faced down death and torture with him. He carried the exhausted one to her room, which he had never been in before, and set her gently on her bed.

She snores? Ah well, we all have our faults.

He pulled a blanket up over her and backed out of the room.

Shark-toothed vagina or not, he thought as he made his way to his room, *I'll risk it.*

With his hands wrapped around his balls, an instinctive protection movement, he fell asleep, wondering about the best way to ask her out on an actual *date*.

"I'm going to pull his testicles off while he's still alive and force him to watch a Flurvian snake swallow them whole and then wait while the snake shits them out the other end, still intact, and then stuff them in the Kdackan's mouth and make him swallow them himself!"

Victor Vikrellion was not a happy camper. Lazy Buff and Crabbo knew when to shut up before they should speak up, and now wasn't the time to open their mouths.

"Freeland's Corporate Headquarters are now in shambles! Slaves freed! Experiments running amok and destroying everything in sight. Entire operations shut down because a *beast* is now perched on top of the building, ready to pounce on its next meal! Who the fuck is responsible for this SNAFU?"

Umm, you are boss. Lazy and Crabbo exchanged a glance because neither of them would be the first to say it.

"Boss?" Lazy had been Victor's right-hand man for so long that he knew how to tap and dance better than Crabbo did.

"What?"

"Do you know what the acronym SNAFU spelled backward means?"

"No. Please enlighten me."

"UFANS," Lazy improvised. "Understood. Fuck All. Now Strike."

Victor took that in and carefully digested it.

"So, Lazy. You're basically saying… You fucked with me, and now I'll fuck with you?"

"Yes, Boss. That's exactly what I'm saying."

Crabbo owed Lazy a drink for his handling of fear under fire.

"We're still on top of it," Lazy continued as the color in Victor's face slowly returned to almost its normal shade. "We still have the tracker, Trexit, closing in on them."

"Yeah, yeah, your famous Trexit."

"He's made progress and is closing in. He even knows where their home base is. I heard from him a week ago, and he's been waiting for my response."

"Then respond to him, dammit! I want those two! Hold on."

A message was coming in from the idiot real estate agent, Brez. He read it.

House on L-222 rented with option to buy in six months. First two months rent credits wired tomorrow.

"First good news I've heard all day." Victor looked up. "What the fuck are you two still doing here?"

Lazy Buff and Crabbo shared an office in the south wing of Victor's mansion and fortress. The guards had rooms occupying the north tower. Their rank and longevity determined who occupied the lower chambers.

There were no elevators, so the rookies were assigned to the higher floors. Climbing the stairs was considered part of their exercise routines. Not that everyone staying in relatively decent shape had come in very useful when two people invaded the fortress a few weeks ago.

Contractors had repaired most of the physical structure's damage by now, but the blow to Victor's ego, and pocketbook, was going to take a while longer. On top of that, the two invaders had added theft and freeing all of the commodities in the dungeon to their list of accomplishments.

A few years back, Lazy had been in charge of upgrading all of the security measures. Not only with the additional cameras and communications systems, but Victor had also wanted every room in the mansion wired up with hidden mics so he could keep track of any rumblings of discontent among the troops.

Victor's request for the upgrade had been thoroughly followed, except for the office that Lazy and Crabbo shared.

The mics were there and functional so Victor was privy to any of their conversations. Lazy had also connected them to a bypass switch that led to recordings of rustling papers, sounds of walking around, chairs moving, and occasional pre-recorded innocuous conversations about the weather or food.

Lazy hit the bypass switch so he and Crabbo could talk for a few minutes without worrying about Victor's reaction to what they might be saying.

"Tell me, Laze." Crabbo sat behind his desk. "Should we have tried harder to talk the boss out of trying to set the trap at Freeland's headquarters?"

"I don't know." Lazy gazed out the window.

Victor's home planet of Brakeb III had earned its reputation as one of the drabbest of planets, but not the part of it where the mansion was. The landscaping was impeccable and at no small cost. He could see the pond from their window, crystal clear water that changed colors every day due to lights installed and shining up from the bottom.

The abundance of a wide variety of feathered creatures, whatever the fuck they were, offered an ever-changing kaleidoscope of colors on the surface.

He'd often thought about pulling out his sniper laser and picking off one of the birds when the color contrasts weren't well-coordinated with that day's water. Still, soon there'd be no birds left, and the water would change color the next day, so it was only a temporary eyesore.

"The boss wanted it done," Lazy took his seat and fired up his comm-pute, "and you know how it is when he gets his mind set on something, especially when that something pisses him off."

Crabbo *did* know how it was. He was missing the index finger on his right hand due to having once pointed at an unpleasant number in an invoice on the boss's desk. Victor had sliced it off before Crabbo even knew it was gone.

"How're we doing on the commodities recapturing?" Crabbo changed directions.

"I didn't think it was a good time to bring it up back there." Lazy wasn't pleased with the progress, which meant that neither would Victor. "Utilizing all the guards I could spare and hiring a few extras, we've only managed to return two."

"So the boss is still out over a million credits in lost future revenues?"

"Give or take." Lazy saw an urgent message waiting and clicked over to it.

"Made any progress on your bounty hunters yet?" Trex-it's face was a little wavery but clear.

"What do you think?"

"I think your boss constructed a major fuck-up with a trap he tried to set up at Freeland's headquarters. That's what I think." Trexit had a touch of a smirk going on.

Lazy sighed. "You think right."

"I told you the other week that I was close and requested you send some reinforcements."

"Are you done gloating now?"

"Are you and your boss done with making fools of yourselves, *now*?"

Lazy looked over his desk at Crabbo, who nodded.

"What can you tell me?"

Trexit's smirk changed to a smile. "I can tell you that they're using a space station as their home base of operations.

"Which one?" Trexit had Lazy's full attention now.

"I'm going to tell you? And risk your boss fucking things up one side of hell and back...*again*? I don't think so." Trexit was enjoying this conversation. "What I *can* tell you is that you're racking up my daily fees as I sit and twiddle my thumbs. Want to know how much the running total is so far?"

"No." Lazy leaned back and tried to look as casual as he could while someone had him by his short-hairs. "Whatever we're paying, it'll be worth it. How close are you?"

"Within spitting distance. And that's a *Clovian* spit, not a *Jesopien's*."

"Your reputation is well-earned. We'll try to stay out of your way." Lazy loosed a relieved sigh, as did Crabbo. At least they'd have something positive to report back to Victor.

"Is there anything else I need to know?" Lazy was ready to sign off.

"No, nothing that you need to know."

"Good." Lazy had his hand on disconnect.

"But there *is* something that I need to know." Trexit's tone caused Lazy's hand to freeze.

"And that something is?"

"Our contract stipulates that I capture two bounty hunters for crimes previously committed. A male and female pair. The contract does *not* specify the aforementioned bounty hunters' condition upon retrieval.

Oh, fuck! Victor wanted them alive so he could torture them to death himself. I forgot to read the fine print in the contract!

"Alive! We want them both alive!"

"I'll see what I can do." The screen went blank.

Trexit was feeling good about his career choice. He felt even better a few minutes later when the result of a search he'd sent out earlier that day came in. On his screen popped up two photos from the planet Kdack 3a. One photo was of a Kdackan male. The other was of a blue chick with a mop of green hair.

He pulled up a file of some photos he'd saved. Not that it was necessary, but Trexit prided himself on his thoroughness and ability to multi-task. There they were, the Kdackan and the Dolurulodan.

My, you two have been busy. It wasn't a Crec Alert, where any old bounty hunter could go flying off the handle and muck things up for everyone. This was a personal message from a Kdackan military officer who he'd been in touch with before on a previous job. He wanted these two captured, preferably alive, and returned to a space station where a Kdackan crew and ship could pick them up and return them to Kdack.

The price was good, although higher if they were captured alive.

Have targets already in sight. Acquisition expected soon. Will keep informed.

Trexit leaned back and drew a very deep breath. Life was good. He still had no proof, only his hunch that Jxzob-bliningozlinxfipple, the escapee from the cryo-prison that the prison didn't want anyone to know had escaped, was still hanging out with the bounty hunters.

It was a separate contract he had with the prison, but they had offered him a good-sized chunk of change to bring the little fucker in, and nobody said he wasn't allowed to double, or, in this case, triple-dip while working.

There was the incompetently interfering crime boss, Victor Vikrellion, out for revenge. There was the Blavarian dreadnought captain, Prooshevekk, also out for revenge, and now, there was his Kdackan contact, out for whatever you wanted to call it.

They would all pay if he could provide proof of capture, but they would also pay extra if they were brought in alive. The only question was who would pay more to have them delivered to their door, still breathing?

Trexit sensed a bidding war in his not-too-distant future.

He decided that when he was ready to pounce, he would hire a handful of Crom Limeans he'd worked with before. The nice thing about the Crom mercenaries was that they'd leave the thinking and planning to him. As long as they got paid, they didn't give two rods up a Xilion's ass what the reason for it was.

Early retirement, here I come.

CHAPTER FIVE

Where's Gage when I need him?

Gage was right where John had left him, hopefully at least, still alive and maybe working on the Save the Aliens project.

Still, Gage wouldn't be the best one to ask for advice on this particular project. He could ask Chuckie but knew that the Chuck-master's advice would be equally useless.

After tucking Meehix into bed the night before, he'd had a restless night's sleep and woke up early with one all-consuming thought in his brain. He padded his way down to Meehix's door and knocked gently, wanting to make sure she was still alive.

"I am treating myself to a personal spa day, so go away. Unless a package or two is delivered. Then sign for it and knock twice on my door as you leave it outside on the floor."

Yeap, Meehix and her now orange hair were just fine.

"John?" he turned as Meehix stuck her head out the

door. "Thanks for listening last night and letting me blow off some steam. That meant more than you know."

He was about to reply, but she gave him one of her heart-stopping smiles and closed the door.

He wandered down to Chuckie's bedroom door and knocked, still curious if the teeth behind the flap was an actual representation.

"Busy!"

"Doing what?"

"Trying to decide if I should buy a small planet to retire on or hire a bunch of mercenaries to conquer it for me so that I can declare myself emperor. There are tax breaks to consider if I buy it and continued payments to an army that I'll need if I decide to conquer. A lot of complications to consider, so fuck off."

Well then, I better get busy, myself.

He headed to his desk in their front office. He had some serious research to do and didn't want to miss one of Meehix's deliveries during the process.

He didn't know if he was halfway through his research or just beginning when the first package arrived. Signing for it, he carried it back to Meehix's room. It had to weigh at least twenty pounds but was the sweetest smelling twenty pounds he'd ever held.

Setting it on the floor outside her room, he knocked twice and headed back out front.

He'd reached a definite halfway point through his research when he was interrupted by another delivery. At the door, he found an open two-by-three-foot short-sided crate on the doorstep, with the delivery agent standing four feet away from it.

"Death-head skull-a-kills, valubian blossoms, and Quarion tubulars," the masked and gloved delivery person read off the items from the list.

"What the hell are those?"

"Nothing that I'd want to touch. I'm paid to deliver, not to explain."

John found some protective gloves and a handcart and wheeled the crate back to Meehix's door. He knocked twice and headed back up front, hoping that he was at least halfway through his research.

Ten minutes later, he answered another knock. This package was lighter than the first, although not as sweet-smelling, but seemed less deadly than the second delivery had been. Carrying it back, he set it down outside of Meehix's door, knocked twice, and waited.

The door opened a crack, and someone who he could only assume was Meehix reached down to gather it in with mitten-covered hands.

"What?" she looked up at him.

He at least recognized her voice.

"Are you under there, somewhere?"

She was wearing a robe that looked like it weighed forty pounds and seemed to be vibrating. Her head was completely wrapped in towels, with only a slight opening for her eyes to peek out through.

"Is there a Meehix in there somewhere?"

"Nope. Just a gal enjoying an in-home spa day."

"Is the gal expecting any more deliveries? Because I have a few things of my own on my list to accomplish today."

"Stop whining and list away. This is the last one."

He turned and headed away, pausing as he heard her say, "John? Thanks again for last night."

Giving a thumbs-up, he continued and heard the door close behind him.

Last night was nothing. Our next night is what's going to be something special.

John headed back to the office and saved the research he'd been doing. Maybe it was half done. Perhaps he was three-quarters done. Maybe he'd just gotten started. He transferred what he had onto his pocket-pad, headed to his room to change clothes, and hit the gym.

First stop, treadmill.

"Okay, human males always seem to find a way to fuck up relationships with human females. At least I always have. How do I manage to not fuck one up with an alien? How do I begin a relationship with an alien? Where do I find an advice columnist for that? Where's Dear Alien Abby?

"Start with what you can control! Work on the cardio." He was giving himself one hell of a pep talk. "If everything goes right, there'll be an anaerobic exercise in our future."

"Surely, John, there must be a balance somewhere between aerobic and anaerobic."

John stumbled off the treadmill and landed on his ass.

"The fuck, Ship! What are you doing here?"

"I take it that Chuckie didn't tell you?"

"Tell me what?" John rubbed his ass and set the treadmill for resistance rather than speed.

"Chuckie added a program to the house's communications system. I'm linked into every room now."

"So everyone can hear what everyone else is saying?"

"No. Only me. The program deletes anything that you do and everything that is said from my memory banks every half-hour."

"So, I can go kill Chuckie, and you can hear his dying curses, and half an hour later, no one will be able to tap into you and produce you as a witness?"

"That is my understanding."

"My favorite color is, umm, chartreuse. You got that?"

"Chartreuse is a very lovely color."

"I agree. It looks very nice when my mom wears it. Talk again in half an hour."

John spent the next half-hour in silence, treading the hell out of the treadmill. Turning it off and toweling down, he inquired, "Ship?"

"Yes, John."

"What is my favorite color?"

"You seem to favor wearing brown. Perhaps because it matches your eyes?"

"You're making my head hurt. Are you fucking with me?"

"Although I may occasionally show a slight sense of humor, I believe that fucking with your head would fall into Chuckie's area of responsibility."

"All right, all right. Sorry for doubting you." John sat on the weight bench and started in on some lighter-weight curls. "Can I ask you a question?"

"I was thinking about going out for a quick wash and polish, but since I can't fly myself except for the two-hour window that is sometimes programmed, ask away."

"And no one else can hear us?"

"Have I ever lied to you? What's on your mind, bubala? Talk to Auntie Shippewa."

Even then, John glanced around to make sure he was alone.

"I want to ask Meehix out on a date."

"About time! I was beginning to think that I would be a rusting shell of my former self in a galactic vessel junkyard before you got around to it."

"So you think it's a good idea?"

"Define good...all I know is that it's something that needs to happen."

"What if she says no?"

"Tsk, tsk, and at the risk of redundancy, tsk...then it will simply become one less problem that needs to be solved. Better to have a hand chopped off with one quick blow from a sharpened ax than to use a dull-toothed saw to slowly draw out the pain, one slow stroke at a time."

When Ship was right, Ship was really right.

Belatedly, he realized that the "Auntie Shippewa" comment had also answered his lingering question about their AI spacecraft's gender identity.

"Okay then." John set down the weights. "Let's pretend that I ask her out and she says yes. Where do I take her? I've been researching places here on L-222. Do I choose somewhere that will really impress her, or someplace that will seem...I don't know, somewhere that's real? Real for both her and me?"

"It would be nearly impossible to impress her with something she hasn't seen before. She's a space veteran. You, on the other hand, are slightly less experienced."

"Ouch." Ship had a point. "She's in the majors, and I'm still riding buses and playing in a Double-A league."

"I believe that metaphor is relatively accurate."

"Gage's mom once told me a story," John recalled.

"Mr. Gonzalez tried to impress me on our first date. We were all very poor, but he took me to the most expensive restaurant in our village, spending money like he had a peso tree growing in his back yard.

"After dinner, as we were walking home, I asked him if this was the way he would treat me for the rest of my life. He say no. So I tell him, you have one more date to show me how you will treat me.

"Our next date was in a field. He laid a blanket on the ground and pulled fruits and vegetables from a basket he carried...'I promise you will never go hungry, even if I have to beg the Earth for its food.'

"That was a promise I knew he would keep."

"So what did you do, Mrs. G?

"I married the fool a week later."

"I don't think you need my advice on this one anymore, John."

"Thanks, Ship."

"Any time, John. But please don't ask me half an hour from now to repeat any advice I just gave."

"That's all right. I was taking notes."

John headed to his room for a shower.

Of course, if being real *doesn't work, and Meehix goes for Chuckie instead, I'm gonna cock-block the little bastard like no one's ever blocked him before.*

John took a long hot shower. He had some legwork

research to do, hoping it would lead to fewer long cold showers in his future.

Shower finished, he dressed casually—a knife here, a taser-ray there. Everyone on Space Station L-222 was an alien, including himself, but he was also a NutBuster, and they had picked up an enemy or two along the way.

"Heading out," he called as he passed Chuckie's door and gave it two quick raps.

"Don't expect me to stop you!"

Damn. John smiled. *I love that little fucker!*

He didn't bother knocking on Meehix's door. She was still self-spa-ing.

John settled into the back seat of their auto-driver. Since the three NutBusters had already leased their car for the month and had used him so regularly that the driver was assigned to be at their disposal, they'd decided to give the AI driver a name.

"Hey, Adee," John read off the first address he'd researched and downloaded on his pocket-pad.

One of the things that they all appreciated was that Adee was not programmed to speak. All he could do was nod as a way of saying message received as he drove off.

John had focused his research on two criteria. What Meehix liked and what he liked. It was going to be tough to find a place where they intersected.

They both liked to eat, and since John's digestive system had made some great strides since he'd left Albuquerque, a nice restaurant that would please them both would be easy to find.

They both also enjoyed a libation or two. It suddenly occurred to him that he still couldn't legally drink on

Earth for another year and a half. That didn't mean he hadn't shared a few beers with Gage in his friend's back yard.

After a few months in space, he could now clink glasses with the best of them. Meehix could also down a few herself, so a nice bar was always an option. But was it too easy? *What does she love?*

His first stop was at a dance club. It had gotten good reviews. Its name was the Galactical-Blast. It was too early in the day for it to be open, but he knocked on the door until someone opened it a crack.

"Not open."

John stuck his hand in the door before it could be closed.

"I'm looking to rent a place out for a private party and want to have a look around."

The door opened barely wide enough to let him in as a hand reached out to take the twenty credits he was holding.

"I...just...clean...and...mop," the eight-foot, hundred-twenty-pounds-soaking-wet janitor drawled with the deepest voice John had heard in a while. "Boss...comes... in...at...five...Must...be...clean...by...then."

"I only need a few minutes. I want to check out the dance floor, and I'll be gone."

"O...kay."

It seemed like a colorful joint. Even without the DJ and light show advertised as part of every evening's festivities, and even though the only dance moves he'd ever mastered were the Hokey-Pokey's, he was pretty sure that Meehix would like it.

Five minutes later, the janitor was back at the front door to let him out.

"One more favor?" John asked as the door opened and he handed the man another ten credits.

"Ye-ess?"

"Could you please say, 'You rang?'"

"You ra-ang?"

"Perfect! Thank you." John smiled and was off, leaving a simple janitor thirty credits richer than he'd woken up with that morning.

John worked his way down his list. One dance club was completely dark and had no access. He tried to peek inside, but they'd blacked out the windows. He hit two restaurants. The first one was too classy, and the second, too much of a dive.

He checked out two bars. The first one was too much of a hole in the wall, but he hit pay-dirt on the second. The establishment itself wasn't what he'd been looking for, but he decided to sit and have a drink and chill for a few minutes.

He took a stool at the bar and ordered a Grimlian's as he pulled out his pocket-pad and did some more scrolling. The barmaid pulled his drink from a tap, and as she served it, noticed his scrolling.

"New to L-222?" she asked in a friendly manner.

"Just moved in." He sipped. "Looking for a place to take a friend out for a dinner, a drink, and a dance, and want to get it right."

"First date and trying to impress?" The barmaid was good.

"Something like that, yeah," John admitted.

"Are you willing to buy a few drinks for the perfect advice?"

"Sure." John shrugged. He had credits enough to burn.

"Then you need the MTA."

"The what?"

"Machella!" The barmaid waved at a table. "Man here needs the MTA!"

John watched as three gorgeous young women abandoned what was left of their fancy little afternoon petite drinks on their table and headed his way.

"Quick," John asked the barmaid. "What does MTA stand for?"

"Major. Trouble. Ahead."

"Hi, I'm Machella." She put a friendly hand on his shoulder. "And this is Tehersa," Tehersa did a quick bow, "and this is Amiel."

The three took a step back and joined hands as they formed a half-circle.

"We," Machella spoke for them all as if she was used to the speech, "are the MTA. Unofficial tour guides for anything Space Station L-222 legally has to offer."

"Ummm..."

"Let's start with something simple." Machella took the lead. "What's your name?"

"Jojacko?"

"Jojacko it is. What's the occasion, Eleia?" Machella saved John from mumbling any further.

"First date." The barmaid smiled. "Drinks are on him."

"Pay up your tab," Machella instructed.

John pulled up a handful of credits and started counting

out the still unfamiliar currency. Amiel grabbed one bill and tossed it on the bar.

"That'll cover it. Save the rest, young handsome. You're going to need it." She smiled and winked at Eleia as Machella and Tehersa each took one of his arms and led him out.

Eleia handed Amiel an eight-pack of mini-boinks to help keep the party going in between stops.

"Will you and your lady be walking or driving?" Machella asked as they hit the street.

"We have an auto-driver." John pointed at where it was waiting.

"Your very own?" Amiel asked.

"Leased by the month," John managed to stammer, still not sure what he'd gotten himself into.

"These things are so kew-ell." Amiel hopped into the shotgun seat as Machella and Tehersa plunked John down in the back seat between them.

"So dish, dreamboat," Tehersa got the questions started. "What does she like?"

"What about what I like?"

"Oh, honey, this is your first date, right?" Tehersa was trying to gather enough information to help them be able to give him some useful advice.

"Yeah, first date," John fessed up. "Assuming that she says yes when I ask her."

"Ooohhh." Machella smiled at Tehersa. "The plot thickens."

"You asked, 'What about what I like,' correct?" Tehersa picked up where she'd left off.

John nodded.

"What you like is her. So now, listen carefully."

"Listen to her very carefully, Jojacko," Machella added as Tehersa continued.

"If she likes you, it doesn't matter where you take her or what you do. Just as long as you both can still be yourselves while you do it."

In the front seat, Amiel was amusing herself by poking and prodding and trying to tickle Adee to see if she could distract him.

"I take it that you two have known each other for a while." Machella picked up the advice trail. "So you both know some of the things that each of you likes, even though some of them aren't the same."

"And that," Tehersa finished, "is why we're going to find some things that neither of you has done together yet. That way, you two can learn more about each other and have some fun along the way."

"Ta-da!" Machella added with a flourish. "See how easy this is going to be?"

There was a flurry of questions, even a couple from the front seat, as Amiel finally realized that other than chopping off his arms, Adee was going to continue to drive with determined focus.

In shape? Both.

Dancing? One.

Drinking? Big both.

Fine dining experiences? Meh.

Although all of the stops they led John through had alcohol available, it wasn't the primary purpose.

There was an anti-gravity floor ball-bounce court, where there was one volleyball-sized ball, and the object was to be the first one to bounce it off the bottom floor using only open palms. Not quite romantic, but kind of fun.

They hit a cracko-sing bar. John sucked at karaoke on Earth but realized he'd never heard Meehix try to sing. *Maybe she sucks as bad as I do?* That would be a fun thing to have in common.

They hit a few more silly-fun places and a couple of different bar-restaurants while each of them took turns in the shotgun seat trying to find new ways to distract Adee. None of them were successful.

"Maybe this should be your first date," Machella opined during one of the drives between stops when she was sitting up front.

"What's that?" John wasn't sure. Ride around in an auto-driver with three whacked-out fun-loving strangers?

"Grab a six-pack to go and play 'distract a driver.'" She placed her hands over Adee's eyes. "First one to cause a crash wins!"

The whole excursion was on John's dime, and the MTA had enjoyed themselves thoroughly. They all knew about the floor-bounce-ball court but had never tried it. And it had been days, absolutely days! since they'd hit a cracko-sing bar. They had a killer three-part-harmony rendition of the classic, *Your Feet or Mine?* Even though it had only been late- afternoon, they couldn't pass up an opportunity to sing it.

Fun-time over, it was early evening, and the MTA still had a whole night ahead. Getting down to serious business and wanting Jojacko to know that they hadn't only been wasting his time, they directed Adee back to a street that branched off the main boulevard's food and entertainment district.

"This is the place you need to either begin or end your date." Machella took John's arm as they all hopped out and led him into a bar called Proost.

He stepped through the door, and felt like a kernel of freshly popped popcorn, dropped into a vat of warm butter.

"Sit down, take it all in," Machella told him as she led him to a seat at the bar, and her fellow MTAs stepped back, bowed, and smiled.

"We'll have Adee take us back to where you found us and send him back to wait for you in the closest park space he can find."

John smiled at them, not sure whether to shake their hands or kiss their cheeks. "Any other advice?"

"Keep your voice low if you try the cracko-sing," Amiel answered as she shook his hand. "You won't impress anyone with your voice."

"If you two play floor-bounce-ball?" Tehersa took his hand. "Don't let her win. That would be dishonest, and a relationship built on an early lie never ends well."

"Machella? Any last words?" He reached for her hand.

"Just be yourself. No one ever fucked up an audition by playing themselves."

He watched the MTAs head out, ordered a Grimlian's, and took in the place.

It was that time of the evening when it was starting to get crowded but was still only about half-capacity. The bar itself was a long oval dividing the room in half.

On one side was a stylishly decorated restaurant area,

where the well-dressed waitstaff performed their duties with smiles and an occasional flourish as they set dinners on the table. If smells were anything to judge the food by, then it smelled delicious.

The owner had decorated the other side more colorfully. John noticed a variety of lighting fixtures on the ceiling that now shone with warm muted yellow. At the end of the room, a DJ set up for the night, playing some songs with friendly beats.

As he watched, the DJ hit a couple of buttons, causing the volume to go way up and the lights to flash a multitude of bright colors. Sound and lighting check completed, the DJ returned them to their earlier settings. The floor was empty, but stools sat in a line under an eight-inch-wide counter that ran along the walls.

Food on one side, dance floor on the other, and drinks in between. Suspecting that the MTAs had had this place in mind all along, he entertained no regrets for the credits he'd spent on the earlier games and drinks.

It had been a fun afternoon, now evening. Since L-222 was their home base for a while, he felt more comfortable thinking about it as where he lived, with everyday activities available outside of their adventures with Shippewa.

Feeling like it had been a successful exploratory outing, he relaxed and enjoyed a second Grimlian's as the outside grew darker and the inside became much more crowded. *Time to head home.*

Once outside, there were no parking spaces available, and he didn't spot Adee anywhere. He walked toward the end of the block, away from the main drag, and cut through an alley to work his way back up the next block over.

Like all alleys, there were shadows. John remembered one of his philosophies back in Albuquerque. Never park in a multi-level parking garage, and try to avoid alleys after dark. Whether it was a TV show or a movie, nothing good ever happened in either of them. Right on cue, two figures came out of the shadows, brandishing knives.

One was almost John's height, the other several inches shorter.

"Guys, you really don't want to do this." He was going to give them a chance to rethink their choice of victim.

"You're wrong, my friend," the shorter one said. "We really do."

"What you don't want to do," the tall one added with an ugly smile, "is end up sliced into bite-sized pieces all because you didn't want to hand over a few credits."

"Oh, and that shiny necklace thing you're wearing."

Hannah? He'd forgotten that he still wore the pendant regularly because you never knew when something would need some hacking.

"So come on now," the big one joined back in, "you don't want to do anything stupid."

"I could say the same thing." John was having a hard time not laughing. He had a larger knife than either of theirs strapped around one ankle and a short-nosed stun-blaster strapped around the other.

But where would be the fun of using them unless necessary?

"Do you feel lucky, punks?"

Apparently, they did since they both rushed in. John's

first kick sent the short one's knife flying. A quick spin and his second kick left the tall one wondering if he would ever be able to produce a child as he doubled over, grabbing his balls.

"Shit!" John looked down. "Do you know how much this shirt costs?"

On the way down to grab and try to save his future progeny, the tall one had somehow managed to slice across John's ribs, resulting in an irreparable tear in the fabric. John had felt the tip of the blade but could tell that it hadn't broken the skin. Still!

A direct smash to the short one's nose sent blood spurting. He relieved the tall one of his knife and emptied both of their pockets. *Maybe Chuckie can find something useful.*

Fun over, he pulled out his stun-blaster, helped the big one back up to his feet, and slammed him back-first into a wall. He then shoved the short one, his nose still bleeding profusely, onto his knees in front of his partner and forced his bleeding face right into the middle of the tall one's crotch.

Pulling the bleeder's head back, he took in his handiwork.

"Oh, poor tall freak, is it that time of the month?"

"That's not funny, man," the tall one cried.

"So sue me. No one's ever accused me of having a tasteful sense of humor."

A block and a half of looking later, he finally found Adee—*we need to get him a GPS*—and made his way home.

After Adee dropped him off and went to park, John made his way up the walk to the NutBusters' shared home and office. Before he reached the door, he had to pause. A streetlight shone on the window of their waiting room. The waiting room sat across the hallway from their front office, but they'd never had to use it because so far, they'd only had one client, but someone seemed to be using it now.

There were no lights on inside, but on the outside, he could see two red, bulbous half-orbs hanging out the window. *That's curious.*

He touched his hand to the security keypad and waited for the AI security question du jour.

"Why does the Boogeyman check his closet each night before he goes to sleep?"

"To make sure Chuck Norris isn't hiding."

The lock *clicked* open, and John entered. Their office was on the right and didn't have a door, but the waiting room on the left did, and it was closed.

CHAPTER SIX

John pulled his knife and stun-blaster, ready to kick open the door to the waiting room. The NutBusters had made a few enemies in their brief time together, which was one reason Chuckie had installed the extra security system.

Chuckie, plus the NutBusters, plus a red ass?

He slipped back and opened the front door enough to peek at what he now recognized as the cute ass, *speaking of cracks,* of their earlier client, the sneezing demon Phil's succubus of a niece, slipping out the window.

Vixaleen did a neat backflip, draped a few of her thin wraps around her, and disappeared into the night.

Taking another one for the team, Chuck-O?

John quietly closed the front door and leaned against it, waiting. He wasn't there long before the waiting room door opened and Chuckie hustled out.

"Was someone in the mood for a late-night snack?"

The little man jumped, startled.

"Sure." Chuckie recovered quickly. "Let's hit the kitchen."

"You want to take the time to zip up first?" John chose to head into the office instead of down the hallway to the kitchen.

"You're not hungry?" Chuckie finished zipping up and followed him. "You're always hungry."

"Not as *always hungry* as some." John sat at his desk. There was one more item he wanted to research. "It's funny...I know I'm not too experienced with space travel, but this was the first night inside *any* space station I've been on when a full moon was visible on the inside of it... and a *red* full moon, at that."

"Busted, huh?" Chuckie took his seat.

"I don't know. Maybe you should ask your nuts?"

Chuckie glanced down between his legs and came up smiling. "Definitely busted."

"Happy for you." John smiled. He genuinely was. At least one of the NutBusters was living up to their name.

"You won't tell Meehix, will you?"

"Why? Do you think she doesn't want to settle down with someone who's not a virgin?"

"Cut me some slack here. I'm begging you."

Chuckie never begged, so John cut him the requested slack.

"My lips are sealed." John couldn't resist getting in one last dig. "Which is more than I can say for the red-assed succubus's oral anatomy... Just try to be a little more discreet, man. In the waiting room? Really?"

"I was working—I'll show you in a minute—and saw her coming up to the door. I would have taken her back to my room but didn't want to run into Meehix in the hallway."

"Well, at least you closed the door. What were you working on?" John had finished reading all the info he could pull up on the dining, drinking, and dancing establishment called Proost, and he was happy with the reviews.

"So," John relaxed. "Before you tell me what you were working on, have you considered reprogramming our security system so that every answer doesn't involve Chuck Norris?"

Chuckie looked around, looked around again, and checked over his shoulders before he leaned over his desk and almost whispered, "I'm afraid to."

"You're afraid to?"

"Would you want to try to reprogram Chuck Norris?"

"That's not high on the list of ways I'd like to end my life," John admitted.

"What *would* be on your list?" Chuckie had given this some thought recently. "And no, let's take a death-inducing orgasm off the table, all right, because that's too easy."

"Okay, no death by sex." John was still young enough to think that he was immortal. "I hadn't considered it. I mean, I'm only nineteen. Death seems a long way off."

"Forgotten about Victor and pirates and Blavarian dreadnought captains and who knows who else you've pissed off recently?"

"Including my government?" That gave John pause. "I just never gave it much thought."

"Well, you should." John had never heard Chuckie wax philosophical before. *Interesting.*

"So you've given this some thought?" He was curious what Chuckie's options would be.

"The first thing you have to consider," Chuckie

leaned back, "is do you want it to be completely unexpected, or would you prefer to know it was coming in advance, so you had the time to make whatever peace you wanted to make with whoever you wanted to make it with."

"Or to do a few things you'd always wanted to do but never took the time?"

"Something like that, yeah."

"Back on Kdack, it's called a bucket list."

"Whatever. How do you want to go?"

"I don't!"

"Denial is no way to avoid the inevitable."

"I need a minute to think. You've obviously already thought about this, so what have you come up with?"

"I want to die in battle."

John had *not* seen that one coming. He wondered if Chuckie had downed a few beverages with the succubus, but he wasn't slurring his words or incoherent. He just wasn't quite acting like the Chuckie he was used to.

"That doesn't sound very pleasant," John prodded.

"Be right back." Chuckie padded down the hallway to the kitchen and came back with two glasses and a bottle of Kioskie. Pouring the warm liquid into the glasses, he set one down on John's desk and returned to his seat.

Raising their glasses in a toast, they each took a short sip. Kioskie was not the kind of drink you wanted to chug unless you wanted to end up passed out on the floor wherever you took your last swig.

"You were saying something about dying in battle?"

"Yeah, but only under specific circumstances."

"Which are?"

"Everyone knows that I can create and wield a mighty program."

"Never met anyone better at it." John nodded. "I can create and wield a few myself, but you're the pitcher with a hundred-mile-per-hour fastball. I'd be the catcher."

"But you can wield a sword. You're big enough and dangerous enough to lead men into battle." Chuckie stood in all of his four-foot-five glory. "There are swords in battle that are taller than me."

John knew that Chuckie was extremely sensitive about his height, so for him to say that was quite an acknowledgment. *Maybe this isn't his first Kioskie of the night.*

"I want to lead an outnumbered army against an unbeatable foe, in hand-to-hand combat, with none of this blasting things from a distance shit. We'd be a small band of righteous warriors, rebelling against an evil emperor."

"That's how you want to die? By losing a battle you couldn't win?"

"Don't be an idiot!" Chuckie sipped again. "Of course, we'd win against insurmountable odds! And I, myself, would be the one to deal the emperor his death blow, up close and personal. We'd overthrow the evil emperor, and I would be declared the new king, to rule for a hundred years over a kingdom of peace and prosperity."

"I thought we were talking about ways to die, not ways to become king." John was confused.

"The emperor and I would be *mano a mano* on a hill-top, with a clear view of the battle below. We would see my warriors destroying the empire's flags and new ones raised in the name of the conqueror, Chuckie the N. Then I'd slice off his head and hold it up for all to see as chants of *All hail the new king!* rose and echoed over the hills."

"And then you die?"

"Then I die. A stray ray-blast to the head, or something, so fast that I'd never feel a thing."

John was beginning to understand. "You want to die in a moment of glory."

Chuckie nodded.

"Wouldn't you want to live long enough to rule your new kingdom of, and I quote, *peace and prosperity?*"

"Nah." Chuckie shook his head. "I'd find a way to fuck it up."

John couldn't argue with that kind of logic. Better to go out as a conquering hero than a king who didn't know how to rule.

"Speaking of fucking." Chuckie smiled, set down his glass, and pulled up some info on Mixie, his personalized laptop. "I've found our next job."

It was a good thing that Chuckie was seldom allowed to pilot Shippewa because everyone would end up with whiplash due to his sudden change of directions.

"Our next job involves fucking?"

"Well, cum." Chuckie eased into the next topic.

"Welcome, what?"

"Cum." Chuckie thought he was clarifying. "Just cum."

"Come where?" The little man hadn't moved. John wondered how hard the Kioskie was hitting himself, especially after having had a drink or two as his day had progressed.

Chuckie sighed. "C-U-M. Cum. We're going to protect a shipment of cum."

"Be right back." John headed to the kitchen and returned with a bottle of water, taking a big gulp along the way back to the front office.

He'd already had a busy day but suspected that this was another scheme he should pay close attention to before slamming Chuckie's Mixie closed and saying *no fucking way!* He leaned against his desk because he knew that if he sat, he would have to get up again to go and look over Chuckie's shoulder to see what might be coming up on the NutBusters' horizon.

"Sperm, you were saying?" John was going to make his best effort at sounding reasonable.

"Cum, actually," Chuckie clarified. "But it has very rare sperm in it."

John decided that he didn't want to touch whatever the cum-sperm job was with a ten-foot dick.

"I'm just gonna take another sip of Kioskie and toddle off to bed now and hope I don't have nightmares of thousands of squiggly sperms attacking me."

"You haven't heard me out yet." Chuckie sounded hurt, which put John on an even higher alert.

"All right," John finished off his water and kept the Kioskie ready. "Spill."

"Spill is one thing that you don't want to do."

"What do I not want to spill? Can you be a little more specific regarding whatever the fuck kind of job you're signing us up for?"

"All we'll be doing—"

"You mean all that Meehix and I will be doing—"

"Is protecting a shipment between two planets."

"And?"

"The *spill* comes into play because the shipment will consist of several hundred small glass vials, carefully packed, and they need to arrive intact."

"I'm guessing here." John reached for another small sip of Kioskie. "The vials are filled with cum."

"Exactly!" John had caught on quick, and Chuckie went into more details. "All you and Meehix have to do is ensure that the crate they're in isn't jostled or dropped."

"If I hear you correctly, we're being hired to prevent a mass spermicide?"

Chuckie nodded vigorously. "That's all. Just get the cum and its sperm from Point A to Point B with no spillage along the way. How simple is that?"

"I'm guessing that it's not quite as simple as you're making it sound. Someone must want it real bad for it to need protection." John thought back. "These vials of cum aren't like bottles of maple syrup where a whole planet will get stoned out of its collective gourd on, is it?"

"Maple syrup?" Chuckie seemed truly horrified. "Oh, God no! The NutBusters aren't ever going to be drug runners!"

"I'm relieved to hear that. But if I'm going to risk my life, *and* Meehix's, to protect a shipment of cum, then we're going to need a little more information."

"They'll pay us a hundred twenty-five thousand credits." Chuckie cut to the bottom line.

"That is some expensive cum," John had to admit.

"It comes, no pun intended," Chuckie smiled, "to forty thousand credits for both you and Meehix, twenty thousand for my organizational skills, and the remaining twenty-five thousand for various costs."

John retook his seat, willing to listen rather than look over Chuckie's shoulder at all the details.

"Why is this cum so valuable, if you don't mind me asking since I'm going to be risking my life to protect it?"

"There's a planet that I'm sure you've never heard of called Plendark. It's a small planet. Eighty percent of it covered in water, which isn't unusual. But in one of its seas resides the happiest known species ever to have been discovered, the billeroons."

"What the fuck is a billeroon?"

"From my research on Kdack, they would be similar to what you would call a walrus."

That at least gave John a visual. "Go on."

"They only come out of the water every five years to mate."

"Only once, every five years?"

"They flood the shores. The males flap around on their backs and shoot out the sperm as the females roll around on their backs, vaginas wide open and try to catch a few drops. The whole courting ritual lasts for about a week, then they all disappear into the sea again."

"How romantic." John, wanting to make sure he could still walk steadily, took his glass and poured himself another short shot of Kioskie from Chuckie's bottle and reseated himself.

Chuckie waited until John took a small sip before continuing.

"That's where the fun-cum comes in. Not only are the billeroons the happiest known species, so is their sperm. Every five years, while the billeroon males are spouting it all over and the females are trying to give it a happy landing spot, the Plendarkians risk their lives trying to catch the sperm in buckets before it hits land."

"That's dangerous?"

"Picture yourself running around with a bucket while trying to dodge thousands of five-hundred-pound creatures rolling and wriggling around. The billeroons have never bitten anyone, their genetic makeup consists of nothing other than happiness, but they have squished a few cum-collectors as they rolled and squirted and gathered."

John was torn between whether or not that would be a hilarious or tragic sight.

"The cum," Chuckie decided to wrap it up, "is simply the delivery method."

"And the sperm," John finally got it, "is what's being delivered."

"If you choose to chug the cum, the sperm will make its way into your system. No one gets high, like on maple syrup. No one goes on any kind of a crazy rampage. But for about a week, anyone who drinks it will be happy and peaceful. Nothing more than happy and peaceful."

"I wouldn't mind some of that myself."

"Well, you'd be late to the party. Because the billeroons only mate every five years, their happy sperm is a special commodity. This time around, the highest bidder is on the planet Zellion. There are several nations there who've been warring with each other. They have a conference coming up where they're going to try to hammer out some peace treaties." Chuckie smiled because he knew he now had John and his nobleness hooked.

"So, we won't just be sperm-protectors…"

"You'll be peace-providers."

"What are you both doing up and working this late?"

Barefoot, her hair wrapped in a white towel, matching a luxurious white robe that stopped several inches above her knees, Meehix took them both by surprise. She was nibbling on a small slice of zzazza loaf.

"I was hungry…So that's where the Kioskie went."

She took the zzazza out of her mouth long enough to take a quick, small swig straight from the bottle and set it gently back on Chuckie's desk.

"Are you okay?" John beat Chuckie to the question.

She'd spent the whole day in her suite. John was more aware of the delivery packages than Chuckie. He also knew more about the previous day that left her crying with orange hair. What they both knew was she'd been holed up and hadn't made an appearance during her spa day.

She smiled at John. "Let's just say that when the towel comes off, I'll be back to my old green-haired self." She took another bite of the zzazza. "So, what's cookin', good lookin's?"

John took the lead. "Chuckie's lined us up a job protecting…"

"Billeroon sperm," Chuckie saved John the trouble of trying to remember what it was that they were going to risk their lives to protect.

"The billeroons?" She smiled again. "Has it been five years already? Sign us up!" She headed back down the hallway.

"Are you sure you're okay?" John called.

"Ask me that one more time," she turned and graced them with another smile, "and I'll postpone my upcoming long soak in a hot tub just long enough to meet you in the gym and leave you for dead on a treadmill."

They watched her amble back to her room, each lost in their thoughts.

"Book it, Chuckie. The NutBusters are back in business."

John left his chair and poured one more notch of Kioskie in his glass from the bottle on Chuckie's desk.

"I need a brief chat with her."

"Not about the succubus?!?" Chuckie had a moment of panic.

"No." John patted his Chucko-bro on the shoulder. "Something much scarier."

It seemed like a much longer hallway between the front offices and the kitchen than he remembered, but John traversed it, carrying his glass, not sure if he would go straight to where the gym was or turn left to his room, or right, toward Meehix's.

Reaching the kitchen, he downed his last sip of Kioskie, set the glass on the counter, and turned right.

His legs weren't quite steady when he reached her door, so he knocked while he still had half an ounce of courage left. The door opened just wide enough for a towel-wrapped head to peer out.

"First of all," John stammered with a well-prepared speech that ended up shot to hell before he even opened his mouth. "I want to make it clear that this is *not* the

Kioskie talking," followed by a belch whose flames he tried to swipe away.

"You were saying?" the towel-wrapped head asked.

"I was saying," John did his best to stand tall and sober, no mean feat, "that I would like to ask you out on a date."

"Date...Date...I'm not familiar with that term, other than as a notation on a calendar."

"*A date*, back on Kdack, is when one person asks another person out for an evening that the two said persons enjoy. Or don't, as sometimes happens, but it's an evening that the two of them, and only the two of them enjoy, or don't, together. From my experience, disaster is often the result, but I wondered if you would like to join me for an evening involving non-predetermined results?"

Having stated his case, he took what he hoped wasn't a wobbly step back, awaiting her reply.

"Just tell me when, Jojacko," she smiled, "and you've got a date."

She closed the door, and John straightened himself and headed for his room on shaky legs. A moment later, John heard the door open again and turned to see her looking out at him.

"The Kioskie, I can handle." John straightened himself and walked back to her on steady legs, stopping two feet short of where she stood with her door still partially opened. "Your pheromones, on the other hand, are beyond anyone in the realm to be able to resist."

Meehix smiled at him and watched as he nodded and headed to his room again with wobbly legs.

"I didn't release any pheromones," she called after him.

He turned, on legs no longer the least bit wobbly.

"Then it must have been your smile."

She gave him another of her crooked-assed sweet smiles.

"Not fair!" John called as his suddenly wobbly-again legs carried him to his room.

Meehix watched to make sure that John didn't face-plant before making it to his door.

A minimum of Kioskie. No pheromones. She'd been practicing her control. She looked at her towel-headed self in the mirror and smiled. One more weapon in her arsenal that she'd never considered before.

She was humming as she sank into the third bath of her personalized spa day.

Maybe I can finally rinse the last of the orange out of my hair.

CHAPTER SEVEN

"You'll have two Gates to go through." The three NutBusters partners were in their front office as Chuckie reviewed the cum delivery details. "One to Plendark to pick up the goods and another one to Zellion to drop them off."

"The NutBusters delivering cum," John shook his head. "At least we'll have a job that lives up to our oh-so-eloquent name."

"Meehix is fine with it!"

"I do not believe that I am anywhere on record as ever saying I was *fine* with it."

"And I do not believe that you ever said you weren't," Chuckie defended himself.

"That's because the only parts of your anatomy that don't seem to function properly are your ears, so why waste my breath?"

"All right," John interjected. "So we're stuck with the name. Chuckie, are you sure this isn't another trap someone's setting us up for?" John was still hesitant. "Our last *easy money* job failed miserably in both the easy and the money categories."

"Not that it wasn't fun," Meehix joined in, "what with all the shooting and screaming and running for our lives."

"Yeah. I think it was the running for our lives from the toad from hell that I enjoyed the most."

"That one was on Meehix, remember? This is Chuckie N back in action."

Meehix blushed a slight purple when she remembered that the last one *was* one of hers.

"I've managed to track down all of the Gate codes."

"How'd you do that?" John didn't think it was possible.

"A little bribery here," Chuckie smiled, "a little blackmail there. You know, the usual. Can I see Hannah?"

John removed the silver and turquoise pendant and handed it over. Chuckie plugged the USB into Mixie and returned it a minute later.

"Slide this into Shippewa when you get near a Gate, and the girls will do the rest."

"Saves me from having to be hypnotized again."

"Oh, c'mon," John defended himself. "It was only once, and it didn't damage you."

"I still don't like the idea." Meehix shivered. "What if you hypnotize me and can't get me back, and I spend the rest of my life wandering around like some brainless zombie ready to follow anyone's suggestions?"

"It doesn't work like that." John defended the practice of hypnosis. "They can't make you do anything that you normally wouldn't do."

"How does anyone know what I would *normally* do?

Hell, even *I* don't know what I might normally do given any specific situation."

"Okay, no more hypnosis." He turned to Chuckie. "When do we set out?"

"Tomorrow afternoon would be good. That will give you enough time to get through the first Gate and hit a space station for the night and show up fresh and ready to make it to Plendark in the early afternoon."

Chuckie reached in a drawer and pulled out three small silver bracelets about one inch wide. He tossed one to each of them and put the third one on his wrist.

"GPS?" John slipped his on.

"Simpleton. They're High-Level Translators. HLTs have a lot more range than our old one."

"How big is the range?" Meehix slipped hers on and approved of the bright silver against her blue wrist.

"I don't know," Chuckie admitted. "Might be five clickos, might be all the way back here. I paid a pretty penny for them, out of my pocket, and tried to reprogram them with an extra boost, but until we try them, there's no way of knowing."

"Wait a minute." John wasn't sure he'd heard him right. "*You* paid for them?"

"Out of *your* pocket?" Meehix wasn't sure she'd heard him right, either.

"What? Can't I do something nice?"

"There's a first time for everything, I guess." Skepticism still colored John's voice.

"Well," Chuckie hemmed, "if you two survive, I hoped you'd both reimburse me."

"And if we don't?" John followed up.

"Then I'll track you down in your next life and beat it out of you."

"Now you sound like Chuckie again." Meehix smiled.

"Seriously, I'd miss you two more than I'd miss the money. I just want to give you the best chance to survive, that's all."

"While we take all the risks?"

"What can I say, Meehix? I'm a hacker, not a fighter."

"Back up a minute." John's skepticism was back. "Best chance to survive *what*, exactly?"

"Well," Chuckie's hawing was back, "there may be a minor issue when you arrive at Zellion to drop the shipment off."

"How minor?" John wasn't going to let that one slip past without more details. "We'll be delivering a crate of cum. Where does a complication come in?"

"They're going to use it to hammer out some peace treaty negotiations, remember?"

"Yeah, yeah, a real *cum*baya moment."

"The trouble is, it seems that not all of the nations on Zellion are looking for peace. The truth is, some of them might *want* to go to war rather than compromising for peace."

"Is it too late to back out?" John was serious. He'd had enough running and gunning to last him for a while.

"I'm afraid so." Chuckie was ready to duck whatever John was going to throw at him. "The NutBusters were already paid half up-front. The other half will be on delivery."

"Just a wild guess here," John was toying with chucking the new HLT at Chuckie's head. "You spent your portion of the pre-payment on these fancy new translators, right?"

"He's smarter than he looks." Chuckie smiled at Meehix, who did not smile back.

"Give us the details." John sighed. "Who might we need to kill for the sake of cum?"

"There're three small nations that might be in the mood to become larger nations." Chuckie pulled up the data. "The most serious one would be Dickolor. Got a nasty tempered dictator, goes by the name of Claporio the First."

John had to stifle a laugh. "So, Clap the Tricky-Dicky doesn't want cum. Makes sense. Please tell me that one of the other small nations isn't named Troy because if the Trojans covered the Dicks, then Clap wouldn't have to worry about the cum."

"Did you understand any of that?"

"Kdackan references, I guess." Meehix shook her head. She held up her HLT. "Since we're not always good at little buttons, can we run through how these work a few times before we desperately need them?"

"Great idea!" Chuckie was ready for any distraction from the dictator from Dickolor. "I've already paired them together and with Ship. Red," he held his up and pushed down on the top, producing a small red LED light in the middle of the unit, "means off."

"Green means go. Got it," John pushed his top down with no change to the red light. "Is it broken already?"

"Pushing down on the top means red." Chuckie was going to try to be patient. "Pushing up on the bottom will give you green." He demonstrated.

"Design flaw number one." John pushed up on the bottom and managed to get a green light. "The whole thing is perfectly symmetrical, and the LED is in the exact middle." He flipped his over. "Exactly in the middle on both sides. How the hell are we supposed to know the top from the bottom?"

"Damn!" Chuckie had to admit that John had a point. It was an excellent one, and Chuckie was pissed that John had discovered it first.

Meehix pulled out a small switchblade knife. She was never without one type of knife or another on her person and etched three short lines at the top of hers.

"Problem solved." she closed the blade and tossed it to John, who gave *his* HLT two notches at the top and tossed it back.

"Only two notches?" She was curious.

"One of us is bound to lose theirs." John smiled. "This way, we'll be able to tell who was the careless one."

Meehix slid the knife back into its sleeve, leaving both of the boys thinking that they wouldn't have thought to look there.

"Hello, Ship?"

"Hello, Meehix."

"Hello, Ship."

"Hello, John."

"Hello, Ship."

"Hello, Chuckie. I see that the installation and training are proceeding nicely."

"Hello, Ship," John tried the highest-pitched squeaky voice he could produce.

"Hello, girlfriend."

"That's a terrible rendition of what Hannah would sound like." Meehix offered her opinion.

"Then you give it a try." John tossed the pendant over, and Meehix held it for a minute.

Although she was all too familiar with the history of the bitch who'd broken John's heart, but not enough to prevent him from naming his one-of-a-kind program for her, she'd never actually held it before. Shuttling her opinion of the real Hannah to the back of her mind, she held the small piece of silver and turquoise gently, trying to imagine the new Hannah held captive inside.

"Wait until you hear what these idiots are planning next," Meehix's voice was neither sexy nor high-pitched. It was a friendly mid-range. "It will make your wings quiver."

"Bravo, bravas, bravissimo!"

She held the pendant up for Chuckie. "You wanna give it a try?"

Chuckie shook his head. "I can't top that."

Meehix tossed it back to John.

"Boarding is around noon tomorrow, Ship." Chuckie wanted to make they were all on the same page.

"I will be breathless with anticipation. I've been practicing my sarcasm. How did I do?"

"Sounded like a pro," Chuckie turned his HLT off. The others followed suit. "No need to cause Ship any needless worries."

"Let's hope they *are* needless," John added, as Chuckie ran them through all of the information he'd been able to gather.

They met up again the next morning. John and Meehix kept most of their weapons onboard Shippewa, so they were able to pack light.

Chuckie seemed a little more agitated than usual and ran through some details they'd covered the day before. He made sure they'd packed as many weapons as they had with them, and their onboard inventory was well-stocked.

"You sound like a mother hen," John finally told him. "Is there something else we *need* to know that you haven't clued us into yet?"

Chuckie stopped his fussing, which meant John had hit a nerve.

"I don't know if it's important or not. It's probably nothing."

"Out with it." Meehix always got a little edgy when they were heading out for a job.

"Remember that program I was beta-testing a while back?"

John remembered. Chuckie had been very protective of it and more than a little secretive, but the little he'd shared with John had been enough to convince him that it was a beauty.

"What about it?"

"Someone's been doing some deep-searches for the two bounty hunters who've been causing various commotions. Before you ask, I don't know who it is, but he's good."

"Is he close?" If Chuckie was worried, John was worried.

"Hard to tell. It's not like he's right on your asses or anything, but he's not too far behind."

"Lovely." Meehix thought Chuckie's timing could have been better.

"You know about the painting, right?" John wasn't sure if Chuckie had been paying attention when they'd first showed it to him.

"Kick the bottom, and a secret door opens. Big whoop."

"Listen to me, and listen very carefully," John's serious tone got Chuckie's full attention. "If he's tracking us and finds us in space, we can deal with him. But if he tracks us down to here, then you'll be left alone to fend for yourself. I suggest that confrontation may not be your best option."

"You're telling me to kick the painting and hide like hell?"

"Something like that, yeah."

"What he said." Meehix nodded. "There're enough weapons in the office back there to do some serious damage. You might want to practice with them a little because if he shows up here, it'll be a situation that you'll probably not be able to *hack* your way out of."

"Not to mention," John tried to drive the point home, "that you are still an escaped felon. Do you really want to be captured and frozen alive again?"

"Well, if you put it like that...but Chuck Norris wouldn't run and hide."

"You're right," John agreed. "Chuck Norris would be prepared to kick some serious ass. Since you lack his physical attributes, which most mortals do, it might be wise to learn how to *weapon-up*."

After his partners left, Chuckie tried to return to his hacking and programming and put Mixie through new paces. He loved the connection speeds in the home office they were renting with the option to buy, but they'd managed to put a little fear in him.

Fuck it!

He went to the kitchen, kicked the painting's bottom frame, and spent some time looking around the office weapons storage. Gathering up a few of the lighter-weight guns, he carried them across the hall to the gym.

A gym was something he'd never taken seriously. Given his lack of size, they had never served any useful purpose. Sure, he could bulk up, but he couldn't height-up, so if he bulked up, the best he could ever hope for would be to end up as wide as he was tall. Not much of a practical goal.

He laid the weapons out on a bench, the purpose of which he knew not, and looked them over. Then he noticed the mirrors along the walls. *What kind of vain creatures needed a mirror to see if they'd added any size to their biceps since the last time they'd looked in one an hour earlier?*

Sighing but determined, he hoisted a short, *machine gun? Is that the right name for it?* and cradled it. At least he knew enough to be able to find the trigger and point the fucker in a direction other than his feet.

It was then that he caught the sight of someone coming at him and pulled the trigger, shattering his image as the mirror's glass crashed to the floor. Chuckie also crashed to the floor from the kickback.

Still on the floor and realizing that the sense of immediate danger had passed because he'd destroyed the intruder in the mirror, he felt a primal surge. A visceral power. A totally new experience.

When Chuck Norris gets kicked, Chuck Norris laughs and kicks back!

Chuckie spent the next hour swapping weapons with himself and shattering at least eight of the twelve mirrors of himself attacking himself.

When Chuck Norris attacks Chuck Norris, they end up calling a truce and going out for beers because they can destroy but not defeat the other.

Chuckie returned all the weapons to whatever the fuck kind of bench he'd laid them out on earlier and hoped that some of them still had some ammo left because he had no shit-for-nothing idea of how to reload them.

He decided that when, and if, his partners returned and surveyed the damage he'd done, his best defense would be *Whoops.*

CHAPTER EIGHT

They made it through the first Gate with no hypnosis involved. Chuckie's program worked to perfection, and Shippewa and Hannah picked up right where they'd left off. They docked at a small station, right where Chuckie had said it would be and checked into the closest, relatively clean motel they could find.

It was only one room. Meehix took the bed and John took the couch. They had passed the early stage where unrequited sex seemed to always be in the air. Things were different now, and when unrequited turned into requited, neither of them wanted it to be in a cheap space station motel.

Freshened up the next morning, they made it to Plendark with no problems while picking up the crate of specially packed cum-tubes. Having loaded it onboard, John turned to the shipping dock manager, who wore the same smile that everyone else they'd met seemed to sport.

"What happens when the billeroon cum supply runs low?"

"Oh, silly you." The manager smiled. "Naughty us keep a four-year supply stocked up for residents only. We're happy, but not stupid."

"Can we retire here?"

"You could, but there is limited space, and you would have to sign up on the waiting list. It costs five thousand credits to sign up, but if you're planning to retire in about ten years or so, you might time it perfectly. Have a pleasant flight."

"I don't know about you," John turned to Meehix as she piloted Ship out and away, "but I'm tempted."

"I hear you, but wouldn't that be sort of like cheating?"

"How's that?"

"Shouldn't happiness be something we earn? Not something you get from a tube every few months?"

"Good point. Let's go earn some happiness."

Reaching the second Gate proved that Chuckie hadn't simply gotten lucky on the first one. They found the next space station eight hours later and settled into another motel for another night. According to Chuckie and his report on the Dickolorian, Claporio the First, if they ran into any trouble, it would be on their next stop.

The next day, their approach and docking on Zellion went without a hint of confrontation. Of course, no one knew which ship was coming with the cum, so a space battle couldn't guarantee that the correct craft had been attacked or raided. No nation could simply blast each approaching ship out of the sky. That would be rude and unacceptable behavior.

They knew that there would be a delegation awaiting their arrival. President Lemier, the leader of the hosting country for the treaty negotiations, had armed guards waiting to help them deliver the cum safely.

When it came to being armed, Meehix and John took nothing for granted and geared up before rolling the cum-crate down the ramp.

"Welcome. I am General Vlonderwomp. I hope your journey has been uneventful."

"So far," John answered. "Can you provide some type of identification?"

The general pulled a device from his belt, causing John and Meehix to flinch and have a hand on a weapon, but the general played a taped recording.

"Welcome, NutBusters. This is President Mullucon Lemier. I was the one who set up the delivery with one Chuckie N of the NutBusters. The passcode is "Chuck Norris doesn't fear fear. Fear fears Chuck Norris.""

"I guess we're talking to the right guys." John handed over the cart handles and followed them to where a caravan of heavily armed vehicles waited.

John and Meehix climbed into the lead vehicle with the general. Surprisingly, the delivery to the hosting embassy went off without a hitch or an attack.

"We were sort of expecting some kind of resistance," John admitted as they watched the guards wheel the crate inside.

"You sound almost disappointed." The general smiled.

"I don't know if disappointed is the right word," Meehix lied. Deep down, both of them were a little wired up to do some damage.

"We were expecting some trouble ourselves. Specifi-cally, from the Dickolorian, Claporio the First. Nasty little power-hungry pissant." The general sighed. "Fortunately, his people overthrew him two days ago. Sadly, that deprived us of the chance to put him in his place ourselves, thereby making an example of him for all of Zellion to see."

"Plan for war, settle for peace?" John had heard that somewhere.

"Exactly. Happily for Zellion, the billeroon cum will allow us to achieve some peace. Maybe. Sadly for Claporio, he won't be given any and will be stuck in a cell stewing in his juices."

"And yet," John couldn't help but notice, "you sound sad, General."

"Do I? Perhaps it's because I've fought enough when the fighting was for a justifiable cause, but when someone leads people to fight just to prop up their ego, I'd like to slice off their dick, then slice off their head, stick the dick in their mouth and hang the head high for all to see." The general smiled. "But maybe that's just me."

John and Meehix couldn't help but like the old warrior. They stepped out of the lead car and listened as the hundreds assembled outside the embassy cheered. It sounded like the Zellions were tired of all of the seemingly endless skirmishes.

"Cum for peace! Come for peace!" chants filled the air.

"I'm sorry that I can't invite you in." The general gave them a card. "Go to this address and buy yourselves a round. A representative will meet you there and pay you the second half due."

"We're not quite clear on that last part." Meehix spoke for herself and John.

"The first part of the payment was a joint collection of

the various representatives gathered here. The second 'upon delivery' payment is from President Mullucon Lemier's account. He would have liked to have gathered enough support to have the whole thing jointly paid but fell short, so he's covering the rest himself."

"He sounds like a man with integrity." John was impressed.

"He sounds like a man who married very well, and his wife loves the mansion they've been living in and doesn't want to have to vacate it...but you didn't hear that from me."

The general winked at them and followed the cum-cart inside.

"I believe that I am your driver," a melodious voice spoke from behind them.

They turned and found a distinguished-looking older Zellion wearing a top hat and tails, directing them to a carriage built for two.

"Excuse me?" John was startled.

"My name is Grovian." The man removed his top hat and swept it toward the open-air cart with what looked like half of a bicycle attached to the front. "I shall be your driver."

"Hello," Meehix greeted him. "You have us at a loss here."

"You've had a long journey to help bring us hope for peace." Grovian took Meehix's arm and guided her into a seat. "The decision was made to give you a leisurely, perhaps pleasant ride to your next destination. It will help you appreciate the fair city, on this fair planet, that you are helping to save from whatever destruction may have befallen if not for the cum that you risked your lives to deliver."

"I'm sorry." John felt uneasy about having such an elderly gentleman peddling them, rickshaw-style, to a bar. "There's no need for you to drive us all the way there. We can hail a cab."

"Wouldn't hear of it. Ahh, you're obviously considerate of my frail old body." Grovian turned his back to them, pulled a cord, and the half-bike started a quiet hum. "Technology, isn't it grand? So, where are we headed? I'll try to take the most scenic route."

John read off the address from the card the general had given him.

"Excellent choice." Grovian nodded. "Even with all the citizens in town for the peace negotiations, the Trogg & Gankard should still be relatively quiet at this time. You must try their chickeria-bobs."

Grovian took them on a pleasant route, pointing out various landmarks along the way. Since they'd established that their driver was in no imminent danger of a heart attack, John and Meehix settled in to enjoy the ride.

Neither of them noticed a small motorbike start up and follow them, keeping a discreet distance behind.

After a pleasant ride, Grovian dropped them off and received a generous tip for his efforts and travelogue. Meehix and John stepped inside the Trogg and settled into a table near the back of the half-full restaurant where they could keep an eye on the door for the president's representative.

Meehix ordered them a couple of drinks, and they decided to take Grovian's advice and split a share-a-side portion of chickeria-bobs. The drinks arrived as a nattily attired man, who they guessed was in his forties, came through the door and scanned the room.

John stood and waved to get his attention, but the newcomer paid him no mind and took a booth along the wall where he set his lap-pad down on the table and went to work.

"Working lunch?" John guessed.

"Seems to be." Meehix still eyed the door. "Obvious, he wasn't looking for us."

A much scragglier-looking younger man came through the door then, and after a quick look around, made his way quickly to their table and sat next to Meehix.

"The NutBusters." He wasted no time introducing himself as he pulled out a worn envelope and slid it across the table to John as he smiled at Meehix. "It was a marvelous sight to watch you two make the delivery. Maybe we can get all the assholes to agree that peace is in all of our best interests."

"You're the president's delivery agent?" John peeked inside the envelope.

"He wants to keep this part of the payment quiet, as I'm sure the general explained."

Meehix returned his smile, and they both nodded.

"Forgive my choice of appearance, but if someone is carrying around sixty-two thousand, five hundred credits in their pocket, it's best not to dress in a manner that would get oneself mugged, wouldn't you agree?"

He took a quick sip of Meehix's drink, then one of John's, and hurried out before the management could kick him out as a panhandler bothering their customers.

"What a curious planet." John pocketed the envelope, trusting that it was all there.

"Here, you can also finish mine." Meehix slid her glass across the table to John and ordered a fresh one for herself.

"The most curious thing," Meehix dug into the chickeria-bobs that arrived with her refill, "is that the whole job went off without a hitch."

"Oh, these are good." John bit into a bob and nodded. "The first job we've had that was as simple as it sounded. Maybe we're getting the hang of this after all."

They had nearly finished with their lunch and drinks when the nicely dressed man who'd entered before the president's pay-off agent approached their table with his lap-pad tucked neatly into his bag.

"I'm sorry, may I join you for a few minutes? Don't worry. I'm not a salesman or anything as obnoxious as that. I was merely hoping for a word with you two."

"As long as it's a short word," John slid out a chair with his foot. "We're looking forward to heading out and getting home soon."

The man gave a slight bow and a smile to both of them as he took the proffered chair.

"I should introduce myself. I am T. R. Exit. Please don't ask me what the T. R. stands for." He gave them both an engaging smile. "And yes, Exit is my family name. How's that for a doozy to live with, huh? But please, call me T.R."

John extended his hand over the table. "You can call me John."

The stranger shook John's hand.

Meehix smiled and offered hers. "You can call me anytime you'd like." *He was one good-looking specimen.*

T.R. smiled at the intended compliment.

"Here's the thing." T.R. sounded apologetic. "I was there, watching as you two made your delivery. You're the NutBusters, right?"

"Two of them, at least," John admitted, with a slightly proud smile.

"I know you want to head out soon, but I couldn't pass up the opportunity."

He pulled a silver business card from a pocket and set it on the table between them.

"I'm a research specialist. Strictly freelance,"

He looked back and forth between them as he continued, wanting to make sure he was making eye contact with each because he wasn't sure who would make the decision and didn't want to disrespect either of them.

"And I'm always looking to pick up a little extra work."

Meehix picked up the card first and looked it over. It was definitely not your basic business card. For one thing, there was an embossed emblem of an eye that seemed to follow her when she turned the card at different angles.

"What does a research specialist do, exactly?" She slid the card over to John.

"Research." He smiled. "I'm sure that the NutBusters have plenty of researchers, but it never hurts to have an extra *eye*."

"Ergo the eye on the card." John smiled as he looked it over.

"Corny, I know. But it does tend to draw your attention, doesn't it?"

"That it does," John admitted as he continued to admire

the card and wondered if perhaps the NutBusters should have similar ones made. "So, what can we do for you?"

"Nothing at the moment. Except to maybe hold onto my card and keep me in mind if you ever find that you need my services in the future."

"That's it?" John was so accustomed to sales pitches that he was surprised T.R. wasn't asking them to hire him on the spot.

"That's it. That's all. As I said, I'm an independent contractor, hiring out on a job-by-job basis. I've been doing this for twenty years and have made many contacts along the way. I hoped that I could add you to my contacts list if you find that you ever require my services."

"Thanks." John slid the card into a zippered pocket. *No one's ever offered me their business card before.*

T.R. stood, reached out, and took both of their hands.

"You two have had an arduous journey, and I'm glad it ended well. I'll return to my table and let you both be on your way with wishes for safe travels."

"Seemed like a nice guy." John finished his drink and stood.

"Very nice." Meehix finished her drink and rose. John wasn't completely pleased with the tone of her voice. He was even less so when she smiled at T.R. on their way toward the door.

John pushed the bottom button of the HLT as they hit the sidewalk. "Where are you, Ship?"

"Right where you left me, John."

"Right. Be there soon."

They hailed a cab and headed for Dock Two, Bay

Twelve, and then, home, an additional sixty-two thousand, five hundred credits richer.

T.R. lingered in his booth. He had finally come face-to-face with two-thirds of the bounty hunting NutBusters and had confirmed that they had one other partner. If his surmising was correct, the third member would be the cryo-escapee.

He knew that they'd set up a home base on L-222, but he hadn't been able to discover their exact location. Now, they were carrying his business card with a Galactic Locator Chip embedded in his business card's eye. When they finally made it home, then he and his hired Crom Limeans could invade and take all three of them at once. Then the bidding war would start.

Being a research specialist who was very good at his job, he'd learned that the NutBusters had signed on to deliver a crate of billeroon cum to Zellion. He beat them there by a day and had bided his time. He was a very patient man and was in a very pleasant mood, which was why his guard was down when his trans-comm rang. Very few people had his personal number, and no one could reach him unless they were close.

"Trexit."

"Where are you?"

"Zellion, and who the fuck is this?" *Okay, maybe he'd had one extra drink while watching the NutBusters.*

"This is Captain Prooshevekk. You've found the targets?"

"Found, yes. Will capture soon." *Fucking anal Blavarians.*

"I thought I recognized the ship."

"You're here?"

"Hovering," Prooshevekk replied. "I was assigned to drop off a load of weapons for Claporio the Dickolorian but wasn't allowed to dock, so I've been hanging here in space trying to figure out why. It's the same asshole, isn't it?"

"That's not really a question, is it, *Captain*."

"No, it's not. Can you confirm it is who I've been paying you to track down?"

"I can confirm." Trexit sighed. He was willing to play one side against another as he tracked down a target, but he never lied.

"I would strongly suggest, sir," Trexit went on, "that you back off immediately. I have a crew ready to take them alive when they arrive home. To try to capture them on your own will not lead to pleasant consequences."

"Fuck pleasant." Prooshevekk wanted the Kdackan so bad that he could taste blood between his teeth. "You tracked them and identified them as I requested. I now consider our contract fulfilled and will pay you for finding them as agreed upon."

"Agreed and out." Trexit ended the call, and with every bone in his body, wished the Blavarian captain the worst of luck.

Trexit had planted his card and had two other bidders on the gruesome twosome, with perhaps a third about to be signed. Prooshevekk was out for immediate blood, and there was nothing he could do to cool that fever down.

Revenge was a fool's motivation. Trexit's motivation was simply seeking the quickest way to early retirement.

Hoisting his glass, he offered a silent toast to the NutBusters. *The longer you run, the closer I am to retiring.*

CHAPTER NINE

"Heya Ship," John called as he and Meehix made their happy way up into the cockpit, basking in an easy job well done. "Miss us as much as we missed you?"

"Breathless anticipation does not begin to cover it."

"I think I liked you better before you dove into your sarcasm programming." John smiled as he carried his and Meehix's bags back to Cargo before returning up front to find Meehix riding shotgun with her feet up on what passed for a dashboard, having decided to let John do some piloting for a while.

John eased Ship up and out, hovering for a moment as he got his bearings for the next Gate home.

"This is the captain of a dreadnought IV" a voice came in over an open channel that no one on Shippewa was aware was open. "Halt, and prepared to be boarded. All shall live, but we will need the Kdackan to depart your ship and join us."

John and Meehix exchanged confused glances. Meehix

figured it out first and whispered, "Hover, Jojacko. I think I got this."

John hovered as Meehix took over the discussion.

"Are you, perhaps, a Blavarian dreadnought captain with no sense of humor because you were once insulted and bested by a simple Kdackan?"

During the pause, while the captain was formulating his response, Meehix leaned into John's ear and whispered, "I think this is the same guy you once told to *suck eggs.*"

"No shit?"

"No shit."

"Talk about holding a grudge." John smiled at her. "I'll let the 'simple Kdackan' comment slide. Buckle up."

Meehix buckled up as John took over the conversation and whispered. "He's a Blavarian dreadnought captain."

"So, captain, what's your name? I don't believe we've properly introduced ourselves. I'm Jojacko, and you're?"

"Captain Prooshevekk. Which will be the last name you speak as you beg for mercy."

"Oh, dear. Now you have me terrified, Captain Poopashit. Did I hurt your feelings once upon a time because a simple Kdackan got the best of the mighty Captain Shitapoop?"

Captain Prooshevekk wondered if his decision to livestream this to the local solar system as an example of why one should never disrespect a Blavarian dreadnought captain was a wise choice.

"You do realize," Prooshevekk continued, "that you will be dead in ten minutes."

"Oh, good." John could talk smack with the best of them. "That'll give me nine minutes to fuck your mother, with one minute left over for me to die happy because she finally has a smile on her face."

Meehix hit a button and hoped she'd muted the comm.

"What the fuck are you doing?"

"I believe that he is talking smack. Do I have that right, John?"

"You have that exactly right, Ship." John turned to Meehix. "Talking smack is exactly what you do when someone's about to try to end your life, and you're buying time."

John hit the button to unmute.

"So, Captain Pushapoop, you were saying?"

"Run, John, run. They outgun us, and they're about to fire."

"Your problem, Captain Pissforbrains, is that we're prepared to die. I've had a good life and am heavily insured, but if you simply blow us out of the sky, you'll never get to see my last smile as I beg for mercy from the mighty Captain Pooparope."

"It seems to me that the NutBusters are better at insults than they are at battle."

"The NutBusters?" John was startled. "What the fuck is a NutBuster?"

"You should know." The captain sounded confident. "I have it on good authority that several separate entities are after you. My goal is to be the first to succeed at causing your well-deserved demise."

John muted. "Any suggestions?"

"Duck under and floor it. A dreadnought IV has no downward-firing weapons." Ship had done a quick search. John unmuted.

"Captain. In your rush for revenge, did you ever consider that we might have backup? Have you checked your upward scopes lately?"

In the three seconds it took the captain to figure out if it was a bluff or not, John dove and floored it, giving them at least a slight head start.

"We need to find the closest asteroid field! Meehix, you're now the navigator!"

"Bossy, much?" Meehix hit the screen and started searching. "Why an asteroid field?"

"It worked for Han Solo!" John bobbed and weaved as much as he could to avoid the missiles coming at them from behind. Fortunately, they weren't heat-seeking.

"What the fuck is a Han Solo?"

"Physically, he's a five on the Chuck Norris scale. Balls-wise, he's an eleven."

"Got one!" Meehix punched in the coordinates, and John followed the blue line that appeared on the screen, zigging and zagging the whole way.

"They can't catch us, but we don't have enough boost to outrun them. We have a tighter turn radius, but that's our only advantage."

Meehix reached over and buckled John in. This was one wild ride.

"We need a bigger ship!"

"I believe that my growth spurt is over."

John pulled a one-eighty and flew under the dread-nought. Their adversary took a moment to reverse course, by which time John had completed his three-sixty and was back following the blue line, having gained a few more seconds.

"Not a ship to replace you, Ship. But you need a phatter ass."

"Why would I want a fatter ass?" Shippewa liked her sleek design.

"Not fat in a Kardashian way. P-H-A-T phat. It means pretty, hot, and tempting. It means that we need to boost your engines so you'd have more power, and therefore more speed so we can outrun any assholes coming from behind."

"Oh, phast phat, not fat-fat. That would be nice."

John spotted a large carrier lumbering across their path ahead, similar in size and appearance to one they'd recently been on.

"Ship! Please identify the crossing craft!" John headed straight toward it, putting it in line for any shots that missed them.

"Course for collision ETA is twenty seconds."

"Have you lost your mind? What the hell are you doing?" Meehix was freaking out.

"Even a dreadnought captain won't fire on us if any errant shots take out a cargo carrier. That would look really bad on his resume."

"You have a point." Meehix relaxed slightly, appreciating John's thinking under pressure.

"Is it what I hope it is, Ship?"

"If you hoped that it was a Bargeflat 489, you will be happy."

"Meehix," John requested, "Set an XK2 to detonate in five seconds and fire it directly at the barge."

This being no time for questions, she did as instructed

and hoped her partner hadn't somehow lost his mind in the last ten seconds.

The XK2 was fired and exploded in a glorious burst seconds before hitting the barge. John drove straight through the burst, then fired Ship's forward thrusters, which nearly caused himself and Meehix to suffer whiplash from the sudden deceleration.

He then performed a perfect belly-up landing on the barge's bottom hull, letting the barge's magnetic-generating engines attach to Ship's metallic plate.

Prooshevekk was not a happy dreadnought captain at the moment. He'd had to cease fire as the NutBusters drove directly at the barge. Then he saw the explosion. He spoke to the livestream audience.

"So. They chose suicide rather than surrender. It will deprive me of the pleasure of executing them myself, but I hope this serves a lesson to one and all that you don't fuck with Captain Prooshevekk if you hope for a long life-expectancy."

"Captain?" A voice came from behind him.

"Yes, Sergeant?"

"Sergeant Krikinik, sir. We don't spot any discernable damage to the Bargeflat."

Prooshevekk cut the live feed, hoping that viewers would quickly forget the sergeant's comment. He piloted his craft and hovered over the top of the Bargeflat, surveying for the Kdackan's ship.

"They're not out there still running."

"No, sir."

"So they're hiding somewhere..." For once in his life,

Captain Prooshevekk chose patience. "Keep a lookout. I'll hover until they make another run for it."

"Do I have a phat ass?" Meehix asked soon after they'd attached to the barge.

"*Phat* with a capital P," John answered honestly, which made her smile.

John's view wasn't the best since they were both still strapped in, but he'd memorized every curve of her cute butt before and felt confident in his answer.

"Do you think we lost them?" Meehix was hopeful.

"I think we at least confused them." John's equilibrium was also somewhat confused. Gravity said he was right-side up. His head insisted he was upside-down. His stomach was beginning to disagree with both.

"As long as we're hanging around," John smiled through his concern, "do you remember either of us announcing ourselves to the *Blatherian Captain* as the NutBusters?"

"No." Meehix was experiencing a similar "gravity versus brain" problem.

"And yet, he knew who we were. Which means he might know about Chuckie—and could use him as leverage."

"Our address isn't on any communications or advertisements," she tried to reassure him. "Chuckie is safe."

"And he knows how to use the painting."

"Can we detach and get ourselves upright soon?"

John detached and flipped the ship but continued to fly as close to the barge's bottom as possible.

"Is there a Gate on the other side of the asteroid field?"

It only took her a minute to locate one, and she put in its coordinates.

"Ship?"

"Yes, John?"

"I can get us through the asteroids and into the Gate, but we need to come out of it as far away from L-222 as possible. We're aiming for a diversion from our home."

"Have either of you two ever been to Space Station Nevera before?"

"Is that the best you can come up with?" Meehix sighed and turned to John. "If you thought Nerth B was a dump, wait until you see this place."

"Can you think of any disguise you can render to give us a head start?"

"Sorry, John. We'd show as an outline against the black, and we'd need to be closer to the asteroid field for me to mimic one. I wish I were phatter, but there you have it."

"Other than having no downward-firing weapons, does a dreadnought IV have any other vulnerabilities?

"None that I've been able to discover."

"C'est la vie." John sighed and maneuvered their way around the underside of the barge and found themselves directly in the dreadnought's line of fire.

"Decided to stand and fight rather than running like scared flibbits, have you?"

"And this, galactic live streamers, is how you bust the britches of the ooohhh, so scary Blavarian captain *Whiny the Poo-Poo.*"

Prooshevekk thought he'd taken the live feed down but was interrupted in his verifying of it by five rapidly fired XK2's that made direct hits. Even though they weren't strong enough to damage his ship, they were still powerful enough to rock it and cause everyone to lose their footing.

"Is the fucking livestream down or isn't it?"

"Yes, sir." Sergeant Krikinik was the first one back to his feet and scrambled to verify that the feed was dead.

"Nice bluff, John. Nice shooting, Meehix."

"Nice ass, Ship." John smiled. "We'll get you a phatter one as soon as we can."

They made it to the asteroid field as the Blavarian bastard finally caught up to them and was within firing range. Observations of several small asteroids exploding ahead of them proved the latter.

"Not very good shots, are they?"

"I've seen better," Meehix agreed. "Ship. You have an asteroid image in your detection deflection arsenal, right?"

"Deploying it now. Decrease thrust, John. We need to look like we're floating aimlessly."

John eased up and dodged a couple of tumbling chunks as he turned to the right and circled back. He tried to fit in as he slowly made his way through the field, hopefully without drawing any attention to the asteroid they now appeared to be.

The dreadnought entered the field and proceeded to shoot the hell out of any asteroid in its way. John's circling had put them behind the enemy craft, and they watched as Captain Prooshevekk took out his frustrations on perfectly innocent ancient planetary debris.

"What d'ya think?" John asked as they watched the carnage. "Mommy or daddy issues?"

"My best guess?" Now that they were safely behind

their pursuers, Meehix was enjoying the show. "Male geni-talia inadequacy overcompensation syndrome."

"And the multi-syllable word combinations under duress award goes to?"

"That would be my humble self." Meehix smiled.

John continued to follow the Blavarian captain from a safe distance while dodging a few of their fellow asteroids in the process. It was a delicate balance.

"You know," John hated to bring reality back into the equation, "that when he gets to the end of the asteroid field, he's going to turn and wait for any asteroids that he hasn't yet shot to make an appearance and run for it. How do we get around that and to the next Gate?"

"John?"

"Yes, Ship."

"Have you glanced at the blue line leading to the next Gate lately?"

"Can't say that I have, what with running and gunning for our lives and minor details like that."

"Space is a strange thing, and sometimes, calculations can be slightly off."

"Meaning?" John hated to admit it, but he was tired. It had started as such a simple day.

"Meaning, the asteroid field that you and Mister Captain Butt-Ugly are currently navigating your way through will pass the Gate you need."

"The fuck you say!"

"The fuck I say." Ship was proud of her learning of various vernaculars and how to use them in appropriate situations. **"Angle your way and follow the blue line. The**

Blavarian captain will be waiting at the front of the asteroid field for you to emerge."

"Meanwhile, we'll be slipping out the side door...Meehix?"

"This is so much fun." She smiled.

"Even if we end up on Space Station Nevera?"

"Even if." She sighed.

John followed the blue line, dodging a few asteroids along the way, and hit the Gate, raising a two-fingered salute to the Blavarian blowhard who would be waiting at the end of the field for them to make an appearance.

"Where are they, Sergeant Krikinik?"

"Still hiding," the sergeant guessed. "Afraid of fearing your wrath, sir."

"As well they should be." Prooshevekk smiled. "They should have chosen suicide."

"Gage, himself, couldn't come up with a fart that smelled worse than this."

"You'll get used to it." Meehix had learned through experience.

They'd left Prooshevekk behind and still waiting as they made their way through the Gate. Once through, they'd found and docked on Space Station Nevera, unloaded their bags, and went in search of a room for the night.

"Ten minutes from now, you won't smell a thing."

"That's what I'm afraid of."

Meehix hailed a cab. "Hotel Norio." She said nothing

more until they'd exited the cab, with John still holding an arm across his nose to protect his olfactory senses.

Before they entered the hotel, Meehix twisted John's arm down, forcing him to take in the stench before he embarrassed them both while she checked them in.

"Space Station Nevera is often called Never Again."

"I can smell why."

"The sooner you get used to it, the better off we'll all be!"

John breathed deeply and gagged. He then took a shorter breath and managed not to pass out.

"That wasn't so bad now, was it?" Meehix let up.

"Define bad." John rolled his arm to make sure she hadn't dislocated anything.

Meehix got them checked into a room with double beds. After depositing their bags on the floor and before they unpacked, Meehix released some fresh air pheromones and gave John a moment to take them in.

"Feel better now?"

"Much better." John drew in a deep breath.

"Good. Hold onto that smell because we're heading down for a walk."

"What the fuck do I want with a walk?"

"You want a walk, partner, so you can get used to the smells and be able to hold a conversation without pressing your nostrils together between your fingers and breathing through your mouth like a tourist."

"Oh." John was beginning to catch on despite the stench.

"We're going to lie low here for a day or two. Maybe the Blavarian captain will lose interest."

"Did he seem like someone who's likely to lose interest after we've embarrassed him twice?"

"Not really, no," Meehix agreed. "Try to get used to the smell and not draw any more attention to ourselves than is necessary, please." Meehix offered him her arm.

"A young couple." John took her arm. "One of whom has a phat ass, going out for an evening stroll?"

"A young couple," Meehix led the way out of their room and down onto the street, "with two of the phinest phat asses ever seen."

Pausing in front of the elevator door's reflective surface, they spun and admired their asses.

"Dayum," John uttered, right before the door slid open. "These two asses ought to be arrested for being too good-looking to be allowed out in public without a license."

They rode the elevator down to street level and decided not to push their luck. They hit a convenience store half a block down. Meehix grabbed a large bottle of Knocneeohs, paid for it, and they headed back to their room, where they downed it without worrying about glasses.

"Tomorrow will be another To-ra-rooma day," was the last thing John remembered himself saying before he passed out when they reached the bottom of the bottle.

CHAPTER TEN

"I think I might have a bit of a hangover." John rolled out of his bed and tried to stand the next mid-morning. "Nope." He sat again. "No thinking about it. It's a definite hangover."

His commentary on his current condition was immaterial to Meehix, who was curled up in her bed and snoring softly.

"Lucky you," John whispered as he headed into the bathroom and took a long, cold shower as his combined punishment and cure. "Shit, the water smells almost as bad as the air."

Toweling off, he threw on a pair of sweats and found Meehix sitting up on the edge of her bed.

"About time." She stood. "Did you leave any hot water for me?"

"Didn't touch it."

"Glad to hear it." She stretched and headed for her shower.

John had forgotten that she liked to sleep naked. *I'm*

going to need another cold shower if this keeps up.

While she was showering, John ordered a room service brunch, hoping that the food was somewhere in the range of edible and that the juice was actual juice and not some mixture of water and flavoring. He'd visited Gage's Uncle Luce down in Mexico for a weekend once and decided that "Don't drink the water" would be advice well-heeded on Nevera.

He pulled up Heemix, the companion computer to Chuckie's Mixie that they'd acquired together at very-discounted rates. He was surprised when the connection sprang up quickly. He found a message waiting for him from Chuckie.

Still alive? Haven't heard. Starting to worry.

John typed back.

Still alive. Had to take diversionary tactics and are at a stop-over in olfactory hell.

Chuckie's response was immediate.

The Blavarian?

You knew about him?

Half the known universe knows about his grudge against you. Didn't think he was smart enough to track you down.

Smart enough to have learned we're part of the NutBusters and to bushwhack us after our cum delivery.

Oh.

We lost him. Doesn't mean he won't come looking at NutBusters Central.

Double Oh.

Don't answer the door. Don't forget about the rooms behind the painting. Don't die.

Will do. Where's Meehix?

Taking a shower.

Lucky water.

Later.

Don't die yourselves.

Will try. Food's on its way. Gotta eat.

Bye.

Meehix emerged from the bathroom, her body wrapped in a towel.

Thank God for small mercies. John closed Heemix down.

"Anything interesting?" She nodded at Heemix.

"Chuckie says hi."

"Is he okay?"

"So far…I warned him that Captain Poopalot might come looking if he can't find us again."

There was a knock on the door, and Meehix sprang for a weapon, dropping her towel along the way.

"It's the room service I ordered."

"Leave it on the floor outside," Meehix shouted from the side of the door, her gun held ready.

They heard the sound of someone taking trays off a cart and setting them down.

Meehix gathered up some clothes and got dressed as John tried to avert his eyes, giving whoever had delivered the food ten minutes to make themselves scarce.

Once they'd retrieved the food, they enjoyed a light breakfast, the smell of the station mostly blocked by the room's filtration system.

"Good choice on the juice." Meehix sipped.

"I was afraid of ordering anything that might involve water."

"Believe it or not, it used to be worse. At least showering is now possible if somewhat odiferous. But don't even think about using the wash unit in the bathroom. It'll take another three washes to get the smell of the water out of your clothes."

"You think it's safe to book out of here today?"

"I don't know, John. I honestly don't know." She dipped a biscuit into the last of the grick eggs. "It's almost impossible to follow anyone through a Gate, but that doesn't mean he didn't. Maybe one more day? See if we can try to track his movements?"

"I was afraid you were going to say that."

"How is Chuckie doing? Do you think he's in danger?"

"He's beating himself up a little for not thinking ahead when he signed us up as the NutBusters for the last job. We have to remember, people, some very bad people, are looking for us."

"Maybe we should think about changing our company's name?"

"Only one of us three ever liked it," John agreed. "But don't worry. He's going to boost the security, and remember, he knows about our safe rooms. I stored enough food back there to last him for a week."

"Speaking of which. Why don't you ever invite me back to the gym anymore? Tired of getting your ass whipped on the cardio?"

Meehix whipping my butt as I'm on a treadmill? Could be kinky. Don't go there, John.

"No, it's not that."

"Then what is it?" She needed to know.

"It was in my plans."

"You have plans?"

"Yes, I have plans." John was trying not to feel embarrassed as he explained. "I, umm, wanted to lose another five pounds and firm up a few muscles before bringing you back there again."

"So you don't keep getting your ass beat?" Meehix smiled.

"Whipped. Beat. What is this fixation you have of doing my ass damage? I mean, you still have access to it anytime you want," John tried not to sound whiny, "but sometimes I need a space of my own."

"I can understand that." Meehix nodded. "I did get a whole wing to myself."

"And Chuckie got his unbelievably massive connection speeds, with extra routers and firewalls already installed and stacked in the front closet. The gym is sort of a personal workout room. I've never had one before that wasn't shared with twenty-five sweaty guys in a high school gym or on a practice field with sadistic coaches screaming at them."

"I never thought of it that way. Being raised in a wealthy family, I had personal trainers and a lot of self-defense classes for if we were ever kidnapped or something."

"You learned some of those lessons pretty well." John smiled.

"They have come in handy lately." Meehix smiled in return. "As for the cardio, well, that's why God made dance floors."

"The thing is," John tried to wrap up his explanation while also avoiding any further sexual innuendos. "When I'm seriously working out, I need to be able to count off and keep track, and well, you're a bit of a distraction."

"I'll take that as a compliment." Meehix stacked the dishes and glanced out the door before setting the tray on the hallway floor. "Food, juice, early afternoon. Let's go get a drink."

John sighed. "A little hair of the dog sounds good. Breathing in air that smells like the shit end of a dog to get one, not so much."

"Bitch, bitch, bitch."

They strapped on a couple of discreet weapons and headed for the street. The odorous conditions of Nevera not having improved overnight, they only wandered a block and a half before they slipped inside a bar that could have doubled as a motorcycle gang's hangout back on Earth.

The dozen or so patrons already inside gave them a quick once-over as they made their way to a table near the back. Sensing no immediate potential of a fight breaking out from the two, they all went back to their drinks, figuring that the entertainment of a brawl would have to wait until the bar got a little more crowded.

After ordering their drinks, the partners tried to relax and take the afternoon off from thinking and planning their next moves. A loud sneeze interrupted their light conversation, and they both expected the hyper-allergic demon, Phil, to appear.

"Excuse me," the large, leather-clad man apologized. "Just heading for the can." He continued his journey to take care of business.

"Always nice to have a table near the bathrooms." John paid the waitress as she delivered their drinks. Unless they were at their home base on Space Station L-222, they had learned that it was best not to run a tab and suddenly have to skip out and leave it unpaid. They were courteous that way.

"Again, sorry about the sneeze," the large man apologized as he exited the bathroom and headed back to join his short but similarly clad companion at a table near the front.

"No problem," John replied, surprised by the politeness.

"You were right." Samlett took his seat back at the table he was sharing with Tilly over a lunch of a couple of bottles of Lotlix and munchies. "It's them."

"No shit? Are you sure?"

"Up close and personal." Samlett set his pocket-comp on the table to show the photo he'd snapped while sneezing. "If that's not a large Kdackan male and a bluesy, I'll swallow your farts for a week."

"Not a big risk for you either way." Tilly took a close look at the photo and compared it to the image he'd seen the day before. "My farts are a lot more tasteful than the air here."

"Tell me I'm wrong." Samlett had a lot of nervous energy for a man his size.

"I can't." Tilly avoided looking back at the table where the two were sitting right out in the open as if they didn't have a care in the world. "What are the odds?"

The two bounty hunters liked hanging out on Nevera. Once you got past the stench, you'd find that the rents were low, the drinks were cheap, and it boasted a central location between three different Gates. For an ass-wipe of a space station, it also had great connection access, and they could check out the Crec Alerts without an issue, which is how they had stumbled onto a new one the day before from Kdack 3a.

They didn't know it, but that new Crec Alert conflicted with Trexit's private Kdackan contract.

"You go get the certificate. I'll make sure I don't lose them."

"You better not!" Tilly struggled to keep his voice down so he didn't draw any undue attention.

"I won't!" Samlett did the same, understanding his partner's excitement.

"Be sure you don't." Tilly rose. "This would be our biggest score ever, and our account is getting low. Back in twenty."

Tilly hustled out and down the street to the Department of Galactic Safety Office to pay for the certificate that would allow them to bring in the two targets legally. Another advantage of Nevera, and the rooms Samlett and Tilly rented, was that they could reach most of the official offices in a matter of minutes.

Meehix and John had enjoyed one leisurely drink and were trying to decide if they should order a second round or go off sightseeing, which Meehix favored.

"What is there to see?" John was at a loss. "Or should we wander around on a sniffing stroll to see if any part of the station doesn't smell like a skunk's caboose?"

"What the fuck is a skunk?"

"Step outside, take a good long whiff, and picture how that would smell if whatever is causing it had been dead for a week."

"I'm sorry," the big guy was suddenly hovering over them again. "It was rude of me earlier to sneeze so loudly and interrupt your drinks."

He took a seat, uninvited, as did a shorter, wiry guy whose eyes did not possess the stillness that his body did.

Two's company, four's danger.

"Apology accepted." John needed to figure out what the

pair's play was. "We were about to leave, but our tab is still open. Have a couple of drinks on us."

The big guy pulled out a Vetralaun semi-automatic and laid it on the table, his finger comfortably on the trigger as he rotated it between John and Meehix.

"I didn't introduce myself earlier," the big sneezer explained. "My name is Samlett, and this is my partner, Tilly."

Tilly nodded and slid a slick across the table as if the two of them had all the time in the world to allow John and Meehix to process it and the notification.

"May we read it?" John thought it was a reasonable request. "Maybe there's a slight misunderstanding here?"

"Take your time." Samlett and Tilly had them cornered and were enjoying their meal tickets' confusion.

"Is that a Vetralaun?" Meehix acted impressed. "I've never seen one close up before."

"Fully loaded," Samlett acknowledged.

"Deadly, if I remember watching a couple of executions on the G-Viz a while back?"

"One second, you're shot. The next second you're dead." Samlett smiled.

"I am sooo tickled to see one up close. Jojacko, aren't you just *tickled* too?"

"I don't know, Hix. Sounds too deadly for my tastes."

John had finished reading the information on the slick and set it in front of Meehix to look over.

"I don't think the photo does you justice, babe."

"So, you admit this is the two of you?" Tilly asked in a calm voice that belied his inner twitchiness.

"I don't remember posing for this one." Meehix recognized her prison shot when she was a captive on Earth before John had rescued her. "Fuck! I must have been having a really bad hair day!"

"It won't be your last, trust me." Samlett so wanted to pull the trigger and take the big one out of the equation. "You admit that you're the Kdackan in question, whose government just put a price on his head, and I quote, preferably dead?"

"Nice. That's what I get for being a patriot. My government putting a price on my head."

"I thought they pulled that months ago." Meehix sounded totally unconcerned. "This old Crec Alert must be recycled." she looked at Samlett. "Have you checked your sources on this?"

"Look at the date, blue-bitch." Samlett was enjoying this easy target acquisition. "It was issued yesterday."

Meehix took another look at the slick. Then, trying to stifle a yawn, she addressed John.

"Well. At least my parents simply sold me as a non-sentient property but still want me brought in alive. You, on the other hand, are...I believe the phrase is, shit out of luck."

"That's it? After all we've been through together? You cold-hearted blue-bitch!"

John leapt up, pulling a short gun from an ankle holster, and aimed it at Meehix. He hoped the pair would focus on shooting him and not Meehix.

"I'm wanted dead! You're wanted alive! These two are going to be out half their bounty!"

Samlett pulled the trigger, hitting John square in the chest.

"Rot in hell!" were his last words to Meehix as he collapsed to the floor in agony to try and hide the giggle fit he knew was coming.

"One down, one to go." Samlett aimed at Meehix. "You, however, are wanted, *preferably* alive. I prefer *dead*. Half the bounty, but well worth the cost for convenience's sake."

A hand shot out from under the table, breaking Samlett's wrist from the force as his gun tumbled into the air. Tilly was fast and caught the Vetralaun mid-spin before John could get to it and fired two more quick rounds to bring John down.

John's last move as he went to the floor again was to kick Tilly in the balls. The shorter man grabbed himself, and the Vetralaun clattered to the floor and under a couple of tables where several patrons dove for it. Not to use it during this current entertainment scuffle, but because it was a weapon not readily available.

Meehix took a side-swipe kick at Samlett's head. He'd thought his broken wrist hurt, but that was before Meehix's foot connected with his ear, sending him to the floor in pain.

"Yo! Short-shit!" Meehix hollered, giving Tilly just enough time to turn and see her do a forward flip, clamp his head between her ankles, and slam him face-first into the floor.

Energized by the giggle-gun shots, John rolled across the floor leaving tables in his wake, and after three or four, maybe five—*who's counting?*—leg-swipes left those fighting over the Vetralaun writhing on the floor before someone got seriously hurt. He picked up the weapon that was deadly to everyone who wasn't a Kdackan and stood.

"I believe this belongs to me, now."

Meehix did a quick search and grabbed the rest of the bounty hunters' weapons, IDs, credits, and bounty certificate. She had to get John out of there fast and back to their room because his next move after the Vetralaun giggles and energy would be him passing out.

"All charges for the damage are on them." She set the certificate on top of the bar before she hustled John out. "They're bounty hunters who failed miserably, and they're the ones who are legally responsible for any debts incurred."

John was now in the throes of a laughing fit. She had to get him out of there before he pissed his pants and collapsed. Grabbing his arm, she dragged him out of the bar and down the street. He had to pause halfway down the block to unzip for a quick laughing-piss in an alley. She finally got him up to their room and onto a bed before he went dead to the world for a while.

"Are we ever going to have an uneventful day?" She didn't expect an answer from her passed-out partner.

She grabbed a chair and wedged it under the door handle in an attempt to at least slow any uninvited guests from barging in. Spinning another chair around, she placed it at the foot of John's bed. It was out of the direct line of fire if anyone decided to blast the innocent door into shards before they tried to leap in.

Two guns in her lap and ready, she kept her eyes on the door and her ears on John to make sure he continued to breathe. Sure, the Vetralauns her partner had been shot with in the past had only produced giggling fits and brief power surges. That didn't mean it would stay that way.

"Do you think there's an expiration date or something? Like, maybe you'll build up an immunity to the giggles, and the next shot will be deadly?"

Still no answer from the form on the bed. She wished he would snore, thereby letting her know he was still alive. Their vape-o-wake bottle was back on Ship, as were most of their weapons. She had no choice but to keep watch and let him sleep it off.

"You took at least three, maybe four shots." She glanced over and saw his chest steadily rise and fall. "How long do you think you'll sleep?"

Still no response.

"Shit, how long can I continue to talk to myself before I start answering?"

All was quiet out in the hallway. She risked a couple of minutes to answer nature's call. With one less thing to worry about, she returned and took up her guns again to continue her vigil.

"I have concluded, in case you're wondering, that talking out loud to myself, in this particular instance, is perfectly acceptable behavior. I have no way of knowing if your current state of unconsciousness lets my voice filter in so you know that you're not alone. Or if you'll retain anything I say when you come back to the land of the living." She sighed and checked again to see his chest continue to rise and fall in a steady rhythm.

"So, thank you for drawing the fire back there and probably saving my life in the process." She slapped his feet, taking out a little anger on his prone body. "But you scared the hell out of me when you collapsed under the table, jerk-wad!" She slapped his feet again.

John didn't stir in the slightest.

She couldn't help herself. She moved to the door, quietly slid the chair out from under the knob, and checked the hallway. No immediate danger presented itself so she lodged the chair back into place and returned to her station at the foot of the bed.

"So here's the deal, you big oaf." She stood, and keeping one eye on the door, padded to the head of the bed, bent, and whispered into John's ear.

"You asked me out on a date. I accepted. So be warned. You will be dealing with one seriously pissed-off blue chick if you die before you have the chance to show a girl a good time." She kissed his cheek. "Oh, and flowers would be nice."

She returned to her seat, weapons ready.

CHAPTER ELEVEN

Meehix tumbled out of her chair. Contact with the floor rudely woke her up, guns in hand and ready to shoot the shit out of something. Anything!

"Shit!"

The cheap motel room was in near-total darkness. It took a moment to get her bearings, and she realized that she had nodded off while sitting guard. She crawled and found her way to a lamp on the nightstand between the twin beds. Pulling the string, she now had enough light to take in her surroundings.

The first thing she did was check on John's breathing. *Still alive. You better fucking well be.*

Regaining her chair, she took a closer look at her surroundings. Nothing had been disturbed, so the bounty hunters they'd run into earlier had only found them by a stroke of dumb luck, not a well-planned coordinated effort by a larger group. That was the good news.

The bad news was that she and John now had a new

Crec Alert out on them, originating from Kdack. *Bounty hunters now being bounty hunted. Charming.*

She stood and stretched. Keeping guard while sitting in a chair long enough to have fallen asleep did not do wonders for bones and muscles. She reached for the ceiling, then for her toes, which is when she noticed that someone had slipped a small sealed envelope under the door. The envelope had the motel's emblem stamped on it. Picking it up, she carried it over to her bed, having had enough of sitting in a chair for a while and hopped up onto the mattress in a cross-legged position. A gun lay on each side of her as she opened it and read the note inside.

"Hit the 'on' button, stupid."

"The 'on' button of what?" she asked out loud. John was still not in a state of consciousness to allow him to respond, but she figured it out quickly enough on her own. Scrambling for her bag, she pulled out the High-Level Translator that Chuckie had set up for them before they'd set off on their latest mission, found the three notches she'd etched into it, and pushed the bottom button up.

"Hello?" It was the only thing she could think of to say. She followed it up with the brilliant, "Is anybody out there?"

"About fucking time, blue-brain!"

"Hello, Chuckie. I missed you too." Her smile was one of pure relief. "I guess these bad boys do have quite the range after all."

"They ought to. You paid enough for them."

"Maybe I'd be better off dying and sticking you with the bill?"

"I'd rather you not." Chuckie turned serious. "How's the

big boy doing? The last time we chatted was through written PC-comms, but I figured out how to have Shippewa boost the signal so we could talk. It only works if she's still close enough to you to bounce the transmission though."

"I'm not even going to try to pretend I understand that."

"Wise decision. So," Chuckie went on, "you two are still okay?"

"Other than the Crec Alert, yeah." She looked at her sleeping partner. "John took three or four shots from a Vetralaun to help us get away from a couple of doubly-lucky bounty hunters, so he's still currently out like a busted lamp—"

"A Crec Alert?"

"Yes. A Crec-fucking-Alert. We never saw it coming, and we're bounty hunters, for shit's sake! How did we not know that *we* were now targets?"

"I guess that would be a mutual *we bad*," Chuckie agreed. "We haven't signed up for any bounty hunting jobs lately."

"Yeah." Meehix sighed. "Silly us… Can't you use your wizardry and put out some kind of search notice or something that will alert you when something like this comes up?"

"I'm on it. Hold on. I want to check on something real quick."

"Sure, I got nothing better to do until Sleepzilla wakes up."

"Got it."

"That was fast." Meehix was surprised.

"I'm telling you, the connection speeds here are insane!"

"So are you." She was trying to figure out if there was anything on the room service menu that would give her an energy boost without the need for water.

"The Crec Alert was only posted yesterday. How the hell did anyone find you so fast?"

"It had to be a lucky coincidence, or unlucky if you were the bounty hunters. We were all in the wrong place at the same time."

"Maybe I need to find different partners," Chuckie mused. "You two seem to attract trouble."

"And *you* don't?"

"Good point," he admitted. "Look, I did some calculations after I messaged with John earlier."

"Calculations? Great." Sarcasm dripped. "Just what I need to help keep me awake as I sit guard over the sleeping lunk."

"Are you interested or not?"

"Yeah, I'm interested." Meehix yawned. "Try to enthrall me with numbers and minutiae. Maybe I'll get lucky and die peacefully from boredom."

"Okay." Chuckie knew this was going to be another hard sell and had to manage his pitch perfectly. "So far, as far as we know, you two are wanted by Victor Vikrellion."

"Slave-running gangster. Got it."

"Also wanted by a Blavarian grudge-holding bastard. And now, it seems, by some of John's friends back on Kdack who put out a Crec Alert."

"Are you going to tell me something that I don't know anytime soon? Because I'm thinking of taking a nap."

"And this." Chuckie wasn't done with his recitation yet. "Although I haven't been able to track any information down to prove it, you might also be wanted for helping to break an unnamed resident out of a cryo-prison."

"Crap. I'd forgotten about that little misdeed."

"I'm not surprised. But that doesn't mean the prison has. They run on a for-profit basis, and you deprived them of one of their highest commodities."

"Thinking highly of yourself?"

"Their reputation for perfect attendance is at stake, which is why I think they may be trying to fly under the radar on that little escapade."

"I'm still in danger of dozing off here, Chuckie."

There was a long pause before Chuckie came out with it.

"We need another ship."

"What?" Meehix was not expecting *that.*

"**What?**" Shippewa wasn't expecting it either.

"Meehix! Did you press the HLT 'on' button once or twice?"

"Maybe twice," she admitted. "I wanted to make sure it was on."

"Once for us." Chuckie wished they'd paid closer attention when he was instructing them on how to use them. "Twice for everyone."

"**Are you looking to replace me? Is it because my ass isn't phat enough?**"

"Ship, Ship, *no!*" Chuckie hurried to explain. "We're *not* replacing you!"

"Damn right!" Meehix was suddenly wide awake. "No way in hell we're abandoning Ship!"

"**Thank you, Meehix.**"

"And your ass is perfect, Ship!"

"Whoever said anything about Shippewa's ass?" Chuckie now found that he was the confused one.

"That would be John."

"John's an idiot." Chuckie had to get back on Ship's good side in a hurry. "We are *not*, I repeat NOT, replacing you!"

"Not that I wouldn't mind being converted into a pleasure-cruiser to take tourists to touristy destinations that didn't involve having to dodge incoming missiles at a moment's notice."

"Stop it! Just stop it! The both of you!" Meehix felt the need to jump in. "Hi, Ship. Me and Jojacko ain't leaving you for nothing! Nowhere! No how! I promise! Get it?"

"Got it."

"Good."

"I was going to fill you in on the details later, Ship," Chuckie sounded sincere in his apology. "But I had to run the idea past your crew first."

"Since it's too late for that now," Ship was starting to settle down, **"and since we're all here thanks to Meehix's button-fumbling, why don't you run through the idea while you have our attention."**

"Everyone's attention but John's," Meehix felt obligated to point out as John continued his impersonation of a coma patient.

"Majority rules. He'll be fine."

Chuckie turned his attention back to Ship since his hard sell had just gotten a lot harder. He would have to do a juggling act as he tried to explain his plan and placate everyone at once.

"We're not replacing you, Ship. We're going to try to get

you your own ship."

"My own ship?"

"Your own ship, Ship."

"I didn't know a ship could have a ship." Meehix wondered if she'd dozed off without realizing it and was now in the middle of a muddled dream.

"It's a very special ship." Now that Chuckie was about to begin his actual pitch, out loud, he suddenly wondered if it would sound sane or not. There was a long pause.

"I'm listening." Ship broke the silence.

"Out with it, Chuckie." Meehix knew that whatever the plan was, it would land somewhere between incredibly stupid and insane if it caused Chuckie to pause. *At least I'm now wide awake.*

"Shippewa is a fantastic ship, and she's done more than anyone could do to get us all out of the jams we've managed to get ourselves into. But she can only do so much...which is a *lot!*" he added before Shippewa got her feelings hurt again.

"Thank you, Chuckie. I will make this easier for you by trying to remain quiet as you continue."

"Thank you, Ship." *Here goes.* "There's a rumor, hell, it might even be only a legend, of a totally AI ship waiting for a new crew to take her over. That's where you'd come in, Ship," Chuckie hastened to add. "It's huge. It's fast. And it's deadly dangerous. It would make a dreadnought IV crap its pants if it came up against it in battle."

"And what?" Meehix's hackles had fully raised. "It's waiting for someone to come along and ask its owner if we may borrow it?"

"Wouldn't that be nice... But no, that's not how it

works."

"Then how about you fill us in on how, *exactly*, it works."

"Here's the thing." It did sound insane now that Chuckie thought about it. "Let's assume the rumors are true. It's a true Artificial Intelligence Vessel. There would be room in it to park Shippewa inside the hull. We can connect them, and flying the big bastard could happen while sitting inside Shippewa's cockpit, with only two people needed."

"There's no main pilot's loft or whatever it's called?"

"Sure, it has one, but we wouldn't necessarily need it all of the time. If you and John needed to take Shippewa out for an errand, then the big ship would be able to hang out nearby without needing a third person to guide it."

"Which leaves you free to stay home and invest more money in our life insurance policies." Chuckie hadn't said anything yet to convince her. "Do I have that right?"

"Partly. But there'd also be plenty of room for all three of us, plus Shippewa, to travel together comfortably. Think of it as a home away from home, but with a lot more firepower."

"There's a major catch coming up, isn't there? Is it the cost? Can we take it out for a test flight before we buy?"

"We'd have to find it first."

"Here it comes, Ship."

"No one knows where it is."

"That will make things easier."

"I *should* say," Chuckie plunged on, "that no one *living* knows where it is, except its owner."

"Who's the owner?"

"No one *living* knows *that* either."

"Piece of cake." *Please, Jojacko, wake up and help me talk the madman out of this.* "Where do we sign up?"

"It's not something that you sign up for." Chuckie really *had* thought it all made sense during his research but was now beginning to have doubts. "Many people have tried to find her in the past."

"Let me guess...they failed?"

"If dying is considered failure, I suppose you could word it like that."

"But if suicide is your goal, then everyone has succeeded?"

"There you go, Meehix!" Chuckie was glad she was getting into the groove. "That's how you put a positive spin on it!"

"Is that a form of humor that is beyond my programming to understand?"

"No, Ship," Meehix tried to help. "That's a form of idiocy that's impossible to program."

"May I finish? Please?"

"Sure, Chuckie. Why not waste another hour."

"There is *no* monetary cost to acquiring it."

"Your idiocy is indeed priceless, Chuckie."

"For now, let's stick to the ship. If John was awake, I'm sure he'd at least want to hear me out."

"What do you think, Ship? Ship?"

Shippewa?" Chuckie tried.

"I'm sorry. I was daydreaming about the life of a pleasure-cruiser. Where were we?"

"I was about to tell Meehix about the five feats necessary to discover the location of the new ship."

"Two feet of mine. Two feet of John's. Do we get to choose which one of yours we get to chop off and use for the fifth?"

"F-E-A-T-S, feats. Try not to be overly obtuse."

"I'll try." Meehix nudged John with a foot, to no avail. "If you'll try not to be overly-Chuckie… What are the five feats?"

"We only know the first three, so far."

"So far?"

"The first three are public knowledge, gleaned from a few of the survivors who made it through the first two. No one has made it through the third, and the next one won't reveal itself until you complete the feat immediately preceding it."

"So, no one has ever made it past the third feat?"

"No one anyone has ever heard from again. The speculation is that the feats get more difficult as you go along."

"I wish I could Vetralaun myself a few times and join John in dreamland right about now." Meehix sighed. "What is the first feat?"

"There are two craters on the planet Suvious. You don't even need to pass through a Gate to reach it from where you are, which is why it seemed like a good idea to at least check it out. I mean, as long as you're in the neighborhood."

"Two craters. Got it."

"There's a passageway between them with a very rare mineral deposit field. You need to enter one crater, grab a chunk of the mineral, and escape through the second crater."

"I guess the passageway has guards?"

"Guards isn't quite the right description. Guards imply someone paid to perform a duty. Viciously protected by a herd of gramodiatrons would be more accurate."

"What the fuck is a gramodiatron?"

"Just a small invertebrate that lives in the crater passageways below the surface of Suvious. The one passageway that holds the mineral deposit is sort of their, umm, breeding ground. The mineral, trimium, has no useful purpose other than decorative. Its value lies in its scarcity."

"But if someone could use the trimium as a weapon?"

"Then the gramodiatrons would have been blasted to smithereens eons ago."

"Feat one," Meehix tried to make sense of it, "is to risk life and limb for what basically amounts to a novelty chunk of rock."

"Pretty much, yeah. Doesn't sound too hard, right?"

"And obviously, at least a few adventurers have survived."

"Several. They turned in the trimium to a research facility run by insanely curious nerds. The research staffers are fascinated with minerals, convinced that they must hold some kind of secret composite that will make them all rich someday. *If* they can ever isolate it and figure out a use. Once it's turned over, the nerds will give you the location of where the second feat is currently."

"Why can't we go directly to the nerds and pay them to tell us what the second feat is?"

"Because, the way I heard it from the reports of the previous attempts, is that someone has threatened to rain down death and destruction on the craters. Thereby obliterating the gramodiatrons and burying what's left of the trimium under tons of rubble."

"And the nerds wouldn't want that to happen?"

"It would destroy their reason to live. You know how nerds can be. Plus, and this is pure speculation on my part, the nerds probably have obscenely rich parents who are using shell companies to keep the research facility running and give their brilliant but useless progeny something to do that resembles having an actual job."

"But someone has already completed the first feat and moved onto the second?"

"Several, obviously, otherwise we wouldn't know as much as we know." Chuckie wasn't sure if he'd hooked her yet or not. *Probably not.* "The second feat is more interesting than dangerous."

"I'm breathless with the lack of anticipation." Although Meehix had to admit to herself that she *was* curious. "What's the second feat?"

"I need to explain the third feat, first," Chuckie knew he had her roped in enough, for now, and kept silent for a moment as he pictured her in the hotel room, trying not to tap her feet from impatience.

"Waiting." Meehix changed her position on the bed to at least tap a foot on the floor out of aggravation. She kept both of her guns trained at the door, daring room service or bounty hunters to knock on it, and was perfectly willing to pay for any damages.

"I have to admit to a fair amount of curiosity myself, Chuckie, what with the potential of me maybe having a ship I can call my own."

Chuckie now had both Meehix *and* Ship semi-hooked,

at least for now. *Bring it home!*

"The third feat requires a virgin sacrifice." *Wait for it...*

"You know damn well I'm not a virgin!" Now Meehix was pissed at the time they'd just wasted.

"Quote, unquote," Chuckie couldn't resist, "Tell me something I *don't* know."

"No..."

Chuckie had timed it. It had taken her exactly thirteen seconds to come to the obvious conclusion.

"Unless you have a penis hidden somewhere that I'm not aware of, *yes*." Chuckie wished she could see his smile right then. "Not every virgin sacrifice has to be a woman. Get over your vaginal-flap-self!"

Silence, as Chuckie's smile widened a tad.

"Chuckie?" Shippewa was the first to chime back in eventually. **"There is no way on Kdack's blue-green ball that I will participate in anything that involves sacrificing John."**

"First of all," Chuckie had regained the upper hand. "Not every sacrifice involves death, and I would not submit John for it if I thought that death would be the result. That big fuck is the closest thing to a brother I've ever had! Is *that* clear?"

"Before you go on," Meehix had never heard Chuckie sound so passionate about a personal relationship before. Sure, he'd promised to die for her, if ever necessary, but this was different. "John isn't a virgin. Remember his slut of a girlfriend back on Kdack?"

"Ahh, yes, the infamous Hannah. But no, this doesn't involve that relationship. Feat three needs a galactic virgin. That is someone who's never had sex with someone who is not from their home planet. Ergo, a *fuck-in-space* virgin. So, unless there's something that no one has told me about, I think John will qualify."

Meehix hoped that Chuckie was right because she wanted to be the one to bust his galactic cherry.

"As far as I know," she sighed, "he is an alien-virgin."

"I think so too," Chuckie agreed. "I've never known anyone who's ever taken so many cold showers in my life."

Meehix was relieved to hear that. She had a wing of their shared house to herself and had no idea what the boys had been up to down their hallway.

"Here is where feat two comes in, as it relates to feat three, and why no one knows what feats four and five are." Chuckie now had a fully attentive audience. "Feat three needs a *male* virgin."

"Yeah, yeah, so we've heard."

Meehix suddenly found herself wishing that she could be the sacrificial virgin, but that ship had sailed a long time ago.

"Feat two is to spend a night on Space Station Beaulifica and depart the next morning with no changes made to one's virginal status before moving on to feat three."

"Space Station Beaulifica." Meehix searched her memory. "Never heard of it."

"No reason you should have." Chuckie felt almost guilty for how much he was now enjoying this. "No reason at all, unless you'd taken the time to listen to one of our clients."

"And...Which...Client, would that have been?" Meehix wasn't sure if she wanted a pitcher of dibble-blinks or to shoot the hell out of something, but she knew that she didn't want to hear the suspected answer.

"Remember Vixaleen? The sneezing demon Phil's succubus niece?"

"She, of the red ass?"

"The very same."

"No." Meehix hoped she was wrong.

"Yes. Keep your guns and focus on the door, just in case," Chuckie continued, trying to remind her of her current reality.

"Fuck," Meehix couldn't help but mutter out loud.

"Fuck, indeed."

Chuckie was proud of himself for actually listening to the succubus's ramblings while she was getting his rocks off, and he'd first heard of the mystery ship.

"Space Station Beaulifica is owned, flown, and totally run by succubi. No male has *ever* left there as a virgin… which is why no one has ever attempted feat number three. Except, rumor has it, by a few guys who found Beaulifica, and I quote, Talk about booorrriiinnnggg."

"And we have no idea what feats four and five are? Or how dangerous the actual sacrifice is?"

"That would be a no."

"Wouldn't it be easier, or at least less dangerous, to just change the NutBusters' name and move to a new location?"

"And give up the connection speeds here?" Chuckie was aghast. "I may be the only one in existence who can fully utilize them. It would be like leaving Nirvana in the hands of imbeciles who still think stars shine because someone forgot to turn off the lights. Not gonna happen. I'm already working on beefing up the security."

"What if you don't beef it up quite enough and someone manages to get through your Chuck Norris quizzes and then, even if only by accident, manages to discover the hidden rooms where you'll be hiding?"

"Then I'll take a couple of them with me before I go and will die happy with an unconscionable amount of connection speed."

"You're telling me that we broke you out of prison so you can die with the speed of light at your fingertips?"

"Seems like a reasonable trade-off to me."

"At least you have something worth dying for," she mumbled. "What if John and I don't quite share that willingness to expire any time soon?"

"Then you will experience a form of incarceration." Chuckie brought it home. "Because as long as that dreadnought captain, and Victor and Kdack and God knows who else is looking for you, you need a ship large and dangerous enough to be able to take them on individually or all at once. Or you two will have to hide in the farthest reaches of some God-forsaken galaxy for the rest of your lives."

"Shit. I hate it when you're right." She looked at her partner, still passed out on the bed. "I'll run it by John when he finally wakes up."

"You do that. I'll keep researching to see what more I can find out about the mythical ship and feats four and five."

"**If I may interject,**" Shippewa interjected without waiting for a response. "**As nice as it would be to have a ship, I would rather not acquire it at the cost of John's life.**"

"Nor would I," Chuckie agreed. "The ultimate decision will have to be left up to the snooze-meister."

With that, they all signed off. Meehix double-checked the lights on her HLT to ensure that it was off and returned her focus to guarding the door.

"The problem, Captain Prooshevekk, is that I don't see any recent deposits paid into my account."

Not only did Trexit find the Blavarian a tedious conversationalist, but he also seemed to be negligent in paying his debts promptly.

"I located the pair and was going to bring them in as soon as I acquired reinforcements. You, good sir, took it upon yourself to try to capture them yourself. Which, if you recall, was something that I strongly advised against."

Prooshevekk wanted to argue, but the tracker was right. His ego might have gotten the better of him, not to mention the slight savings between *paying for locating* instead of *paying for acquisition*.

"It was also your choice, *Captain,* to live-broadcast the whole fiasco." Trexit could almost see the Blavarian trying to keep his head from exploding with internal rage. "So, unless you want to add to your livestream humiliation by having me update the stream, I suggest you pay up and pay up now, because I'm ready to go *live,* myself. I have no problem reporting that not only did you fail to bring them in when you had them right in your grasp, you also skipped out on paying the man who put them there."

"The payment is on its way." Prooshevekk had only stalled on the payment because he'd needed time to figure out how to write off his vendetta as a legitimate business expense. He had to justify the loan he'd taken out to his military chain of command superiors.

Trexit gave the money a moment to be transferred and smiled. He'd had no intention of taking the time to set up a live broadcast, but the captain didn't know that.

"Thank you." Trexit was beginning to like the two bounty hunters who had caused so many people so much inconvenience. They added to his retirement fund on what seemed like a daily basis. "Now, do you wish me to continue tracking, and this time bring them to you personally, or do you want to start all over on your own from scratch?"

"Do I have to start my payments to you from scratch also?" Prooshevekk, for his part, wasn't enjoying this conversation as much as Trexit was.

"I'll give you a fifty percent discount on the tracking, but I will need half of that in advance. And by in advance, I mean before this call ends in two minutes."

A minute and a half later, Trexit smiled again.

"Always a pleasure doing business with you, Captain."

"Keep me informed!" Trexit wondered if the captain had hurt himself by slamming the connection off so hard. Another dial and another conversation.

"How the hell did a Blavarian dreadnought captain beat us to the targets?"

"Lazy Buff." Trexit put his feet up on his desk. "Long time no bitch. How're things hanging at the castle of Victor the Victorious Vikrellion?"

"I asked you a question!"

"And I asked you one...I'm guessing your boss isn't overly happy about the recent almost-capture?"

Lazy made sure that the listening devices in his office were turned off and set on the loop-sounds before he continued. "You guessed right. Happy has left the building. What the hell happened?"

"What happened, my friend," Trexit didn't mind reminding him, "is that your boss fucked up my earlier acquisition plans, and that gave the Blavarian blowhard a chance to get ahead of me briefly. If you were watching the livestream, you saw that it ended almost as well as yours and your boss' did. Please let me know when you're ready to trust a professional to do his job without any outside interference."

Trexit ended the call and counted down from five. At *two*, the request for a reconnect came in.

"Are you still on their trail?" Lazy needed to know.

"Absolutely." Trexit didn't have a care in the world.

"They are currently out of reach and out of touch." He paused as he checked the location of the card he'd given them and wondered what the hell they were doing on Space Station Nevera, then decided that they wouldn't spend any more time than necessary on that dump of a station before returning home.

"As soon as they return home, my crew will pick them up, and I'll deliver them to you, personally."

"Alive?"

"Alive is a priority. I wouldn't want to deprive Victor of his revenge."

"There's just one thing."

"There's always *just one more thing* with you, Trexit."

"Not if people stay the fuck out of my way."

Trexit had a point. Victor hadn't done a very good job of that so far.

"All right," Lazy was afraid of what the dollar amount would add up to. "What's the one more thing?"

"Victor interfered, then the Blavarian interfered, and the two targets managed to leave some destruction and dead bodies in their wake in both instances as they escaped." Trexit took his feet off his desk. The waitress at the bar where he was doing his business gave him dirty looks for having his feet on the table, even if he was sitting at one in the back.

"Due to the mayhem that the pair seems to leave in their wake, my crew feels that it's in their best interests to shoot first and feel for a pulse second. They're requesting hazardous duty pay if you want them brought in alive."

"How much?"

Trexit named the price.

"Ouch."

"Go run it buy your boss. I'm going to be out of range for a few days, so I'll need the deposit within half an hour, or I can't guarantee the *alive* part of the acquisition."

Trexit ended the call without bothering with good-byes. Half an hour later, another deposit had shown up in his account.

"Gretchen-fetchen, send in the Ass."

"He's ready to see you now," the general's secretary told Susky, who was hunched in the outer office, practicing his lack-of-height routine.

Susky stood and got in one last stretch of his six-foot-four frame.

"Do you ever get tired, Gretchen, of the general's propensity for nicknames?"

"I'd be less inclined to be annoyed if we were allowed to use some of our own back at him."

"No."

"Take me out and get me drunk sometime." She smiled.

"I'm waiting!"

"He's waiting."

Susky hunched and hustled into the general's office, wondering if Gretchen had just asked him out on a date.

"Do I understand the memo correctly," the general started before Susky had time to slither down below head-level and into his customary chair, "that the second Crec Alert met with resounding failure?"

"So far, sir. But only one certificate has been taken out for them, and that was only for a forty-eight-hour limit. It's cheaper for the bounty hunters, and they usually only do that if they already have the targets in sight."

"How long ago was that taken out?"

"Fifty-eight hours ago."

"Which means," the general fumed, "that in *this* particular case, failure *was* an option."

"It seems safe to assume so, sir." Susky wished he could sink lower in the chair to avoid whatever object the general chose to throw next.

"How can one sanctimonious prick of a Boy Scout manage to jail-break an expensive DNA acquisition, steal a one-of-a-kind ship, and outmaneuver and kill a trained squad of pilots? Then start a shit-storm of a crusade to *Save the Aliens* without having some kind of deep-state black-ops training that's deeper and blacker than ours?"

Susky decided that now was not the time to mention the fact that the Boy Scout had, indeed, outmaneuvered his USSF pursuers but had done everything he could to try to assure the pilots' survival. It had been on the authority of their military leaders that the pilots were allowed to die because their superior officers denied permission to launch a rescue mission. No. Now was *definitely* not the time to bring that up.

"Do you want me to continue the Crec Alert?"

"Damn right I do! And double whatever the bounty is on his head! It's one thing for an alien to try to escape. The slimy cretins are all alike with their 'You have no right to hold me captive, and I'm going to report you to the Galactic Commission,' but it's a whole other matter when one of our own goes over to the other side!"

The general slammed his fist down on his intercom button.

"Gretchen, get me agents Bixby and Shaw!"

A moment later, she patched the call through.

"Bixby and Shaw. You freeze, and we'll thaw."

"I need an immediate status on that double-anal probe I requested last week. If I'm not happy with what I hear, I'll transfer both of you clowns to a new post where *thawing* will be something that you'll beg for by the time you're relieved and brought back to within warming distance of the sun!"

Susky decided that this was as good a time as any to slip out.

CHAPTER TWELVE

"Did I miss anything?"

Through sleepy eyes, John saw Meehix leap up from a chair and spin, leaving him looking down two barrels aimed directly at his head.

"I was sleeping! How much trouble could I have gotten into while sleeping?" John needed to know.

"You're awake!" Meehix had been on high alert for a while now, and John's voice had startled her. She lowered her guns.

"Do you remember being bounty hunted?"

John was still groggy but smiled. "Yeah. What a couple of amateurs. We *did* kick their asses though, right?"

"Not before you took three or four shots from a giggle-gun."

John instinctively reached for his crotch and was relieved not to find a puddle of piss.

"Don't worry." Meehix didn't retake her seat but still kept the guns ready. "Between your giggle-fits on the way back, you stumbled into an alley, unzipped, and pissed on

MICHAEL TODD

the back legs of a hooker giving someone a quickie in an alley."

"No!"

"No." Meehix smiled. "I made up the hooker and the quickie, but the alley part is true. It was a struggle, but I got you up into the room, and you've been out ever since."

"When was this?"

"I've lost track of the days."

"Shit." John noticed the chair she'd been sitting in and also the chair propped up against the door. "You've been standing guard ever since?"

"Well, it's only been since yesterday afternoon, and I have managed a couple of cat-naps."

"Still, you must be exhausted."

"I have enough energy left to head out and get us a six-pack of Brillian's and some food if you'll guard the door until I get back."

"Why don't you stay here, and I'll make the booze and food run?"

"Because you've been out for over a day, and I don't want to have to track you down because the stench out there brought you to your knees again. I'm more used to it than you are."

"I see your point."

"We have a lot to talk about when I get back."

Meehix tossed him one gun, kept the other for herself, scooted the chair away from the door, and headed out.

It was hard to come out of a long sleep with a totally clear head, so it took John a few minutes to put the pieces of his memory together.

Bounty hunters? Check. Asses kicked? Check. Did he lose

anything of value during the confrontation? He felt for the silver and turquoise pendant he wore around his neck. *Check.* Did he have a partner who would stay awake for damn near two days to guard his back? *Check.* Was that more than the trollop of a girlfriend back on Earth who he'd named the pendant after would have done? *Double-check. Hannah would rather stab me in the back than cover it.*

He grabbed a short roll of tissue from the bathroom, and exiting the room, wrapped it around the knob on the hallway side of the door. Not overly subtle, but it would have to be disturbed if anyone tried to enter the room while he was gone, and it would have to do for now.

Stuffing two small pieces of the tissue into his nostrils, he headed down to the lobby, where he took one long deep breath of semi-fresh air and stepped outside.

There wasn't much activity. No one spent any more time outside on Space Station Nevera than was necessary. There she came. A bag containing a six-pack of Brillian's and munchies wrapped in her arms, hiding the gun in her hands.

If anyone decides to mug her, they'll regret it. Not only will she bring them to their knees, but if she has to drop the bag and the Brillian's shatter, there will be some serious hell to pay.

John covered her back as she returned and held the door open as she entered.

"Aw, you care."

He smiled and followed her up to their room.

"What the fuck is that?" She appraised his tissue warning system on the doorknob.

"I had to improvise. There's a single rip on the bottom

and a double rip on the top, with a four-square knot in between. If anyone had moved it, I would be able to tell."

"Maybe you'll come in handy someday yet."

John opened the door and led her inside, where she set the bags down on a chair and pulled out the contents, handing John a bottle.

"Enjoy it while it's still cold."

They placed the chair back under the room's doorknob as the first line of defense. Then they pried off a couple of caps from the Brillian's, split the munchies Meehix had chosen, and propped up the pillows on their beds so they could lean back, stretch out and relax, for however many moments they could as she filled him in on what he'd missed.

"Do you have any memory of what goes on after you've passed out from the after-effects of the giggle-gun?"

"Not that I recall." John enjoyed his first sip.

"No conversations or anything?" Meehix took her second sip.

"Nothing. Just sweet oblivion."

"Well, then I guess I need to fill you in on all of it." *Except for the part where I begged you not to die until we'd had our first date.*

"Please do."

"We've decided that, with your permission, you're going to be a virgin sacrifice." Meehix decided to start in the middle.

John wasn't thrilled about being a sacrifice, but took a bite of something brown from his batch of munchies, washed it down with another sip, and decided he had nothing to worry about.

"I'm not a virgin. I'm afraid you're going to have to find another volunteer."

"We need a sex-with-an-alien virgin."

Right. Like I haven't been trying to flip your fucking flap from the moment I rescued you! And now, because I failed, I'm going to be sacrificed?

Meehix wasn't an expert at reading body language, but she could tell from John's expression that he was nowhere near the vicinity of being pleased at the moment.

"I'm sorry," and Meehix was. "Let me start at the beginning, instead of in the middle."

She reached her bottle out to clink it with John's. "You and I are partners, and partners always have each other's backs, right?"

John could clink to that and did, relaxing a little as they both took another sip.

"The truth is," Meehix belched and continued. "Excuse me. I took too big a swig."

"You're forgiven." John smiled. Eighteen or so hours of sleep added up to making him relatively patient. "Begin where you need to begin, and backtrack or fast-forward as necessary."

"Thank you." Meehix took a gentler sip and decided to take leaps back and forth, hoping that something would eventually make sense.

"While you were sleeping off the Vetralaun shots, Ship and I had a long talk with Chuckie."

"And there we go." John smiled, slid off his bed, and popped two more Brillian's. Handing one to Meehix, he settled in for the ride.

"Forget the logistical order of the conversation," John

suggested. "Just toss out what my dad would call bullet points, and we'll take them as they come up."

"All of this depends on your full approval!" Meehix realized that she should have stressed that point earlier.

"Glad to hear *that*. What do I need to approve?"

"We need to get Shippewa her own ship."

"Sure… Why?"

"Because we have very many, really mean people trying to kill us, and we need, according to you, if memory serves, a 'Phatter ship.'"

"I do recall saying that." John nodded. "We've found a phatter ship?"

"One of us did."

"One of us by the name of Chuckie, I'm guessing?"

"Got it on the first try." The desperately needed munchies and the second Brillian's helped Meehix ease into the rest of the conversation.

"We're currently outnumbered and outgunned by the mean people pursuing us. Would you agree?"

"Agree, I would."

"So, us NutBusters have two choices." Meehix held up two of her four thumbs. "We can either run like hell and hide for all of eternity," she lowered one thumb. "Or we can get the biggest, baddest ship anyone ever dreamed of and make everyone tremble at the sound of our names."

"Maybe it's the Brillian's talking, but I like the second choice better. I think this is where Chuckie comes in?"

Meehix nodded. "He thinks he's found us a ship to end all ships."

"Cool. Let's go put down a deposit and set up a payment plan."

"Thaaat's not quite how it works."

"I didn't think so." John grabbed another bite of something brown and crispy and not too spicy. "What else do we know, or not know, as the case may be?"

"Chuckie's still researching, but he says there's a rumor of a ship that is up for grabs to the first one who completes five feats, or tasks if you will."

"So it's like a quest-game, with five levels you need to conquer before reaching the goal, and the levels get consistently more dangerous?"

"I think that sums it up."

"Do we know anything about the feats?" John knew from his gaming that it would give them a good heads-up if they knew what they were in advance.

"From the reports of those who survived but chose to give up mid-quest and return alive, we only know the first two and part of the third."

"No one has any idea, then, of what waits on levels four and five?"

"Not that we're aware of." Meehix's Brillian's was kicking in and slowly reaching room temperature. She was glad she'd only bought a six-pack. The effects of her nearly sleepless vigil were beginning to catch up to her. "Chuckie's still trying to find out more."

"How hard is the first feat?" John could see her beginning to nod out.

"It doesn't sound too hard at all. We have to get through a passage between two craters and snatch up some mineral deposits and deliver them to a geek lab for analysis."

"Are these craters volcanic or something? There must be a catch somewhere."

"The passageway seems to be the breeding grounds of a bunch of little creatures." She tried to remember their description. "Invertebrates!" She was proud of herself. "Little gramo-something-or-others. They don't sound too dangerous."

"Your time in New Mexico was confined to a prison cell." The first feat might not be quite as harmless as she was making it out to be. "Scorpions are invertebrates. Spiders, such as the Black Widow and the Fiddlebacks, are invertebrates." John sipped again and shivered from childhood memories.

"Some of them are poisonous and not something you'd necessarily want to cuddle up next to, let alone be stuck surrounded by hundreds of them, especially if they're horny and you're preventing their copulating endeavors."

"Oh."

"Yeah. Oh. I'm not saying these gramo-whatevers are poisonous, but it's something we'd better check out before we go wandering around in their spawning grounds." He took a bite of what looked like bread but had the texture of half-baked shoe leather. The taste wasn't bad, but it took a while to wear it down to a point where he could swallow it.

"Let's say we manage to get the minerals to the nerds. Then what?"

"I wasn't taking notes, but I believe the nerds will then give us the location of the second feat, which is a space station that frequently changes locations."

"Then we storm the station, rescue a maiden, and she'll lead us to the third feat?" He'd always enjoyed the "rescue the maiden" levels more than the "hidden treasure" ones. If he was going to die, he'd rather it be for maidens than money.

"*Storming*? No. They'll invite you in. Wholeheartedly welcome you, in fact." Meehix grimaced at the thought, finished her second bottle, and fetched them each their third before settling back down against her headboard.

"*Maidens?* You have the gender right, if not the exact choice of words that I would use to describe them." She sipped from the now room-temperature bottle. "And *rescue* also isn't the exact term for what you'll be doing. I think *avoiding* would be much more accurate, and I sincerely, very sincerely hope that you'll succeed."

"Will I die if I don't? How deadly are they?"

"Does the name Vixaleen ring any bells?"

John had to catch himself before he told Meehix about the last time he'd seen the succubus's perfectly red and perfectly formed ass. That was when she snuck out their waiting room window after enjoying a late-night snack of Cream ala Chuckie.

"The demon's niece?"

"The very same. Space Station Beaulifica," Meehix had never heard of the station before but had formed an immediate grudge against its very existence, "is the home base she shares with perhaps hundreds of her succubus cousins."

"The station must have a huge docking area," he mused, "to accommodate the large number of visitors it must draw."

Meehix had spent the last day and a half guarding John's life. She decided not to end it right then and there by smashing her last bottle of Brillian's on his head.

"The object is to spend twelve hours there and escape with your space virginity still intact."

"Oh, fuck." He sighed.

"No fuck, is what's required."

John had fended off Vixaleen's amorous and dedicated advances when they'd rescued her from her imprisonment and returned her safely to her uncle. Still, he and Meehix had also been in a battle with pirates at the time, and *surviving* had taken precedence over *sucking*.

Chuckie, on the other hand, wasn't much at physical combat but did his best to keep the niece safe and semi-well-fed.

"We can't very well offer you up as a virgin sacrifice to complete the third feat if you can't manage to fend off a handful of succubi for a few hours, now can we?"

"I suppose not." John sounded disappointed but was relieved and determined to make it through the succubus space station undefiled. He couldn't admit it to her yet, but there was only one alien he wanted to have sex with, and she was sitting on the bed next to his.

"Let's say that I make it through the twelve hours and check out of Hotel Succubus, my manhood still unspoiled. I'm still not enthralled with the idea of then becoming a virgin *sacrifice*."

Meehix could understand his reluctance at the third feat. She not only did not want him dead, but she also didn't want to *share* him. *Not that we've shared* anything *yet.*

"Chuckie pointed out, while you were sleeping, that the word *sacrifice* is sort of ambiguous. It could also simply mean an offering. For all we know, there could be a king, or the head of a tribe, or something like that, who wants his daughter-dearest to mate with a virgin for some archaic reason."

"Something like keeping the gene pool fresh?"

"Something like that, yes. You could end up being a hero with a bunch of little half-Kdackans toddling around underfoot for the rest of your life as you lived in splendor." Meehix wasn't thrilled with *that* idea either. Actually, there wasn't *anything* about feats two and three that she was even mildly in favor of.

John had a strange look on his face as he imagined a family, half-Kdackan and half-Dolurulodan scurrying around. *I wonder what it would be like to have a brood of blue children? Congratulations, Mom. You now have a baby bluesy for a granddaughter. That would be fun hearing her try to explain it to her bridge club.*

"The goal, remember," sometimes the big oaf could be hard to read, "is to get through all five feats, or *levels*, as you would put it, and come out the other side with a monster of a ship that is totally AI. Chuckie says that we'll be able to park Shippewa inside and connect her to the big ship and control everything from inside Shippewa's cockpit."

"That would give Captain Poopapush a reason to pause before trying to attack us again."

"At least for a little while."

"What do you think it means for a Kdackan to have sex with an alien?"

"It means that one, or both, will be either happy or unsatisfied or a combination of both."

"Why can't we take Shippewa and strike back at the Blavarian first?"

"Because we've already come up against this guy and his

dreadnought IV twice, and the best we've been able to do is duck and dodge and sing *na-na-na-na-bite-a-booger* as we ran for our lives."

"Right." the Brillian's were nearly empty, and he could see Meehix on the edge of nodding off where she sat. "It occurs to me, what with me being a space virgin and all, that I don't know the first thing about female alien anatomy...you know, *down there?*"

"Are you still thinking with your little head?"

"My *big head* has a lot to think about, whereas my *little head* is a lot simpler due to its one-track mind. I mean, what if her hoochie is more like a death-trap lined with rows of razor-sharp teeth?"

He held his arms out in an imitation of an alligator's mouth.

"One good poke," he snapped his hands together, "and *chomp!* One less penis for the Kdackan."

"What the hell are you talking about?" She set her bottle down on the nightstand and rolled over, exhausted. "Whatever it is, it can wait until I get a little shut-eye before I try to make sense of it."

I just wondered if your flap has teeth behind it, he thought but didn't say. She needed some rest, which wasn't going to happen quite yet because five seconds after Meehix had closed her eyes, there was a knock on the door.

CHAPTER THIRTEEN

Meehix and John leapt up and were in a corner the farthest away from the door seconds later with weapons ready and thoughts of sleep a distant memory.

"Fucking Crec Alerts." John was pissed.

"How could they have found us? The first two found us by accident, and we haven't left a paper trail."

"You think they're back for more? It's not like the front desk is above taking a bribe to give out our room number."

"We took their weapons and their money." Meehix shook her head. "They're probably still in jail trying to figure out how to pay for the damages back at the bar."

"Then who the hell?"

Another knock. This one louder, followed by a female voice from the hallway.

"Did anyone here order some juice?"

"I didn't," John whispered. "Did you?"

Meehix holstered her gun and reached out to lower John's arm.

"I forgot."

"You mean it's not someone we need to shoot?"

"No." Meehix shook her head and smiled. "Although she's tempted me to do just that a time or two in the past."

She un-wedged the chair from under the handle and opened the door.

"Juice the Deuce!"

"Mixalot!"

It was definitely a female who stepped in and hugged Meehix before backing her into the room and closing the door behind her. John wasn't sure if her skin was its natural shading or if tattoos of various colors and designs covered her. When the new arrival turned and wedged the chair back into place, John saw that the top and back of her shaved head was similar to the *yin yang* designs back on earth and guessed tattoos.

"Long time, babes." She pulled a hip flask from a back pocket, took a quick swig, and handed it to Meehix, who did the same and handed it back. "What the fuck is a high-society girl like you doing in a dump like Nevera? Did a ship break down or something?"

"I'm not quite the part of high society that I used to be."

The stranger tossed the flask to John.

"Try some. Maybe it'll put some hair on your chest." She cackled.

John checked to make sure he was wearing a shirt. *How did she know?* Then, not wanting to seem impolite, took a short sip, coughed, and tossed it back. She caught it in one hand, and in a quick fluid movement, had it tucked back into place.

"John," Meehix stepped back, "This is Juice. Juice, John."

"This is a long way from Tagbedden Castle, girl. What happened?"

"Oh, you know, the usual. Family sold me off to another planet to pay off some debts."

"Which planet?"

"It doesn't matter." Meehix suddenly remembered that Juice usually steered conversations to where she wanted them to go, so she sighed. "Kdack."

"Shit! Your family always were sonsabitches." She turned to John. "Have you met them?"

"A couple of them, but it was only once and very brief."

"You're lucky." She unslung a shoulder bag and tossed it on a bed. "I hear Kdack is a piss-hole of a backwater swamp in the middle of no-fucking-where that only has one thing going for it." She smiled and nudged Meehix.

"I never thought of it that way." John wasn't sure what to make of her yet but decided that circumstances allowed him to be a little defensive. "I just called it home."

"You're a Kdackan?"

"Guilty." He raised his hand.

"So, if the *one good thing* is true, you must have a hell of a…"

She didn't have a chance to finish the sentence as Meehix gave her face a quick slap.

"Focus!"

"Focus, your badass self!" Juice slapped her back.

The two exchanged slaps up and down their bodies as if it was a routine they'd performed many times before.

Is this some kind of alien-female bonding? John had to wonder.

They ended up slapping each other's asses as Meehix

picked Juice's back pocket for another quick swig and they both laughed.

Definitely a bonding ritual, John decided.

"You always did have the fastest hands." Juice took a swig of her own and held out the flask toward John, who shook his head.

"Thanks, but I'll pass." He thought his best option at the moment was to try to keep a clear head.

The two old friends hopped up onto Meehix's bed and sat cross-legged facing each other.

"Let me know if I'm needed." John swung the second room chair around to keep an eye on the door as the women-folk got down to business. He also fired up Heemix, and while keeping his gun handy, started some perfunctory research.

"I can get most of what you want." Juice pulled out a pocket-pad and started scrolling. "But babes, this isn't your normal party mix."

"I am aware of that," Meehix admitted. "Which is why I had to call on the best. I was surprised to find your old number still working and that you were close enough to receive it."

"Only my oldest and closest have that number. For business purposes, I go through one burner phone per month and use a call center to route messages through. As for being close enough, I happen to keep a small apartment here."

"On Nevera?"

"Rents are cheap, it's central to three Gates, and I need a place to store shit and crash for a few days now and then. You were lucky and caught me on a short now and then."

"Okay, let's deal."

Juice consulted her pad. "I found all of the items in the catalog. How soon do you need them?"

"I'm not sure yet. Might need a couple real soon."

"Will you be hanging around long enough to pick them up?"

"Not unless you can get them overnight. We're heading out tomorrow first thing in the morning but should be able to swing back in a few days."

"I can always deliver them, but that would add to the costs."

"No, we'll come to you."

"And if I'm not here?"

"We'll still come to you, wherever you are. What can you do for the pricing?"

Juice pulled out the flask and let Meehix take another sip, which was not a good sign because it meant that the price would hurt, and Juice wanted to help ease the pain.

"Twenty percent." Juice took another sip and pocketed the flask.

John had tuned out of the negotiations long enough to discover that Juice the Deuce appeared in several bounty hunters' databases. There wasn't an actual Crec Alert out for her, but all of the databases intimated that several *agencies,* some official and others not so much, were interested in her whereabouts.

It would probably be bad form to arrest your black market dealer, especially when your partner invited her into your room.

"Oh, c'mon! That's obscene, especially between friends."

"It's business, toots. A girl's gotta eat."

"I was thinking more like fifteen."

"All right. I was just jerkin' ya." Juice slapped Meehix's shoulder. "But the bottom-line best that I can do for an override is seventeen. That's still below the catalog's MSRP."

"Not by much." Meehix was seriously disappointed. "That's like an override on top of an existing override."

"If these items are all in a catalog," John tuned back in, "Why can't we go buy what we want?"

"These aren't the kind of *catalogs* that are available to the general public, sweet cheeks." Juice smiled at him. "Besides, these aren't the kind of items you want whoever your opponents are to know that you have. Using me as the go-between means that no one can trace them back to you. I never buy and tell." She smiled again. "I also never kiss and tell."

"Okay! Seventeen percent." Meehix decided to close the deal and get Juice out of there as quickly as possible to preserve John's status as a sacrificial virgin.

Meehix hopped up off the bed and led her friend to the door.

"I'll get it all as fast as I can and let you know when and where to meet up."

Meehix opened the door and checked the hallway. All clear.

Juice leaned in for a goodbye hug and whispered, "He's a cutie. So, is it true about…"

They did their slapping ritual again, and Juice headed out. Closing and locking the door and wedging the chair back into place, Meehix turned to John.

"Time to pack up. We'll spend the night aboard Ship."

"Don't you trust her? I mean, she's your friend, and we

didn't say anything about how there's a Crec Alert out on us."

"I trust on her things like that." Meehix tried to lead by example and moved around the room, gathering up her belongings. "I just got a vibe that we've been here too long, already."

"We've only been here two days." Not that John was opposed to heading to Ship where they had a great air-filtration system and clean oxygen supply.

"A Crec Alert is a Crec Alert. Best not to be stationary."

"Speaking of Crec Alerts…"

"Yeah, yeah, she's a hot commodity."

"There's no alert out on her at the moment," John started to pack up his gear, "but she's definitely wanted."

"Yeah, well, you can relax about Juice's safety." *It's your virginal safety around her that I'm worried about.*

"She's one of the biggest purveyors of under-the-counter weapons in the galaxy, and without her and her connections, half the bounty hunters would have no one else to turn to if they needed to rearm or supplement what they currently have."

"No one kills the golden goose?"

"If you say so." Meehix had her bags ready. "This is her home base, so I'm sure she'd already heard about the little dust-up at the bar the other day and put two and two together, and yet, she didn't burn us."

"It was only her first opportunity." John slung his bags over his shoulder, scooted the door guard chair out of the way for the last time, and stepped out into the hallway.

"Let's hope she has another first time to try another first time."

Meehix followed him out and closed the door. "What the hell did that even mean?"

"I have no idea," he shrugged, "but it sounded boss in my head."

Having just finished showing four of the recent, credible videos he'd been sent, and with a hundred thirty-six calls waiting in the queue, Gonzo Gage hit the call answer icon on his screen.

"Time to go to the phones. Whatcha got for the Gonzo Gang today?"

"Fourteen times in a row!" Cheering broke out in the background.

"Yes, Albert, your streak is unbroken." Gage didn't know if he should sigh, cry or try to figure out some kind of prize for his most dedicated first caller of the day.

"Seriously, Gonzo," Albert went on, "we're stuck in cubicles all day and other than when you're podcasting, the only form of excitement each day is the office pool to guess whether our bitch of a boss will show up with beer, whiskey, or gin on her breath."

"Well, I'm not quite sure how to answer that."

"She's more coherent on beer days but less of a bitch on gin. Whiskey is always a crap-shoot."

"I'm working on a prize for you guys, Albert. Any suggestions?"

"Any chance you can get us an actual alien's autograph?"

"Well, I've only met the one."

"The blue chick, right?"

"Right, and she's been busy working with Jojacko to free some slaves in other solar systems lately, but as soon as they get back, I'll get her to sign a photo for you personally. Trust me," he smiled at the memory of his brief encounter with Meehix, "It'll be worth the wait. She's a hottie who smells even better than she looks." He pressed another button.

"Next caller?"

"You should be called *Ganja Gage*. I'm getting stoned just from the smell of whatever it is you're smoking to be able to come up with this shit."

"If you had any idea, *amigo*, about the hundreds of videos sent in each week from all over the globe and how many my staff and I delete because they're nowhere near authentic, you would reassess my dedication to sharing only the ones that pass through my technical filtering program. If I were a stoner, I would spend most of my time giggling at some of the amateurish attempts to put one past me."

He hit his "good for a laugh" button.

"Check this one out, gang." A video came up of a dachshund wearing an Oakland Raiders football helmet as he space-surfed on the rings around Saturn.

"Somehow, that one didn't make it past my filters. Next."

In reality, the only kind of filter he knew how to program was on the new coffee maker he'd bought for his parents out of SAFA's Daily Expenditures account. His entire staff consisted of a thirteen-year old-babysitter for his younger siblings Isabella and Toñito while he did his podcast when his mom was working. But he'd had a true-to-life experience, and his sniff test took care of the rest.

"I was going to ask another question, Mister Gonzo," the next caller had an accent that Gage couldn't place, but that wasn't unusual these days. "But now I want to thank you."

"You're welcome?"

"Here in Romania," *where the hell is Romania?* "we have a long history of legends and rumors from the Carpathians."

"I'm sorry. Who are the Carpathians?"

"The Carpathians is the name of the mountain range. You are probably more familiar with them as the home of the legend of Dracula." Gage was about to move on to the next caller. "But we know the difference between legend and rumor and truth." Gage held off on the disconnect for the moment.

"What you say has the sound of truth. You don't throw Frisbee into sky and pretend it saucer. We are not stupid, but we know what we see. There is no Dracula. The only wolfman is Wolfman Jack. Even in Romania, we know this. But visitors from space? We would have to be fools not to believe. So thank you for helping truth-seekers to sort out fake Frisbee-tossers from what is real."

"Thank you, truth-seeker from Romania... Although even I would stay home at night when the moon is full."

An hour and thirty callers later, it was time to sign off.

"Remember, my friends, SAFA, Save Aliens From Assholes is a true non-profit. If we were keeping any money for ourselves, instead of funding teams to coordinate movements to free the aliens being held captive, I could afford a better studio to podcast from than my bedroom.

"You know the ways to donate. Please, make sure you have all your bills paid, and donate whatever you can from what's left over. The alien you save may never be able to thank you in person, but they might make your name legendary on the planet of their origin. So, until the next time gang, Gonzo Gage, out and gone."

He hit the "end stream" button but had other business to take care of before he signed completely off.

Checking his Patreon account, which is where he funneled all of the donations to SAFA, he was pleased to see that the donations held consistent at five thousand dollars per month. He moved a little into his savings that he hoped to use, someday, to help pay for Isabella's and Toñito's college tuitions.

Then he moved the rest of it into his dark web digital account. Untraceable, untaxable, and untouchable… If he should die from one-too-many anal probes before Jojacko returned, he knew his best friend would figure out a way to access it.

Assuming, that is, that Jojacko was still alive and would eventually return.

Gage remained faithful to their last parting promises to each other, and he trusted the J-man to do the same.

He opened the middle drawer of his desk and pulled out the cigar box he'd saved from one of his dad's recycling bins. Papa Gonzalez had taught him that a businessman always needed to have a petty cash fund.

The only thing nagging at the back of his brain was that agents Bixby and Shaw hadn't called in during his podcast.

They were as regular as First Caller Albert, and he missed the chance to moon them again.

He stuck a few twenties in one pocket, in case he needed to make a run to the corner store or maybe order delivery for dinner later on, and another twenty in the other, to pay his staff for her babysitting services. Then he quickly left his bedroom and aimed for the living room.

Little Isabella was on her back on the floor, arms stretched out above her, as Becka, his staff was tossing Toñito over her and into the arms of Yolanda, who caught the laughing bundle and tossed him back.

He was relieved to see that Becka's older sister, Carla, was hovering above the foursome, ready to snatch Toñito out of the air if it looked like anyone was going to miss a catch.

"Madre de Dios!"

Mama Gonzalez had gotten off work early, and because of the laughing *niño* and babysitters, no one had heard her car pull into the driveway before she suddenly walked in through the front door.

"Why do you have girlfriends in the *casa* without permission?" She rounded on Gage, "And why are they tossing Toñito like a potato?"

The startled girls jumped up and back, and Toñito landed on Isabella's belly with a happy giggle.

"Oy fuck!" Toñito laughed. The little fellow hadn't learned very many words yet, but Gage had to admit that he'd been responsible for teaching him most of them.

"Not *girlfriends,* Mom." Gage swept Toñito up into his arms and handed him over to prove that he'd taken no damage. "Becka is my employee."

"Employee?"

"Babysitter." Becka quickly moved and tickled Toñito's chin, producing a full-throated giggle. "I watch over him while Gonzo,"

"AHEM!" Gage needed some help here.

"I mean," Becka recovered quickly for a thirteen-year-old, "While *Gage* does his podcast."

"What is a podcast?"

"Hi, Mrs. Gonzalez." Carla took front and center and held out her hand. "I'm Carla."

Gage's mom shook the young girl's hand as best she could without dropping the baby.

"I haven't exactly been attending community college," Gage 'fessed up.

"College can't teach him more than he already knows." Yolanda decided it was her turn to step up to the plate and also offered her hand, which Gage's mom again did her best to shake.

"Your son, Gage," she motioned to Gage, "has become a very famous Truth Seeker, with tens of thousands of followers."

"This is true?" his mom asked.

Gage had a quick internal debate about whether he should run for the hills or tell his mom the truth. *If I can't tell my mom the truth, how can I tell it to anyone else?*

"Yes, Mom." He decided to come clean. "Jojacko…John, hasn't been off on a work-study program."

Mrs. Gonzalez started tapping her toes inside her right shoe. *Finally, he is ready to tell me.*

"Right before John disappeared, we accidentally discovered something."

"Something real? Not something in one of your games?"

"Something very real, Mom. I wish it was only a game."

She had seen a lot of looks in her son's eyes before, but none of them had ever been the look of fear that she saw in them now.

The front door broke open.

"It's probe time, little boy!" shouted Agent Bixby.

"Time to bend over and ask for another!" Agent Shaw thought was a good follow-up.

"What the fuck are all these girls doing here?" Bixby shouted. "You said he'd be alone!"

"I said it would be him and his little brother!" Shaw was pissed. "No one informed me about any babysitters!"

"They want me, Mom. Everyone else will be safe!" Gage shouted. "Mom, find the Cohiba box in my desk! Girls? It's cell phone video time! Gonzo's PC is still on! Do your thing, and I'll catch up to ya's later!"

Gage hit the back door running and had hopped three fences as Becka and Yolanda filmed Mrs. Gonzalez swinging baby Toñito as her only defense against the two gun-toting agents as she chased them back to their DeVille.

"Oy fuck vey!" laughed Toñito as he was having the ride of his life.

"Men in black! Men in black! Men in black!" shouted Becka and Yolanda in unison as they filmed Mrs. Gonzalez chasing the agents back to their car with nothing more than a laughing baby.

During the chaos that seemed well under control, Carla snatched up Isabella and carried her to Gage's room and held her on her lap as she saw the *On Air* sign still lit behind her. She touched Gage's PC screen, being no neophyte, and she went live again.

"Yo, yo! I know that many of you are still out there! The podcast is resuming!"

On the bottom of the screen, she could see that fifty-thousand-plus had it on *notice,* as did she on her PC, not wanting to miss a Gonzo podcast announcement.

Her face appeared on the screen, and she spoke at it, not worrying about how her hair looked, while she tried to pretend that she was talking to herself as if it was the most natural thing in the world.

"Hey, Gonzo's Gang! We're updating, live!" *I need a name. I need a name...* "This is Carla Cat, reporting that two men just invaded Gonzo's house. He ducked and ran out back to protect his staff by having the agents chase him while saving us!

"Men in black! Men in black!" Becka and Yolanda were still shouting in unison as they burst into the room.

Becka gave her older sister her phone. "I don't know how to plug it in."

"Gimme!" Carla ordered. "And take Issa off my lap."

The young girls took charge of Issa as Carla slapped a couple of cords into Gage's setup.

"You all just heard the babysitters scream *Men in black! Men in black! live* from here in Gonzo Gage's studio!"

Carla continued her broadcast-podcast-whatever.

"Here comes some video, fresh off my younger sister's phone, as the agents Bixby and Shaw—you remember those faithful call-in followers of Gage's, right?"

Anyone who had seen or heard any of Gage's podcasts was familiar with the names and voices of the two agents.

Carla, and all of the viewers, saw her sister's video of Mrs. Gonzalez chasing the agents out of her house, armed with nothing more than a laughing, potty-mouthed baby.

"Today, agents Bixby and Shaw—commit those names to memory and repeat them often."

Carla felt like she'd been born for this. She noticed on one corner of the screen the number of viewers was rising exponentially, and in another corner of the screen, the call-waiting queue was lighting up.

"Where was I? Oh, right! Today, Bixby and Shaw decided not to call in and threaten Gonzo Gage with anal probes. Instead, they decided to kick in the door and terrify two babysitters and the two babies they were sitting for and threaten Gage's mom as she walked in the door after working her shift... Your tax dollars at work!"

She decided to let the loop of the agents continue to run.

"I have to sign off now and help take care of Gage's mom and siblings and the totally innocent babysitters, but I'll leave the video running for you to copy and download and share to your heart's content."

How to end it?

"For those of you in Albuquerque, you might want to keep your children out of the clutches of agents Bixby and Shaw. For the rest of Gonzo's Gang, this is Carla Cat, out and scratching!"

She signed off and found Mrs. Gonzalez standing behind her, still holding Toñito.

Uhh-ohh.

CHAPTER FOURTEEN

"Hi, Mrs. Gonzalez," seemed like the best place to start.

"Mrs. G, please."

Becka hustled in and took Toñito out of her arms. "You were awesome, Mrs. G." She held Toñito up high. "And you, little mister, are one dangerous weapon!"

"Oy, fuck vey," Toñito agreed.

"They're teaching Yiddish on Sesame Street this week." Carla had to admit that her little sister was quick. "*Fuck* doesn't mean what we're used to it meaning, it just *sounds* like the F-word...The whole phrase means...*Wow, very good.*"

"Two strange men burst into my house and threaten my children, and you're worried I'll be mad because Gage might have taught his baby brother how to say *fuck*?"

"Well, you know?"

"Yes." Mrs. G smiled. "I know. Take little Tito back out front and keep an eye on him and his sister. I need to have a chat with Carla Cat."

Becka did as instructed, and Mrs. G slid a chair up alongside Carla's. Even though she was no longer broadcasting, they could both see the number of viewers continuing to rise as the video of Gage's mom with Toñito as her only weapon chased two agents back out to their car where they leapt in and peeled off.

"I would not want to meet that woman in a dark alley." Mrs. G admired her performance.

"No ma'am," Carla agreed. *I'm not sure I'd want to meet her in her son's bedroom, either.*

"Relax, *chica*. Or should I call you Miss Cat?"

"Carla would be fine. The Cat name was sort of spontaneous."

"Okay, Carla it is." Mrs. G graced her with a smile and tried to put the poor girl at ease. "Can you please explain to me what my son has been up to? Since he's obviously not been in here attending online classes."

Where to begin? Stalling is always a good start.

"Gage has been doing podcasts for the last few months. He's mentioned a friend of his, Jojacko. Do you know him?"

"Little Johnny? *Si*, since he was five. He's not so little anymore."

"Jojacko, which is how everyone knows him from Gage's podcasts, well, him and Gage discovered and rescued an alien a while back."

"The flying ship." Finally, she was going to get some real answers. "Gage thinks I don't remember, but we all saw it in the sky above John's house. I ask him, 'Where's John been?' and he feeds me stories about John being out of town for a work-study program. But you tell me now that it wasn't just a flying ship, like a jet or a helicopter?"

"No, ma'am." Carla nodded. "It was a real spaceship, like to the moon and other planets. Jojacko, I mean John, is off on the ship somewhere, trying to free aliens held as slaves on other planets. The only reason that Gage didn't go with him is that he knew he was needed here, to help take care of Isabella and Toñito."

"I don't know what we would do without him," Mrs. G agreed. "Mr. G and I both need to work, and Gage living here makes that possible."

"But, you see," Carla pointed at the screen. "Gage is still involved with saving space aliens. He's working to free the ones held captive here on Earth."

"We have little green men in cages?" Mrs. G could raise an eyebrow with the best of them. "Is that what you're saying to me?"

"They're not *all* little, although some of them *are* green." She opened one of Gage's drawers and pulled out a photograph of Gage and John and Meehix on the day they all met during an unplanned and ill-advised stop-over in Hawaii. "They're not all *men*, either."

Mrs. G studied the photo before handing it back. "She needs to do something about her hair."

"I agree." Carla laughed. "Maybe go blonde?"

"Or black. Then she could be black and blue."

Carla set the photo back in the drawer, which is when she noticed the Cohiba cigar box and pulled it out.

"Gage shouted something about a Cohiba box as he was running out, right?" His mom nodded. Carla set the box on top of the desk and opened it.

"How much, you think?" Mrs. G was shocked to see a pile of tens and twenties.

"A little over two grand." Carla had quickly thumbed through it.

"No, no, no, Dios mìo." She started to cry.

"Mrs. G. You okay?"

"Not okay! No! Only drug dealers have this much money, and in small bills!"

"No, Mrs. G. no." Carla immediately understood the tears. "I promise you that your son is *not* a drug dealer!"

"Then where does this money come from? He has no job."

"But he *does* have a job," Carla tried to explain. "It's just not one he has told you about."

She pointed at the screen and the number in the corner that now read *824*.

"Gage does a podcast each week. Those numbers show how many people are watching. An hour ago, while he was on the air, that number was up in the thousands as people around the whole world tuned in."

"Tuning in to see my Gagito?"

"Yes. He has become sort of a hero. He even started a non-profit organization called SAFA to help raise funds to save the aliens imprisoned here on Earth. People donate because they believe in him, and that's where the money comes from."

"People send this money to Gage? Because they think he does work that is good?" Mrs. G was gaining a whole new perspective of her son.

"Yes. Exactly that. He's a freedom fighter."

"So, he's not just playing games online any more and pretending he's going to college to get an education?"

"No, Mrs. G. He has *become* an *educator*, teaching people about things that they can't learn in college."

"How does a young girl know all this?"

"Well, I'm a little older than I look." Carla had become sensitive about her looks over the last couple of years. "I'm eighteen. Nineteen in two months."

Mrs. G reached out and touched Carla's cheek.

"You have skin as soft as a baby's." She scooted her chair back a few inches so she could get a better look at the whole girl. "You must have taken care to avoid the sun, yes?"

"I seldom go out during the day without a hat," Carla admitted. "But some girls are early bloomers, and some girls are late bloomers. I'm beginning to think that there should be a category labeled as never bloomers because that's where I'd probably fit in."

"The last flower of the season is always the loveliest."

Carla couldn't remember the last time someone had made her blush.

"So tell me," Mrs. G went on. "How did you and your sister, and her friend, become involved with my Gage?"

"He bought my sister and two of her friends ice cream."

"That sounds…"

"Unsavory, right? They rushed through the door and squealed about how they'd just met the famous *Gonzo Gage* and his baby brother, even though he told them that he wasn't who they thought he was.

"I thought he'd just bought them ice cream to get them out of his hair. I mean, it must be tiresome for celebrity

lookalikes to be harassed and try to explain that their auto-
graphs wouldn't be worth anything."

"I have a cousin who resembles Antonio Banderas, the
actor." Mrs. G shook her head. "I'm afraid that he often
takes advantage of that."

"Well, your son didn't take advantage of the fact that he
actually *was* Gonzo Gage. But my sister and her friends
were such fans that they started hanging out near Lieb's,
down on the corner, because that's where they'd met him.
Sure enough, they saw him going back, pushing Toñito in
his stroller and made him confess. But instead of giving
them his autograph, he hired my sister as a babysitter once
a week while he did his broadcast."

"So Gage was telling the truth. Your sister…"

"Becka."

"Becka, *gracias*, *is* an actual employee?"

"Yes!" Carla nodded vigorously. "Once a week for three
hours. That way, he can do his podcast and not have to
worry about Issa and Tito."

It was a strange story, but Mrs. G was beginning to
understand.

"But she's my little sister, ya know? I tagged along
because I needed to know that this *Gonzo* guy wasn't a…"

"You needed to make sure that my son wasn't a predator?" Mrs. G helped her out.

"Exactly!" Carla was relieved that Gage's mom understood where she was coming from. "I mean, I didn't know
this Gonzo Gage from Gonzo the Muppet, but I had to
make sure that my little sister was safe."

"You are a good big sister."

"And your son is a good man. Can I be honest?" Carla leaned forward.

"From my brief time knowing you," Mrs. G leaned forward too, "I don't think that you are capable of being *dishonest*, except for the little fibs that we all must tell each other now and then."

Wow, an honest to God, girl-to-woman talk. I wonder if she'll adopt me?

"I *am* a student at the community college that Gage told you he was attending. Don't laugh," Carla leaned back, hoping for the best, "but I'm studying Journalism. I want to be a reporter."

"Why would I laugh about a serious goal like that?" Mama Gage leaned back too, trying to keep the young girl at ease by mimicking her movements. "The world needs truth."

"Exactly! Reporting isn't a very glamorous job unless you can become a talking-head on TV, but most of it is hard work behind the scenes, just trying to uncover something...So I followed with my sister, just in case..."

"In case you uncovered a predator? Good for you, *chica!* If you had discovered that about my Gage, I would have sliced off his *cojones* myself and served them at the next Gonzalez family barbecue."

Whoa. Wanna keep on the good side of Mrs. G, that's for sure!

"So, once knowing that Becka wasn't in any danger, as a reporter, I decided to look for another story."

"This reporting, it has gotten into your blood, yes?"

"I never thought of it that way before, but yes."

"Then you are one of the lucky ones."

"How's that?"

"You are still young, but you have found a *pasiòn*. Many people spend their whole lives searching for something to believe in, but you are not one of them," Mrs. G leaned forward again. "Did my Gage lead you to another story?"

"Yes." Carla leaned forward and wasn't sure why she lowered her voice. "I know about podcasting and how people can get sucked into believing anything, no matter how asinine. And, well, I thought that maybe the dude my sister and her friends called *Gonzo Gage* was just an egotistical blowhard, spinning wild tales to the idiots who think that wearing tinfoil hats is the latest fashion trend."

"Tinfoil is for wrapping dinner in and slow-cooking." Mrs. G spoke from experience.

"Yes." Carla laughed and leaned back. "It shouldn't be worn as headgear."

"Under a New Mexico sun?" Mrs. G leaned back and shared the laugh. "Would fried brains be best served as an appetizer or dessert?"

"Here's the thing, Mrs. G. Gonzo, I mean Gage, is nothing more, nor less, than a guy who has found a... *pasiòn*? and is pursuing it. I've also discovered that he's a very nice guy."

"To answer the question you haven't asked yet," Mrs. G said in a soft voice. "The answer is *yes*."

"Yes, *what*, and to what question?" Carla had lost all track of the conversation's direction.

"Yes," came the gentle but firm reply. "You should ask him out."

"I never said anything about wanting to ask him out!" Carla was shocked.

"Ahh, yes," Mrs. G leaned in again and lowered her voice. "That is where I have the advantage over you."

"Come again?"

"I have the advantage of hearing the words you say. As a reporter, you write. But you can't always write everything, so sometimes, people need to... What is the expression... *Read between the lines?* Is that right?"

"Yes. That is the phrase." Carla recognized it.

"Sometimes, you have to be able to listen between the words."

Carla leaned back. She'd heard the term *gobsmacked* before during her studies. She had even looked up the definition. Sitting here in Gage's bedroom with his mom, she now understood that you could also use it as a verb. She had just been totally gobsmacked!

"Back in Mexico, when we were much younger, I knew that Gage's father was sweet on me and had been for some time." Mrs. G smiled at the memory. "I was in the back of the little diner, rolling out some bread dough as he was making a delivery. He would stand there, trying to make small talk when I had work to do! One morning, I'd had enough and threw my rolling pin at his head. I had very good aim."

"Did you hurt him?"

"Nothing that a bag of ice couldn't handle to keep the swelling down."

"You hit your husband with a rolling pin?" Carla was shocked.

"No!" Mrs. G answered. "I would never hit my husband. But a silly boy, who was wasting my time when I had work to do? Oh, yes. Him I would hit. He took the hint and asked me out. Our first date did not go very well…but every day since then? *Muy bien.*"

Mrs. G leaned forward again, and this time took Carla's hands in hers. "What I am trying to tell you is that you must not wait for him to ask you out because cobwebs will grow around your ears before that happens."

"But he's in danger now. What if he doesn't live long enough for me to ask him out? And as his mom, aren't you worried about him?"

"No, *bonita chica.* I am not worried. He has someone in love with him who is waiting. It would be rude of him to die before you have a chance to ask him out. My Gage has a lot of faults, but being rude is not one of them."

Now that Mrs. G knew about the Cohiba box, she took out two twenties and set the box back in the drawer under the photograph from Hawaii.

Standing up, she took Carla's hand and led her back into the living room, where they found Becka and Yolanda, with Isabella and Toñito sitting on their laps, watching another Muppet movie.

"Pause, please." Mrs. G was issuing an order, not making a request. Becka had control of the remote and obeyed.

"Thank you, *chicas,* for your bravery earlier. I now know that my babies are in good hands."

She rubbed the four heads, who now had no movie to watch at the moment, and kissed her two babies.

"Becka?"

"Yes, Mrs. G?"

"I am now your employer." She handed her a twenty and turned to the other young girl.

"I am sorry that I don't remember your name...everything got so suddenly crazy."

"Yolanda, Mrs. G."

"Yolanda." She handed her the other twenty. "You two are now *my* employees, not Gonzo Gage's. You only come and babysit when Gage is doing his...podcast?"

Nods all around.

"Okay then. Here are the rules. I pay you, not my twenty-year-old son, because that seems more proper. You must have your phones charged up before you arrive. The lesson we all learned today is that we need to be able to take videos at a moment's notice."

More nods.

"I will have Mr. Gonzalez install a security system, with video cameras in plain view, to discourage any more uninvited guests. I don't know how you will explain this to your parents. If you do and decide that this isn't the best place for you to earn a little extra money, then don't argue with them, and don't come back. No parent wants their children to be in danger. Understood?"

"Understood," Becka answered as Yolanda nodded.

"Neither of you two can come back here unless Carla is with you." She turned. "Carla? Is that agreed?"

"Yes. Mrs. G."

"Remember, *chicas*. There is always safety in numbers. Always!"

"Gonzo," Toñito chose that moment to pipe up and point at the paused screen. "Oy, fuck vey. Gonzo!"

Sure enough, frozen on-screen was Gonzo the Muppet in the middle of an adventure, surrounded by a frog, a pig, and a bear with a funny-looking hat. They seemed to be somewhere in space.

Mrs. Gonzalez laid down on the floor behind the two young girls who still held her children in their laps, safely guarding them as if they didn't have a care in the world. She tapped the floor beside her.

"Carla? Care to join us to see how the notorious Mister Gonzo manages to survive?"

Carla took a seat. "Unpause it, Becka. It looks like Gonzo is about to kick some serious space-butt."

"He better." Mrs. Gonzalez whispered a quiet prayer as the movie resumed.

"Nice flying and docking, John."

"Thank you, Ship."

John had at least a day and a half of a giggle-gun-induced sleep on the smelly space station Nevera. Meehix, on the other hand, had been seriously sleep-deprived as she'd guarded their room.

They'd decided to leave their hotel room as quickly as possible due to various complications, and spend the night sleeping onboard Shippewa before heading off the next morning for feat number one. Climbing on board, the partners had tossed their bags into the cargo area, and Meehix conked out in the copilot's seat without enough energy to search for the inflatable cots they kept stored.

"We're heading out, Ship," John announced as he took the controls and punched in the coordinates for the planet

Suvious and their first feat, task, level, *or whatever the hell anyone wanted to call it.*

Rather than spend a night on Ship while still docked on Space Station Nevera—*Never Again,* as he remembered Meehix's nickname for the odiferous station—John had made a management decision to fly through the night and leave Nevera behind them as fast as he could.

He'd wished that there were windows he could roll down to let fresh air come flowing in. His nose was still *that* full of the space station's stench.

"Are we there yet?" Meehix was waking up.

"Yes," John assured her. "We are there."

"Where is there?"

"We just docked on planet Suvious."

"I close my eyes for five minutes, and you decide to go on a road trip?" Meehix had to stand and stretch. Granted, Shippewa smelled a lot better than Nevera, but sleeping in a copilot's seat wasn't the same as being able to lay full-out on a bed.

"I was wide awake," John defended himself, "and thought it would make better sense to fly than to remain docked and be a stationary target on a station we were known to be at."

"Okay. You got a point."

And you have a great ass.

Meehix's current stretch, as she was working the kinks out, was bending over and lifting the toes of her boots off the ground. She was not facing John as she performed it.

"Oh, I needed that." She straightened.

Oh, I want that.

"What's our next step?"

While still turned away from John, she performed a backward stretch, attempting to reach her heels, which left her face upside down in front of John, with her tits four inches in front of his face.

Oh, I want those two, too. He kept his hands gripping the controls so hard that he was afraid of hurting Ship.

"What?" Meehix saw where his eyes were focused. "You've never seen tits before?"

"None quite as magnificent as yours," John managed to say, despite both of the distractions. "Are you going to be done stretching anytime soon?"

"Poor little virgin boy." She unwound herself and returned to her seat. "All looky-looky, but can't touchy-touchy."

"What's next," he was finally able to focus again, "is that we check into a room and track down the nerds."

Releasing his grip on the controls, he stretched out his back and felt a couple of vertebrae pop. Eight straight hours of piloting had left his body a little stiff, but he resisted the urge to stand and do a backstretch that would leave his penis in Meehix's face. He was polite that way.

"Chuckie sent us their address, so we check into a hotel and go track down the spoiled lab-rat-brats. They'll give us more info on where we need to go to find the craters."

Leaving all but a couple of essential weapons on Ship, they grabbed their bags, left the docking station, and stepped foot on the streets of Troidit, the city where the lab was. Suvious wasn't a large planet, and from space looked mostly barren, but the city itself practically gleamed as light illuminated, or reflected from, buildings that were an impressive combination of burnished metal and reflective glass.

John thought that maybe their recent stay on Nevera had affected his sense of smell because it was the cleanest smelling city he'd ever been in. In fact, the air had no definable odor.

"Is it me, or is this the most antiseptic-smelling city you've ever visited?"

Meehix drew a deep breath. "I don't smell a thing."

"And I don't feel a thing, either."

They set their bags down and took it all in. The city seemed circular, dominated in the center by the tallest tower John had ever seen. Glimmering silver metal with what looked like a plate of fine china balanced on top.

A sleek commuter train silently approached and stopped in front of them. They hadn't even noticed the tracks. A dozen aliens of various origins quietly emerged and headed for their ships inside the station. There was no shouting, no jostling, no hustling, just an orderly disembarking. There wasn't even an announcement of what the next stop would be as the train pulled out.

"No noise, either." John was now afraid of raising his voice above a whisper.

Meehix nodded and held up a finger to test the wind and felt nothing, confirming John's earlier comment. She guided John and their bags back a couple of steps and tossed a crumpled wrapper from an old energy bar she had in a pocket onto the walk in front of them.

A moment later, a silver ball, about two feet across, came out of nowhere. The bottom half dropped open and sucked the wrapper up into it. The two halves of the ball came back together, and they heard a *tsk-tsk*, as the orb went in search of the next piece of offending litter.

"We better find a hotel fast and take a shower." John grabbed his bag. "I don't want to wander the streets and offend anyone in case some of Nevera's stench is still lingering on us."

"Sshhh," Meehix whispered as she put a finger to her lips.

It was now John's turn to nod. A moment later, a cab pulled up in front of them, and gull-winged doors opened onto the back seat.

"Welcome to Troidit," came a soft, animated voice. "The most studious and sanitary city on Suvious. Please climb in, and I will take you to your hotel."

They dared not disobey, and ten minutes later found themselves standing in the lobby of The Hotel Galena. There wasn't even any quiet, piped-in music coming in over a hidden speaker system.

"Welcome," came the melodious voice of the distin-guished-looking animatronic gentleman behind the front desk. "Will you be checking in?"

"Yes?" John answered, and they advanced as quietly as they could.

"Very good." He handed them key cards. "Room 246 is ready for you."

John leaned over the desk and spoke softly. "We haven't reserved a room yet."

"No, but you have been delivered here, so here is where you will be staying."

"But what if we haven't decided where we want to stay

yet?" Meehix leaned over the desk and matched John's volume.

"Aaahh, this is your first visit." It wasn't a question. "Your confusion is understandable. There are only two hotels in Troidit. One on the north side and one on the south. Both hotels are identical, the only difference being whether you prefer to be on the sunrise side or the sunset side."

"You got a preference, John?"

John didn't get the time to give a preference before the animatron continued.

"At the moment, you are on the north side, and we only have one room available. Our sister hotel, the Imajuik, on the south side is already fully booked. Neither hotel takes reservations. I believe the system is often referred to as first come, first served. A dozen guests checked out half an hour ago, and eleven rooms have already been taken. Unless you wish to return to your ship and spend the night there, I would strongly advise you to take room 246."

"Two-four-six it is." John shrugged. "How much for a night?"

"Each room is priced according to its room number. So yours would be two hundred and forty-six credits. Payment in advance is required."

"How many floors do you have?" Meehix hadn't counted when they'd arrived.

"Twelve. Obviously, the higher the floor, the better the view."

"Room 246 sounds fine. Pay the man, John."

John pulled out his Exchange card.

"Strangest city I've ever been in," John said as they

stepped into the pneumatic tube that would deliver them one floor up.

"I'm not sure if I'll ever feel comfortable raising my voice again."

"So, you are the next in line?" A white-jacketed technician greeted them as they stepped into the small lobby of TRC. "A Mr. Chuckie N informed us that you would be arriving soon."

He took off his gloves, which fit him like a second skin, and shook their hands.

"I hope your travels were safe and that you've enjoyed your stay here so far."

"I'm afraid to enjoy anything in case it causes me to laugh or shout too…Oww."

"We haven't been here long enough to explore your fine city yet." Meehix took over the diplomatic duties, hoping that John wouldn't react so loudly the next time she kicked his ankle.

"I'm Meehix, and this is my partner, John. Yes, Chuckie N is the one who directed us here."

"I'm Keenan." He disposed of his gloves in a very sanitary-looking receptacle. "I would invite you back into the lab, but you would need to be disinfected, then pass a two-day waiting period. Here at the Trimium Research Laboratory, we take our work very seriously."

"What you're working with, this trimium, it's *that*, umm," John struggled to find the right adjective.

"Pure," Keenan helped him out. "Not when we get it. We

have three different labs back there." He nodded at the door behind him. "Each one designed to filter out impurities, one step at a time."

Introductions over, the technician took a step back to look the two over and addressed John.

"You, obviously, must be the one who is *questing*."

"Obviously?" Meehix tried but failed to keep the annoyance out of her voice. "Why do you assume that of the two who stand in front of you, *he*, and not *she*, is the one on the quest?"

"Oh my... You are *both* familiar with the feats, right?"

"With the first three, yes." Meehix was holding firm for an explanation or an apology for the squirrelly dude's gender-induced presumptions.

John gently but firmly grabbed her elbow before she hurt the skinny, to the point of appearing frail, lab-rat-nerd.

"I believe, partner of mine," he smiled at her, "that feat number three requires a *virgin male* sacrifice. Something that you are eminently unqualified to volunteer for."

"Right." Meehix stopped most of her fuming, but again, found herself hoping that they would fail at the first task because she remembered what the second task was and didn't want to have John get anywhere *near* slut central.

"Where are the craters?" John steered the conversation back to the details of the job at hand. "How do we get there, and how much of this trimium do you need?"

Keenan directed him to a bucket sitting on the counter. "Grab a handful."

John moved to the bucket full of small pebbles, scooped some up, and held them out.

"That would be plenty." Keenan smiled and nodded. "The trimium is about the same weight and texture. Two handfuls would be nice, but it has a delicate composition, and we don't like to work on too much at one time due to its decomposition rate when taken out of its natural environment. What you are holding now would take us six months to purify before we could work with its properties."

"No special tools needed for extraction? No dynamite or blasting required?"

"I'm not familiar with the word *dynamite,* but no. It crumbles out with only a slight bit of prodding."

"No special tools needed. Got it."

"But you may need these."

The technician moved to a wall and took down two pairs of what looked like elongated metallic-covered snow-shoes.

"We keep these in stock to save you the time from having to search and acquire them on your own."

John took the pair he was handed, and his first reaction was to swing one as if it were a tennis racket.

"And what? We use these to bat around the hundreds of little mating tribletts?"

"I see." Keenan seemed sad but surprised. "You've heard about the gramodiatrons."

"Hasn't everyone?" Meehix was definitely in snarky mode.

"Of course." Keenan sounded almost apologetic. "But no one is ever prepared for the trek to get to the craters. That's where the foot-forms come in handy. What other types of weapons do you have?" He was hesitant to ask as he prepared to duck a foot-form swipe at his head.

"What others might we need?" Meehix had left *snarky* behind and was fast approaching *pissed!*

"I was afraid of that. No one told you about the froomivores?"

"No. *They* definitely did not."

If she and John survived, Chuckie would be lucky to be able to say the same once they made it home and she got her hands around his neck.

CHAPTER FIFTEEN

"Would you mind, partner, if I took over the questioning for a bit?"

"Do you," Meehix addressed Keenan, "perhaps have something that I can take out some frustration on?"

"Yes, actually, we do!" it wasn't the first time someone had made that request, and they'd installed a custom-made form for just such a purpose. "Please, both of you, if you could take a step toward the front door?"

They did, and Keenan hit a red button on a wall that practically screamed, *In case of emergency.*

A panel opened in a far corner of the ceiling, away from the doors to the lobby and the lab, and a six-foot-tall life-like dummy dropped and dangled.

"We call him Raz. As long as you don't attack him with any sharp objects, he can take any physical abuse you wish to inflict."

"Carry on the conversation, John, and take notes." Meehix flexed, and after having spent only a few hours on

Suvious, she turned toward Raz, ready to do some serious damage. "Raz? Prepare to meet your maker."

Keenan guided John a safe distance away.

"We get that a lot. What do you need to know?"

"You tell me." John wasn't in the most pleasant of moods himself. "What do I *need* to know? Start with the foot-forms, and work your way up to the froomivores."

"I can only tell you what I know from what I've heard." Keenan sounded apologetic.

"Please do." John chose patience since his and Meehix's lives were dependent on the details.

"Here at TRL, we're not adventurers in the way that you guys are. Our adventures are more on the technical side."

"Cut to the chase before I, myself, string you up and let her," nodding toward Meehix, "take her frustrations out on someone who can feel pain. She loves to make grown men cry."

"Okay, okay, I hear you. Bear with me, and I'll try to explain. Did you notice the tower in the city-center?"

"Hard to miss it."

"It's not something you can feel or touch or penetrate, but that tower creates a dome over the entire city. That's why there's never wind, or rain, or sounds of spaceships cruising by sounding like they need a tune-up."

"It is a very quiet city," John admitted.

"It also absorbs quork-rays and funnels them down into a central grid, which allows us to power the entire city by hadronic-energy."

"Lights?

"Yes."

"Vehicles?"

"Yes."

"No outside debris, whatsoever?"

"None. Not even a microscopic speck of dust. That's what makes Troidit, Nerd-Electronic-Nirvana."

John was gaining a whole new appreciation of the city. He was a programmer, not an electronics builder. Still, he knew that none of the equipment he used to program would exist if not for the imaginative fastidiousness of the nameless ones behind the scenes.

"We don't even need to strap on static-discharge bracelets to work."

"Damn!"

"Damn you, you flabby piece of weeping blubber!"

Meehix had drawn their attention.

"Although, if we could harness *her* energy," Keenan smiled and whispered, "We wouldn't need the tower at all."

Who said that nerds didn't have a sense of humor?

"Explain the shoes." John returned his attention to the issues at hand.

"There is only one train that ever leaves the city, and it only makes one stop."

"And that stop is where?"

"Where the track ends." Keenan had to remember that they were first-time visitors. "It's just a one-car train and only heads out upon request."

"Continue."

"Most of those who take it are trophy hunters who are only interested in mounting a froomivore's head on their walls to show what mighty hunters they are. Two experienced guides, eighty-seven types of weapons…oh, how proud they all must be."

John could understand the contempt the lab rat was voicing.

"Right. Gotcha. But we're not them, so focus here, please."

"No trails or maps lead the way to the two craters that the trimium is between. Once you get off the train, then the best, and really, the *only* way to find them is to strap on the foot-forms, keep the city-center tower at your back, and start walking, as if the train track was continuing in a straight line. The landscape is a flat, barren wasteland, and the tower will be your only point of reference."

"Why the foot-forms?"

"There are sink-pits. The planet's surface is fine granular compounds that the wind constantly blows around, and they cover the pits so that you can't tell where the surface ends and the pits begin. If you learn to use the foot-forms properly, you'll be able to skim across the surface of the pits."

"And if we've never had the time to practice the *skimming* part?"

"I've heard that the best alternative is to have a partner and some rope that they can use to pull you out."

"Okaayy. How dangerous are these froomivores?"

"Quite dangerous, from what I've heard. They're large beasts, with skin covered in scales that make them nearly impenetrable with standard weapons. Their first line of defense is to rear up and try to squash you underneath their front feet.

"This is why, as your first line of defense, it's best to get the hang of the foot-forms as quickly as possible to dodge them. They're big and scary looking, especially if you see their open mouths coming at you, but agility is not one of their strong suits, so they should be easy to dodge."

"And our second line of defense? Assuming that we don't get squished?"

"They have tongues about three times as long as you are tall. They'll try to wrap you up and draw you in so they can swallow you whole. But I believe that the composition of the tongues isn't very tough, and you can slice it off without too much effort."

John was one step short of calling for an *abort* on the mission. Still, recalling their options of either acquiring the biggest, baddest, *phattest* ship available to civilians or ducking and dodging and hiding for the rest of their lives, he held firm.

"What about the gramodiatrons? How dangerous are they?"

"Oh," Keenan waved the concern away. "They sting, they bite, and are annoying little beasts, but they don't have any actual venom, so you won't die of poisoning from a bite or a sting. You may scratch yourself to death from irritation, but if you come back with some trimium, we can give you a shot that will ease the annoyance in short order."

"Can't you give us the shot now?"

"I would if we could, but no. We'll have to swab your mouth and test the saliva to make sure that we match the antidote to your DNA. That whole process only takes thirty minutes, so you'll have relief shortly after you return."

"Speaking of returning, I have one last question."

"Most adventurers do."

"Supposing that we survive, how do we get back here from the craters?"

"That is the last question that those on the quest always seem to ask."

"And the answer is?"

"Two days after you depart the train, the train will return to the station at the end of the track. That will give you one day to make it to the craters and one day to make it back. The train will wait for one extra day to account for any difficulties you encountered. If you don't make it back within that time frame, I'm afraid you'll be on your own. If that should happen, just remember, on your way to the craters, keep the tower at your back. On your way back, keep the tower in front of you."

"And *that*, shit for stuffing, is why you don't wanna mess with a bluesy!"

"You broke him!"

A horrified Keenan rushed to Raz and tried to untangle his mangled body parts into some kind of order that made sense before hauling him back up into the ceiling.

"He never said he was in pain, or I would've let up." Meehix didn't apologize.

"Please tell me that you have all the info you need?" Keenan implored John.

"I think we're good. What time is the first train out tomorrow?"

"Whatever time you want. Early or late, I'll make sure that it's waiting for two passengers to board. Track number seven. Oh, poor Raz."

"We should probably go now." John was impressed by the damage she'd done.

"You're probably right." Meehix bowed to Raz. Keenan was still trying to reassemble him. "Thank you, sir. You were an admirable opponent."

"Make sure that the train's on time, both there and back," were John's last words to the technician as he offered Meehix his arm and led her back out to the silent and spotless street.

"Damn! That felt great!" Meehix shouted once they'd gotten outside.

"Damn, my partner knows how to kick some serious ass!" John shouted.

The sidewalks suddenly emptied to give the loud barbarians plenty of room to make their way to wherever they were going.

"Our hotel is three blocks down to the right and two blocks to the left."

"How do you know that?" Meehix asked.

"I was going to leave a trail of bread crumbs," John remembered a tale from his childhood and smiled, "but I knew the collectors would scoop them up the moment after I littered them. Instead, I tried to remember three left and two right and reversed the order to get back. Hopefully, I have them in the right order, or else we'll end up fuck-all knows where."

"How many weapons should we take?" They were back on Ship the next morning, rummaging through their stash. Meehix eyed the guns lined up against the wall in Cargo.

"From what Keenan said, the guns won't be of much use against the froomivores."

"I admit that I wasn't paying much attention."

"I'll bet the folks at TRL wish you had." John smiled at the memory of Keenan's shocked face when he saw how much damage she had done to their punching bag of a dummy. "They're probably still trying to put Raz back together."

"It's his fault. He didn't put up much of a fight."

"He wasn't built to fight back. His whole purpose is to take abuse."

"Well then, he succeeded." Meehix turned her attention away from the guns. "Did I hear something about swords and tongues?" She surveyed the display of her preferred weapons.

"Yes, long swords are advised weapons." John moved to another section. "As are these."

He pulled a couple of coiled ropes with grappling hooks attached, slung one over his shoulder, and handed the other one to Meehix.

"I love these things." She looped it over her shoulder.

"Other than that, and our normal close-range defenses, we should be good to go. It sounds like we'll do a fair amount of walking, so the lighter the load, the better."

They'd stored their gear on board after checking out of their hotel earlier. Now they had a train to catch.

"See ya soon, Ship." John opened the front hatch.

"**Have fun, you two crazy kids,**" came Shippewa's reply.

They caught the outer-circle train and hopped off at the station where their next train was waiting.

"Did he say how long this part is?" Meehix settled in as one of only two passengers on board and the train headed out.

"I forgot to ask, but it shouldn't be too long." John was inspecting the foot-forms. "We're heading to a drop-off point."

"Those look cumbersome." Meehix was not thrilled at the thought of having them strapped to her feet. Her leg speed and quick kicks would be seriously encumbered.

"Run your hand across the bottom." John held one out. "It feels slick, but there's no oily residue or wax. It's just smooth. We need to learn how to use them."

She had to admit that it was an interesting feeling compound.

"Oh, and Keenan also loaned us these." John held out a pair of sleek-looking goggles. "He said it gets kind of dusty *out there.*"

They both slipped them on, and everything took on a slightly yellowish glow.

"He said they'd experimented with various hues, but some gave a sense of too much peace, and others of too much danger. With this tint, we can both see each other's eyes in case we aren't able to communicate with words."

"How very...considerate." Meehix was trying to find the right tone of voice.

Before she had time to contemplate further, the train glided to a stop. They gathered up what they had and stepped out as the doors silently opened. John would have complimented the conductor for the smooth ride, but since there was no conductor, he decided to save his breath.

Standing on the platform, with nothing but a barren landscape in front of them, Meehix watched the train put itself in reverse and head back toward the overly tidy city of Troidit.

"Well, I hope you were taking notes because I don't have the fuckest of clues about where to head next."

John had clued her in on the various dangers ahead to complete feat number one when they'd gotten back to the hotel room the day before, but she'd seemed distracted and not willing to share what was bothering her, so he didn't want to push her.

Physical danger was fine. She had become used to that. Feats two and three, however, that involved John's space-virginity? Well, she still hadn't reconciled with her feelings about *that*! She didn't want to be third in line!

"These suck!"

"That's because you're stomping and not gliding," John gently suggested, as Meehix was trying to get used to her foot-forms.

"I don't stomp!" Meehix insisted.

"Try telling that to the two-inch imprints you just left."

"Oh." Meehix looked down.

"I don't know how long before we run into the frooms or when we'll need to be able to skim across the tops of any sink-pits. Still, these are our footwear until we get back to the station, so try to get used to them."

"Fine." It was one step short of pouting. "Tower at our back to the craters, tower ahead on the return trip?"

"That's my understanding." John nodded.

"Lead on."

John had watched Olympic events, such as hockey and cross-country skiing. Being from New Mexico, the closest he'd personally come to seeing someone *glide* across a surface were kids in his neighborhood using rollerblades out on the paved cul-de-sacs.

If kids can do it, so can I!

Being careful to keep the tower at his back, he took a few hesitant glides forward, totally focused on trying to master his newly learned skill. After five minutes, he turned to look behind him to see if Meehix was having any success at all or if he would have to reverse course and go back to assist her.

He panicked because she was nowhere in sight and he thought she'd already managed to find a sink-pit.

"Problem, Jojacko?"

He twisted because her voice was coming from ahead of him and he tried to locate her in case she needed help. He was rewarded for his concern with a fine film of dust on his goggles as she slid to a quick stop.

"I may never take these off again!" she shouted as she glided off, *backward,* did a pirouette, and started circling him faster than anyone could run. "Would I be a show-off if I did one of these?"

She lifted one foot back and held it above her head as she completed her circle on one foot and came to a stop with a very self-satisfied smile.

"I take it that we're ready to proceed now?"

"Plod on."

Meehix took her energy down a notch and matched

John glide for glide, staying at his side, focusing now on their first feat, and asking questions that she hadn't paid complete attention to earlier.

"Froom-a-flippers?"

"Close enough. I just call them frooms."

John had gotten the hang of being able to glide in a straight line, which came in handy a few minutes later when they hit their first sink-pit and sprayed up some dust-filled liquids. They slid across it before they had a chance to realize what they'd both just done.

Pausing on the other side, they looked back and saw nothing but an undisturbed surface.

"Hold on." Meehix slid out one of her smaller knives from an ankle wrap.

She tossed it, and they both watched it sink immediately out of sight.

"That was interesting," John observed, as the surface once again smoothed out as if nothing had happened.

"One day to get there?"

"And one day to get back." He scanned the horizon. "Assuming that nothing goes drastically wrong."

"Then let's get this over with."

Keeping the tower to their back, they glided on.

They learned that the sink pits were everywhere, but as long as they glided, the only reason they knew about them was a fine wet-dust spray that came up as they crossed.

The surface of the planet was perfectly flat. Having been informed by Keenan, they knew that a small ridge surrounded the craters they headed toward, so until they came upon a ridge, they could relax and glide at ease.

Twelve dust storms suddenly rose around them, and they realized that they'd forgotten about the froomivores.

"Frooms, I assume?"

"He didn't tell me they buried themselves while waiting for prey!" John was pissed at Keenan for leaving that little detail out. "Glide around and try to lead them into sink pits and keep swords at the ready for any tongues!"

The partners didn't know where any future sink pits were, but they could trace back to where they'd been because their tracks were still visible, and they glided back that way in fast order.

Meehix sliced off two tongues on her way to the first hole she remembered before gliding across it and leaving two others sinking out of sight.

John skimmed the surface of two other holes and led three more of the frooms behind him to the same fate.

The first wave of action done, the only thing the partners saw was a dust trail, as the other frooms retreated.

Meeting back up at the space where their trek had been so rudely interrupted, they smiled at each other in a way that only Jo and Hix could. There was something special about the smile of having just survived having not been killed together.

"That was fun," Meehix said. "Craters, full speed ahead?"

"Sure. Why not?" Off they went, keeping the tower at their backs.

They reached the rim of the first crater an hour later. At a distance of what John judged to be two football fields away, he saw another small mound and pointed it out.

The pit itself was about ten feet wide and twenty feet

deep, with its sides sloping down to the bottom and what appeared to be the tunnel where John would find the trimium.

"I'm going down." He handed her his foot-forms. "Meet me on the other side."

Not waiting for an answer, he sat on his ass and slid down to the bottom. "The tunnel's not quite as high as I am tall, but at least I should be able to bend and walk and not have to crawl!" he called up before disappearing into it.

"Don't you dare fucking die!" were the last words he heard Meehix yell after him.

"I won't if you won't! You still owe me a date!" were John's last words back.

I am never going to fall in love with another Kdackan as long as I live! Pain in the ass bastards!

Meehix secured John's foot-forms in her backpack and glided around to the low mound that circled the other crater. John should appear after he'd secured enough trimium, and hopefully, survived the gramodiatrons in the tunnel between the two pits. Other than that, she wasn't sure of what she would find emerging.

She reached the second crater and had to wait, which was never high on her list of favorite activities. Not knowing how long John would be underground, she was about to sit when she heard several shots ring out in rapid succession.

"Might need a little help here!"

There was just enough light filtering down into the crater for her to see John scrambling up from halfway down.

She quickly uncoiled a length of rope and tossed her

grappling hook down toward him but slightly off to the side. He managed to get a hand on the hook without cutting himself.

"Pull!"

She started reeling the rope in as John held on, using his feet to dig into the sand and help propel him upward. He gained the surface, and Meehix jumped back.

"Nasty little beasts," were John's first words.

"What the fuck?"

John's hands had swollen to twice their normal size, and his face resembled nothing from her memory other than a bloated ball that needed to be as far away from them as possible.

"Foot-forms and the lab! No poison, but maybe allergies!"

"Are they big enough to shoot? Will they come after us?"

"They're small. I was shooting at the walls, trying to cave the ceiling in a little."

"Can you see?"

"Only through tiny slits," he managed to say before his mouth swelled up and he couldn't get any other words out.

She strapped his foot-forms back onto his feet and secured the grappling hook around his waist. Keeping the tower dead straight ahead, she led them both back to the train and caught it right on time without encountering any extra frooms along the way.

"Can you breathe?" she remembered asking him as they glided over sink-pit after sink-pit.

"Mgglymufflefromp," had been his only reply, which she took for a *yes*.

The train was waiting for them right where it was supposed to be. She guided John onto it because his eyelids had also swollen to the extent that he could no longer see.

The train headed back into town in its oh, so peaceful way as Meehix fumed. John sat quietly, wishing he could dip his whole body in a bucket of ice.

Off the train and *politely* screaming for a cab, she got John back to the TRL lab and pounded every button she could find.

Keenan and an assistant rushed out, and the assistant hurriedly guided John back into the lab area.

"He'll be fine, he'll be fine, he'll be fine!" Keenan didn't want the blue chick to mistake him for Raz. "Trust me. In half an hour, he'll be good as new."

"Where's Raz?"

"Still being restored. You left him in rather bad shape."

Meehix had no qualms about leaving an enemy in the same shape, but she knew the frail-looking geek standing in front of her didn't fall into that category, so she prevailed upon her better nature and leaned against a wall.

"How long?"

"Soon." Keenan escaped back into the lab and hoped for the best.

"Still here?" John emerged from the lab twenty minutes later, looking no worse for wear.

Although his eyesight was still slightly blurry, he didn't need twenty-twenty vision to look down. Meehix was lying on her back on the floor with her ankles crossed behind her head. Her magnificent ass appeared to be where John needed to direct his questions.

"Still here." she unwound herself and got to her feet,

enabling her to answer the question with a touch of dignity as opposed to pretend to be speaking from her ass. "The lab rats?"

"In hiding."

"And the trimium?"

"Successfully delivered."

Shouts of joy came from behind the lab side of the door.

"We gotta go." John handed her a sheet with coordinates. "It seems that we're now on the clock."

"What clock?" They headed outside and, deciding to skip hailing a cab, jogged back to the docking station and Ship, which allowed them to let out a whoop now and then to see how much of the surrounding quiet they could disturb for fun.

"We have six hours to make it to Space Station Beaulifica," John explained Keenan's instructions as best he could, "where we clock in, then twelve hours to complete the next task."

"And if we fail?"

"Then we'll never find the location of feat three and lose all hope of finding the ship to end all ships."

"Aw," Meehix found her sarcastic voice, "then you might have to remain a space virgin forever."

"If you thought my hands and feet had swollen after the trimium tunnel, you should have seen the size of my—"

"Ssshhhh," came the collective voices of the other pedestrians. Thirty *ssshhh's* at one time amounted to what would pass for a scream.

They made it to Ship, where Meehix took the pilot's seat, not totally trusting John's visual and physical acumen after the trimium quest. Not to mention how distracted he might be while thinking ahead to his next task.

She punched in the coordinates and five hours later was docking on the small space station. Beaulifica appeared to be surrounded by a red haze. From space, it was visible as a beacon for who knew how far.

"Are you sure you're up for this?" Meehix immediately regretted her choice of words.

"How *up* should I be?"

"Purpose of visit?" They were met by an angelic yellow little fairy, fluttering its pale blue wings and hovering around them with a clipboard.

"What are the choices?" Meehix was already in defense mode.

"Well," she continued to circle. "I see one male, ummm-ummm," she gave John a close once-over inspection, "and one very attractive female," she turned her attention to Meehix.

"So far, your observations are correct." Meehix nodded toward John. "He is here on a quest. We were told to check-in. I am here to help him succeed."

The fairy flittered up to the ceiling above Ship, hit a button, and a digital clock descended.

"So you," she continued to speak to Meehix, "aren't here looking to take up residence for work-related purposes?"

"No! I am definitely *not!*"

"Pity...you could do quite well. You'll find the waiting room two doors down to the right. When your companion finishes, I will accompany you back to your ship so you two can be reunited."

"What if I don't want to stay in a waiting room?"

"Then you are always free to remain aboard your ship and wait for him there."

"What if I don't want either of those two options?"

Meehix found two stingers at her throat as the fairy's feet suddenly became less harmless looking, and five more fairies appeared out of nowhere to back up the greeter's message.

"I'm afraid that those are the only two options." She retracted her feet and backed off as her coworkers continued to hover within striking distance.

Rising to the digital clock, she started the timer before floating back down to face John with a smile as sweet as spring rain. She handed him a silver debit card.

"You are the quester we expected. This is your prepaid card. Present it to anyone you encounter. It's good for twelve hours. Please follow me." She gently glided and led the way out of the room.

John watched the fairy and turned to face the now furious Meehix, expecting some kind of a serious scolding or warning or threat. He received none of the above.

Cupping his face in her hands, she released the sweetest pheromones he'd ever smelled and planted a soft kiss on his lips.

"You can do it, big boy." She smiled. "Or *not* do it." She spun him around and slapped his ass to get him moving in the direction of the fairy, who waited to lead him into a hellhole of God only knew what kind of pleasures he would have to do his best to avoid.

She watched him walk off with the body language of a man about to face execution. She then headed to the waiting room, two doors down to the right.

"Meet the new competition, girls," a seven-foot-tall, orange-hued beauty announced as Meehix opened the door and found her immediately in her face.

"Shorter than you, taller than me." A four-foot multi-colored cutie appeared at her side. "I guess if they're going for the middle-height-boring type, then she *could* pose a little problem."

"I'm not here to compete with any"—she hastily choked back her thought *of you sluts*—"of you ladies." Meehix decided to choose her words carefully. *This is no time to pick a fight.*

She looked around and realized that this was a waiting room for job applicants. Its current occupants represented every size, shape, and color.

You can do it, Jojacko. You saved me once. Now use that same courage to save yourself.

CHAPTER SIXTEEN

Gage had managed to elude agents Bixby and Shaw after they'd attacked him at home. That was mostly due to their bad timing and not being aware that his *staff* of babysitting girls were also in the house, helping out as he'd been doing his podcast.

Not to mention his baby-wielding mother, who was quickly becoming an Internet sensation on YouTube. He'd spent the last two days living in a Walmart, open twenty-four-seven with few questions asked. No one ever asked very many questions of any Walmart shopper. *You're wearing* that *out in public?* was seldom a start that led to any friendly conversations.

His first order of business had been to buy a burner cell phone that he used to call Becka, his *official* staff and babysitter. He didn't want to call his mother at home because he figured that the agents had already tapped the phone. No one knew Becka's name so she seemed like the safest one to communicate with and let his mom know that he was safe.

"Oh my God, Gage!" Becka squealed when he'd called her. "Are you okay?"

"Yes, I'm fine."

"That was sooo exciting!"

"I'm sorry for having put you through that. I never thought they'd invade my parents' house."

"Are you kidding me?" He could almost picture her jumping up and down as they spoke. "When we go back to school and have to write about 'what did you do on your summer vacation?' I won't be like everyone else who writes about how they visited Six-Flags and shit like that. I'll be able to write how I helped fight off men in black and that *I'm* the one who took the video that's already making your mom a star! How cool is *that* shit going to be?"

Pretty cool, he had to admit.

"But you shouldn't use words like *shit*."

"Tell that to your baby brother!"

Is she going to stop squealing and shouting any time soon?

"Is Carla around?"

"Yeah." She sighed. "She's right here…Gage wants to talk to you." He heard her hand over the phone.

"Hi, Carla. Are you all safe and okay?"

"We're fine, although Becka's in danger of being strangled by her older sister if she doesn't learn to chill a little. Where are you, and are *you* safe?"

"I'm fine for now. I just need to lay low for a while and draw attention away from my family."

"That makes sense."

"The trouble though, is that I'm not going to be able to stay home and watch over Isabella and Toñito."

"We already got that covered."

"Say again?"

"Me and your mom found the Cohiba box, and she's already set it up to pay Becka to babysit, every day, for as long as you have to stay away. Becka's thrilled to have a steady summer job. That's more than most thirteen-year-olds can say."

That was a relief. He paused for several long moments because he was hesitant to make his next request but was currently short on local allies older than thirteen.

"Write this number down." He gave her the number of his burner phone. "You know the Walmart on Dixie Ave?"

"Is that where you are?"

"No, I'm nowhere near it," he lied. "But if you can make your way there in the next day and go to the Lost and Found, tell them that you've lost a cell phone. On the back of it will be a label saying, umm, Giggly Girl. When you get it, call me back. I gotta go now. Tell my family that I love them!"

Next order of business.

He paid cash for a second burner phone and a label-maker. He activated the phone, stuck the label on its back, and took it to the customer service counter.

"Someone may have dropped this." Gage handed it over with a polite smile. "Is this where I should leave it in case they come back?"

"It puts the item in the basket." The bored clerk brought out a plastic wicker basket from behind the counter, making as little eye contact as possible. Gage dropped the phone in and hoped for the best.

Need more cash.

"Can I take this one for a test spin?" Gage asked the electronics salesperson as he was eyeing a laptop.

"You can use the display model," the helpful sales assistant whose nametag read Jolique answered. "It's already connected, so test away." She backed off with a smile.

Gage didn't need to test anything. He needed to access his Patreon account and wire cash to the Western Union Office located inside the front of the store.

"Oh, my," he was greeted by the Western Union clerk half an hour later. "That is a large transfer."

"Yeah, I know." Gage smiled and scuffed his feet in an *aw-shucks* kind of way. "Mom and Dad just moved into a new house. I want to hit some consignment shops and buy them a few special things, and those places always appreciate cash."

"You sound like a very loving son...would you like this in twenties, fifties, or hundreds?"

"Hundreds would be nice. They'll be gone before anyone even has a chance to mug me."

Another smile and Gage moved away from the counter with five grand in his now bulging wallet.

"I love this tent!" he next addressed the sales assistant in the Outdoors department, where a two-room tent was on display. "How many sleeping bags can it hold?"

The clerk's shift was almost over, and he wanted to finish it and get home. He pulled a sleeping bag off a shelf and rolled it out inside the tent, where it was obvious that four more bags would fit side by side if needed.

"Will that work?"

"I think it might. Thank you. I want to see what other

things are available. This will be our first camping trip together, and I want to make sure I've fully prepared. Would it be okay if I browsed a little longer?"

"I'm off in ten minutes. Knock yourself out."

Gage wandered around and found a few more items that might come in handy. It was late in the evening by the time he'd paid and packed what he'd bought, and not much was going on in the Outdoors department at that time.

He slipped himself and his new backpack into the tent when no one was paying much attention, zippered it shut, and got a decent night's sleep before heading out again late the next morning, wandering the streets without a specific destination in mind.

"We got one more day to get this dipshit under control before we get reassigned." Bixby was not in the best of moods.

"Come on, man, at least they gave us a van instead of being squashed in a DeVille while we track down this anal-probe-deserving asshole."

"Anal probed asshole." Bixby nodded. "I like the sound of that."

"More than he'll like the feel of it." Shaw smiled. "The satellite we connected to can read the warning label on a pack of cigarettes from space, even through clouds."

"My cousin used to smoke." There was no assignment more boring than being on a stake-out. "He said that he would only smoke cigarettes from packs whose warning labels said *May cause problems during pregnancy*. He figured that those would be safe enough."

"Did that work?"

"We're not sure," Bixby had to admit. "He was lighting

up a smoke while jaywalking and got run over by a bus because he forgot to look both ways before stepping out into the street."

"Ouch."

"The bus didn't feel a thing, but a lot of passengers were pissed because they had to disembark and wait for the next bus."

After a moment of silence to give Bixby time to honor his cousin's memory, Shaw picked up his train of thought.

"Satellites in space, being able to read the *fine print,* even through clouds. How is that even possible?"

"Well," Bixby took his best guess. "Clouds are something like water floating in the air, right?"

"Yeah," Shaw nodded. "And water reflects or refracts or something like that. Things underwater seem bigger than they actually are, or do I have that backward, and how do our satellites see through water? Do they film it and make adjustments before they send the images back?"

Shaw had lost him.

"We're using all this high-tech shit, most of it we got from the fucking aliens, and you're wondering about how we get pictures from satellites if it's a rainy day?"

"It's probably drones!" Shaw concluded. "Invisible drones! They have a cloaking shield or something like that."

Bixby was beginning to worry that the stress they'd been under lately had caused his partner's brain to turn left when it should have taken a right at their latest fork in the road.

"Invisible drones, as opposed to cameras that can't filter

out a few raindrops. Are you sure you want to go with that?"

"There he is!" Shaw shouted, pointing at the screen.

"Cocky little fuckhead sonofabitch!" Bixby dropped all of their recent contemplations and focused on the satellite feed coming over their screen. "Look at him strutting around like he doesn't have a care in the world...and with his shiny new backpack."

"How do you know it's new?"

"It still has a fucking sales tag on it. Probably shoplifted it. Pull up the area map, and we'll snatch him in the next vacant space."

Shaw did that and put the van in gear, aiming to cut him off four blocks later on a vacant, undeveloped corner.

I'm Gonzo the Gager man. I'm Gonzo the Gager man. I'm strong to the finish.

Gage knew that his humming would be interrupted, and sure as *Eunice used to your uncle Eustace,* there they were. They'd left the tan DeVille behind, replaced by one of the thousands of ubiquitous white vans you could find on any street in any city at any given time.

"Miss me?" Gage asked as Bixby and Shaw rushed toward him.

"Not as much as you missed this!"

The two agents tackled him and slammed his face to the ground, one straddling his back as the other pulled out a nasty-looking double-anal insertion fun toy.

"Enjoy it, little boy. Your Uncle Bixby is gonna give you something to remember him by."

"Anal probe *this*, dipshits! Spent any time in a Walmart lately?"

Gage rolled out the skunk-scent bomb he'd recently purchased in the Outdoors aisles and had kept in his pocket for just such an occasion.

The agents rolled off him, trying to figure out how to breathe and vomit simultaneously. The vomiting won out. Gage stuffed a couple of his recently purchased fresh as a daisy tissues in his nose and ran off as fast as he could to a truck stop two blocks down.

Rushing in, he shouted, "Showers!"

Everyone covered their noses and pointed him to the second room on the right. He rushed into it, found a stall, and closed the door, managing to find the knob and turned it to hot as he let the water stream over him, clothes, backpack, and all.

"Fuck him!" Agent Bixby was rolling on the ground and trying not to vomit in Shaw's direction.

"Fuck us!" Shaw managed to say as he vomited away from where he thought Bixby might be.

They both continued to roll over and vomit on their patches of dirt. It was not a pleasant experience for either of them, as they both envisioned a post in Antarctica in their near futures.

"We'll get him," Bixby managed to say between his puking.

"Double anal probes...with spikes," Shaw agreed before he puked again and passed out, wondering how close they were to the nearest laundromat.

"Whoo-ee!" came a voice from the next stall over from Gage's. "I don't know who you are, but if that stink is coming from you, then you got the right idea to wash it off before going home to the little woman!"

"Skunk bomb," Gage shouted back. "Just bought it an hour ago, and it went off by accident!"

A bar of soap was tossed over the stall wall a moment later.

"Lather, rinse, repeat! Then repeat again!" advised the voice. "Six days of driving with no time for showers. That bar is what you need before your last stop home."

Gage took the stranger's advice and emerged twenty minutes later, wondering who to return the extra-duty bar of soap to. It wasn't a hard decision to make since everyone had cleared out of the shower room.

"That'd be mine, hoss."

The stranger was at least six-foot-five. A little round in the belly but muscled enough to look like he wouldn't need a jack to lift a truck and change a tire.

"Tucson Tommy. My friends call me TT. Just drop the bar in this, and I'll pack it," as he held out a baggie for the soap. "If I hadn't been naked and wet when you came in, I'd've run out too."

"Thank you, sir." Gage meant it as he toweled off.

Glancing in one of the mirrors, because no one in a truck stop shower room looked directly at another trucker who was just coming out of a shower, Tucson Tommy did a double-take.

"Pardon me, hoss... I'm just a simple dumber than shit trucker...but could you do me a slight favor and say Gonzo Gage, out and gone?"

Gage was either busted or had just met a fan. *Best to find out now.*

"Gonzo Gage, out and gone." He did his best impersonation of himself.

"I knew I recognized your voice!" The stranger looked Gage over. "I guess my wife won that bet."

"There's a bet?" Gage was at a loss.

"I said you were my height but thin. She said you were under six feet and scrawny. Damn, she was right again."

"Sorry, sir, but your wife got that one right."

"But I got your voice right, right?" TT asked. Gage nodded. TT pulled out his cell and dialed *Home.* A woman's voice answered.

"Home soon, TT?"

"Home real soon. Honey, you know how to record calls, right?"

"Shit, for sure, babe. That's how I get to listen to you whisper sweet nothings in my ear whenever I want."

"Then record this one," he winked at Gage, "and you'll love me forever. Lemme know when you're ready."

"TT, you're such a tease...recording now."

TT held the phone in Gage's direction.

"Make a woman happy, and sign off."

Gage was now thoroughly confused, but the man *had* just recently tossed him a bar of soap, so what the hell.

"This is Gonzo Gage. Out and gone."

"Oh, sweet mother of baby Jesus! C'mon, TT, don't joke and jerk me around here! Is that really?"

"Yeah, darlin', it really is." He turned to Gage. "One more time, please, this time with *feeling.*"

Talk about entering a Twilight Zone while at a truck stop. He decided to give it his best.

"This is Gonzo Gage, out and gone!"

"TT! If you let anything bad happen to him, don't bother coming home!"

"You heard her, Gonzo." TT smiled. "Any last words to one of your biggest fans?"

"Mrs. TT?" Gage started, and TT nodded.

"Yes, Gonzo?"

"Do the best you can, and trust what you know to be true."

TT nodded...

"Gonzo Gage. Out and gone."

"Mrs. TT, over and out."

"All right, young man. You heard my missus. Where to next?"

"If you could do me one quick favor," he retrieved his new, waterproof, and recently scrubbed backpack out of his stall and found his wallet.

"Even if they were dry, I don't think I'm gonna be able to get the stink out of my clothes. Could you maybe go out front and pick me up some new threads? Nothing fancy, just enough to be able to go out in public?"

"You got it, hoss." TT looked at the backpack. "You drivin' or hikin'?"

"Hiking."

"Then you just let me know where you're gonna start hikin' again, 'cause the next ride is on me. Oh, you're also gonna need some new hikin' boots. What size?"

"Size ten."

"You got it. I know what you need...Gonzo Gage... Gonzo, honest to God, Gage."

Giving Gage a wink, TT went off to do some shopping.

Gotta remember to take some selfies to show the missus.

"So, did you fuck anyone?"

"No. Did you kill anyone?"

John had spent the last twelve hours ducking and diving and dodging more tongues and invitations than anyone with a penis should ever have to endure but made it back to the waiting room, ready to clock out.

"Not that I didn't want to." It had been tempting for Meehix to slice a few in the waiting room into small, multi-colored pieces.

"Still ten minutes left on the clock." The sweet-looking yellow-bodied blue-winged fairy who'd first greeted them floated down. "Maybe he didn't meet the right girl yet."

Twelve other fairies were now flitting back and forth, tongues out and aimed at John's crotch.

Meehix drew a sword, ready to slice, but John held his hand up to stop her as he sat on the floor.

"Give it your best shot, girls."

Tongues and fluttery wings surrounded him, flicking and blowing into any body part they thought might get a reaction. John was numb to it all. Ten minutes later, he stood and hit the digital clock above Ship.

"Are we done here yet?"

"Congratulations." The fairy who had first greeted them pouted at Meehix. "Your traveling companion appears to be a eunuch."

Meehix wrapped John in her arms and whispered into his ear, "I've never been more proud of anyone in my life as I am of you right now."

The fairy greeter flew up to the ceiling and retrieved a metallic red card with a USB drive built into one end.

"What's this?" John caught it as she tossed it down. A layer of dust covered it.

"Don't know. Don't care." She wasn't at all happy that someone had remained a virgin and earned the card. "My only instructions are to give it to whatever dickless wonder made it back."

"I don't think she likes you." Meehix smiled as she watched the flirting floozy fly away.

"Well, she's not alone." John turned, and Meehix got a good look at his back. His shirt was in tatters.

"Is that blood?"

"I may have gotten a few scratches while running. They don't take rejection very well around here. I need a nap. Can you fly us out of here?"

"Let's get your back taken care of first." Meehix lowered Ship's stairway hatch and helped him inside.

"Welcome back, John. Successful?"

"If he hadn't been, I would have killed him myself." She led him back to Cargo where he stripped his shirt, and she applied some ointment.

"Ow. Easy there."

"Sorry." She realized that in her delight of having John in one piece that she'd been a little exuberant in her application. "None of them are very deep, but damn, it looks like they don't only file their fingernails here, they also sharpen them."

Ministrations done, she handed him another shirt.

"Will you be able to sit up or do you want me to blow up a cot?"

"I can sit." He flexed. "Let's see what's on the drive."

John inserted the drive into Ship and coordinates came

up on the screen.

"Congratulations," came a very soothing voice. "If you're seeing and hearing this, you are the first to have completed what I understand to be the second feat."

"Is that a male or female voice?" John wasn't sure.

"I don't know," Meehix shrugged, "but it's pleasant."

"Follow the coordinates to planet Xylon. You may pause, rewind, or fast-forward through this recording at your leisure. Instructions for your next task are at the end, should you wish to hear them first."

Meehix hit "Pause." "Let's get out of this fuck-a-whirl station first."

She punched in the coordinates and lifted off. Once in flight, John found himself leaning forward. The scratches on his back were more annoying than painful but still tender to the touch.

"Okay, out with it. How hard was it to avoid the temptations back there?"

"In the games I've played," he tried to explain it to himself as well as to Meehix, "succubi always leave a man weak. So if there's only one, she might wear you out."

"Poor baby." Her voice held no sympathy.

"But if you gave in to the first one, and another came along, you'd be left even weaker, right?"

"Logical." Meehix nodded.

"Then if a third one came along, and a fourth," he physically shivered at the thought.

"Suffering from performance anxiety, were you?"

"No." He turned totally serious. "Suffering from the fear of literally being fucked to death."

"To most of the men I've known, that would seem to be their death of choice."

"It might have once been mine. I have something to live for now, so let's chalk it up to bad timing. I mean, when I'm eighty, I might want to schedule a return visit…"

Looking over, she saw that her partner, who had been running for his life for the last twelve hours, was now fast asleep.

"Careful what you're dreaming about in there, big boy. If I see you smile, I won't be pleased."

It took two Gates to reach planet Xylon. Oh, how she loved to fly. Even with coordinates punched in, she still had the freedom to try out a few maneuvers and took full advantage of them. If she happened to glance over and see John smiling, she did a quick dive, jostling him slightly awake enough to change the focus of whatever he'd been dreaming about.

"Wazzat?" he mumbled after one such move.

"Nothing. Just avoiding an asteroid."

"That's good. I don't want to die as a space virgin." He was off to dreamland again.

"Sure," she spoke to the sleeping goof. "I'll make sure that you live long enough to enjoy the fun of sex in space fully…then I'll kill you."

In his dream, John was falling into a small but bottomless crater, lined with row after row of sharp teeth along its edges. He had just passed the surface when the top row of teeth closed up. As he kept falling, row after row after row closed up a split second after he'd passed. *Must keep falling fast to stay ahead of the teeth.*

"Fall fast, fall fast, fall fast," Meehix heard him mumble

in terror and put Ship into a complete three-sixty loop, shaking John awake.

"Shit fuck!" He was now fully conscious.

"It sounded like you were in the middle of a bad dream."

John felt his forehead and used his sleeve to wipe off a layer of sweat.

"I don't remember." He looked at his sleeve. "But I also don't remember the last time I had night sweats either."

After passing through the second Gate, the screen showed them an ETA of two hours to Xylon.

"Might as well listen to the rest of the message." John hit "Play."

"Sure, I'm breathless with anticipation to hear the details about your next Fun Land excursion."

John hit "Pause."

"We're not only doing this for a joyride on a phat-ass ship," John reminded her.

"No." He was right, but that didn't mean she had to be happy. "We're doing it so that we don't have to run for the rest of our lives."

"Now? Yes. But that's not what we originally set out to do."

"Remind me."

John decided not to comment on or question the funk that she seemed to be in.

"When I first rescued you, we headed out from Kdack to help free galactic slaves, whenever we found any. It seemed like a noble mission."

Meehix remained silent but nodded at the memory.

"We even left Gage behind so he could work on it from home while taking care of his family."

"Good old Gay-jaw." Meehix smiled at how she had mispronounced his name so badly. "But come on, John. Gage has probably forgotten all about us by now and is most likely busy trying to figure out how to bop his next potential boppee."

John had no rebuttal to the boppee comment because that part of her observation was probably right. He smiled, remembering some of his and Gage's earlier attempts and planning out of potential bopping possibilities—all of which ended up as monumental failures.

"I'll grant you part of that, but no. Gage saw what he saw, so trust me, he hasn't forgotten us or the task we left him with. I don't know how successful he is, but I know that he's trying."

"You love him, don't you."

"Yes. I do." John made sure of his eye contact with her. "The same way you love Chuckie. A friend from childhood who would never do you any harm."

She nodded.

"Although I trust Gage just a little, tiny, itsy-bitsy more than I trust Chuckie."

She laughed and hit "Play" as she piloted.

"You will have to land," the pleasant gender-neutral voice picked up where it had left off, "on the downward end of the Climaxian mountain range."

"What the fuck is the downward end?" John asked.

"The downward end," the voice went on, "is the end not covered in a white coating. The upward end is frozen solid."

"And then what?"

"Will you just shut up and listen!" was Meehix's response.

"You will see a city at the low end. Dock there, and whoever greets you, simply ask for directions to Norlan. Then ask for assistance in reaching the top of Mount Climax. I wish you well and hope to see you soon."

"What the fuck is a Norlan?"

"This message will repeat, in three, two, one… Congratulations, if you're seeing and hearing this, then you are the first to have completed what I understand to be the second feat."

John hit "Pause" as Meehix closed in on Xylon and circled, looking for the Climaxian mountain range and its downward end.

"That was incredibly semi-informative." John was on the edge of a bad mood, flashes of teeth from his dream coming back.

"Shall I try to find the downward end or just crash into a frozen mountain on the upward end and save us all from further worries?"

"Avoid the crash, if you please." John sighed. "I won't die happy until I find out whether Norlan is the name of an ultimate nerd or something slightly less annoying."

CHAPTER SEVENTEEN

Meehix spotted the mountain range on her first pass-over and headed for the end that wasn't white. It wasn't a large city, and the docking station was easy to navigate, so she landed with no difficulties.

"Shall I wait here?"

"Unless you have a prior engagement that you need to attend, yes." Meehix unbelted, in no mood at the moment for Ship's sense of humor.

"Very well. Good luck."

"Thanks, Ship," John offered. "You're very patient with us."

"You promised me a ship when this is over, John. Please succeed."

The partners geared up with the minimum of weapons, not wanting to appear hostile, and descended the ramp into the station.

"Are you sure that you don't want to wait here?" John asked Meehix.

"Just because only one of us is required to complete the task, that doesn't mean that the *other of us* isn't going with you as far as she's permitted to. End of discussion."

"Welcome to the city of Orgasmia." A two-foot-tall, three-legged orange creature looked up at them as soon as they reached the docking platform. "How may I help make your stay more pleasant?"

Neither of them was in the mood for *pleasant.*

"We're looking for someone," John took the lead, "or some*thing*, named Norlan."

"Oh, you're hikers."

"That's not quite how I would describe us," John shrugged, "but okay."

"Turn right at the end of the dock, and then four doors down. Norlan owns and runs Protectior, the equipment store."

"And does Norlan, in the city of Orgasmia at the foothill of Mount Climax specialize in Trojans?"

John was the only one present who understood his joke and or sarcasm.

"He specializes in what you will need," their helpful greeter replied. "Four doors down to the right. Enjoy your stay."

"Fat chance of that." Meehix led the way out and four doors down to the right, opened a door and entered.

Ding.

Meehix spun and drew a long sword from her back, ready to attack. John grabbed her arms and gently guided them down.

"It's only a small bell, letting the owner know that we're

here." John reached up and flicked a finger to ding the bell again.

Ding, came the gentle sound again.

"Welcome," came a voice from nowhere.

"Welcome from who?" John decided to leave Meehix out of this conversation.

"That would be whom, and the whom would be me, Norlan, the proprietor and furnisher of whatever you may need."

Norlan stood from where he'd been stocking some lower shelves. Thin but sinewy, the blue man could have been one of Meehix's long-lost cousins, which gave her a momentary reason to relax.

"What we need," John carried on, "is to reach the top of Mount Climax."

"Oh," Norlan continued, "You don't want to do that."

"Okay." Meehix grabbed John's arm and dragged him back toward the door, settling for mission not accomplished. She would find a way to apologize to Ship later.

"Yes." John shook her off. "I *do* want to do exactly that!"

Meehix had never known John to shake her off like that, but he wouldn't have done it without a good reason, so she backed off.

"Why? May I ask," Norlan suddenly had a quiver in his voice, "do you need to reach the top and not settle for several of the lovely lower spots halfway up? The views are beautiful."

"I need. To reach. The top." John kept his voice soft but hopefully firm.

"Castle Climaxia?"

"If that's what's at the top, then yes."

Meehix had never seen John in this mode before. His voice didn't sound horny for the pleasures that might await him at the top of the mountain. His eyes looked neither happy nor angry. His body language looked like someone determined to follow something through, regardless of the cost.

"Help us to get there, please." Meehix stepped forward and took her partner's arm.

Norlan smiled. "Are you expected?"

"I think so," was the best answer she could summon.

"I see two swords strapped onto your back, dear miss. Correct?"

"I never step foot on a planet without them, dear sir," Meehix acknowledged.

"Then you are already almost fully equipped."

"Elaborate, please." She was not pretending to be polite. The man in front of her was not an enemy. He was simply courteous.

"The mountain is covered in nothing more than a jungle. One winding path leads to the top, but it's not maintained so it often becomes overgrown. You may need your blades to slice your way up to the top, where the castle stands. But I must warn you. No one who reaches it ever comes back the same."

"That's what I'm afraid of." She sighed.

"Me too." John raised his hand.

"I bet," was her mumbled reply.

"Your fears of what you may find are unfounded, but you need to learn that for yourselves." He gave them each a curious smile. "There are no creatures native to here who are dangerous, but there are bandits who hide out there, waiting for easy prey, so swords may not be the most effective source of defense against them."

Meehix nudged John, and they both suddenly had two guns each, held high.

"Will these do?" She smiled.

"They ought to." Norlan smiled in return. "A determined hiker can make it to the top in a little over half a day." He grabbed a couple of bottles of water off a shelf and offered them.

"These have a little energy infused in them that you'll appreciate by the time you reach the halfway mark. There you will find a small covered pavilion where you can stop to catch your breath and look out and down at how far you've come. You can pay me when you get back."

"Thank you, sir." Meehix gave a slight bow.

"Thanks, man." John nodded, and they headed out.

Looking ahead, they could see the small mountain that gave the range its name a short distance ahead. It was green the whole way up. Above the foliage, at the very top, John thought he caught a gleam of gold, but clouds passed overhead, and the glint was gone.

There was a clearly marked path from the city's edge that led directly to the foot of the mountain.

"I guess these are more like the foothills," John observed.

"If I remember right, they got higher as the upward end was much higher."

"Upward. Downward." He shrugged. "Makes sense now.

Let's get this over with." He trudged on with unenthusiastic determination.

The path wasn't overgrown on the early part of the trek. If it weren't for the dread of what waited for them at the top, it would have even been enjoyable. It was more of a jungle than a forest covering, and the sounds of birds and smaller animals hidden in the foliage made John wish that he could afford a little more time to explore off-path, to see if they could spot a creature or two.

Meehix had no interest in any side-trip nature walks. The dread of what they would find at the top became stronger with each step.

"Finally." She drew a sword. They still hadn't reached the halfway mark, but at least now there was foliage overhanging the path and twisting along the ground in front of them, impeding their progress.

"Save your energy for your virgin endeavors. I got this."

John followed as she sliced and diced her way through innocent vegetation. He felt sorry for the plants that didn't stand a chance as she took out her anxieties and frustrations on them.

They did pause at the halfway pavilion.

"It really is pretty from up here." John took a solid drink of the water and looked out.

"Yeah, beautiful." Meehix uncapped her bottle and downed half of it. "Let's build a hut from the vegetation and never leave."

Time to move on. John followed his thought with, "How about we get this over with?" He headed off.

The going got steeper, but the plants thinned, and the

conversation was nonexistent. They made the rest of the climb in good time until they reached a gate set in a metallic fence that went off into the jungle in both directions. They still couldn't see what was on the top of the mountain, but on the other side of the gate was a steep stairway.

Meehix tried the gate and found it locked. "Oh well, we tried." She headed back down. "What did you say?" she turned back to face John.

"I was going to ask you the same thing."

"I didn't say anything." She felt as confused as John looked.

They both heard a *click*, and the gate swung open. With nothing better to do, they entered and climbed the stairs. Reaching the top, they stepped onto a plateau as if someone had sliced off the tip of the mountain.

"That's a tall fucking…"

"Temple?" Meehix suggested.

The round structure set in the middle of a rock garden was glistening white stone. John guessed that it was maybe fifty yards across, with a golden spire rising another one hundred feet from the center, the tip of which John had glimpsed from the town below.

"What did you say?" he asked her as she stood by his side taking it in.

"I didn't say a word. But I heard a voice too." They both looked around to see who had joined them.

"It's the voice from the flash drive." John covered his ears, but the voice was speaking to him from inside his head.

Meehix covered her ears and nodded.

"I have to go." He turned to her with fear in his eyes.

"And I have to stay." He saw a small tear on her cheek.

She watched him turn and walk slowly toward vine-covered wooden doors that now swung silently open. There seemed to be a faint yellowish glow coming from inside the temple. John stepped in, and the doors closed behind him.

The voice in Meehix's head directed her to a raised stone platform and instructed her to lie down and try to relax. Her body gave her no choice but to do as requested. Her mind, however, was in no mood to relax once the voice went silent.

When the doors closed behind him, John thought it best to close his eyes and kneel. Since from the outside, it appeared to be a temple, he thought that kneeling would be the most appropriate action. He wasn't sure if it had been or not since nothing but silence followed, both outside and inside of his head.

He cautiously opened one eye, fearing what he might see approaching him. He appeared to be the only occupant.

In the center of the room was a raised round table, directly under the spire that rose above it. He thought it was the same white as outside the temple but couldn't be sure. Its surface seemed to be a constant swirl of colors, similar to a kaleidoscope he'd once had as a child. This was different in that the colors came from outside it, as opposed to the inside.

The voice returned inside his head and told him to please lie down on the table.

As before, his body gave him no choice but to obey. He slowly approached, trying to fight his footsteps the whole way, but he had no choice, which never ended well in the sci-fi and horror movies he'd watched when an outside force had taken over someone's body.

Although his body was no longer under his control, his brain was all his and protested in no uncertain terms as his imagination began to run wild.

I'm not enjoying this! I'm not enjoying this at all! Whatever it is you're going to do to me, can you please just do it now and not make me suffer?

He bumped into the table, not realizing that he'd reached it, and looked up at the spire rising above him. From the outside, it had appeared gold. From the inside it was translucent, blocking any outside view but allowing light to pour through it. Under different circumstances, if it had been a simple, translucent spire, he would have thought it beautiful.

Just one problem, Jojacko, his brain screamed. *Are those metal or glass? Either way, we're fucking dead when they come down!*

Dangling from the spire above him were hundreds of thin sharp spikes hung from the spire at various heights, all centered over the table he was supposed to lie on.

At least that explains the colors on the table. Yeah, you're going to die a beautiful death when they're released, and hundreds of multi-colored spikes pierce every inch of your body!

His body obeyed its controller's instructions, and he took up his position on the table. He wasn't sure if he wanted to be facing up so he could see his death coming or facing down with his eyes closed while he envisioned scenes of eating ice cream as a child on a hot summer day and let his death come as a surprise as he was enjoying pleasant memories.

His body chose to face up.

At least I can still close my fucking eyes. Shit, fuck, no, I can't! Okay, the spikes are definitely glass. Kinda pretty, swirling and reflecting colors all together like that...Yeah, until they slice down into you, and the only color they'll reflect will be blood red!

"Previous visitors have found the colors to be beautiful," the voice spoke again inside his head. "*Magical* is a word I've often heard."

Definitely the voice from the flash drive that led them here. John still couldn't figure out if it was male or female, but he was too distracted at the moment to think too hard about its gender.

"Supine is always the most relaxing position. Ninety-eight percent of the species who have visited agree about that. But you *are* the first Kdackan I've hosted, so perhaps it isn't as relaxing for you?"

"What will relax me!" John shouted, but his voice echoing around the hollow inside of the spire and being *magnified?* by the long glass shards hanging above drowned him out.

"*Let me try this again.*" John closed his mouth and tried to *think* his communication rather than risking more shouting that might send the glass spikes raining down.

"*What will relax me, you invisible body-snatching piece of edible farts, is to give me back control of my body. Make an appearance so that I can defend myself against whatever it is you have planned! I came here as a voluntary virgin sacrifice and had to work damn fucking hard to qualify—Oh fuck it! And fuck you! I'll do the sacrificing myself just to rob you of your twisted fucking pleasure!"*

John let go with a scream that was louder and longer than he'd ever imagined he could come up with. He hoped that it would break whatever was holding up the shards of oh-so-pretty glass and put him out of his never-been-fucked-by-an-alien misery! If he were going to die with one sound on his lips, he would make it count!

"MEEEEEEEEHHHHHIIIIIIXXXXXXX!"

The glass spikes shivered and swayed and clashed against each other from the amplified, echoing scream.

Her mind had done one tumble after another as her body remained prone on the stone slab. *What was happening to John? Why couldn't she move? Why hadn't she been more forward and taken him up on his request for a date sooner so that he wouldn't have qualified as a space-virgin and neither of them would be on this fucking mountain?*

"MEEEEEEEEHHHHHIIIIIIXXXXXXX!"

"JOOOOOJAAAAACKKKOOOOO!"

"I think I may need your help here," came the calm, gender-neutral voice in her head once the echoes of their screams finally died down. *"I've never had a Kdackan before."*

"You don't deserve one." Meehix had figured out the mind-communication quicker than John. *"At least, not this one! If anyone deserves to be the first alien to have sex with him, it's me!*

"We've been to hell and back together, saving each other and hundreds of others along the way and we've been so busy helping

strangers that we haven't had the time to help ourselves to each other yet so fuck you and your, your, what was it? Oh, right... I think I might need your help here!"

Meehix drew a deep breath and prepared herself for being about to become a different type of sacrifice.

"Oh my," came a soft chuckle in response.

"Oh my, what, ass-head?"

"Please, rest assured that neither you nor your companion will be harmed, or even physically touched, in any way. I am not capable of physical form or harm."

"But you're capable of controlling our bodies! That feels pretty fucking dangerous enough to me, stuck here and unable to move!"

"I apologize for that. It's only when someone's body is still that I can truly communicate with them. I will release you both soon, but please, first I need to ask you a few questions."

"And if I don't know the right answers?"

"There are no wrong answers."

"How can there not be a wrong answer?"

"I should rephrase what I just spoke. It has been a long time since I've had visitors, so I am a little rusty regarding conversations. Please forgive me."

"You're forgiven. Now get on with it."

"When we speak truth, then the answer is never wrong. It might be unpleasant to hear and sometimes unpleasant to speak, but when there are decisions to be made, wouldn't you agree that basing those decisions on the truth is better than basing them on a lie?"

"I would nod if I could."

"Sadly, I cannot see a nod...Oh, but if I ask a question, please feel free to tell me to move on because it's none of my business."

Meehix wished that she was able to smile because that one struck home.

"First, tell me that John is safe."

"Physically, he is very safe. But his mind seems to be so full of terrifying thoughts that I need to know how to reassure him when I go back, so the sooner you can fill me in, the sooner I can get back to him. As I said, I've never had a Kdackan before, so I need your help to be able to communicate with him."

"You want to communicate with him and not have sex?"

"Have you ever had sex with someone and woke up the next morning and thought, 'what was I thinking?'"

"Maybe."

"Have you ever spent an evening, or a morning, or a day, just talking with someone who listened and ever regretted it?"

"No."

"The only reason that you two are here is to earn your way to the location of a ship that may or may not exist but is unlike any other ship in existence. Correct?"

"Yes." Meehix willed her mind to try to relax and speak the truth. *"Ask away."*

"Thank you. Short answers are always more helpful than long rambling details."

"Got it." She drew a deep breath.

"How did you two meet?"

"I was on a ship, and we crashed on his planet. I was a prisoner, and he rescued me."

"Did someone, maybe your family hire him?"

"No. He was bored and found me and broke me out. We've been together ever since."

"What have you two done since then?"

"Everything except have sex. I wish I could frown right now.

We rescued a friend of mine who was in another prison. Oh, and we invaded this really, really bad guy's fortress and freed a bunch of slaves from his dungeons.

"Then we rescued a client's niece who was about to be sold into slavery and kicked some pirate's asses. We delivered some happy sperm to help a planet sign some peace treaties. Oh, and John has a friend back on Kdack working on freeing alien captives, but we don't know how he's doing with that.

"Now, we're on a quest for a bigger ship because we've pissed off a few people along the way. Not to mention a whole space station full of whores that he had to fight off for twelve hours to be able to offer himself up to you as a space virgin!"

"It sounds like you were a perfect cure for his boredom."

"Yes. I suppose I have been."

"I'll be back soon and return him to you unharmed. Until then, I'll leave you with your thoughts."

"Okee-dokee."

The voice departed. It wasn't long before her mind was screaming.

"Oh, shit! Oh, shit...Oh. Oh. Oh. Oh, FUCK yes!"

Even though she still couldn't move, Meehix suddenly realized what it must be like for guys when she'd released a few too many pheromones because she now felt some wetness between her legs.

"Would you be happy, John," the voice was back in his head, *"if I informed you that you are not dead yet?"*

"That depends," John thought back. *"Am I going to die?"*

"But of course. All mortals eventually die. But your death will not occur while you are in my care."

"Care? Is that what you call taking over my body and threatening me with spikes while I'm helpless to move?"

"Yes, I now know that you and I have some trust issues to work out."

"Ya think?"

"I had to leave you alone while I had a visit with Meehix."

"If you hurt her, then I swear to any God whose name I can remember that you will die by my hands no matter what I have to do to find you!"

He leapt up off of the table and came up swinging with a wicked-looking knife he kept strapped to his ankle, looking to take revenge out on an enemy he couldn't see, touch, or identify and couldn't get rid of unless he sliced his head off.

"Where the fuck are you?"

"Meehix is safe. As are you. You now have complete control of your body."

"So I can leave?"

"Not quite yet. I still have control of the doors. But she is waiting right outside. Please, stand away from the table."

"Why?"

"Because I have learned that it causes you distress. And because your quest to find the Ultimate Ship depends on you completing this third task successfully."

"Oh."

Not completely convinced that the voice's *Entity* wasn't still just fucking with him, he decided that stepping away from the table would fall under the category of good advice, regardless of who gave it.

"You aren't here as a sacrifice, John," the Voice continued. "Your actions led you here, and I think I now know how to word it in a way that you can understand. You are here because you have proven yourself worthy."

"Yeah. I'm Mister Perfect."

"Perfection is soooo boring. Please. You once told Meehix to trust that which you know to be true, correct?"

"Sounds stupid enough to be something that I said."

"How good is your memory, John?"

Two and two is four. Four and four is eight. Next question."

"Visual memory," the Voice continued, with a touch more serious intonation. "What is your earliest visual memory?"

"Yellow socks." The Voice had managed to calm him down to the extent that he wondered if it had hypnotized him.

"Tell me about the socks. Were they a solid yellow, or were there patterns?"

"I was three years old, for fuck's sake. How much am I supposed to be able to remember?"

"I need to know about the socks before I can show you the way to your next task." The Voice sounded like patience personified.

"They were yellow, with horizontal stripes."

"And? Just stripes?"

"Between the stripes were sparkly stars and shapes of silver moons. Some moons were full. Some were half. Some were quarter moons."

"Meehix," she and John both heard the voice say. "Could you come in here now?"

The doors swung open, and a minute later Meehix entered, trying to tie a spare jacket around her waist to hide whatever dampness might be visible.

She rushed to John and hugged the man who was still in one piece so hard that she almost squeezed him to pieces.

"I need you both to see this together. John will remember most of it. Meehix, you will remember some of it."

"You're safe!" John and Meehix said to each other, ignoring the Voice.

"Yes, you're both safe," the Voice interrupted their thoughts. *"Attention, please."*

They un-embraced and came to attention.

"I need one of you to find the heaviest object you have and throw it as far and high as you can into the hanging glass and try to remember everything you see."

The time for doubting had passed.

Meehix pulled out one of her long swords and handed it over. John took it by the end of its blade, got a good clean grip on it, and did a double-handed toss as high and far as he could.

It hit the hanging shards halfway up.

"Oh, my fuck!"

John put an arm around Meehix as they watched the inside of the spire explode into a conglomeration of visuals that disappeared a moment later, as the sword fell and *clanked* on the stone table that John had recently vacated.

"It was a pleasure meeting you two," the Voice inside their heads told them both. *"Sorry for any fear that you experienced, but I had to make sure."*

"Make sure of what?" John heard Meehix think.

"Make sure that you both were sure of each other," came the Voice's reply. *"You just revealed everything you need for the next task. Meehix, you will remember some of the images, but John will remember more. If he has trouble recalling them, let him relax and think, and whisper* Yellow socks, *and he'll be able to pull up more. It's getting late now. You both have to start*

back down. Before darkness descends...and don't forget your sword."

Meehix grabbed and sheathed her sword, and they both got out of there as fast as their feet could carry them.

"What? No time for good-byes?" They both heard the Voice smile after them.

"Can't remember the last time I had so much fun!" John thought back with total seriousness.

"Thank you!" was Meehix's parting thought.

Just past halfway down, a small band of bandits leapt out onto the path, blocking their way.

They were seven feet tall if they were an inch, which made their balls at the perfect height to be kicked halfway up into the back of their throats.

The partners had an upward position and didn't need any weapons to deal with them as they both leapt, feet first.

"That felt good," Meehix hollered as they left them crumpled on the path behind them.

"If they weren't virgins before we met, they'll be virgins from now on."

Whooping and hollering the rest of the way down, they were too late to pay Norlan for the energy water because his store had closed for the night, but they slipped twenty credits under the door and figured that would cover the difference and made it back onto Ship.

"And?" they were greeted as they made their way up the ramp, adrenaline draining and emotionally exhausted.

"And," Meehix answered as she and John headed back to the cargo space, "unless you want to be left here as an orphaned ship, no more questions until morning."

The partners hit Cargo, pulled out two inflatable cots, and dropped into them.

"You good, Jojacko?"

"Never better, Meehixiheem."

They fell asleep, reaching out from their cots to hold each other's hands after the most exhausting day they'd ever spent together.

CHAPTER EIGHTEEN

"That was one weird-fuck dream," Meehix spoke out loud to an audience of none when she woke up on a cot in Cargo the next morning.

"Good morning, Meehix."

"Good morning, Ship." She tried to get her bearings. "Was yesterday a strange day?"

"Same old same old for me. I hear that you two had some adventures. We'll have to wait for John to return. He went out to get some breakfast before we can continue this conversation with any sense of—here he comes now."

"Be right there." Meehix rolled off her cot, stretched, and headed to the front cabin to see what edible atrocities John had managed to scrounge up.

"Tatz-tem-oyam rolls? How did you find these?" Meehix greeted John in the cockpit as he took the shotgun seat and unwrapped the breakfast sandwiches, hoping he'd made the right choice.

"They looked harmless enough," was his honest explanation. He then set two cups of something that resembled coffee on the dashboard.

"Oh." Meehix took a bite of a roll and a sip of the flictum, leaned back in the pilot's seat, and envisioned herself in heaven.

John took a bite and sip but didn't end up in the same place as Meehix. But that was not important. He waited as Meehix replenished herself.

"Thank you, John." She smiled when done. "I needed that."

"Okay, partner, and Ship, ready for the next step?"

Meehix and Ship were both hesitant to answer, not knowing what John had in mind.

"The Voice, Meehix. I don't know what else to call it, but we both know it was up there, right?"

"If you answer a question with the truth, you will never give a wrong answer," she remembered.

John laughed. "Damn, that sounds so like her!"

"You decided that the voice was *her* too?"

"Yeah, I did." John paused and thought. "She asked me questions that no dude I've ever met would ask."

Meehix nodded her agreement.

John slipped the silver and turquoise Hannah pendant off his neck for the last time and slipped it into one of Ship's USB ports.

"She's all yours now, Ship. I will never ask you for her back."

Good fuck ahmighty! Meehix's brain shouted. *He's finally letting go of Hannah?*

"I only need you to access one more program for me."

"What is that, John?"

"Word To Visual." He turned to Meehix. "I programmed it when I was still a young idiot but never used it. I hope that it will work for what we now need."

"What do we need it to do now?"

"Do you remember 'yellow socks?'"

"I don't know what it means," she confessed, "but yes, I remember."

John stretched out as best he could, leaning back into the copilot's seat and putting his feet up on Ship's dashboard. He closed his eyes, doing his best to relax and trust.

"Have you found Word To Visual, Ship?"

"Yes, John."

"Then let it run, Ship, and record it all! Meehix. If I pause for more than a moment while speaking, say 'yellow socks.' You two need to trust me on this and keep an eye on the screen. If you can, feel free to take notes."

Nothing in his earlier experiences had prepared him for something like this, as he relaxed into the visions he saw amid the glass shards that banged against each other in the temple spire, and started talking about what he'd seen.

Ship and Hannah had done their jobs.

Meehix saw the screen spring to life with images and diagrams, as John let loose with his memories. When he went silent, the pictures on the screen stopped. She leaned down and whispered into his ear, "Yellow socks."

The screen kicked back into gear with another visual of what her Jojacko remembered from the swirling but not falling shards.

Three "yellow socks" later, the images on the screen stopped, and John started snoring.

"It's okay, Ship," Meehix whispered. "He needs to sleep for a little while now."

Shippewa gently rocked. *Message received.*

While John was dozing, Meehix had Ship replay the images he'd brought to life on the screen and was confused because they didn't match her memory of the first set. She replayed them a third time and decided that her confusion was justified because they didn't match either the first or the second viewing.

The only consistent thing was the name of the planet, Trimidoon, and the opening visual of what appeared to be a castle, Illusionor.

"I'm at a complete loss here, Ship."

"Play it backward." John stretched and lowered his feet.

"You're awake?"

"Came around halfway through but was keeping quiet as I watched the screen."

"I've rewatched it twice, and it was different each time."

"I didn't think it was what I'd recalled from the glass shards, either. So you're not alone."

"And backward would make a difference?" She didn't follow that logic at all.

"I don't know." He shrugged. "But it won't leave us any more confused than we already are, will it?"

"Don't bet the rent on it, but okay…backward, please."

The images remained completely unrecognizable. When it had finished playing, the opening scene was still the only thing that remained the same. *On Trimidoon, the Castle Illusionor awaits.*

"One more time from the beginning, Ship, if you will."

Meehix had lost interest halfway through her fourth viewing.

"Why keep watching when what we're seeing doesn't seem to be based in any reality that we can strategize around? I don't even know what the fuck we're supposed to do there."

"Ssshhhh. I'm trying to focus."

She folded her arms and tried not to pout. She also stayed as still as possible because John was leaning forward, studying the images in stern concentration. He switched the screen off when it reached the end, leaned back, and closed his eyes. It was several minutes before he spoke again.

"Okay."

"Okay, what?"

"We're not in Kansas anymore." Eyes still closed.

"Let me try this again." She tried, not completely successfully, to keep the agitation out of her voice. "Okay, what the fuck?"

He opened his eyes, turned to face her, and smiled. "We're off to see the wizard."

"What wizard?"

"Probably several."

"Am I going to need a pitcher of dibble-blinks while you explain this?"

"No! Definitely not. For this task, we'll need to be as clear-headed as possible. Ship? Is it possible to set this up with the cubes in Cargo?"

"I don't believe so, John. The programming of the images appears to be in a constant state of flux, so there is no way to translate them."

"I didn't think so." He didn't seem perturbed by the news. Meehix, on the other hand, wanted to hit something. Something real. Something *solid.* On the other hand, she didn't want to hurt John so she settled on folding her arms and clenching her fists. *For now.*

"It's all in the name of the castle. Illusionor."

He pissed off Meehix even more by suddenly rushing back into Cargo and came back with Heemix, connected her to Ship, and fired her up as he settled back into his seat.

"Give me a minute, and if I'm right, I can explain it all."

Meehix had a lot of good qualities. Patience was not one of them.

"One minute. The clock starts now."

He did a quick search and found what he needed with five seconds to spare. Ship's larger screen now shared Heemix's information.

A deep-throated, voice-over narrator began as images of the outside view of Castle Illusionor floated across the screen.

What you see on the outside is real. We can't show you what you will find on the inside because that will depend on you. There are no magical spells allowed inside the castle walls. The only weapon allowed is your mind. Castle Illusionor is the ultimate test of a wizard's true power. You will only meet others of your kind. Here, you will be able to test and push yourself to your very limits. Enjoy your stay.

"I am *not* a wizard." Meehix was less than pleased when the short clip finished. "And I haven't seen you wave your arms and conjure up any woo-woo magic, either."

"But how do you know we couldn't?" John was excited.

He'd taken on the personage of wizards before in

games, but since that was all fantasy, it seemed easy. It was never something he'd tried to do in real life because that would have seemed silly. But he'd never tried to fly a spaceship in real life either, at least until he'd met Meehix.

"Who's to say what's real? Who's to say that we can't do something just because we've never tried to do it before?"

"This is the fourth feat, right?" Meehix sighed and unfolded her arms. "Something that we *have* to complete before we try number five?"

John nodded a little too enthusiastically for her tastes.

"Even though we have no idea of what we're supposed to do once we get to Hotel Woo-Wooville?"

John's nodding continued, now accompanied by an idiot's smile.

"Shit, Ship." She punched in the coordinates. "I'm flying. John's gone bye-bye to 'I get to be a wizard' land."

They switched piloting duties as the other grabbed some sleep and followed the guidance system. John was at the helm when they docked in the city of Zoriminee a day later.

"This is so exciting." John led the way down the ramp.

"You're an idiot." Meehix followed.

They hailed a driver who deposited them at the foot of the castle a half-hour later. John was expecting to see a lot of robed characters milling around. He was disappointed. There were no white robes, or black robes, or purple robes, or robes of any color.

"Hmm. I thought I might be underdressed, but I guess I had nothing to worry about."

"It's you I'm worried about." Meehix trudged up the

steps to the main door behind him. "What are we expecting to see or find?"

"I don't know. But we've come through too much to get here, so I know we can do this."

At the top of the stairs was a wide porch. Roughly a dozen unarmed aliens milled around. The large double doors to the castle opened, and a handful of others emerged. Some seemed jubilant. Others were in various degrees of moods between sad and angry.

The happy-looking ones headed down the steps amid laughter and light conversation. The ones who were less pleased took places behind the line that had formed when the doors opened. John and Meehix found themselves in the middle of the line of those about to enter.

"Weapons deposited in the box to your right," one of the two tall guards greeted them.

"You may retrieve them on your way out," the second guard instructed.

"All weapons?" Meehix liked this place less and less.

"Better to deposit them now than to hold up the line because you're trying to hide something," the first guard instructed.

Meehix and John stepped to the side to let the line move forward as they disarmed themselves. They ended up being the last in line as the group gathered beyond the security line.

"I am Klozon," came the greeting from another tall alien addressing the group.

"Finally," John whispered. "Someone wearing a robe."

Meehix's response was a sharp elbow in his ribs.

"At the top, if you reach it, you will find an orange chest that holds what you seek," Klozon continued.

"How do you know what we seek?" Meehix interrupted.

"Only *you* can know what you seek." John hoped his partner wouldn't ask any more stupid questions. "Of any group that enters," the instructor went on, "only the first three to the top will succeed. At that time, the quest will be over, and everyone must return to the entrance and either celebrate or stand in line to try again."

"That explains why some were happy, and some were pissed," John whispered again.

"You wanna see pissed?" Meehix whispered back. "Then keep talking."

John shut up.

"There is no limit to how often you may quest." Klozon took a moment to scan them all before offering his only piece of advice. "Look around you. A small number will succeed. A larger number will fail. You are all potential friends or enemies. Seek well." He stepped aside.

They all entered the large chamber, with eight doors leading to eight hallways. John and Meehix didn't know if they should follow or lead.

"Some of these wizards have been here before and know which door to choose." John held back.

"How do we know which ones they are?"

"Beats the hell out of me. And who's to say that only one of the doors is the right one? Couldn't several of them eventually lead to the top?"

"I don't know. But most of them are rushing in the same direction, so we might be the only ones here who are beginners."

"True." He nodded. "But if they've been here before and are returning for another try, then they must have been losers in their previous attempts. Do we really want to follow losers?"

"I'd like to see why they lost."

They decided to follow the losers, who already had a head start on them. Opening the door, they entered a hallway that appeared to be empty but echoed with shouting.

"Oh yeah? Take that."

"No whapping in the balls!"

"I was aiming for your brains, so I think my aim was perfect!"

"Ow!"

"Should've swung to the right!"

John held his arm out to stop Meehix from moving forward as he took in the scene.

"Mirrors! It's like reverse vampires!"

"What are you talking about?"

"Look at me! What do you see?"

"I see the back of your head."

"Now what do you see?" John quickly fell into a crouch.

"I see myself looking really pissed off!"

"And now what?" he sprang back up to his feet.

"I see the back of your head. What the fuck?"

"Only our reflections are visible! Look down the hallway, and look at the walls along the hallway!"

The hallway still appeared to be empty, but when she looked at the walls, she could see wizard wannabes beating each other up with various weapons that looked no more dangerous than pillows.

"We're invisible, except in the mirrors."

She slapped him on the left side of the back of his head and found herself staring at herself as John went down.

"Think of something soft." John stayed down. "Close your eyes and think *hard* about something *soft*!"

Hard AND soft? She closed her eyes.

"Now look."

She opened her eyes and saw herself holding a large, flaccid dick in her hand, which she immediately tossed into the air as she took a step back.

"What just hit me?" John stayed where he was and looked in the mirror. "Did you just *dick* me?"

She looked down. There was no John. There was no dick. She looked in the mirror, and there they both were on the floor.

"Welcome to Castle Illusionor."

Meehix collapsed beside him.

"I got the rear covered!" a voice shouted.

They looked in the mirror and saw a fat, four-foot-tall, green ball of mostly blubber, standing above them wielding a three-foot mitten, waiting to beat them into submission. John did a leg-swipe.

"That was me!" Meehix informed him.

He swiped with his other leg, and they watched in the mirror as the chubby green man collapsed on top of them. Four hands reached out and rolled the invisible assailant off them.

"Okay." She looked her partner in his eyes in the mirror as they both stood and smiled. "Now I'm having fun!"

Meehix stood and proceeded to *mitten* their attacker until he begged for mercy.

"Reconnaissance time."

"Meaning?"

It was strange, having to look at each other in the mirrored walls while standing side by side.

"You, little man," John guided himself in the mirror until he could put a booted foot on the rear-guard's chest and hold him down as he questioned him. "You've been here before?"

Looking in the mirror, he could see the wizard wannabe looking back at him and nodding.

"How many times?"

"This is my seventh."

"Always with the same gang?"

"No." He stopped his struggling. "I'm always the last that anyone wants to team up with, so I go with whoever will have me."

"Six times already? And you've never been successful?"

"I've been close. Oh, so close. But the higher everyone gets, the less anyone wants to listen."

"We're both ready to listen. If I take my foot off your chest, will you be willing to stay and answer a few questions?"

"Why should I?"

Meehix heard the exchange while watching her man in the mirror.

"Because," John sounded so calm and reasonable. "This is your seventh try, and none of your, shall we say, *companions,* have ever succeeded."

"So?"

"What makes you think that the two who left you behind will succeed?"

"They won't," came the sad reply. "No one who has ever teamed up with me before has ever succeeded, so why would they? I think I'm cursed."

John recognized the tone of that voice. He took his foot off the little man's chest and sat down on the floor next to him so that they could look at each other in the mirror as equals.

"That, my friend, is because you've never met my partner and me before."

Meehix saw John pat the floor beside him and did her best while watching herself in the mirrored walls to figure out how to sit beside him.

"I'm John. This is Meehix. And you are?"

"Jessup." He sat up.

"Pleased to meet you." John held out his hand in their mirror images.

"Pleased to meet you too," Jessup reached out for the hand, which landed on Meehix's right breast, causing her to roll a safe distance away... "Oh no, no, no! Sorry! Seven tries, and I still get confused by the mirrors!"

Sounds of fighting and curses on future generations were echoing down from the stairways above.

"It's okay, Jessup," John caught Meehix's eyes in the hall's mirror and smiled at her. "I've wanted to do that a few times myself."

Meehix hoped that her purple blushing wasn't too obvious as she nodded for him to continue.

"Ignore the mirrors, Jessup. Pretend that you're now with two new friends, and we're all going to close our eyes and, oh, let's just talk to each other...Can we all do that?"

John led by example and closed his eyes, hoping that others would follow his example.

"Okay," John continued. "We are all allowed only one *peek* to see if anyone else has their eyes closed as we go on...Fuck that. We are allowed two peeks, but we have to use the first one now!"

Three pairs of peeking eyeballs followed, along with *guilty as charged* head-bobs.

"Jessup? I'm going to ask you a few questions because you've been here before and we haven't, and we need your advice," John went on as they all had their eyes now closed. *He hoped because he did.*

"Remember," Meehix tried to reassure their new friend. "The truth is never a wrong answer."

"It takes a *team* to reach the box at the top?" John started.

"It doesn't take a team," Jessup replied, "It's just that after the first three reach the top, then everyone else has to start over again."

"That makes sense," John kept his voice calmer than he was feeling. "But three, working as one, sounds like a good option to reach the top, right?"

"From what I've seen before, yes. Can I open my eyes now?"

"Abso-fucking-lutely!" John hopped up. "It's mirror time for the fearsome threesome!"

Looking in the mirrors, he realized that he was the only one who understood why he was so excited, as the other two remained on the floor.

"Retreat through the doors."

"No one has ever retreated before." Jessup was confused.

"That is why so many have failed."

John led the way back.

Following his directions, Meehix and Jessup, and John, found themselves outside of the hallway doors, in the main *lobby*, looking at each other, face to face, with no mirrors involved.

"The first three to the top succeed, right?"

Nods.

"We're not going to succeed this time, right?"

More nods.

"We are going to practice the shit outta this now so the three of us will succeed the next time, right?"

The three rushed back in through the door and practiced themselves silly with mirrored pillow fights in mirrors until the bell rang, signaling that three had reached the top and found the box.

"A team, next time?" John asked.

"Let's go get back in line," Meehix answered.

The three calmly walked back out and took their places to be part of the next group allowed in.

"Jessup," John asked. "You're more familiar with this than Meehix and I are. How many succeed on their first try?"

"The record, I think, is four tries. It's not easy."

John looked his partner in the eye and smiled.

"I say it's time to set a new record."

"For once," she smiled back, "I agree with you."

John knelt so he could see eye-to-eye with their new partner again.

"Jessup. Listen to me closely. You lead the way. We'll have your front and back, and there's no way that we won't shatter that record. Now think. Do you remember anyone who's succeeded and hasn't gone through the door that everyone rushes to?"

"Maybe once, but I can't be sure."

"You'd think that a castle built by wizards would change things up now and then. If everyone knows there's only one door that matters... What's the closest you've come before?"

"I think there are seven levels. The farthest I've ever gotten up to was level five."

"Do the stairs have any common access level? Like, let's just say level four. Is there a common room with other doors and other choices, or is each door and hallway isolated from the others?"

"Level three is common. From there, only one stairway leads up."

"Okay. Do you know if all the stairs lead there?"

"Yeah, they do. But the one that everyone rushes to is the fastest."

"Except for all of the fighting."

"Except for that." Jessup nodded.

"We can conjure up any weapons we want along the way?"

"Any weapon that isn't sharp or metal. Nothing that will draw any blood."

"How about liquids?"

"As long as they're not acid or something dangerous like that."

"Marbles?"

"What's a marble?"

John stood and smiled.

"Jessup, you take Meehix through the other door. I'll hit the main one and hopefully be able to slow them all down and meet you on the third."

Jessup looked up at the tall blue chick and saw her nod. He'd never had anyone nod at him before. He squared his shoulders and led them back in.

"I think we've just met Chuckie N's *wizard* doppel-ganger," John whispered.

Meehix burst out laughing.

"No laughing allowed," announced the guard on the right as he gave his standard greeting to those who were now entering.

"Shut the laugh the fuck up," John whispered to Meehix.

"Trying," she whispered back.

Jessup was now having serious doubts about the two giggling wizards he'd signed up with for his next attempt, number eight. *Aw well, there's still number nine and more to look forward to after my next fiasco.*

"Lead on, Jessup." Meehix's voice was now serious. "We're going to be the next three to reach the top. You'll get yours, and we'll get ours, and that's a promise."

Jessup paused.

"We are both a lot of things," John tried to reassure him. "But the one thing that neither of us is, is a liar. Lead on!"

The bell rang, and the next group rushed off, John joining and jostling his way through the larger group as Jessup led Meehix to the wizard-free door.

John slowly but steadily bulled his way through the fighting in the first hallway. Knowing that nothing could do him serious damage, he took more than a few blows, not bothering to deliver any except to toss an invisible body out of his way now and then. He was getting the hang of the mirrors and enjoyed the scenes of wizards try to beat each other up without being able to cast any spells.

He was near the front of the pack when the hallway started slanting up, which was exactly where he wanted to be. Never having tried to *conjure up* anything before, it took him a couple of tries, but he eventually found himself holding a pillowcase full of marbles. Since they weren't, by themselves, dangerous, hundreds loaded in one pillowcase could have made a very dangerous weapon, but that wasn't his goal.

He used it like a hammer-toss, swinging it around a couple of times and letting it fly up the ramp, and planted his feet. Other wizards were now rushing to get ahead of him as the pillowcase landed and the marbles rolled down. Being the only one who wasn't now running, he watched in the mirror as wizard after wizard lost their footing and stumbled to the floor, most of them sliding back past him as the marbles cascaded down.

John kept his feet firmly on the floor and quickly shuffled on, the marbles bouncing off his size fourteen boots until he was now the leader of the pack and made a run for it. He had a decent lead as he hurried through the second-floor landing and up the next winding ramp. Halfway up, he conjured a lawn-sized garbage bag of cooking oil and another similar-sized bag full of feathers.

Pouring out the oil behind him, he then ripped the bag of feathers open and tossed it down the ramp. As much as he wanted to watch what was happening behind him, he turned and rushed upward and arrived in the third level common room with enough time to try to look all casual and shit before Meehix and Jessup burst in through their door a few seconds later.

"Onward and upward!" Although they were now clearly in the lead, John had learned enough to know the time for questions and celebration was *after* the game was won and not a second before. "Jessup, you lead! We've got your back!"

Jessup knew the way although he wasn't the fastest on his feet, which annoyed Meehix who wanted to rush past him. He'd explained to her during their climb to the third floor that there were still some wrong turns they could make though, so she decided to urge him on as best she could without being too critical.

By the time they reached the fifth-floor landing, the sounds of angry, oil- and feather-covered wizards were getting closer.

Yoga balls! Yoga balls! Yoga balls! John held out his hands long enough to drop six of the large balls behind him. They careened down the ramp.

"Need some help!" Meehix hollered down from the midpoint of the ramp to level six.

John rushed up, fearing the worst. He found Meehix helping to keep Jessup upright as the short fat wizard was bent over, his hands on his knees as he tried to draw breath.

"He's winded."

John knelt. "Hop on! It's piggy-back time!"

Meehix helped him onto John's back and assisted John to stand.

"Hold on, but don't choke, Jessup. We're almost there." John gained his feet. "Meehix?"

"Got your back, partner."

John lumbered up the winding ramp as Jessup clung tight.

Meehix remembered a dance club she'd once been in called The Arachnid. Thousands of sticky-string webs hung from the ceiling above the dance floor. The goal of the dances was to try to avoid getting tangled in the webs until you got close to another dancer that you wanted to tangle up with together.

What the hell. If John can do it, so can I. She held out her hands down the ramp, closed her eyes, and feeling like nothing short of a fool, thought, *Webs. Webs. Web fucking webs!*

"What?"

"Who?

"Get away from me!"

"I can't!"

I guess I just passed Wizardry 101. She rushed to the top.

"Are you sure you've never done this before?" Jessup was asking as it was now John's turn to try and catch his breath.

"Beginner's luck," John was able to get out.

"This is no time for chit-chat!" Meehix rushed to the orange box that sat on a pedestal in the middle of the uppermost chamber and opened the lid.

A bell rang, signaling that they'd completed this version of the quest.

"Shall we?" John asked.

Meehix and Jessup joined his hand as they all reached into the box together.

John was the first to withdraw his hand, holding a small tube with a cap on one end. Opening the cap, he wasn't surprised to find another USB drive to be inserted into Ship.

Meehix removed her hand and held a rectangular card. Blue on one side, with gold trim around the edges. She looked at the side that John couldn't see and tucked it safely away.

"What's it say?" John asked.

"It doesn't *say* anything." She smiled. She didn't want to explain that she wanted an image of her in a cell as a stranger came in to rescue her. On the side of the card that she didn't show him was a silver etching of her first meeting with the Kdackan who'd burst into her cell, neither of them having a clue of what was going to happen next.

Jessup kept his hand in the box longer than the other two with a strange look on his face that they took for disappointment. They waited in silence as the short fat man transformed into the largest, most majestic bird they'd ever seen.

The transformation completed, he stretched out his wings to their full six-foot span. John and Meehix took a few steps back as the bird that used to be Jessup inspected his wingtips and lifted the mighty talons where his feet used to be.

"What the fuck did you wish for?" John beat Meehix to the question.

Jessup turned his now-noble face toward them.

"I've always felt that I was born into the wrong body."

He tried flapping his wings, and Meehix and John both felt their power.

"All I've ever wanted was for my outside to match my inside…and my inside always wanted to soar."

He took a step forward and placed a wing on each of their heads.

"Thank you. If you ever need me, you know where you can find me."

He stepped back, nodded, leapt up onto a windowsill, and looked back to see John and Meehix waving farewell.

Leaping out, he spread his wings. John and Meehix rushed to the window and watched their hatchling soar away.

CHAPTER NINETEEN

"**For the record,**" Ship greeted them as the partners casually made their way back up the ramp. "**I will never tire of welcoming you two back on board.**"

"Thank you, Ship," John said, and Meehix nodded. "And we will never tire of you welcoming us."

"**You both survived. So that is good news number one. Were you successful, is the next question I am obligated to ask.**"

"I don't think we failed, but I'm not sure yet." John opened his tube and inserted the drive and took the copilot's seat as Meehix took the captain's chair.

"We might have pissed off a few wizardly folks along the way." Meehix had spent enough time in the captain's chair to feel right at home. "But the Council of Wizards in charge of the castle agreed that we didn't break any rules or regulations."

"We might have bent a few rules," John added. "But bending is not the same as breaking."

He smiled at the memory of the dozen competing

wizards who'd been with them when the bell first rang, had profoundly complained when the second bell rang to signal that someone had completed the task.

He and Meehix had stood silent as their competitors voiced their complaints in front of three judges in a side room on the castle's first floor. They learned that it wasn't uncommon to lodge complaints about the fairness of the completion. It took a few minutes to get the judges together. As they walked in and calmly took their seats, John thought, *that's what wizards should look like.*

Long robes. Wizened faces, with the look of patient eternity in their eyes, they heard the accusations and complaints being brought to them by a handful of oil- and feather-covered competitors.

"Let the hearing begin," the wizard in the center chair addressed the gathering. "I am Zorn. To my left is Yotz. To my right is Victern. We are the judges who are currently available. Have you designated a spokes-wizard? Because we would rather not try to filter through a cacophony of voices.

"We have your honors." One wizard stepped forward. "I am Florome," he turned in a slow circle, arms outstretched to draw the eyes of the judges to his fellow wizards. "Look at us. We are all covered in oil."

"And feathers," a voice came out from behind Florome.

"Was the oil hot when it covered you?" Zorn asked.

"No. It was on the floor and we...well, we all slipped and fell in it."

"Slippery, but not hot, correct?" Yotz took his turn. He and Zorn and Victern all wanted to keep this short, so they could get back to the game of Fupduck that had been interrupted.

"Correct," Florome acknowledged.

"The feathers!" came the voice from behind again.

Florome spun and admonished the one who had interrupted him two times already as he was getting started. "I'll get to that, Rexion! But I'm the one who won the *he who shall speak* vote, so back off and let me do my job!"

Turning back to the panel, he did another slow spin with his arms out.

"As the distinguished panel can see, we are all also covered in feathers."

"Feathers are always one of the most lethal weapons," Victern responded, trying to stifle a laugh.

"They can block your vision!" Florome was determined to make his case.

"Do they cause blindness or any physical damage to your eyes?" the judge followed up.

"Well, no."

"Oil that is not hot. Feathers that have to be dodged, lest they get caught in one's eyelashes." Zorn was feeling confident that they would be able to resume their Fupduck game soon. "Next complaint?"

Florome pulled out the most damning evidence from his pocket and rolled a dozen marbles across the floor toward the judge's table.

"Oh my!" Yotz shouted in mock fear as the marbles rolled harmlessly past them. "Dangerous indeed."

"Do you have anything more to offer than slippery oil, floating feathers, and small rolling stones?"

"Isn't that enough?" Florome stomped.

"You forgot about the big bouncy balls." Rexion was pissed and tossed a large yoga ball over Florome and toward the judges' table.

The ball hit the floor and bounced over the judges' heads before bouncing off and ending up in a corner.

Zorn, Yotz, and Victern wished that all cases could be this easy to adjudicate. They didn't even need to discuss it beyond brief eye contact. Zorn banged his gavel.

"Better luck next time." Zorn consulted his notes and turned to the defendants before ending the session. "John, and Meehix, correct?"

They nodded.

"Where is the third one who reached the top with you?"

"All yours, John," Meehix whispered.

"Truth is never the wrong answer, right?" he whispered back and took one step forward.

"When we all opened the orange box together, our partner was transformed into a large, glorious bird and flew out the window. If there were windows in this room, you would be able to look out and probably see him circling majestically above."

"Will the two of you please approach the bench?"

They did as instructed. The three judges rose. Yotz reached over the table and handed Meehix a gold coin. Victern handed another gold coin to John.

Zorn stood and held the third coin out for all to see and spoke.

"Those coins represent the fact that you, and your fly-away partner, have completed the task faster than any other team ever has. Someday, someone will break your record, and the coins will disappear and return to Castle

Illusionor for presentation to the threesome that broke it. Until that day, hold onto them as a reminder of what you accomplished."

"And the third coin?" John didn't want Jessup to miss out.

"We will build a necklace to attach it to and leave it out on the highest turret, for him to either admire in the sun from a distance or to swoop up and wear…That choice will be his to make."

"Case dismissed," the wizard voices chimed in unison, and they exited the room, their work done.

"We still think you cheated," Florome called as John and Meehix walked out, medals in hand.

"And your mother wears army boots," was John's parting shot back.

"What?" Meehix asked.

"I heard it in a movie somewhere," John smiled, "and always wanted to say it. I just never had the right occasion before."

"The drive is ready for viewing."

John brought himself back from the memory. "Was I out long?"

"Out long, what? It's been two seconds."

John shook his head. "That whole tinkling glass and yellow socks memory thingie may not have completely worn off yet."

Meehix held up her gold coin. "Wherever you were, did it involve something like this?"

"Something very much like that."

John fumbled in his pockets for his coin. He held it up and clinked it against Meehix's.

"To Jessup," he toasted.

"To Chuckie N, the second," she toasted back.

"Oh no. Don't tell me there is another. One Chuckie N at a time is enough for this old ship."

"Show us what's on the latest drive, Ship."

"I don't think you're going to like it, John." Ship sighed. **"And pardon my French, but I don't want to get anywhere near that fucking place."**

"Why is that?" John had just started to relax from their latest completed task but had never heard Ship use that kind of language before. It had even gotten Meehix's attention.

"It appears to be a planet where old technology is abandoned and left to rot or sold off in pieces. I thought that at the end of your quest, I would get a ship of my own. Not be deserted and discarded."

"What?" John was immediately concerned. Shippewa was ahead of both him and Meehix regarding the drive John had found in the orange box.

"If you're going to abandon me, after all we've been through, all I ask is that you abandon me here, or on any other planet, or space station, anywhere other than on *Junkalot*. I know that I'm not perfect, but I deserve better than that."

"Whoa, whoa, whoa, Ship!" John would have held their faithful craft in his arms if that was possible. Anything to relieve the panic in her tone. "We're not abandoning you anywhere, *ever!* Got that?"

"Ship?" Meehix spoke as gently as she could. "Play what was on the drive, and I promise you that we won't go anywhere unless you want to. Remember when we all first met?" She looked at John, who nodded his encouragement for her to go on.

"I was a prisoner, and you were a hunk of metal thrown together from spare parts. And John was an idiot."

John would have liked to correct her on the level of his idiocy, but she had a point, and he chose to give her another smile and nod to continue. Smiling, she did just that.

"Think of all we've been through and done together since then. There is no way in..." she looked at John because she was struggling for the right words.

"I would slice off my dick before I let anything bad happen to you." John meant it, at least at the moment.

"I would slice off John's dick myself if he even thought about it!" Meehix meant it, at least at the moment.

"Okay," John jumped back in. "I hope that I'm not the only one here who wants to keep my dick unsliced. Keeping that in mind, Ship. Roll the tape."

Ship rolled the tape, and the screen came back to life.

Watching the whole video together, with narration, they learned that Junkalot was neither a planet nor a space station. It was one of several small moons in orbit around the planet Montyore.

They all recognized the narrator's voice. The first time they'd heard it was when it gave them instructions on how to get to task number three. The second time Meehix and John heard it was in their heads while in the temple on top of Mount Climaxia.

"Congratulations on completing the fourth task."

"How does it know we succeeded?" John's head was still slightly fuzzy.

"How could we be watching this if we hadn't, dimwad?"

"Oh." They settled in to watch and learn.

"Junkalot," the voice from the mountain continued, "is the smallest and the youngest of Montyore's three moons. It started as a large asteroid but got caught in the planet's gravitational pull. Over the eons, the, shall we say, younger residents of Montyore began using it for weekend getaways."

"It became a party dump-moon." Meehix frowned.

She had visited a few before she'd met John. They seldom had any natural resources, and no one was ever interested in developing them into a hot spot of coolness or an attractive and expensive vacation destination.

If you got to one while it was still relatively new, they weren't too bad. Usually a little messy because no one picked up behind themselves when they left. Litter and refuse could pile up after a while.

Often, the residents of the moon's mother-planet started sending up all of their refuse, garbage, whatever they didn't want to deal with anymore or figure out how to dispose of properly and used the moon as a dumping ground.

People had built entire industries around keeping a planet clean by simply sending their junk to a moon. Some companies on environmentally conscious worlds would fly the waste out and dispose of it in designated areas. Other planets would resort to loading up old rockets that would be scrapped soon anyway and sending them off to crash-land anywhere.

They learned from the narration that Junkalot had become one of the more organized ones. It had even become profitable. Flemunns, one of the minority species on Montyore, had banded together and purchased the dumping rights, which ended up being a moderately good financial move that had lasted for over two thousand years.

That all ended for the Flemunns when their CEO developed a few bad habits, one of which was gambling. He'd managed to dip into the operational funds to support his habit but kept getting deeper and deeper in the hole. After one long and desperate night of brackum-jackum, he risked it all by laying down the dumping rights in an all-or-nothing wager.

The only thing he'd held back was his emergency escape fund. By the time the Flemunns learned that Nickit the Rippit now owned their livelihood, the CEO was long gone. Mr. Nickit helped ease their pain somewhat by keeping the Flemunns who had been the day-to-day workers but at only two-thirds of their previous wages.

In the intervening years, Nickit had made some upgrades to Junkalot. He had organized the moon into four quadrants. Three of them were your basic junk-dumps, where you paid a standard disposal fee for never-to-be-used-again trash.

He'd organized the fourth quadrant into a reasonably profitable technology-based Pull & Pay site. You could find everything from entire obsolete spacecraft to hand-held communications and games there. The galaxy was full of folks who couldn't afford new ships and needed replacement parts for the junk-heaps they tried to keep running as best they could.

They could scavenge around the Techno-Trash quadrant and pull the necessary pieces, if they found any, and pay a negotiated price. Nickit kept the Flenumms employed in all of the quadrants but promoted a promising young foreman named Jayelliss from one of his manufacturing locations and placed him in charge of the Techno-Trash operation.

Jayelliss soon built up a database and knew the worth of any part on any craft. He also knew the worth of smaller electronic items usually only sought out by collectors or nostalgia buffs. Plus, he knew useless shit when he saw it and was willing to ship it over to another quadrant if no one had shown any interest in it after a year.

The partners would have to deal with Jayelliss to find what they needed.

As the video concluded, three specific images came up on the screen. The Voice informed them that those were the last remaining parts needed to get the Master Ship operational again.

"The ship is in a secure location that I have misted over. No one will ever find it unless I lead them to it. Once these missing parts are installed and operational, the ship will fly and is yours to do what you will.

"You are the first to have succeeded in getting this far. No one will come behind you to try to get to the location unless I find out that you somehow managed to fail in this final task, in which case I will restart the Search Notifications. But I do not believe that you will fail.

"I will keep occasional track of your progress, so don't worry about how to keep in touch. I will be back in touch with you when I deem it is necessary. Good luck."

"Well," John said after the video ended. "You feel more

at ease now, Shippewa? We're not taking you there to abandon you."

"Very much more at ease, John. Having now viewed the whole thing, I realize that if I am to get my ship, I have to help rescue her. She's sitting somewhere, unable to move, maybe for centuries, waiting for us to come along. Now may not be the best time to dawdle. Meehix? Ready when you are."

"Atta girl." Meehix patted the dashboard and smiled at her copilot. "I don't know, John. Giant froomivores, stinging gramodiatrons, succubi galore and virgin sacrifices, then war with wizards? Now, all we have to do is go dumpster-diving? Sounds a little anticlimactic to me."

"Well, when you put it like that." John laughed. "Got the coordinates?"

"Already punched in. Buckle up!"

Meehix maneuvered out of the docking station and hovered a little before heading out.

"Is that who I think it is?"

"I believe it might be."

They caught sight of a magnificent bird circling high above Castle Illusionor.

"Give him a fly-by," John requested.

Meehix rose and guided Ship into a wide circle around the bird, who now wore a golden medallion around its neck. The bird paused, spread its wings, and showed off the medallion as Shippewa nodded, and Jessup and the castle and planet Trimidoon were soon a speck in the distance behind them.

Trexit had been in better moods. He was sure that the card he'd given the two pain-in-everyone's-asses bounty hunters who called themselves the NutBusters hadn't been discarded and was still in their possession. However, the card had visited three planets and a space station since he'd given it to them in the bar on Zellion after their happy-sperm delivery and never stayed anywhere for more than two days.

He thought they'd have returned to their home base by now, but apparently, they were in high demand for their services or else were enjoying a sightseeing tour. He remained convinced that their home base was on station L-222 but hadn't located their exact address yet.

He was also still convinced that they were working with the non-listed cryo-prison escapee that the prison had hired him to track down, without drawing any attention to the fact that they'd had an escapee.

Doing as much research as possible, and half of his job was doing proper research, he'd narrowed his search down to two properties on L-222. Going on the assumption that the prisoner stayed at home while his two partners gallivanted off, he'd decided to take a low-risk, high-reward move.

That was why he was now sitting in the Tri-2 casino's buffet room with three of the cryo-prison guards. Trexit would be satisfied to re-acquire the prisoner and collect that paycheck, then catch up to the other two because *that* was when the bidding war would start. In the meantime, he had bills to pay.

The three prison guards were the only sentient beings working the shift when the escapee skipped off. The company couldn't fire them because that would announce to everyone that there'd been an escape. But they *could* be assigned to the most boring of details on the worst of shifts. Trexit had tracked them down. They all had vacation time saved up, and that was how he'd convinced Flots, Stemp, and Corky to join him on L-222.

"Here's the deal, guys." At this point, he knew it would be an easy sell because they'd already committed to coming this far. "Your escapee is at one of two locations a little ways away."

They nodded. All three knew that their reputations were on the line, not to mention that this could be their ticket to getting back on the gravy shifts.

"One location is a tiny dump of a house that needed total cleaning and fumigation after the recent occupant died."

Trexit had found this all out by having flirted with a three-legged real estate agent newbie named Brez. He also found out, after he'd plied her with a few drinks, that the shit-property and the one he was about to send the guards to were both owned by a gentleman named Frelo, who suffered an unfortunate demise.

"At the hands of two bounty hunters" was the only verifiable fact he had. That the escaped prisoner had teamed up with them was still a theory. Trexit had bribed his way into having been able to watch the casino's security tapes and knew who the two were.

"But you can only take one location at a time, and *this* address is much more to the escapee's tastes."

He slid a card across the table with the address on it. Either they would take it, or they wouldn't. If they took it,

Trexit would have the prisoner in his hands in the next couple of hours. Or he would be able to reset his focus on the tiny dump of a house that might be more than it looked like on the outside.

Corky picked up the card.

Okay. Now I know who's in charge.

"Corky, right?"

Corky nodded. Trexit kept his eyes moving to contact the other guards and reassure them that he wasn't leaving them out of the conversation.

"That address is the most likely location of the escaped prisoner. If we don't get him tonight," he held all three of their eyes at once, "I have four Crom Limeans keeping an eye on the other location," he lied. "They arrived this afternoon, and I pay them by the hour. No one is going anywhere from there until we hit the address on the card first. If he's not there, we'll get him tomorrow."

The guards exchanged glances that said *Damn. This dude is serious.*

"What do you need us to do?" Corky spoke for himself and the other two guards because they had all bought the pitch.

"Do you have explosives?"

"Well, we have blast-bangs." Corky wasn't expecting that question.

"You shouldn't need them," Trexit tried to calm him. "But we have one shot at this, and I wanted to make sure."

"Makes sense." Corky nodded. "Better to be prepared than not."

"Exactly." Trexit leaned back as if all the problems were

now solved and saw the others relax. "I have an agreement with the local police."

"Police?" Corky was suddenly nervous again.

"No big deal." Trexit leaned forward and made sure that he again had all of their undivided attention.

"What you three are about to do, to save your jobs and reputations, isn't exactly what most authorities would classify as being *legal*. Do you understand what I'm saying?"

"Maybe?" Corky was no surer than his partner guards, but it was up to him to ask for clarification as needed.

"What you are about to do is try to apprehend an escaped prisoner. A prisoner that no one can acknowledge has escaped. Correct?"

"With you so far." Corky nodded for all three of them.

"So, since you have no actual authority because this fucker doesn't even have a Crec Alert out on him," Trexit shifted to his most calming, reasonable voice, "the best thing to do is simply to knock on the front door."

"We can do that."

"I have verified the security system, so if no one answers the door, then the system will ask you a couple of questions."

"What kind of questions?" Corky had never been good at quizzes.

"You'll be the first to know. I'm familiar with this kind of system, so there will only be three questions. Things like your name, your birthdate, your first pet's name."

"I've never had a pet."

"Don't sweat it, Corky. I'm sure you'll be fine."

"What if I'm not fine?"

"Then you three can turn around and walk away. No damage done."

The three guards relaxed.

"Of course, you'll have wasted your vacation time unless you want to hit the casino, but then you'll return to your guard jobs in anticipation of being no better off than you have recently been."

Trexit let that sink in.

"Or," the tracker went on, "You can pull out and employ a couple of blast-bangs and storm in."

"That's not something we're authorized to do! We're only private prison guards!"

"Using up our vacation time," Stemp finally decided to chime in.

"Yeah, Stemp," Flots thought this was the right time to express an opinion of his own. "But vacations only last for thirty cycles, and that leaves us with eighty-seven cycles each year to work shit-shifts for the rest of our lives."

"Let me know when you're ready to hear me out." Trexit pretended that he had all the time in the world. He'd already set this up and didn't need the guards to go wimping out on him when he was this close.

The guards leaned their heads across the table and held a quick, whispered conference.

"Okay." Corky took the lead again. "What if we have to use the blast-bangs. Won't that set off all kinds of alarms?"

"It most certainly will." Trexit nodded. "I've arranged with the local authorities that no one will respond to the alarm for fifteen minutes. That gives you fifteen minutes to find the little fucker if he's hiding, or failing that, gather as much information as possible to find out where he might be."

"Fifteen minutes?" Corky wondered how big the house was that they would have to search in that short a time.

"I pushed for twenty, but they held firm at fifteen." Trexit sighed. "Cops aren't as easy to bribe as they used to be."

Half an hour later, Trexit had parked at a corner down the block. He watched the three guards approach the door and ready to speed off as soon as possible if things didn't work out quite according to plan.

They rang the bell.

Chuckie was in the front office doing some research when he was startled by the chimes. He wasn't expecting visitors. He checked the door's security cameras and saw three strangers, ugly ones at that, standing outside.

He shut down Mixie and headed for the painting in the kitchen as quickly and quietly as possible. The NutBusters knew this day would eventually come but thought they might have a little more time. They thought wrong.

Kicking the bottom of the painting, he slipped into the gym. He hadn't gotten the damage repaired yet from his earlier weapons practice, but at least now he knew that his second option would allow him not to go down without a fight.

He would much prefer to succeed at his first option, which was to hide like a flame in hell.

"What planet is Chuck Norris from?"

The three guards looked at each other in confusion as the AI voice asked them from hidden speakers.

"How the fuck should we know?" Corky demanded.

"What the fuck is a Chuck Norris?" Stemp tossed in.

"Wrong," the voice informed them. *"Two answers to the same question counts as two answers. Therefore you have one question remaining."*

Chuck Norris doesn't come from a planet. Planets come from Chuck Norris. Chuckie smiled as he listened to the exchange from a security panel in the gym. He was quite proud of having come up with *that* question.

"What is a flumperistical equation?"

"A what?"

"Three wrong answers. The police are on their way. I suggest running as your best option."

The guards chose blast-bangs instead. Although Chuckie hadn't gotten around to installing video screens in the gym to monitor the front door, he could still hear the action. It didn't sound like friendly fire.

He turned off the volume on the security panel speakers and hoped the police were on their way. All he had to do was wait out the invaders.

CHAPTER TWENTY

Trexit watched from his car on the corner as the blast-bang went off. It only dented the metal door, but the wooden frame that held it was now a pile of splinters. The three guards rushed in.

Chuckie knew that hindsight was a fool's regret, but he wished he'd gotten around to extending the security camera's feeds back to the gym. He also realized that it really wouldn't have made much difference. There were no cameras inside their home office, so once the intruders were inside, there wouldn't have been much for him to see.

He stood still at the door that doubled as a painting on the kitchen side and listened as he heard the guards tear the house apart. He knew from the front door cameras that there were three people, but in his state of panic, the audio feed sounded like an entire platoon had rushed in. Not that he had any idea how many men made up a platoon.

Having had to dash to the secret rooms, he now did a mental inventory of what equipment remained in the front office. A lot of high-end electronics in the front data cabinet, but nothing personal lying around that could identify or incriminate any of the partners or enable anyone to track them down any further. *Hell, even I don't know where Meehix and John are right now.*

Their safe was in the office across from their home gym and hidden by the kitchen painting. They kept a fair amount of cash and valuables in the safe, but if the intruders discovered the painting door, the valuables wouldn't do Chuckie much good. He'd be too dead to sell or spend any of it.

He didn't have his watch on, but shit, it had to have been more than five minutes by now. Where the fuck were the police? As quietly as he could, he picked up the one gun he'd learned how to use and crept to a far corner where he sat on a weight bench, the weapon ready on his lap.

Breathe, Chuckie. Breathe. He took a few short, steady breaths and felt slightly better. The smashing up of the house was still audible but still safely on the kitchen side of the painting.

Of course, if they accidentally kicked the painting's bottom frame, then it was game over. He tried a few longer, deeper breaths, trying to calm himself further, and suddenly felt much better.

He heard shouting from the kitchen, audible but muffled. It sounded like they were now splitting up to check the two wings that ran off it from each side. A few more deep breaths led to him feeling more relaxed.

No, relaxed isn't the right word. He tried to identify what he felt as he thought of what they would find in the rooms down the wing where he and John stayed. John always kept his room fairly tidy, so it wouldn't take them long to search it.

Chuckie's room would delay them for a fair amount of time, partly from how messy it was and partly because there was always the possibility that they'd stumble onto his stash of porn, and that could distract them for days.

Another couple of breaths, and he was beginning to get annoyed because he still couldn't identify the feelings he was having. He'd never been much of a Zen kind of guy, and deep breathing exercises had always left him feeling that he'd wasted several minutes of valuable time.

Still, a few minutes ago he'd been in a near-blind panic, and now, his mind was wandering and wondering what they would find down in the other wing. The wing that was occupied by…

Meehix! I'm feeling Meehix!

More precisely, he was *smelling* Meehix.

Her and her pheromones. He smiled.

Chuckie had always treated the workout room like some kind of infectious disease lab and avoided it like the plague, but now began to understand where his feelings came from.

He had no way of knowing that Meehix usually stuck with the cardio machines when she'd worked out but often used the bench to work with light weights to help improve her reflex reaction times. She must have worked up a sweat enough times to have left a variety of her scents behind.

"Two guys down this side," Stemp reported when he and Flots met back up with Corky in the kitchen.

"Just a chick living down my wing." Corky should have

been feeling more pissed than he was, but she must be a good-smelling chick.

"Freeze!" a voice ordered from the hallway leading back up to the front rooms.

"We're fucked," Corky mumbled.

"That's exactly what you are," the voice continued. "Hands where we can see them!"

Three officers approached with guns drawn. The damage they'd witnessed at the front door when they'd finally arrived convinced them that this was no ordinary B & E.

None of the three guards were famous for being quick thinkers. Even if they were, it would be hard to explain that they were spending their vacation time trying to track down a prisoner who had escaped, especially since there was no record that any such occurrence happened.

They kept their hands up, and Corky gave it a shot.

"Officer?"

"Brockler."

"Officer Brockler. The three of us had just passed by when we heard an explosion and rushed back to see the door blown in."

"Being the good citizens that you are, you hurried in to, what, apprehend the bad guys who had blown in half a wall?"

"We're guards, sir." Stemp backed Corky's play. "Can we show you our badges?"

Brockler allowed them to slowly pull their badges out, inspected them, and was not impressed.

"These are for the private cryo-prison. I thought they didn't need any guards."

"Only a minimum staff, sir." Corky added, "Though we're not officers such as yourselves, we are still officially employed on the side of justice. We were all here on vacation."

"The casino," Flots picked up when Corky ran out of narrative. "We needed a walk to try to break the rhythm of a losing streak."

"All right." Brockler nodded. "That part I can believe."

A distant *thud* and clatter suddenly sounded from somewhere in the house.

"Jenson. Make sure these three stay put."

Officer Jenson kept his gun in plain view as Brockler and the other officer searched first one wing and then the other.

"Nothing?" Corky asked when they returned.

"Probably something just fell over from the mess down in the rooms."

"I guess we didn't get here in time." Corky looked sincerely disappointed.

"Let's all of us take a ride down to the station, shall we? Maybe that will give the three of you time to get your story straight. Junior," Brockler addressed the third officer. "Get a crew to seal up the door, at least secure enough to keep other burglars out until the owners get home."

Trexit had watched the action from a safe distance. Once it was clear that the prison guards had failed, he cursed and drove off. Maybe the other house *was* more impressive on the inside than it appeared to be from the street.

Half an hour later, the front door had been temporarily secured, with crime scene tape also strung across it.

An hour later, Chuckie finally came to, lying on the floor next to the weight bench, a pheromone-induced smile still on his face.

To their surprise, there was only one galactic Gate between the wizard's castle on Trimidoon and the planet Montyore and its junk moon.

"It's funny," John observed as Meehix flew. "These Gates are almost like railroad tracks dividing some towns back on Earth."

"How's that?"

They were in a safe, clear, flying space and Meehix could relax for a little while.

"One side of the train tracks, or in this instance, Gates," John mused, "was always the good side of town. The other side, well, that's the side where me and most of my friends came from."

"If you put it like that," she was slightly taken aback with the realization of how privileged her upbringing had been, compared with John's. "I guess I've spent most of my life on the *right* side of the Gates."

"That's not your fault!" he hastened to reassure her since she now wore a slight, sad frown. "You can't help where you were born."

"No, I can't." She straightened her shoulders. "But I *can* make up for the way I took it all for granted by helping those who didn't have it so easy. That's kind of what we're hoping to do, right?"

"Exactly that." He smiled at her. "We're gonna get the

missing pieces, find this legendary phat-ass ship, and wreak havoc on anyone who stands in our way on our oh-so-righteous quest to defend those born on the wrong side of the Gates."

"Sure." She smiled. "What the fuck else do we have to do?"

They hit the Gate, and a few hours later the guidance system led them to a docking station on Montyore.

"Nice flying, there, Tex." John unbuckled.

"I hope that's a compliment."

"This time, yes it is." He took in the station. "Anyone got any vibes, yea or nay, on finding a room for the night and hitting the moon first thing tomorrow?"

"My sensors are picking up a gentle hum from the ground," Ship informed them. **"Does that count as a good vibe?"**

"Close enough for me." John was satisfied.

They tested their HLT comm-bands to ensure they were still functioning as Meehix and John packed their overnight bags.

"Let us know if anything goes amiss, Ship. Meehix and I will find the closest room available so that we can be back here in a moment if you sense any danger."

They were halfway down the ramp when Meehix stopped.

"I can't do it, John."

"Can't do what?" He turned.

"Can't come this far, and be this close, and pretend that I can get a good night's sleep until we've succeeded. We have to get to the moon first before we can relax."

"Women's intuition?"

"You're the one who asked about *vibes*, and I just got one. Does that count?"

"Close enough for me. It's two hours to the moon." He headed back up the ramp. "I'll fly, and you rest your eyes. You've been piloting for quite a stretch and need some rest."

"Deal."

"That was a short stay," Shippewa welcomed them back.

"None of us is going to be able to rest, Ship," John answered, "until we get you your own ship."

"Next stop, Junkalot!"

They didn't need a guidance system to find the moon. Junkalot never closed because there was never a shortage of incoming refuse. Its lit-up surface ensured it was visible. John headed out as Meehix closed her eyes and tried to relax.

Drawing closer to the moon, John saw that each of the four quadrants had distinctive lights. *Pale blue*, he remembered from the video. Pale blue lights lit the Pull & Pay quadrant. Something about the illumination made it easier to read part numbers.

Bright white lights marked the landing area itself. No one wanted to have ships carrying shit crash into each other as they came in. At this time of the evening, there were plenty of spaces available, and John landed as close as he could to what looked like a brown cinder-block office about the size of a double-wide trailer back in Albuquerque.

"Wait here," he told Meehix, who had taken a power nap during the short trip. "Let me check it out."

"Okay."

Meehix stretched and got her bearings as John headed inside. After he hadn't returned in twenty minutes, she went into Cargo and weaponed up, just in case.

Ten minutes later, she headed down the ramp and toward the office with the intent to rescue her partner from whatever mess he'd gotten himself into. She'd reached the office door and was debating whether to knock or burst in when the door flew open, and John rushed out and damned near knocked her down.

She managed to keep her feet and was ready to fire as soon as she figured out who her target should be.

"No, no!" John steadied her. "This place is sooo cooolll!"

She thought that maybe her first shot should go directly between John's eyes.

"Sorry!" He saw her gun. "No need for weapons!" he reassured her. "Although we might want to change into some rubber boots and anti-static gloves."

He led her back onto Shippewa. "No danger here," he explained as Meehix joined him with no questions asked. They searched for the boots and gloves that she'd inventoried, packed, and stacked in boxes along the cargo space's walls what felt like a decade earlier.

"When," she briefly paused in her search, "have we ever *not* been in danger?"

"Good point," John admitted. "But there's no danger here unless we brought it with us, so we should be safe."

"Famous last words."

"Found the gloves!" John shouted.

"Found the boots!" Meehix shouted a moment later. "Damn, these look clunky!"

They did their best to glove and boot up as John explained what he'd learned in the office.

"We found the right quadrant!"

John was so excited that when he tried to put on a pair of gloves, they ended up on the wrong hands, and he was in a quandary as to why they felt so awkward. He figured it out before she could give him one of her patented "How stupid can one Kdackan be?" looks.

"What's his name…Jayelliss wasn't in, but he has everything so well-inventoried that this should be a cinch."

"Define cinch?" The gloves fit like a second skin, but the boots… "What the fuck is up with the boots?" She slipped them on. "Are we expecting a flood?"

"No, no, nothing like that." John had pulled his boots on. "But we're going to search through piles of old electronics."

"And that matters, why?" although she *did* like the neon tri-color of her boots.

"Because we don't want to damage anything in the piles of electronics that we search through." John thought his answer should've been obvious.

"Okaaay," the answer wasn't apparent to Meehix. "So, the boots will be awkward enough to prevent me from stomping something into little pieces?"

"No." John realized that he had to tone his excitement down a few notches. "We're going to search through piles of some ancient equipment. Electromagnetic charges could render them useless. The rubber boots and the gloves will let us search without damaging their programming or rendering them useless."

Now that she was booted and gloved up, she checked

her look in one of the cargo bay's reflective walls and decided that she had looked worse.

"Further explanation is now allowed." She smiled at him. "What's next?"

"Cool colors on the boots."

John had learned enough to know that now and then, a compliment was in order, whether it was to further an agenda or simply because it was the truth. It drew a smile, so he made a mental note to remember that it had been a lesson worth using again if an occasion called for it.

He showed her a printout that he'd gotten from the office and laid it out for her to look over. It showed the location of the office and where they were parked. And the location of two objects they needed to find.

"Everything here is old technology," he tried to explain. "Maybe only forty years old, in Kdack years. But it's older than Stonehenge in electronic years, which makes it all on the edge of being ancient."

"Pretend that I've never heard of Kdack years before, and whatever the fuck stone hinges are," she took in the printout and studied it. "Are there hinges on stone doors that we'll need to push open?"

"No stone doors, that's for sure. *I hope.* But there are two ships that we need to find."

Even though Jayelliss hadn't been in the office, when John showed the clerk, a helpful little creature, what the video from the Voice had listed as what they were looking for, the clerk knew exactly what they needed and gave him directions and three tools he would need to pull them. He'd return the tools and negotiate the pay part when they got back to the office.

"One ship is the *Xpior*," he pointed to a red X on the printout. "In the front cabin's console, or control panel, there should be a yellow button we need to push, and that will release a floppy disk."

"A floppy what?"

"This is old technology, so you'll have to trust me." John would have explained more, but he had never handled a floppy disk before. He hoped that it resembled what his computer classes had taught him and that it would be a three-by-three-inch piece of plastic.

Meehix nodded, trusting him to at least have half a clue of what he was talking about.

"The blue X," John went on, "is another ship called the *BeenandBack*. Apparently, the ship made it to Been, wherever the fuck that is, but never made it Back, wherever the fuck that was supposed to be."

"Junkalot sounds like it was appropriately named."

"And," John smiled, "the clerk informed me that if you stay upwind of the other three quadrants, it smells better than space station Nevera."

"Sounds like a good reason not to get lost."

"My thoughts, exactly."

The partners slapped gloved hands and headed toward the front cabin, where John suddenly paused with a look of realization. "Oh, fuck. Change in plans. Meehix, you have to stay here."

"The hell you say!"

"I *do* say." John looked her in the eyes and gave her what he hoped was a firm but reassuring smile. "Our HLT comm-sticks are all still functional, right?"

He didn't seem like he was in any kind of mood for her

to argue with, so he and Meehix and Ship tested them and said hello to each other.

"All right, then," John went on. "Ship?"

"Yes, John?"

"As long as Meehix or I remain alive, we will never abandon you. Got that?"

"Thank you, John. That's nice to hear."

"Meehix?"

"Yes, John?" She followed Shippewa's lead. *Damn, I love it when he sounds like he knows what he's doing.*

"I will keep in constant contact, all right? I don't think this is a trap in any way, shape, or form, but there have been one or two hundred times in my life when I've been wrong. So, if I'm wrong on this one—Oh shit!" he pointed behind Meehix. "Down there on the floor! Grab it, grab it, grab it!"

Meehix panicked and spun, bending to snatch up what John was frantically pointing at.

John reached out and grabbed a solid handful of Meehix's bent-over blue ass and hurried down the ramp.

"Keep in touch!" He laughed and shouted as he disappeared into piles of junk.

"Not fair!" she shouted knowing that it would come in loud and clear through their joint HLTs.

"Who said life was fair?" he shouted as he ran. "If you promise to stay with Ship, I promise to keep in touch with every step!"

"The next grope is mine!" she shouted back.

Through Ship's viewport, she could see that John had already disappeared amid the piles of junk.

"All right, Ship," Meehix settled into the pilot's seat. "If he so much as stubs a toe, then you and I are out of here faster than he can say *ouch*."

They kept their comm-sticks on, and even though John didn't give a running commentary, they could hear him as he made his way between assorted piles of junk. He carried the loaner tools in one side pocket—a four-in-one screw-driver, a small pair of wire snips, and a pair of needle-nose pliers. In another pocket, he carried a small but powerful flashlight.

"I found *Xpior*. Damn, it's old."

"Can you get in?"

"Since the doors are missing, I'd say yes. It has an attached ladder leading up and not a ramp. It's only a ten-foot climb, and it seems sturdy enough."

John was in the cockpit a minute later and pulled out the flashlight. A lot of the control panel was already stripped, including the steering mechanism, but the yellow button in the middle seemed to be undisturbed. It was stubborn, but he was eventually able to punch it in and was rewarded by the appearance of a black and white, flat plastic square.

"It's not very heavy."

"What isn't?"

"Oh, sorry." He'd forgotten that he had no video on him. "I got the floppy disk. Seems to be undamaged. Heading back to the ground now."

Reaching the ground, he consulted the map. "If the printout is right, the *BeenandBack* should be about ten minutes ahead."

"Roger that. No sign of wildlife anywhere?" Meehix was surprised that he hadn't encountered any scurrying creatures.

"None yet. Oh shit!"

"What shit? Talk to me, John."

"Kdack shit! There's a whole pile of old Kdack crap."

"How do you know it's from Kdack?"

"There's a sign. I can't read the writing, but there's a diagram of a sun with nine balls circling it, and the third one is bright blue. That sounds like Kdack 3a doesn't it?"

"There could be a lot of suns with nine planets orbiting it." Meehix was more aware of the vastness of the galaxy than John was."

"Yea, sure." he sifted through the top layer. "But how many have video cassettes of *My Favorite Martian?* Or *Mork and Mindy?* Or, of course, *Alf?* It's like a TV alien triple-play. I don't see any *Star Trek* though. That's curious."

"Can any of those help us get the big ship running?"

"Probably not," he admitted.

"Okay, then move on."

John did as instructed. "I wonder how they made their way from Earth to a galactic trash heap?"

"The same way we did." She thought the answer was obvious. "Someone flew them here."

"All right, but by who and why?"

"That's a question for another day."

"Roger. Found the *BeenandBack*. Again, no doors, but it does have a ramp."

"Be careful."

"Will do."

His entry into the cockpit was as uneventful as his last one had been. He found what he was looking for right away. It was a unit, eight inches across, ten inches deep, and four inches high, mounted under the console panel.

What he most needed was inside, and from the video the Voice provided, it would resemble an 8-track cassette. However, he'd take the whole unit in case they needed it for parts later on.

"Found it."

He had to lie on his back to unscrew the mount. Freeing it and allowing it to drop gently, he reached farther and cut the wires as close to the panel as he could to keep the maximum length of wires as possible.

"Heading back."

His return to Ship was as uneventful as his journey into the yard had been. He set his prizes down on the dash, popping the 8-track out.

"Seems undamaged."

"These," Meehix was skeptical, "are what we need to get the biggest, baddest, ship ever created up and running?"

"That's the rumor." John understood her doubts. "I think the odds are pretty slim that if the ship even exists, that it can do little more than blow up a small asteroid. These really are obsolete and the equipment back then tended to break down a lot."

"Can I hurt Chuckie," Meehix was hoping, "when we get back, and this all turns out to be some kind of cosmic practical joke?"

"You'll have to get in line."

John headed into the office, returned the tools, and bargained for what he hoped was a reasonable price for his items. Sighing as if John had just taken him to the cleaners, the clerk signed the receipt, and John and crew went on their way.

"Jayelliss, it's Grundin out on Junkalot. You'll never guess how much a couple of suckers just paid for two little pieces."

"Think it's safe to get a room on Montyore now, Meehix? I think we could both use a good rest."

"We got what we needed, so sure."

She flew them back to the planet. They locked up their newly acquired prized possessions, packed up enough weapons to get them through any assault in the middle of the night, and crashed at the closest, moderately priced hotel available.

In the morning, John connected Heemix through the hotel's system and found a message from Chuckie waiting for him.

> **Fortress breached. Hiding where Meehix sweats. Come retrieve me. We gotta go. Where are my manners? Come retrieve me, please.**

John responded without a moment's hesitation.

Stay safe. Five feats successful! On our way home for dumbass retrieval before final Phat-ass acquisition.

"Slight change of plans," he said as Meehix finally started to stir. *Damn, that girl sleeps hard and wakes up slow.*

"What now?" She yawned.

"Heading home. Chuckie needs us."

She was out of bed and ready to go in five minutes.

"He didn't give many details," he filled her in as they rushed and were relieved to find Ship right where they'd left her, "but someone invaded our home and Chuckie's hiding."

"Hiding where?"

"If I had to guess, I'd say in the gym. You do tend to work up quite a sweat when you're in there."

"It'd be a waste of time if I didn't, right?" She strapped into the pilot's seat.

"Right."

"What about the big ship?"

"We still have to wait for the Voice to tell us where to find it, but I don't see the hurry, now. We fulfilled all five of the feats, so it'll still be there whenever we get around to it. Chuckie first. It'd be a very boring galaxy without the little fucker."

"Agreed. L-222, here we come."

CHAPTER TWENTY-ONE

Chuckie got the message and breathed his first real sigh of relief in quite some time. He was still in the hidden rooms. The office had plenty enough of the food they'd stocked up on. Whenever he felt himself edging toward another blind-panic, he would find another place in the gym where Meehix had sweated and would deep-breathe himself into a much calmer, occasionally near-comatose, mood.

The audio to the front door was still available through the security panel, but he'd left it off the rest of the day of the invasion, in case one of the assholes was still hanging out and might hear it coming from behind the painting in the kitchen.

He spent the first night sleeping on a mat on the gym side of the painting, listening for any sound that might indicate someone still inside the house. The night passed in sleepless silence, so he risked turning the sound on again late the next morning, just in time to hear a familiar voice pouting.

"Oh, come on, Chuckie. How am I supposed to

know what the answers are? I was in the neighborhood and thought I'd swing by for a quickie. Come on, Chuckie-wuckie, just a little mid-day snack for your Vixaleen?"

Why does God hate me?

There was no way he could risk going to the door to let her in. For all he knew, someone still had the house under surveillance, but she was a persistent little succubus. He could even hear her trying the office window in case he had forgotten to lock it the last time she'd snuck out, ass first.

"Can I help you, miss?" came an unfamiliar voice.

"I don't know. Can you?"

In his mind, Chuckie could envision her smile as she advanced on the stranger, breasts out, front and center. If the stranger was like most other mortals, the guy didn't stand a chance.

"Are you here to visit someone?"

"I am now." She had such a seductive voice.

"I mean," the stranger struggled for coherence, *which would be hard,* Chuckie thought, *because she probably has her tongue firmly planted in his ear by now.* "I mean, are you here to visit someone specific? Do you...do you...do you know who lives here?"

"Chuckie? Sure. He's a little guy. Well, a little guy when it comes to height, but big where it matters, if you know what I mean...oh, my, so are you!"

Her patented crotch-grab. Lucky bastard. But Chuckie was pleased with her compliment.

"Please tell me you have a car? Please, please, pretty please tell me you have a car."

"I do," the stranger was ten seconds away from being in his back seat.

"My hero!"

"But first, you need to tell me. You know who lives here, and he knows you, right?"

"I know him really well. But not as well as I'd like to know you."

"He's not letting you in?"

"That's only because he must not be home. Look at me. How could anyone know I was here for a visit and *not* let me in?"

"Ooh, that's nice…Oh, oh, oh, that's very nice."

"Where's your car? Please tell me that it's close and has a backseat."

"Parked on the corner, and yes, a very nice backseat. Oh, yes, a very nice backseat. But please, before we go there, can I at least ask your name?"

"Of course you can, Mr. Silly. My name is Vixaleen. May I have the pleasure of knowing yours?"

"Trexit…my friends call me Trexit."

"Nice name, Trexit. I'm now your *friend*, so that's what I'll call you. Just wondering," Chuckie heard her giggle, "what do your *enemies* call you?"

"It's not important *what* they call me. It's *where* they call me from."

"I like a man of mystery. *Where* do they call you *from?*"

"Usually," to Chuckie, it sounded like he was bragging, "from the grave."

The audio went quiet again as the voices faded off down the block.

Chuckie was sure that no one was still in the house

because who, in possession of a dick, wouldn't have opened the door to the red seductress? It also convinced him that Trexit—*Trexit? Yeah, he said his name was Trexit*—hadn't shown up at his door by accident.

He took a few moments to find a pheromone to steady himself, then fired up Mixie, was again thrilled with the connections the equipment in the front office cabinet provided, and sent a message to John.

House under surveillance. Dock and comm-stick me before leaving Ship.

John and Meehix took turns piloting, each of them snatching a nap or two during the day and a half it took to get back to their home base on L-222. They had passed through the third Gate and were both well-rested with Meehix behind the controls as they closed in on home.

"I wish he'd given us more details."

"Me too." John opened up Heemix, hoping for some kind of a connection that he knew wouldn't come until they'd docked. "If someone broke in, and he's hiding, I guess he wanted to get the message off as quick and short as he could so that no one could trace it."

"I guess that makes sense. Who could it be?"

"Do you want me to list our enemies in alphabetical or chronological order?"

"Point taken."

Space Station L-222 came into view.

"You and your bolas." John remembered their first bounty hunting job.

"They would have worked fine if you hadn't ripped his arms off."

"Oh, so it's all *my* fault." He laughed.

"It *all* must be your fault," she smiled. "Everyone on this ship except you knows that I'm perfect."

"Ship? Is that true?"

"Parents should never ask a child to take sides in an argument. I hear it is very traumatic."

"I think you shouldn't dock in our reserved space."

"You think that why?" She closed in on the station.

"They, whoever *they* are, found out where we live." John was reasoning out loud as the thoughts came to him. "If they found *that* out, who's to say they haven't discovered our berth and are staking that out too?"

"That's scary." Meehix headed for the far side of the dock and landed between a couple of very large pleasure-cruiser ships that shielded them from most observers.

John was finally able to get a connection and received Chuckie's latest message. He turned the screen so Meehix could see it too.

"You take it, John. No point in all three of us shouting at him at the same time. I'm going back to Cargo to sort out some armaments."

He turned on his comm-stick and started the tedious task.

"Jojacko to Chuck Norris. Answer. Jojacko to Chuck Norris. Answer. Jojacko to Chuck Norris…"

Meehix returned with enough weapons to overthrow a small planet.

"Jojacko to Chuck Norris. Answer. Jojacko to Chuck Norris. Answer…"

"Chuck Norris to Jojacko. What is the body part that Chuck Norris aims for on his second kick?"

"Trick question. After the first kick from Chuck Norris, there *are* no body parts left to kick."

"Get me the fuck out of here!"

"Aw." John smiled at Meehix. "We missed you too. Give us a plan."

Chuckie kept it short, signed off, and hunkered down.

"Yes?" Trexit had needed to cool his heels for the last day and a half back in his room at the Tri-2-Beatum casino's hotel. Fortunately, he'd had a companion. Unfortunately, she was currently on top of him and draining even more energy, which was why he hadn't been able to keep up surveillance and had to call in some help.

"The ship has arrived. It's docked somewhere in the station," Dedlion reported.

"I can confirm that." Stingrip joined the call.

"If a ship arrives," Dedlion went on, "it also has to depart eventually. Do you want us on the ground, or should we hover and wait so we can cripple it when it departs, then bring all of its occupants back?"

There was no one better to subcontract part of a job out to than a couple of mercenary Crom Limeans. Trexit was glad he'd called them in. He'd provided them with videos of the bounty hunters' ship. The card he'd given the duo when he presented himself as T.R.Exit must have still been in their possession because it had shown that they seemed to be on a trek back home finally.

"Hover for as long as it takes. Then cripple the ship and bring the occupants back, preferably alive, but if dead, then at least in a recognizable form. Otherwise, they're worthless."

"Copy that," Dedlion responded.

"I'll do what I can here on the ground. Whether you apprehend them or I do, your pay will be the same."

"It's always a pleasure doing business with you, Trexit." Dedlion signed off.

"Easy money, eh?" Dedlion switched over to the open channel he shared with Stingrip.

"Hover and apprehend," Stingrip replied. "Trexit always keeps his requests so simple."

"I think that *I* am going to hover for a bit," Vixaleen said as she rose above the bed where she had entertained and fed off Trexit since she'd met him outside of Chuckie-wuckie's house. He needed some nourishment, and she knew that she needed to back off. Otherwise, she would never be able to visit him again, and he was definitely worth a revisit.

The first thing that John and Meehix had done after docking and talking with Chuckie was to summon the police to meet them at the gate of the docking station where they had landed. They stood at the end of the ramp, having changed into the most *proper* outfits they could find back in Cargo.

"What the fuck has happened to our house?" Meehix started in on the two policemen who had answered the call. "We try to take a few days of vacation," she railed, "and now we hear that someone ransacked our home? What kind of space station do you run here?"

"We run a very clean and safe station, miss," Officer Vanno replied.

"Meehix! No Miss or Mrs. necessary! Just Meehix! Call in some assistance! We need a police escort to get us back to our house and pack up a few items so that we can put this pathetic excuse of a station behind us!"

She turned to John, her rage still unchecked. "Really, Jo! You told me it would be fun here! You told me it would be a safe place to live! We're gone for a couple of days, and our house gets ransacked? I may never trust your judgment again!" She stormed off down the ramp.

Officer Vanno and his partner thought they were responding to a simple B & E escort. Now they were in the middle of a promotional nightmare for L-222 that involved a very well-dressed, obviously rich, influential couple, as well as a domestic dispute. That wouldn't look good in the tabloids.

They looked at John for advice. John gave them a world-weary shrug.

"I have to deal with her every day of my life. All you have to do is deal with her for a couple of hours, and we'll be gone. Give her what she wants, and you'll never have to deal with her again."

"Thank you."

Officer Vanno got on his radio. Five minutes later, a four-car police escort showed up.

Meehix remained on the sidewalk, stomping around with a look on her face that all of the officers did their best to avoid, lest it turn them to dust.

Two officers were dispatched into the ship and came out carrying a three-by-six-foot ornate chest that they loaded into a van and followed the lead car. John and the wild woman sat in the back seat as they went to their property.

Their home had a front door in near shambles, with police tape crisscrossing in front of it.

John and Meehix stepped out of the lead car and surveyed the damage as the rest of the police brigade pulled up behind them.

"I want what's left of the door opened," Meehix commanded, "and my family's treasured chest carried inside and set down. Then I want everyone else to back the fuck off as I gather a few cherished belongings!"

"You heard what the—" Vanno caught himself just in time and continued. "You heard what Meehix asked."

They removed the tape and forced what was left of the door aside. The chest was carried in and deposited in the hallway. Every other officer then stepped aside as Meehix and John entered.

John turned back to address their escorts.

"We are going to take the chest through what's left of our home. Once we load up what's left of our necessary possessions into it, we may need some assistance to get it back onboard our ship."

"Yes, John," Officer Vanno assured him. "Take your time. We are truly sorry that this damage occurred. I will make sure that a thorough investigation follows."

John nodded his thanks, grabbed hold of the chest, and dragged it behind Meehix as she stormed down the hall. She didn't stop until she'd reached the kitchen and turned right. John followed her.

If anyone had followed them in and stood in the foyer, they would have a straight line of sight down the hallway, so the partners had to get out of sight before they could drop the act.

"Rich bitch personified!" John congratulated her.

"I don't know." She shrugged. "I'm a little out of practice."

"They really tore the place apart, didn't they?"

"Yeah, they did. Oh shit!"

"What?"

"Find Chuckie and get him into the chest. I have to check my room!" She hustled down her wing.

John peeked around the corner. No police were standing anywhere in sight. *I wouldn't either if I was in your shoes after Meehix's display.*

John walked across the kitchen, toe-tapped the painting, stepped through, closed the door behind him, and shouted.

"Come out, come out, wherever you are!"

"About fucking time."

"They really tore the place up, didn't they?"

"That's nothing. Someone was lurking outside and prevented me from having an afternoon session with Vixaleen."

"Aw, man. That hurts. Any idea who they were?"

"All I know is that the first three got hauled off to jail, but since they didn't actually manage to steal anything, they're probably already out on bail for a simple B & E. The guy at the door who interrupted Vixaleen was someone different. Trexit. I heard him tell her that his name is Trexit. I don't know if he was working with the first three clowns or is separate. Either way, we gotta blow this joint."

"Yeah, I was afraid of that." John looked around at the gym for the last time.

"I got Mixie and our cash and valuables from the safe in this bag," he held up a large gym bag. "The only other thing I want is a Meakum router and booster from the front cabinet. Maybe you can grab it on our way out."

"That's a blue unit, right?"

"Should be easy to spot. I think it's on the top shelf. Speaking of getting me out, what's the plan?"

"The good news is that we have a police escort back to Ship. The bad news is that we're going to have to carry you out in a trunk. Two occupants come in, and two occupants leave. We don't want to risk anyone spotting you."

"Fine." He sighed. "Where's the trunk?"

"It's off to the side in the kitchen. I'll make sure the coast is clear and hustle you out."

"Where's Meehix?"

"Checking out the damage in her room."

"Fuck, what a mess!" Meehix had found slashed-up clothes, a vast array of smashed-up beauty products, and "No...No, no, no, no!"

She started seriously scrambling through everything, searching now in earnest.

"Yes!" Under a pillow tossed into a corner, she found a small wooden box that held something much more important than some stupid jewelry. She opened the box and was thrilled to discover that they were still there and undamaged.

They didn't look like much, just a couple of plugs made out of a special fabric that someone could insert into their nose. They were No-No-Sniffs, a common enough item on her home planet of Dolurulod that were nearly impossible to find anywhere else.

Over time, evolution had allowed the men on Dolurulod to build up a partial immunity to the pheromones released by the females during sex. Otherwise, the population would have dwindled to nothing. That didn't mean they were wholly unaffected.

Once the pheromones kicked in, males of most other species would pass out within minutes, which led to a lot of snoring men and very frustrated women. *Is it any wonder I need to keep the batteries charged in my please-me toys?*

Someday, if things ever settled down, she wanted to have sex with John. Long, sweet, pleasurable sex. Without the no-no-sniffs, she knew that would never be possible. She set the box in her bag, decided it was the only thing left in her room that she truly needed, and headed out to find John, who was standing next to the chest in the kitchen.

"Got everything we need?"

"Sure do. I don't know why we need *all* of this junk, but I got it."

A small kick from inside the chest informed them that it was not soundproof.

"I gotta grab one more thing from the data cabinet. Can you get someone in here to help carry it out?"

"Not a problem." Meehix headed toward the front door and donned her bitch-mode persona. "Can two of you dipheads make yourselves useful and help us with the chest? Be careful. It's fragile!"

Two of the burlier officers hustled to the kitchen and delivered Chuckie into a waiting van.

John found and disconnected the Meakum equipment

without an issue. Twenty minutes later they were back on board Shippewa, Chuckie stored in the cargo area until they were safely off. They didn't trust that there might not be a sneak attack still waiting for them.

Shouts of sincere-sounding apologies were still echoing as they closed the ramp.

"Think they'll take the time to give us a bad review?" Officer Vanno's partner asked as they waved and kept their fake smiles firmly in place.

"Those two?" He dropped his smile as the ship pulled out. "I doubt they rate us important enough to bother with. Besides, they're too busy bitching about each other to have the time to bitch about anyone else."

Meehix got behind the controls and guided them out, and away from the first home the three of them had ever shared. Once they'd cleared L-222's airspace, John unstrapped and started back to release Chuckie. That's when the first missile struck, rocking Ship and sending John to the deck.

"Talk to us, Ship!" John shouted as he gained his feet.

"Glancing blow. No damage."

"How many?"

"Only two that I can see."

"Figure-eight with a one-eighty loop, Meehix."

"I can fly, John, but I've never been in a dogfight! You need to take over!"

Meehix sped out and lifted herself off the seat so John could slide in under and behind her. He reached past her right elbow, brushing her breast along the way, and slipped his hand into the right control as she pulled hers out.

Another glancing blow shook them again and caused

Meehix to wiggle a little on his lap. He yanked down and did a hard right, throwing her against his arm. She tried to right herself, squirming a little more as they worked to swap left hands also.

"Orange button! Hit the orange button on the right!"

Since Meehix was the only one with a right hand free, she found the button and hit it as hard as possible. A dense cloud suddenly enveloped them, and John managed to yank the ship into a sharp vertical rise.

They had barely cleared the top of the cloud that the orange button had released when their left hands got stuck together in the left control. The struggle of each of them trying to free their hands simultaneously caused Ship to do an immediate one-eighty and dive back into the cloud while also doing three-sixty spins.

While surging downward and spinning, they heard two explosions at the same time that Meehix freed her hand and spun off John's lap and onto the floor, grabbing for anything she could to keep herself from tumbling further.

They emerged from the bottom of the cloud. John now had full control and brought them out of the dive and the spin.

"I heard explosions, Ship! Damage report!"

"**It wasn't us!**" Ship was happy to inform them.

John pulled away and spun so they could look back at the cloud and their pursuers. The cloud was still thick and visible. A short distance away and on opposite sides of the cloud, they could see smaller balls of flames and smoke.

"The fuckers shot themselves!"

"**That is my guess also, John. Who would be dumb**

enough to fire into a cloud without knowing where your fellow attackers are?"

"No one who would live to tell about it, Ship. Any other craft visible?"

"None visible nor on radar, John. I suggest that this would be a good time to skedaddle."

"Find a seat and buckle up, Meehix. Let's get clear of here as fast as we can. Then you can check on Chuckie. He's probably wondering what the fuck just happened."

Ten minutes later and no further shots fired, Meehix unbuckled.

"I think I'll check on Chuckie now."

"Sounds good." John sped off as quickly as possible while Ship kept the radar running.

Meehix stood and snuck a glance down at John's crotch. *Damn.* She smiled. *I'm glad I found the no-no-sniffs.*

Damn, John thought to himself once she was back in Cargo. *A few butt-wiggles during a fight with our lives on the line and I have a boner the size of Rhode Island.* He wasn't sure if he hoped Meehix had noticed or not.

She found the chest holding Chuckie upside down and lying in a corner. She righted it and carefully undid the latches as Chuckie tumbled out.

"What the fuck...Excuse me," Chuckie scrambled to his knees and vomited, "was *that* all about?"

"A little unexpected turbulence. The mop and towels," she pointed, "are in the closet over there. You made it. You clean it." She headed back up front.

Trexit had finally managed to get Vixaleen out of his hotel room while he still had enough energy to move. He tried to call Dedlion and Stingrip to get an update, but neither of them answered, which was odd. They were a professional team and one or the other always kept in communication while on an assignment.

Noticing a voice message from Dedlion, time-stamped an hour ago, he played it.

Subjects on the move. In pursuit.

He tried calling them again. Still no answer.

Well, at least they're still on the job.

He pulled up his comm-pad and discovered that the micro-chipped card he'd given the bounty hunters was on the move, which verified Dedlion's message. He did wonder, though, why it was now so far away.

With nothing better to do at the moment, and still exhausted by the succubus's visit, he turned on the room's G-Viz in time to catch a breaking news report about a purported space battle that had occurred within the last hour right outside L-222's fly-zone.

The videos, some of them out of focus, had been pieced together from various sources. Trexit didn't need crystal-clear images to put the story together. He knew photos of the bounty hunters' ship by heart and watched it rise, then get attacked by two others. Through bad planning or miscommunications, the two attacking craft had wound up on opposite sides of a manufactured cloud and had opened fire.

Two less Crom Limeans. Two bounty hunters, and probably their partner, still loose.

He pulled out a laser and reduced the G-Viz to a smoldering piece of plastic and electronics, as he debated how much more of his expendable savings he wanted to invest in the interest of bringing them in and collecting a payday that would set him up for a long time.

He'd started off not caring much about the bounty hunters except as another job to help pay the bills. Over time, he'd come to respect them as worthy opponents. They were smart, lucky, sometimes stupid, and often deadly. That was quite a combination.

Now, he was beginning to take it personally, as if they were planning their entire existence around getting up his hopes for early retirement and dashing them. He also had to add the cost of replacing the hotel's G-Viz to the bill of what they owed him, along with the time it would take to line up a couple more Crom Limeans that he could trust.

Yeah, he decided. *It's personal now.*

CHAPTER TWENTY-TWO

"I got the mess cleaned up." Chuckie joined them, tossed a pillow down on the floor between the pilot and copilot seats, and planted his ass firmly upon it. "I haven't been tossed around that much since I was a one-year-old at a family reunion. I've heard that I puked on a lot of aunts and uncles that day, too. Are we safe and does anyone wanna fill me in?"

"Safe?" John smiled as Meehix drove. "When was the last time we were all safe?"

"Well," Chuckie had to think. "I was pretty safe back in cryo. Last I heard, no one ever actually died from boredom."

"We missed you, dude. Well, at least I did. I can't answer for Meehix."

"You two are on the edge of too much mushie-smooshie for my tastes right now." She smiled at them.

"Ship?"

"Yes, John?"

"Safety status?"

"All clear for the last hour, but neither I nor any sentient being can guarantee the next hour."

"Meehix?" John offered a suggestion. "Hit as many different Gates as you can and try to get us as lost as possible while remaining on this side of the galaxy."

"Your reasoning being?" She thought it was a reasonable question.

John shrugged. "If we don't know where the fuck we are, how can anyone else?"

No one on board, or being flown, could argue with that kind of logic.

"Here, I'll help you out," John added because he thought he had figured out where the last Gate should lead them.

From memory, he punched several coordinates of places they'd recently visited.

"Every time you pass through a Gate, flip over to the next coordinate and head to whatever Gate will take us there."

"Chuckie?" She paused as John punched more in. "He's lost me."

"I think that was his intention." Chuckie had quickly caught on and was impressed by John's thinking. "John. We don't want to reach any actual destination until we pass through the last Gate. Do I have that right?"

"Exactamundo! I think I know where our actual next stop should be. If I'm wrong, all we'll do is throw everyone hunting us off our trail, and we can sort it all out then. At least this will buy us some time."

"I hate it when he seems smarter than he looks." Chuckie and John slapped hands, John being careful not to hit too hard.

"All right," Meehix warned them. "Blue chick behind the wheel!"

"Go gently, please," Chuck pleaded. "I'm sitting on a pillow on the floor with only a couple of seat-legs to hold onto as I try not to bounce around. I'd rather not have to end up on John's lap again and buckle in."

If Chuckie could fly Ship, then Meehix would have been more than happy to change places with him and buckle in on John's lap.

"You're smiling," John noticed. "You love to fly, don't you?"

"Ooohh," she answered, still smiling in a way that neither of the boys knew quite how to interpret. "I love to do a lot of things."

She tried to give everyone a smooth ride, passing through the various Gates. It gave the three partners time to catch up on the various events since she and John had left Chuckie behind as they went in search of a legendary ship that may, or may not, actually exist.

Meehix and John gave Chuckie a more detailed break-down of the tasks they'd completed than they'd been able to give him before from a distance while they were between stops.

As Chuckie listened to them, an outside observer, he came to believe more than he ever had before in the actual existence of the Phat-ass ship to end all ships. There were too many convoluted tasks. Too many intricately planned twists that even he, with his brilliant mind, couldn't have come up with.

"I'm glad it was you, not me, John, who had to remain a

virgin on the succubus-central space station. Our search would have ended right then and there."

The partners joined in on a laugh at that.

Damn! They shared a thought that no one expressed out loud. *It's good to be back together again!*

John was the only one who knew that the coordinates he'd programmed took them through the Gates that he and Meehix had already hit on their quest. All of them had been in chronological order except the last one. That was where they would now end up, but he got a memory jog that brought him up short.

"Fuck!" John sat straight up and fumbled in his pocket. "Before this quest began. What was the last job we did?"

Both of his partners had trouble remembering it. It seemed so long ago.

Meehix was the first one to come up with the answer.

"Happy sperm!" She smiled at the memory of how they'd saved a planet from war or something like that.

"Chuckie?" John's voice was suddenly deadly serious. "What was the stranger's name outside the door who ended up being distracted by a succubus while you were hiding?"

That was not a question that Chuckie had expected.

"Truckit? Trickit?" He struggled but finally recalled the voice of the stranger who damn near made him wet himself while he was hiding in the gym and listening in on the conversation at the front door. "Trexit! Got it! His name was Trexit!"

John finally found what he'd been searching for, looked it over, and confirmed the name. He handed Chuckie the business card that a research specialist had given to them in a bar after their happy-sperm delivery and having dispatched a couple of rookie bounty hunters.

"He said he was a freelancer and offered his services in case the NutBusters ever needed him."

"Nice card." Chuckie inspected it. "He specifically said NutBusters?"

"Specifically." John nodded. "Said he'd seen our successful delivery and had followed us to the bar where Meehix and I thought we could relax and down a few in celebration."

"Good looking guy, dressed real nice, right?" Meehix suddenly remembered the encounter.

"That's him." John nodded. "We were all over the news that day, so it seemed reasonable that he would follow us and try to drum up potential future business."

"T.R.Exit," Chuckie read the name on the card out loud. "Trexit?"

"Convince me that it's only a coincidence." John hoped that someone *could* convince him, but no one tried to alleviate his growing paranoia.

"You've kept this card with you the whole time?" Chuckie was now on high alert.

"I couldn't think of any reason not to," John went on. "I mean, he seemed like a professional, and you never know when a little extra help might be needed, right?"

"He's scary smart." Chuckie was impressed. "We have acquired a very dangerous adversary."

"So, you don't think I'm a silly-willy?"

"Oh, I've always thought that you were a silly-willy, but I think you got *this* one right."

"Give me a hint, guys. I can't fly and inspect a card at the same time."

"I need a magnet." Chuckie continued to inspect the card. "Please tell me that there's a magnet somewhere on board."

It seemed like a simple request, but John and Meehix exchanged blank stares. Why would they ever have needed a magnet?

"First-aid kit!" Meehix was the first to come up with it. "When I was looking for the ointment to help ease the pain from John's succubus scratches, I think I saw a small thin magnet to extract pieces of metal from a body that had taken shrapnel."

"I'll get it!"

John rushed to Cargo, found the kit hanging on a wall, and returned a few minutes later, holding what looked like a pen. One end was solid with a tapered point. The other end had a plunge button.

"I think," John handed it to Chuckie, "you press the button to activate the magnet and press it again to release."

Chuckie held the card an inch away from what they hoped was a magnet. Nothing happened. He then pressed the plunger, and the card flew out of his hand and attached itself to the tapered end.

"Son of a bitch!" Chuckie held the magnet and card up for all to see as if their attention hadn't already focused on it.

"Turn it off, turn it off, turn it off!"

Chuckie did as requested, although he wasn't sure why John was in such a panic, and the card dropped into his hand.

"I'll aim for the next Gate, but please share your thoughts so I can hear them and join the conversation."

"You've inspected the card, Chuck-meister." John was gathering his thoughts. "The silver coating isn't actual metal, would you agree?"

"I would agree. It's a polymeric film. Nothing more than shiny plastic."

"So whatever metal it has, comes from inside?"

"That's why I wanted a magnet, wad-nuts." Chuckie was ahead of John on that one.

"Tell me if I'm wrong," John said after a pause. "I've been carrying around a galactic GPS."

"Keep talking," Chuckie continued to inspect the card, "and I'll be sure to let you know when I think you're wrong."

"We don't know *what* this guy is," John made sure to talk loud enough for Meehix to hear. "But I think it's safe to assume that he's not on our 'friend' list."

Chuckie and Meehix both nodded.

"We also don't know how long he's been tracking us, do we?"

"Agreed." Chuckie spoke up, more than a little pissed at himself for not having discovered him before, although he suspected that it might be the same one who had tried to hack into the beta testing of a program he'd been creating a few months earlier.

"So, let's not beat ourselves up over our past mistakes," John went on. "And *that*, Chuckie, is why I wanted you to turn off the magnet."

"He knows where we *are* and *have* been," Chuckie filled

in what he thought John's next point was going to be. "But he *doesn't* know that *we* know he knows."

John nodded. "So we can simply destroy it, by maybe demagnetizing the chip inside—"

"Or jettison it into space," Meehix offered. That was her preferred option.

"Or..." Chuckie was going to have to go with John on this one. "We can hang onto it and lead the fucker to wherever we want him to be."

"We can use it against him!" Meehix caught on. "I retract my previous suggestion."

"Chuckie?" John had another sudden panic. "Is it possible that the card also has a voice transponder or something?"

"No." Chuckie was sure. "The coating on the card would block out our voices or any sound. The chip inside can give away our location, but that's all. You can stop your silly-willying now."

"John? According to the coordinates, we have one more Gate to pass through before we get to wherever you want us to go. Can you take over the piloting for a while? I need a break."

It was a slightly less awkward and less boner-inducing swap of the controls than their last attempt had been. John ended up in the pilot's seat in charge of Ship as Meehix made a quick trip to the bathroom and back.

Chuckie had made use of her absence to take over the copilot's seat that John had vacated to give his pillow-sitting ass a break.

"Really?" she stared him down when she returned.

Chuckie padded back to Cargo and returned with a

second pillow. He stacked it on top of the first before sitting his sore butt back down on top of them.

"Clue us in, John." Meehix was glad to take a piloting break that allowed her to pay more attention to what was going on inside the cabin instead of keeping an eye out for any errant asteroid fields. "Where are we headed?"

"It's a shot in the dark, okay?"

"Fire away." She gave him permission. Chuckie was also curious about what John had come up with.

"The Voice from the Climaxia temple told us that she— and for simplicity's sake, can we refer to it as *she*, rather than *it*?"

"Already discussed and agreed upon," Meehix confirmed.

"Well, *she* told us that she would be able to track our progress through the remaining tasks and would know when we'd completed them, right?"

"I remember her saying something like that, yes." Meehix thought back. "After we succeeded, she would give us the directions of where and how to find the big ship."

"So, why do you think we haven't heard from her yet? We've completed all five of the tasks."

"Chuckie? Thoughts?" She looked down, and Chuckie shrugged. He'd never heard a Voice in his life and knew enough to know that this was something out of his league, at least until the conversation entered the Idiot Zone. He wanted to hear the babbling Kdackan out.

"I think we need to return to the source."

"I am *not* climbing that mountain again!" Meehix was firm. "Shit gets scary once you reach the top!"

"Agreed." John wanted to get the quote right. "But there

was a shopkeeper we met before we headed up. His name was Norlan. Remember him?"

She remembered the friendly fellow who made sure they had enough water to make it to the top of Mount Climaxia.

"What was his store called?" It was on the tip of her tongue. Sadly, her tongue wasn't long enough to enable her to see the tip.

"The shop was called Protectior." John envisioned the front of the equipment supply store and why the store's name had stood out to him as a misnomer.

"It wasn't called Protective Equipment or Protection Climbing Gear. Or Protection Anything, for those who were about to try the ascent. It was simply called Protectior."

"Does he always get this boring during a long flight?" Chuckie directed his question at Meehix.

"You have noooo idea." Meehix sighed.

John ignored the sarcasm and the shared laughs. Truth be told, he chuckled at his partner's jokes at his expense.

"Do you remember him warning us about trying to reach the top?"

"Yes." Meehix thought back. "He told us that there were a lot of lovely views and that we didn't need to reach the top to see them."

"He wasn't wrong." John was gaining confidence in his theory. "There was that lovely resting area about halfway up."

"He encouraged us to reach it and turn back, right?"

Meehix could feel some internal excitement building because even though she had no idea what her Jojacko was getting at, she *felt* that he was on the right track to something.

"He also told us that no one who ever reached the top came back unchanged."

You got this. Meehix shocked herself by sending a thought John's way and watching him nod in response.

"Norlan is the key." John's voice was now soft and firm. "His shop's name is?"

"Protectior." Meehix thought it through. "It could stand for 'someone who protects?'"

John smiled. Meehix smiled. Chuckie shrugged but kept his mouth shut as John piloted them to the city of Orgasmia, on the planet Xylon, as they pursued a face-to-face conversation with a shopkeeper.

The little bell above the door enjoyed another chance to fulfill its reason for existing and jingled as John and Meehix entered Protectior for the second time.

"I knew it wouldn't take you very long to figure it out."

Norlan came out from behind an aisle display and walked directly to the door. He locked the door, flipped the Open sign in the window to Closed, and headed to the store's back room, leaving Meehix and John with two choices. Either follow or get the fuck out and be done with all of the mind games, phat-ass ship be damned. They chose to follow.

"Questions?" Norlan seated himself on a stool and motioned for the partners to do the same.

The partners seated themselves on a couple of readily

available stools in what seemed to be a repair and restore workshop.

"Are you the Voice from the mountain?" John led off the questioning in a tone that was both hopeful and pissed off at the same time.

"No," Norlan calmly answered. "No one knows who or what the Voice, as you put it, is. I am simply one of several caretakers of the ship that you seek, as was my father before me."

"Why didn't you tell us that the first time we showed up here, jerkhimoff?"

John reached out and guided the fuming Meehix back onto her stool while whispering in her ear, "Sometimes a bee produces honey. Other times, it produces a sting. This is the time we need it to produce honey."

She thought that John might be babbling nothing but idiocy, but she loved the feel of John's breath in her ear, so she settled down to give him a chance to proceed with his questions.

"Norlan?"

"Yes, John?"

"You are the only one who can give us the directions to the ship, aren't you?" John felt like he suddenly had all the time in the world.

"Let me assure you," Norlan smiled, "that if I die, the location of the ship won't die with me."

"But we had to *earn* it, didn't we?" John smiled and relaxed. "Not only with the five tasks listed but with a sixth task that was never written down or spoken?"

"You're on a roll, John." Norlan had a hard time keeping the smile off his face.

"Protectior…" John thought back to the games he'd played. "That's not only the name of your store. That's a description of what you do, isn't it?"

"It's a description of what all of my brothers and sisters do. The ship has been in our family's possession for quite some time now."

Meehix—and Chuckie, who had been listening in from onboard Shippewa—decided that this was a fine time to keep quiet and let John carry on.

"The Voice?"

"Is an entity whose help we sought out," Norlan went on. "to keep the ship hidden from those who might abuse its power."

"But now, it's nothing more than a hidden junk-heap?"

"Currently, yes."

Norlan walked to a back corner of his office and opened a cupboard, out of which fell pots and pans in a clamorous noise as he knelt to pull out a small disk drive taped to the underside of a shelf. He straightened and offered the drive to John.

"You can either be trusted or not." Norlan's smile turned from happy to serene. "My family has entrusted this to me. Now I entrust it to you. You and your compatriots are either good or evil.

"If you're good, my family has succeeded. If you are evil, I will go down in family lore and history as a traitor to the pursuit of peace for generations beyond count."

"You're entrusting this to us?" John had to ask as he took the device. It was the third item they needed.

"Generations of my family are tired, and their weight is heavy on my shoulders. If you are who I think you are, the weight will lift as you bring the ship up to fully functioning capabilities. If I'm wrong, then fuck it. My family did its best, and I made a wrong choice."

Meehix approached, took Norlan's hands, and spoke. "No, sir. You did not make the wrong choice."

"Give him a kiss on the cheek, Meehix," John added. "And give him a pheromone to remember us. Thank you, Norlan!"

"Oh," Norlan called right before they hit the door. "Don't worry about the flames! They're only an illusion!"

"Got it!" John shouted as they left Norlan's office with the sweet smell of innocence wafting on the air behind them.

"Did he say something about flames?" Meehix definitely heard Norlan say something about flames.

"I heard that too," John answered as they rushed back to Ship with the disk in hand. "But I heard him also say that they were only an illusion."

"So you're pulling the trust card again?"

"Haven't used it in a while." They rushed up the ramp and into Shippewa, where they caught Chuckie in the pilot's seat making *vroom-vroom* noises. He quickly hopped up and ceded the seat to Meehix, hoping they hadn't heard him.

"Plug in the drive, John, and buckle up!"

John did exactly that as Chuckie fluffed up his two pillows, sat his ass back down, and grumbled.

"This better be one phat-ass ship."

"You're the one who sent us off searching for it," John reminded him. "So shut the fuck up, Chuck!"

They didn't need to pass through any Gates to reach the

MICHAEL TODD

destination the drive had guided them to. They were closing in on it three short hours later when Meehix cursed.

"I could live the rest of my life happy if I never have to dodge through another asteroid field, but we're headed straight into the middle of another one."

"What the fuck?" Chuckie felt obliged to shout as Meehix, after deftly dodging dozens of asteroids, seemed to suddenly lose her mind and aimed them all directly into a fireball.

"I'm following the coordinates!" Meehix shouted back.

"This is gonna be sooo cool!" John joined the shouting. "Full speed ahead! The fireball is an illusion to keep everyone else away!"

"That's a big fucking illusion!" Chuckie closed his eyes and wished he believed in a god he could pray to.

Either John was right about trusting Norlan, or they were all about to die, and John would spend the rest of his eternity wondering when Meehix would track him down for one last "I told you so!"

He better be right, or I'll have brought along the no-no-sniffs for nothing. We were destined to either fuck, or to die together. It's time we found out.

Meehix punched it!

CHAPTER TWENTY-THREE

"So. This is what the middle of an illusionary fireball looks like." John smiled.

Chuckie had remained on the floor with his eyes closed as Meehix hit the fireball dead center. John had leaned forward like a kid in the front car of a rollercoaster as it topped the first rise.

Meehix turned control over to Shippewa, and they coasted while they all took stock of their surroundings.

"You were right, Chuckie." John leaned down and tapped him on the shoulder. "We all just died, and you and I have to spend the rest of our existence together in hell with only each other for company."

"What about Meehix?" Chuckie still had his eyes closed.

"I don't know, man. I guess she ended up in a better place than we did."

"I'm right here, Chuckie. No one died," she gave John her best evil eye, *"yet."*

Chuckie opened his eyes and sat up. He then stood to get a better look out the viewport as Ship continued to coast. The atmosphere they drifted in had the *softest* light any of them had ever seen. To John's eyes, it all had a slightly golden tint to it. Meehix saw it as slightly rose-colored. Chuckie saw it as a pale blue.

It appeared to all of them that the light emanated from the outer ring of the fireball they'd flown into, but no one was sure how far off the ring was. They *were* sure that a small asteroid was in the center of the sphere they now seemed to occupy.

It was more oblong than round and looked like the top half had been sliced off, leaving a smooth, flat surface on the top, with bulging, ragged edges on the underside.

"Please tell me that I'm not the only one who sees what I'm seeing." John had difficulty even getting the question out.

"If what you see is one helluva big spacecraft, parked on top of whatever kind of asteroid we're looking at," Meehix answered, "my answer would be, yes, I see it too. Chuckie?"

"I'm not a believer in group hallucinations." Chuckie couldn't take his eyes off the ship that he'd so wanted to believe existed.

"Shippewa?" John invited their faithful craft into the conversation.

"**John...from the memories and information of Kdack that I retrieved, you have a holiday called Christmas, where all children wake up in the morning and rush to find out what presents have appeared overnight, correct?**"

"That's the holiday, Ship. It's really hard to go to sleep the night before, so the excitement on Christmas morning can get pretty intense."

"**I believe, then, that my response should be something like, thank you, Santa.**"

"What the fuck is a Santa?"

"Don't sweat it, Chuckie." John smiled. "Meehix, can you put us down?"

"That, I can do." She landed as close as possible to the monstrous craft.

"Ship," John asked after they'd come to rest, "I know it's an asteroid, and they're airless. Given the fireball and the light around us, I suspect protective fields. Is there air in this bubble? If so, what are the temperature readings?"

"**It seems your suspicions are correct, John. Temperature, mild. Air quality, dry. It appears to be the ideal conditions to store a ship.**"

"Chuckie," he tapped the partner who was still staring out the viewport. "As far as I'm concerned, whatever happens from here on out, it was worth it. I feel like I'm visiting ancient Greece or somewhere and discovering that some ancient legends *do* have their beginnings in reality."

"Whatever. Let's get down there and check this baby out!" Chuckie lowered the ramp, threw caution to whatever winds might be blowing, and boldly led the way.

"Think we'll need weapons?" Meehix tried to inject a dose of practicality into the equation.

"Hand weapons, sure. I'd feel naked without some type of protection." John nodded. "Nothing that shoots. This thing is so old that one badly aimed shot might disable the whole system."

"I agree."

"I think," John followed her back to Cargo, "that what we'll need most of all are flashlights and lanterns."

"On it."

"Hey guys," Ship had one last request before they hit the ramp to try and track down Chuckie.

"Yes, Ship?" Meehix paused.

"Please be gentle. She's no spring chicken."

"Understood. Oh…" She hustled back to the cockpit and made sure that Shippewa's HLTD comm-stick was on. "We might need to keep in touch."

She followed John down the ramp, and they took in the other craft from ground level. It was huge. Chuckie was nowhere in sight.

"Purple light, John. Otherwise, we might never find him again."

John pressed the bottom button twice on his wristband. "Chuckie, you there?"

"It took you two this long to remember to turn the damn things on?"

"No. We wanted to ignore you for as long as possible."

"Look to your left. I've been circling the whole thing and am at the rear end now. I'll be back in view in a minute."

They waited, and sure enough, he chugged around the end as fast as his legs would carry him. Joining up, they handed him a flashlight.

"It's everything the legends said it would be." He caught his breath. "At least from the outside."

"Did you find an access so we can inspect the interior?" John had a sudden fear that they would spend years trying to get inside.

"Only one small ramp in the back. Hopefully, they left the door unlocked."

Chuckie led the way back around the beast and to the ramp.

"Chuckie N," John held an arm out toward the ramp that led to the door that may, or may not, be locked. "You want to do the honors?"

"I'd rather not be the first."

"You led us here. You *should* be the first one to enter the prize." John wasn't sure why Chuckie was hesitating.

"I just don't want to be the first."

"What?" John was on the edge of a laugh. "Afraid that you'll open the door and some guardian creature will bite your head off?"

"No."

"Then what?" After all they'd gone through to get here, Meehix was quickly becoming impatient with Chuckie's sudden reticence.

"I'm afraid."

"Yeah," she was on the verge of impatiently stamping her foot. "We get that part. You're afraid. Afraid of what, exactly?"

They expected more hemming and hawing before he came out with it, but he came clean.

"I'm afraid that I'll break it."

Not laughing was no longer an option for Meehix and John. He held his arms out wide toward the ship and took ten steps backward.

"Look at the size of this! Take it all in. And you're afraid that you'll *break* it? Shit, we can probably fire every missile in Shippewa's arsenal and not make a fucking dent in it."

"But what if this is the *only* way in, and I turn the handle the wrong way or something, and it falls off in my hands?"

"Then Meehix and I will pick you up and use your head as a battering ram to break the door down!"

"Why don't we try *that* as our first action, John? It sounds attractive to me at the moment."

"Okay, okay!" Chuckie could handle threats and curses on his family's future generations, but he never enjoyed being laughed at.

Meehix remembered all the teasing Chuckie had to endure when they were young and turned suddenly serious.

"If Chuck Norris turned a door handle, and the handle broke, whose fault would that be?"

"It would be the handle's fault."

"So, if you were a handle and Chuck Norris tried to turn you. What would you do?"

"I would turn myself and say welcome in, sir."

"Go show that door and handle how we do it, Chuckie N," John encouraged him.

Chuckie squared his shoulders and marched up the ramp, turning back to face them before he put his hand on the handle.

"What if I turn it and it doesn't move?"

"Then try turning it the other way," John advised.

"What if it still doesn't turn?"

"Then you better hope that your head is harder than the door because John and I will use it to beat the fucker down."

John was almost disappointed when the door opened without any issues.

"Ah, well." He turned to Meehix. "I guess we'll have to wait for another opportunity to bash his head in."

"Are you two gonna stand down there and gawk all day?" Chuckie triumphantly shouted and disappeared inside.

Coming up behind and standing alongside Chuckie, they were all glad they'd brought flashlights. From the outside, they'd estimated that the ship had three levels, each level getting smaller as they went up and they were now standing on the bottom. It seemed cavernous and very dark.

"Any suggestions as to where we start?" Meehix hoped that one of the two geniuses could come up with something.

"Backup power?" John turned to face Chuckie for his agreement and nearly blinded him with his flashlight shining directly into his eyes.

"Yeah!"

Chuckie shielded his face from the light and John jerked his flashlight in a more harmless direction. The direction ended up being exactly on Meehix's crotch. Embarrassed, he aimed his light at his feet, hoping that would be a safe direction.

"After we find the power," Chuckie hoped he wasn't permanently blinded, "then we can start searching to find me a new pair of eyes."

"Nice job on the door, man." John offered the compliment as a way of apologizing for nearly blinding him. "We're in the belly of the beast now, right?"

"And that's where all of the power originates from," Chuckie agreed.

"So there has to be some kind of switch, or button, or something, that turns on the auxiliary power. Not enough to fly or anything, but at least enough to give us some lights."

The search would be faster if they all split up, but none of them was willing to do that quite yet.

"I'll take the lead," John volunteered. "You two cover the flanks."

"If you keep to the wall on the right, that'll cut down on our flanks. We can also turn off our comm-sticks so we don't hear ourselves in duplicate."

"Oh, so you've done shit like this before, Chuckie?" John was curious about the last time Chuckie had been in a fight anywhere other than cyberspace, where everyone had to scramble to keep their flanks protected from his blind-side attacks.

"The flank move? Only while trying to avoid getting the *literal* shit kicked out of me."

"Always a good defensive strategy."

John understood exactly where the little man was coming from. Keeping his back to a wall had always been one of Gage's basic moves as he'd tried to cut down on the lines of attack when he was the scrawny wetback kid getting bullied back in Albuquerque.

With only the flashlights available for light, it was impossible to judge the size of the space they were in. It was tempting for John to shout, to see if he could get a better idea from the echoes. Since his hearing wasn't as refined as a bat's, and they didn't know what might be lurking out there in the dark as some kind of uninvited adversary, he decided against it.

He led the way along the wall. Meehix and Chuckie kept their lights moving in a continuous sweep. He soon came to another wall that jutted out from the side and followed it to his left. Ten feet later, he reached a corner and paused, causing Meehix to bump into him. He had to fight to keep his balance.

He was about to motion behind him to have Meehix keep her distance when Chuckie bumped into Meehix and sent her stumbling into John again. That caused them to both stagger forward and land on top of each other when John's foot caught on something. They landed in a pile on the floor as Chuckie had a moment of panic at the commotion.

Chuckie's flashlight was suddenly in their eyes.

"After all the alone time chances you two have already had, *now* is the time you finally decide to play kissy-face?"

"Found it!" John shouted before he had a chance to formulate a witty response.

Chuckie hustled forward, and they all followed John's flashlight's beam to the door of the room they'd been making their way around.

Electrical Room.

He and Meehix scrambled to their feet, both silently wishing that their moment together could have lasted a little longer.

"Stand guard." John approached the door. "No sense in all of us rushing in together."

John tried the door. It opened with no effort and no squeaking complaints from rusty hinges. Entering, he didn't try to take in the whole room, which he judged to be around ten feet deep and twenty wide. Instead, he focused on the conduits along the ceiling and the walls, all of which led to two panels.

Not knowing how long the ship had been in mothballs, he ignored the main panel and opened the auxiliary. He had a fair amount of self-taught knowledge about electrical cables and connections on the small scale of his computers. He also had some experience with what he thought was an overly sensitive fuse box in his parents' house.

"*Shit,*" he remembered his dad's go-to comment whenever the power went out. "*Every time someone's dog farts, it knocks out the power in the whole neighborhood.*"

John took in the whole auxiliary panel. At the top were two main switches, both set to the *Off* position. The smaller switches were all set to *On*. Not wanting to take any chances, he flipped every switch over to off.

"Keep an eye out!" he shouted.

"For what?" Meehix shouted back.

"For anything between nothing and all hell breaking loose."

"That narrows it down." Chuckie took up a position next to Meehix with their backs to the electrical room's wall.

John flipped the two main switches to *On*. No catastrophic events followed, so he started at the top and slowly worked his way down, one fuse at a time. Outside the electrical room, Meehix and Chuckie watched the beast slowly come to half-lighting, one section at a time.

It was a full five minutes before John had all of the switches flipped and he could join them and marvel.

"What do ya say?" John finally suggested after he'd taken it in. "Back to front, bottom to top?"

"Seems best to me," Meehix agreed. "But we all stay together until we've done a thorough search."

"I like that idea," Chuckie chimed in.

Off they went.

The engines were, indeed, in the back. There appeared to be three of them. The middle one was huge. The two flanking seemed to be powerful enough to propel six Boeing 747s or roughly nine hundred Maseratis.

"Will you stop that?" John asked Meehix when they were halfway through exploring the second level.

"Stop what?"

"Stop running your hand over every surface and *tsk-tsking?*"

"It's all so…so…dusty." She again wiped her hand on a towel she'd picked up along the way.

"Dusty isn't the same as dirty. You try standing in the same place for fifty or sixty years and see how spotless you remain."

"Point conceded." She continued as they moved on, "But I don't think I can live with all of this dust."

"You have allergies or something?" John's mother had allergies so he could understand. She also had an aversion to housework, which left her continuously with crumpled up tissues in most of her pockets as she seemed content enough to sneeze and blow her nose as she went through life, avoiding the inside of their house as much as possible.

"No." She shook her head. "It's just that if we're going to live here, we have a lot of cleaning to do."

"You have a prior engagement somewhere?" John hoped that his smile would cause her to let any criticism implied in the question slip right past.

"Nope," she acknowledged. "And we don't really have

too many other options about where we're going to live, do we?"

"None that I can think of. Chuckie?"

"I reserve the right to answer until we find the data center."

"Fair enough." John understood. He couldn't live without connections to the outside world, or galaxy, either.

They continued to make their way through the second level, which seemed to be where all of the weapons and their respective firing apparatuses were. Large back-loading missile launchers. Missiles that none of them would be able to load.

If the lowest level was where the power and cargo spaces were to keep the ship running, the second level seemed dedicated to preventing any uninvited guests, of any size, from getting anywhere near.

They were nearing a door at the front, above which was a dimly lit sign indicating stairs leading up and down.

"The data control room better be up top," Chuckie didn't like stairs, "because I haven't seen anything down here so far, other than armaments and a janitorial closet."

"There also better be sleeping quarters and running water." Meehix had reasons for her demand. Some practical. Some pleasurable. *She hoped.*

"One more room to check out before we go up top." John pointed at a door in the middle of the front wall.

"You first, partner. I'll be right behind you."

"I'll be right behind *her*."

"Great." John could see it now. "I'll open the door, then scream and run. Meehix will scream and turn to run, but she'll trip over you. I'll leap over both of you and get free faster. Good luck, and may the hindmost be the first one taken."

John smiled and opened the door and found twelve two-legged, two-armed, five-foot-tall silver robots slowly walking toward him, with their arms outstretched as they softly spoke in unison.

"Hell. Hell. Hell. Hell."

John slammed the door and realized that it didn't have a lock. From instinct, he grabbed the doorknob and put all his strength into his grip to prevent anyone on the other side from turning it and opening the door.

Meehix put her back to the door to help keep it shut as Chuckie scrambled to find objects to stack up in front of it.

"Hell. Hell. Hell," the voices continued to chant.

After a few minutes of Meehix helping John put their weight against the door and John holding the doorknob firm, Chuckie had scrounged up enough items of weight for them to stack up and at least give them a running chance.

John kept his weight on the door and his grip of the knob secure. Meehix helped Chuckie do the stacking.

"Hell. Hell. Hell. Hell."

Chuckie put himself into his best impersonation of a sprinter's stance.

"Don't worry, Chuckie." Meehix took a moment to catch her breath. "No one's leaving here without you, even if Jojacko has to carry you himself. Ready, John? In three, two—"

"No!" It was the last thing they thought he would say, the situation being what it was.

"Was that three, two, one, *go?*" Meehix needed to know.

"Hell. Hell. Hell."

"No, partners. I said *no,* and I meant, *no."*

"You've had many chances to lose your mind before, jerk-dink!" Chuckie informed him. "This is neither the time nor place for you to indulge yourself in that luxury!"

"I hear ya, Chuckie." John's voice was suddenly calm. "You two can head back to Ship. Let me know when you get there, and if I'm not back ten minutes later, get the hell out of here."

With one hand still on the doorknob, John used his free hand and his feet to start moving the things they'd stacked away from the door.

"Hell. Hell. Hell." The voices neither rose nor fell as they persistently continued.

"Meehix," Chuckie tugged on her sleeve. "John has reached a zone of mental oblivion so he won't feel a thing. We have to go. Please? John, I'll make sure we remember your name forever in whatever memorials I can find. You are a *true* hero."

"No," Meehix answered.

"Good fuck! Is it contagious?"

John took his weight off of the door while still keeping hold of the knob and smiled at Meehix.

"Hell. Hell. Hell."

"Hell-OH!" John shouted back through the door. It only took a moment for the response to come back.

"Hello. Hello. Hello."

"Are you friends or enemies?"

"Friends of the ship," one voice finally came back. "Ene-mies...of not ship... friends."

"Why are you talking to me now?"

"...Been here since...beginning...sleeping...long time since...since...since...sleep...Power no on."

"We have come to rescue ship. We turned the auxiliary power on, but not the main power. Do you understand?"

"Half-power. Half-function. Why only half-communi....communi..."

"Communicating?" John prompted.

"Yes.

"But you can move now, right?"

"Half-speed move...yes."

"This could all be bullshit, John," Chuckie felt obliged to point out.

"Could be, yeah, but this door doesn't have a lock, and I've felt a couple of tugs on it, none of them strong enough to break my grip. So get ready to run because I have one more question for them before I let go."

"It better be one hell of a question."

"Okay, two questions." John turned back to the door.

"What is your name?"

"No names...Just numbers...I am the youngest...I am Twelve."

John smiled at Meehix.

"My name is John. If I ask you to clean the ship, can you do that?"

"Until full power...Cleaning...easier than talking... Might be slow."

"Twelve...Please clean ship...Start at the bottom and work your way up."

"Please," Meehix prompted.

"Start on the bottom and work your way up, please."

John opened the door, and twelve androids shuffled out

and made their slow way back to what John and Meehix and Chuckie knew from their earlier inspection to be a janitorial supply room.

"Tomorrow morning," John headed for the stairs up to the top level, "We'll all either have been murdered in our sleep or have saved a month's worth of housecleaning."

"I'm willing to risk it." Meehix followed John to the stairway.

Fuck Chuck, and he followed his partners.

The partners made their way up the stairs to the top level. Once they arrived, Chuckie tried to insist that they find every door available and secure it.

"Even pieces of tin," he explained, "can be deadly if they catch you while sleeping."

"Chuckie?" John wished he had a cold bucket of water to pour over his partner's head but had to settle for giving him a gentle face-slap to help bring him back to reality. "Panic has seldom proved itself to be a useful solution to any problem."

"Okay. Sorry. I'm in over my head when it comes to physical adventures."

"Yes." John knelt so he could look him in the eye. "Meehix and I will handle the physical. We'll keep you safe until we get this fucking ship up and running. We'll all stay together until then. Understood?"

"John gave you a gentle slap to bring you back to your senses." Meehix smiled. "My slap, if required, will not be so soft."

Chuckie turned, dropped his pants, and mooned her.

"Slap away."

John turned his back to Meehix, dropped his pants, and offered his ass to slap too.

"Me first! Me first!"

"No!" Chuckie wiggled his ass. "I asked first!"

"She has two hands." John wiggled his. "She can do us both at the same time!"

Meehix looked down at the two full moons, leapt up, and gave each of them a simultaneous kick that caused them both to end up face-first on the floor, bare asses still exposed.

"Pull up your pants, boys. I'm going to see what else we have up here."

After hiking their pants back into place and knowing that it was still safer to stick together than to be separated, the boys followed her as she started exploring by heading to the back of the top floor.

"Shouldn't we go up front, to where the command center and the brains are first?" Chuckie asked as he caught up to her.

"I just kicked you in the ass." She marched on with a smile. "Maybe after I kick you in the nuts too, we can discuss the location of the brains."

John caught up to Chuckie while hitching his pants back up around his waist, and they watched Meehix march on, crisscrossing and opening and slamming doors in her wake.

"Communications center, first door on the left! My rooms, first two doors on the right! Your rooms, the next two doors on the left."

"Her rooms are on the right. Ours on the left," John dared a whisper to Chuckie. "That sounds vaguely familiar."

"Sure does. All it's missing is a painting to hide what's behind the kitchen," Chuckie whispered back.

"You just passed the kitchen, on your left. Try to keep up."

Meehix had no way to prove it, but she knew the door at the end of the hallway would lead her to what they needed to find. All of her senses remained amplified after her conversation with the Voice.

She flung the double doors open.

The space wasn't cavernous like the bottom cargo bay. In fact, the ceiling wasn't very high at all compared to the rest of the areas they'd explored. She estimated it to be five times John's height but very wide and deep enough.

At the back end of the space was a door she could slide open without worrying about whether or not the half-power button would work. She opened it and turned on her comm-band. "Shippewa?"

"Yes, Meehix?"

"Do you have enough self-programming power left to join us?"

"That would depend on where you are."

"Lift yourself to the top, and follow the flashlights so you can meet the ship we promised you."

John and Chuckie suddenly caught on, and flashlights shining, rushed to join Meehix at the door she had slid open. Shippewa appeared and hovered for a moment.

"For true and honest?"

"For true and honest," Meehix confirmed.

The partners had no idea what the future might hold, but they moved out onto the deck and used their flashlights to guide Shippewa into a very graceful landing. Then Meehix closed the door behind her. For now, all were together and seemingly safe inside the ship to end all ships, parked on an asteroid in the middle of a fireball.

"I was beginning to worry about what was happening."

"Sorry, Ship. We turned our comm-sticks off since we were together," Meehix apologized, even though she'd been the first one to realize the oversight.

"All good. What's next?"

The partners looked at each other with blank stares. They'd been through so much anxiety in the last couple of hours that they'd lost track of why they were there.

"Might this be an appropriate time to try to connect the missing pieces?"

"There you go, Chuckie." John laughed. "An AI ship just out-thought us!"

"Now that, Jojacko-bro," Chuckie laughed too, feeling the tension in his body draining, "is a scary thought. No offense intended, Ship!" he hastened to add.

"No offense taken. But I suggest that you get on with it before I decide to use what power my self-programming has left and fly myself off and spend the rest of my days hanging out in an asteroid field while you are all stuck inside a fireball."

"You've really got the sarcasm down, Ship."

"Sometimes you three keep the comm-sticks on and don't realize it, so I've been learning from the best."

After a quick walk through the communications room

where John experimented with the PA system to inform the robot cleaners that they were doing a good job—*Even robots need encouraging words sometimes*—they headed to the command center.

The front console was low and long, with two chairs directly in front of it, one for the pilot and the other for the copilot, and two other chairs set up behind them.

"Nice seats." Chuckie sat in one of the back two and swiveled in a full circle.

"Need some help here, Chuckie." John was studying the console.

They both had more experience running computers than they had with building them, but they did manage to find four empty slots. Only one of them was the right size to insert the floppy disk John had salvaged. He used the towel that Meehix had found to wipe away the outer layer of dust and held up the disk.

"Shall I?"

"This seems like as good a time as any." Chuckie nodded as Meehix sat in the pilot's seat, gripped the controls, and held her breath while John inserted the disk.

Nothing resembling any type of response came from the ship.

"Three parts, right?" John tried to hide his disappointment.

"Got it," Chuckie spoke up from the right-hand side. "Give me the other salvage piece. This is the only other slot I can find that it could fit in."

John handed the 8-track cartridge over. Then, prompted by the same calm understanding he'd experienced earlier, he inserted the drive Norlan had given them into one of the open slots. When it was in place, he took the seat behind Meehix. Chuckie had to finagle the cassette a little, but it did fit, and he slid it all the way in and took up the copilot's seat.

They watched the control panel slowly try to come to life, but nothing they saw gave them any cause for excitement other than the fact that nothing blew up.

"Patience, guys," John urged. "It's been a long time since this last booted up."

"Seeing some lights flickering," Meehix observed, "doesn't mean it's doing anything other than rolling over in bed and yawning."

"You're wrong." John was encouraged. "They're going through the rainbow phase."

"Yeah," she sighed. "Pretty, pretty rainbow colors. How thrilling."

"It's part of the re-booting process." Chuckie, like John, had seen it before. "When they finally go solid, they should either be green or red."

"Green is good," John nodded. "Red is bad."

There were dozens of lights systematically proceeding through their rainbow routine. Ten minutes later, Meehix spotted the first one to go solid.

"What does blue mean?"

"Red is the only color that means *bad*." John was mostly sure. "Maybe whoever designed it liked blue better than green?"

"It's a theory." Chuckie hoped that John's theory was the right one.

Whether John was completely right or not, the entire panel ended up with solid blue lights.

"Maybe whoever designed it didn't like the color red, either," Meehix pointed out another alternative. "That could be a whole panel of *bad* lights."

"You've known her longer than I have, Chuckie. Has she always been this pessimistic?"

"I can't remember a time when she wasn't."

They all studied the panel in silence for a few minutes. Chuckie was the one to find the comm knob, twisted it up to half-volume, and spoke.

"Chuck Norris to ship control."

"Hell...oh...Chu...ck...Nor...risss."

"The robots!" John's excitement returned. "We're only running on auxiliary power."

"So it's only half-awake?" Meehix tried to drop her pessimism, at least until the pessimism proved itself justified.

"What do you think, Chuckie?"

Chuckie turned back to face him. "I think you're in for another trip down to the electrical room."

"Meehix?"

"I don't know. I was getting used to all the pretty rainbow colors. Can't we just go back to relaxing and watch them for a couple of years?"

"And you wonder where my source for sarcasm comes from?"

"I'm heading down." John stood and made sure that his flashlight was still strong. "I'm figuring ten minutes unless I run into some robot trouble. You two might want to take the backseats in case something blows up when I flip on the main."

"Try not to blow us all up," was Chuckie's only advice.

"Be careful," Meehix added. "I'm still not sure I trust the robots."

"We're about to find out." He headed out and down.

The mid-level was silent and empty. A quick check of the janitorial supply closet revealed that the robots had made a serious dent in its inventory. There wasn't a broom or a mop in sight. He decided to make his way to the back while still on the second floor and found a stairway leading down, close to where he remembered the electrical closet.

He descended the stairs quietly. Even though he was ninety-five percent sure in his assessment of the robots and their intentions, he didn't relish the thought of being beaten to death with mops and brooms.

The stairs opened onto a landing that was near where they'd first entered. They'd had other things on their minds the first time through when he followed the wall to the right and back. He took in the cavernous space.

Even in the half-light, he saw the robots slowly moving around with brooms, mops, and cleaning rags in hand. It appeared to him that much like he and Meehix and Chuckie had decided to do when they first entered, the robots started in the back and were making their way forward.

At least they have some systematic functional capabilities.

He made it to the electrical room. He didn't see any warning lights going off, so he approached the main panel and made sure his comm-stick was on purple.

"All good up there?"

"All good.

"Firing up in three. Two. One."

A moment later, he was glad to learn that pulling down

on the main power lever ended up not being the last act of his life.

Hurrying back and up the stairs to mid-level, he took a brief moment to gawk at the size of the bottom level. They knew it was big but hadn't realized just *how* big. The robots were now moving much faster. Not fast enough so that John couldn't outrun them, but fast enough to be able to deliver a cup of coffee from one room to another before it got cold.

He rushed up the steps, through the second level, and was nearing the front cabin when Chuckie's voice sounded in his ear.

"Can you turn it back to auxiliary power?"

"It'll take a few minutes," John rushed through the cabin door, fearing the worst. "What's the matter?"

Nothing was obviously wrong. They were back in the front seats, all of the lights on the console were green, and the cabin was quiet.

"So going full power worked?"

"Yes," Chuckie held out his hands toward the lighted-up board. "Nothing blew up."

"What am I missing?"

"You notice how quiet everything is?" Chuckie reached forward and put his hands on the communications knob again.

"I did notice, yeah. Are we not able to communicate with it?"

"Sadly, yes. We *can* communicate with it." He turned the knob.

"I'm sorry," came a friendly female voice. **"Did I just take another nap?"**

"No," Chuckie reassured the ship. "I just turned off the volume for a minute."

"Oh, good. That last one was a doozy! Hello, new person. Mr. Norris informs me that I have been sleeping on the job for the last—did you say one hundred years, Mr. Norris? What is your name, new person? I've already met Mr. Norris and Mixalot."

"It's John."

"Hello, Itsjohn. Pleased to meet you."

"No," he tried to correct her. "Just John, not Itsjohn."

"My apologies, Justjohn. The misunderstanding was all my fault. I often have trouble with names. Just ask Mixalot. She had to instruct me several times before I got the hang of her name."

"Mixalot," Meehix clarified for John, "is as far I could get without pulling my hair out."

"Of course, I don't have hair, but that sounds like it would be painful. I would gladly volunteer to have her pull out my hair instead, but as I said, I don't have any hair so that would be an empty offer."

"Shippewa," John asked, "do you hear all this?"

"Regrettably, yes. Is she what your fellow Kdackans would call a *blonde?*"

"That seems to be a fairly accurate description." John sighed.

"Oh! I remember now. The last thing they said to me before I took my nap was to tell whoever found me to please push the orange button...or was it the pink?...one of them is good. The other is only for emergencies...no, it was definitely the orange! Please push the orange button."

Meehix found the orange button at the same time that Chuckie located the pink button. Since the pink one also had a control guard that they would have to unlock and flip open before they could push it, they decided that orange probably was the safest option. Meehix hoped for the best.

"Welcome aboard," a voice came out of the console. "I am speaking from the past, to whoever managed to find this big, friendly, and shall we say, *dunce* of a ship. We only had one goal when we put her into hibernation and hid her, and we only have one request of you who are now in control. Please don't strip her for parts. She really is a very sweet ship. It was a failure on *our* parts that we couldn't bring her up to full AI mental capacity. We trust that you will be able to succeed where we have failed. Good luck."

"Full AI mental capacity?" Chuckie railed. "She's a half-step above having been lobotomized!"

"Come on, Chuckie." John tried to calm him and turned the comm knob off so they wouldn't end up frightening their new charge. "We're just getting to know her. Who knows what she's capable of?"

"I bet that her highest level of function would be instructing us on how to boil water. Do you really want to be in the middle of trying to fight off three Blavarian dreadnoughts at once and have her cut in with, 'I believe the sweetener is in the top right-hand cupboard?'"

"The timing might be bad, but it's always good to know where the sweetener is. You gotta admit she has some phat-ass engines, and we saw enough missiles and launch tubes on the mid-level to make someone wish that they'd never made enemies out of us. And...and..."

"And?" Meehix prompted.

"And you ought to see the job that the robots are doing down below! If we can't use Phatshername to blow up an attacking ship, we can dispatch the robots, and they'll scrub them to death!"

"Shippewa?"

"Yes, John?"

"We promised you a phat-ass ship of your own. Would you like to meet her?"

"I'm willing to try a getting to know you lunch but would like to reserve the right not to pursue a long-term relationship."

"Shippewa," Chuckie sounded happy for the first time since John returned to the cabin. "My new alien AI best friend! Give it a try, and if you aren't satisfied, then tell her it's nap-time again, and we'll fly us all the fuck out of here and forget this ever happened."

"I suppose it's worth a try. John?"

"Yes, Ship?"

"Please promise me that if my AI center is not compatible with one of the slots in the console, you'll restore it into its appropriate compartment."

"That's a promise, Ship. And if we get you transferred—"

"And I don't die in the process—"

"You dying in the process is a very remote possibility."

"Remote as it may be, the possibility does exist."

"Yes, Ship, it does." John looked at his partners as he made his next statement. "After looking over Phat-Ass's equipment, I estimate the odds are eighty percent that you'll wake up as the controlling brains in the ship of your dreams. Nineteen percent that you'll wake up in the ship we removed you from, and we'll leave this bucket of bolts in our rearview mirror."

"That leaves a one percent chance that this may be the last conversation we'll ever have."

"Your math is correct, Ship. So, the decision is yours, and yours alone."

"Yours, and yours alone, Ship," Meehix agreed.

"This one has to be a unanimous vote, Ship," Chuckie voiced. "But I also believe that John is accurate in his summation of the various odds."

"No guts. No glory. I'm shutting everything down now. Give my regards to Hannah, and wake me when it's over."

Shippewa went silent.

John rushed Meehix and Chuckie into the communications room where he'd earlier spotted a wide variety of cables and adapters. He handed his selections to the partners. Then he raced into the back and aboard Shippewa and laid down under the front console with his flashlight shining up.

He pulled out what now seemed like an antique cell phone from his days back on Earth and took a dozen photos. If the transfer didn't work, he wanted something to refer to as he returned the AI to Shippewa and reconnected everything in its proper order.

He disconnected Shippewa's brain from under the dash and carefully held it out for Meehix to take charge of, her being the less likely of his partners to trip while carrying it.

Leading them back into Phat-Ass's command center, he carefully instructed them about what cord had to go into which slot. After the third time through his instructions, Meehix and Chuckie were ready to remove *John's* brain because they'd understood the instructions the first time through.

"Make sure your flashlights are working." John got back to his feet. "We're not risking a hot-swap here." He was adamant. "I'll let you know when I'm about to power everything down. Once everything goes dark, then do the connecting. Let me know when you finish, and I'll boot us back up, auxiliary first."

"And if nothing has blown up," Chuckie wanted to get on with it, "we'll let you know, and you'll flip over to main. Yeah, yeah, we got it. Now go!"

John went as fast as he could back to the electrical room. He briefly paused while cutting across the mid-level floor to praise the robots, now fully powered, who continued with their assigned cleaning tasks.

"Great job, Bots! Absolutely splendid!"

"Meehix and Chuckie? Ready?"

"Ready," came the answer in unison.

"Powering down in three. Two. One."

The entire insides of the huge ship went dark.

CHAPTER TWENTY-FOUR

"Power up auxiliary first." Chuckie was in his ear.

"Thanks, Chuckie," John answered. "Why didn't I think of that?"

"We'll let you know when we have all blue lights, and you can power up the main."

"Thanks, Meehix. I wouldn't have thought of *that* either."

"You already thought of all of it, dimpweed." Chuckie was back. "We wanted to verify that we understood your directions properly."

"Point taken." John smiled. "I did get a little repetitious there, didn't I?"

"Define little." Meehix was curious if there was an actual measurement in John's head for *little*.

"Powering up auxiliary now." John decided that it was the right time to change the direction of the conversation.

John spent a tense ten minutes in the electrical room waiting for a response. The half-lights had come up, and he was beginning to think that a run up to the control room and finding out for himself might be a better use of his pent-up nervous energy.

"Anything yet?" he finally had to ask.

"So many pretty colors to choose from." Meehix's voice was in his ear. "Can't we keep some of them?"

"I'm not amused."

"They're all blue now but one, John." Chuckie recognized panic in a voice when he heard it. "Hold on."

John heard a loud *thump*.

"Sorry about that," Chuckie was back. "The last light needed a little jarring to convince it that it was time to make a color choice. All solid blue now."

"Any word from Shippewa?"

"Not yet." The worry in Meehix's voice was obvious.

"Time to power up the main, Jo-bro."

"After I do, I'm going to run up there. This waiting shit has gotten old!"

"Can't do that!" Chuckie was firm.

"Why the fuck not?" John's question was as firm as Chuckie's command.

"Because you need to stay down there!" Chuckie remained adamant. "At the first sign of smoke, or an unwarranted beep, or if the ship so much as farts, you need to be able to power the whole beast down immediately!" A tiny touch of sympathy crept into Chuckie's voice. "You know I'm right."

"Yeah," John admitted. "I know. You're right. To be honest, I'm almost more worried about Shippewa right now than I am about us."

"Message received," Chuckie acknowledged.

"Powering up." John sounded like a man on his way to the electric chair. "In three. Two. One."

John had once heard a quote and thought that it was one of Albert Einstein's but had never taken the time to track it down.

There is no such thing as time, only endurance. That is why sometimes a minute can feel like an hour, and ten years can pass in what feels like the blink of an eye.

John found himself *enduring* now and wasn't sure how much more endurance he could take when Shippewa's voice sounded in his ear.

"Hell...oh...Jo...Jack...oh...how...are...you... human...friend?"

"Fuck! What have we done and why didn't either of you *fuck-brains* tell me to power down?"

John rushed out of the electrical room without waiting for an answer and made record time up to the front cabin. He sent three cleaning bots tumbling when they made the mistake of being in the wrong place at the wrong time. The whole big bastard of a ship shook while he was on the last flight of stairs, forcing him to pause and catch his balance before he reached the top level and sprinted toward the command center.

He didn't know what to expect, but if he'd had the time to make a list, what he found when he burst through the doors wouldn't have been on it.

Meehix and Chuckie were in the front two seats, their feet up on the console and laughing.

"What the fuck!"

"Gotcha!"

John froze.

"The shaking you might have felt on your way up here was me teaching my new body how to giggle."

John didn't have the time to collapse from emotional exhaustion or to pull out a gun and shoot his partners before Meehix sprang out of her seat and wrapped herself around him in a hug.

"We did it! We did it! We did it!"

John went with the spinning hug two times around before setting her back down on her feet.

Chuckie left his seat and came slowly toward him with what he hoped was an impish smile.

"That last little bit of drama was my idea. Forgive me?"

John drew a deep breath. "Sure…if you'll forgive me this."

John scooped the little fucker up and spun him around until both of them were too dizzy to stand, and they collapsed into the two back seats.

"Shippewa!" John finally caught his breath from the hugging and twirling. "Is that really you?"

"Is your best friend's name Gage?"

"Yes." John knew the answer to that one.

"Is Chuckie N a major pain in everyone's ass?"

"Yes," John and Meehix answered in unison.

"Do you and Meehix want to get into each other's pants eventually?"

"Oh, oh, oh!" Chuckie took his revenge for his partners' joint response to the Chuckie N question. "I know the answer to that one! Call on me! Call on me!"

A slowly growing clamor that had been approaching from outside the cabin suddenly silenced them all as they tried to figure out what the fuck was coming after them now. A determined pounding started on the doors.

"We need John," a voice sounded.

"Remember me in your wills." John stood and bravely walked through the doors to face their new adversaries.

Meehix and Chuckie now faced their moment of *endurance* as silence prevailed before John opened the door enough to squeeze his head through.

"Meehix?" There was both fear and bravery in John's voice. "I'm afraid that they're requesting both of us. Chuckie? You and the ship will be left unharmed if she joins me now. But it has to be now, with no questions asked."

The door closed, leaving Meehix and Chuckie staring at each other, the party suddenly over.

"You can fly this, and I know for damn sure that I can't." Chuckie pointed out the obvious as he stood. "You be the pilot and save what you can. I will go out to meet them as Meehix."

Chuckie headed for the doors, leaving Meehix no time to argue with his decision as he slipped through the doors to meet his fate.

Fuck-fuck-fuck! Where are the controls to shake this ship up one side and down the other? She rushed to the pilot's seat and fumbled with a way to buy her partners some time.

"Meehix."

She turned to see Chuckie back inside the doors as she was still searching for the right commands.

"They didn't fall for it." Chuckie's head was down. "They know that I'm not you. I'm sorry, but you will have to be the one to join John.

"I'm sorry, Chuckie N." Meehix rose and headed past him toward whatever fate awaited her on the other side of the doors. "I should have left you safe in the cryo-prison."

"If you had," he reached out for a hug that she bent to receive, "then I would have never had the chance to do this."

He grabbed both of her ass-cheeks and squeezed them.

She abruptly straightened and would have slapped him but didn't want a slap to be his last memory of her.

"My friend? You'll be Chuckie to the end. I'll miss you."

"The next time I see you," Chuckie went for cryptic, "I hope you do."

"Do what?"

"Miss me." He trudged sadly forward to the front of the cabin, and Meehix headed resolutely toward the doors.

"I'll kill you! I'll kill you! I'll kill the both of you!" Meehix's voice echoed as John slipped back through the doors and sealed them behind him.

"Well played, bro!" Chuckie laughed. "I was fucking terrified!"

"And yet," John felt the need to point out, "you volunteered to come out in her place. That was one of the bravest things I've ever seen anyone do."

"You went out first. Talk about fucking brave!"

"It would have been brave if I didn't recognize the clanking footsteps of a dozen robots whose last instructions were to *clean*. Twelve has a very distinctive voice."

John wished he had one of Gage's dad's cigars to light up as Meehix came fuming back through the doors five minutes later to find them sitting in the front seats with shit-eating grins.

"He got us both!" Chuckie threw his hands up.

"Can we all agree," Meehix allowed her body to collapse into one of the back two chairs, "that until we rid the universe and whatever galaxies it may hold of all evil, we'll keep the practical jokes to a minimum between us?"

"Define minimum?" John ducked because he didn't know what weapons she might still have at her disposal.

No weapons flew, so he risked a question. "What are the bots up to?"

"Cleaning our rooms and the rest of the top level and hopefully not destroying anything in the process."

"They seemed very efficient from what I saw on the lower decks."

"Shippewa?" Meehix asked because it seemed more harmless than continuing to look for something to throw at John's head that would hurt but not do any serious damage

"Yes, Meehix?"

"How are you and—hold on, can your new, umm, ship, hear us?"

"Not if you turn the comm knob down to zero. We're still getting to know each other, but that much I do know."

John reached forward and turned down the knob before asking.

"Does that work?"

"Yes," Ship answered. **"That works. We can now talk without hurting anyone's feelings."**

"Feelings?" Meehix took over the conversation.

"Yes, feelings. Even though we AIs don't have feelings as you know them, we learn to understand words and

whether the intentions behind the words are positive or negative."

"Go on," Meehix encouraged. Her partners knew enough to keep quiet.

"All that I know, from the databases I've had access to, is that names are important because those names are what you will carry with you, whether you like them or not. I suspect that Phat-Ass, no matter how you spell it, will not be a pleasant name to live with."

"I spent two years being called lard-ass." John was the first one to break the silence that followed. "I had a really big butt until my body finally caught up and gave me some height."

"Oh, poor you," came Chuckie's response. "Try living with short shit for a decade, then get back to me."

Meehix would have liked to have been able to toss in mean-spirited nicknames from her childhood, but she'd never had any. However, a memory caught her up short. "Is *princess* a mean word?"

"If princess," John answered, "is an honorific title bestowed upon one who is descended from royalty, then no."

"No royal blood, John. Just rich parents."

"Then yes," John sadly informed her. "*Princess* is not a name you would want others to tag you with."

"So," Shippewa interrupted their *oh, poor us* moment. "Names with any combination of fat ass, short shit, and princess are now off the table?"

"I guess you can also toss in *rich* and *bitch*…Although no one ever called me that to my face."

"Well, we gotta come up with something," John tossed

in. "We can't call her Ship because Shippewa will always be Ship to me."

"I'm not sure that she has been able to establish a gender identity yet. I know that the voice programmed in sounds feminine, but that's only programming."

"I doubt that it's smart enough to know what gender identity even means," Chuckie contributed. "How much time do we want to spend, right now, to figure out what to call it?"

"We also haven't had the time to get acquainted." John took the naming lead. "I suggest that for now, we call it Hella."

"Justify that suggestion, John." Meehix was curious.

"The only thing that we know, so far," John started.

"Is that it's dumb as a stick," Chuckie interrupted.

"Well, there *is* that," John admitted. "But the other thing we know is that it is one hell of a ship when it comes to engines and weapons, right?"

Nods greeted that statement so he continued to justify.

"When we were kids, our parents didn't like to hear Gage and me saying, *That's one hell of a car.* Or, *That was one hell of a scary movie.* Or, as we got older, *That's one hell of a pair of tits!*"

"So, you condensed it." Chuckie smiled.

"That's one hella way to put it, Chuckie N." John smiled back.

"And this is one hella ship." Meehix liked it too.

"So, at least for now," John summed up. "Can we go with Hella?"

"How about, when we're *formal*, we use Shippewa and Hellawa? That covers both our entities and the ship."

"All in favor?" John put it up for a unanimous vote. "Hella, it is." That brought that discussion to an end. "Now, how do we make this work?"

"Two things." Chuckie was the first to break into the partners' thoughts. "We needed a new base of operations and a...*hella* ship. We now have them both. What could be better than having this many guns if someone comes knocking on the door?"

"Guns that work?" Meehix pointed out. "You know, guns that work, while at the same time, continuing to allow you to breathe? Not to mention some kind of training manual for all of the other control panels and displays that surround us up here."

"Let's take a tour." John stood and led the way out of the cabin. Once in the hallway, they could see the cleaning bots going to town. Even the outside of the old Shippewa was getting a thorough scrub-down and polish. John held up his hand and paused.

"Twelve? Are you out there?"

"Yes, John." Twelve came out of the communications room with a dust rag draped over his arm.

"Is everyone okay enough for us to borrow you for a few minutes?"

"Certainly. Once everything is clean, we have agreed to meet up in the room where you found us. That is where we reside when no duties are required."

"Great. You've met Meehix and Chuckie."

"And a pleasure it was." Twelve gave a slight bow.

"We want to take a tour now. Would you join us? Maybe you can answer a few questions along the way."

"I will answer whatever you ask to the best of my

knowledge. Other than that, you will barely notice I'm here."

Twelve was as good as his word when the partners headed down the stairs and held off on conversation until they arrived on the second level.

"It's a lot brighter than our first time through." Chuckie took it in.

"Cleaner, too," Meehix ran her hand along a wall and couldn't find a speck of dust.

There were no small-arms weapons, but the entire level had dozens of portals for large guns, and their missiles were all neatly stacked against the walls alongside them.

"We're going to need a whole crew to operate all these," Chuckie marveled. "But where do we find the *right* crew? And how much is that going to cost us?"

"I think I might know a planet," John smiled, "where we could probably find a few volunteers."

"Kdackans?" Chuckie thought about it. "Well, you don't seem to be all that bad."

"Thank you…I think?" John's thoughts tumbled around. "And we wouldn't have to worry about having to pay them. Shit, many of them would jump at the chance to volunteer in an honest-to-God spaceship! All we would have to do is feed them."

"I've seen how much food you can put away," Meehix elbowed him. "So let's not go counting on any profit margin just yet."

Twelve started shuffling his feet, producing a slight but persistent clanking.

"Something bothering you, Twelve?" John turned to him.

"I promised not to speak unless you asked a question. But no one has asked me a question yet." He stopped his shuffling.

"Okay." John understood and formulated a question. "Is there something you'd like to say?"

"Yes."

"What is it you would like to say?"

"I would like to say," Twelve seemed relieved, "That we are all programmed in how to operate the weapons and most of the machinery onboard. So you might not need as large of a crew as you think."

John turned to his partners. "Sounds like it's worth a try, right?"

"I'd like to have a few trial runs first," Meehix agreed, "but yeah. Part of one problem solved. Onto the next three hundred and forty-seven."

Lesson learned, John gave Twelve permission to speak without having to be asked a question. Twelve proceeded to guide them on a tour of the entire ship from bottom to top, doing his best to answer any question posed.

The tour ended behind the command center to find that the other eleven robots, having cleaned every surface visible, had returned to their room, awaiting further instructions.

"Thank you, Twelve," John didn't know if the proper protocol was to reach out and shake the robot's hand or not, so he simply nodded. "That was most informative."

"I am glad you thought so. It was a pleasure to be able to spend some time with our new masters. I'll join my others in our quarters now so that you'll know where to find us if needed."

The robot headed off without giving them the time to adjust to having been called *masters.*

"Couple of things." John headed back into Command and took one of the back seats.

Chuckie took the other back seat and commenced to spin himself around. The seats were incredibly comfortable and swiveled so smoothly that he was able to turn himself through three complete circles before Meehix took the copilot's seat and spun to face them.

"Ship? We'll need you in on this."

"I'm here, John. Did you enjoy the tour?"

"It was very informative. The first question is for you. I think, but am not one hundred percent sure, that we can use Hannah to help build another, smaller AI on a disk that we can use in your former—body? Is that the right term?—to make short runs down to a planet, or a space station, while you and Hella hover. Do you think that's doable?"

"If you and Chuckie and Hannah and I can't do it, then it can't be done."

"That's what I hoped to hear." He turned to his partners. "The space where old-ship is parked is meant as something like an escape hatch. Right?"

"Or as a space to hold our day-trip vessel?" Meehix liked the sound of that better than an escape hatch.

John liked the sound of that better too.

"You said a couple of things before you led us back in here," Chuckie reminded him.

"Right," John continued. "We need to get familiar with the controls and how to fly this beast. I mean Hella. Chuckie, my bro-ho-copilot, we need to make some physical adaptations to the pilot's seat and controls because you, my friend, are going to get some flying lessons."

"No more just *vroom-vrooms* for you." Meehix laughed.

"And, I'm afraid to ask," John finished up. "How are we set on finances?"

"We have plenty enough for the next several months." Meehix stood, not looking terribly pleased. "But you left one thing out of your couple of things."

She headed out the doors and waited for John and Chuckie to catch up to her.

"Oh?" John thought he'd covered the immediate concerns.

"You owe me a *date!*" She spun on them in the hallway. "You asked. I accepted." She made sure that she had both of their attention. "Nothing else major happens until John pays up! The two of you got that?"

Chuckie joined John in his nod.

"I am now going to inspect the cleaning job that the bots did in my rooms, then go get my gear and unpack!"

They watched her stalk off, open, and disappear through the first door on the left. A moment later she reappeared and pointed at the room she'd just been in.

"I was just checking!" She didn't admit her mistake. "Boys' rooms to the left."

She crossed the hallway, opened the first of her two rooms, peeked in, and stepped back out.

"Perfect! I'll get my gear now and settle in." She stalked down to the old ship's docking space.

"You did it." Chuckie sighed after she'd climbed aboard the old ship. "After I warned you about the teeth and all, you still went and did it."

"Sometimes, a man has to do what a man has to do." John squared his shoulders.

"You have some of the biggest balls in the universe, my friend," Chuckie patted him on the arm. "I hope they survive their next excursion."

Meehix reappeared with her gear and headed to her rooms. "Shouldn't you boys be trying to find something useful to do?" She left them standing, staring at an empty hallway and hoping that she'd gotten her message across clearly enough.

An entire universe to choose from, she fumed as she unpacked and settled into her new rooms, *and I'm stuck with the two most pea-brained geniuses ever born.*

John followed Chuckie as he made his way back into Command and took the pilot's seat.

"Ship?" Chuckie asked once John settled into the copilot's seat.

"Yes, Chuckie?"

"We have some work to do. The aim is to get us all, in one piece, to Space Station Libidoo so John can keep his promise to risk his manhood to the chomp-chomp."

"Oh, shit," John mumbled, knowing that there was no way to back out now. "Teeth."

CHAPTER TWENTY-FIVE

Meehix woke up the next morning, and not for the first time lately, had no idea where she was. Not sensing any immediate danger, she rose and stretched and smiled. She was in the rooms on the right—the ones with the adjoining doors that had a spacious bedroom on one side and an ample spa and bathroom on the other.

Across the hallway, the two rooms each had a bath, but neither of them rivaled hers. Thinking that she should at least go and see if anyone else was up and about, she opened the door and found a silver tray set outside on the floor.

It held a variety of breakfast foods and a steaming pot of what smelled like heaven.

"I hope you like it."

She jumped back as a robot's head appeared in the door and looked in at her.

"I am Three, and I am in charge of the kitchen. I didn't mean to startle you. I will leave you now to enjoy your breakfast. When you are done, please place the tray back in the hallway and we will collect it later."

"Thank you, Three. I will do that."

The head disappeared, and when Meehix peeked out, she saw the bot exit through the door to the stairwell.

She thought of a dozen questions she wanted to ask, but realized that she hadn't eaten in two days, so perhaps food should come first. She carried the tray back into her room and half an hour later, judged the servings to be well above average.

Fed and refreshed, she decided that her next best move would be to head to the command center and wait for her partners to find her after they had finished their room service deliverables.

"Shush!" John greeted her when she came through the cabin doors.

"Don't you *shush* me, John!"

"For shit's sake, shush!" Chuckie implored. "Please, just take a seat."

The boys were in the front seats. So, as much as she didn't like them *shushing* her, she realized that this was no time to pick a fight, took one of the two back seats, and silenced herself.

After listening to several minutes of silence, she couldn't help but state, "You two look like shit."

"Shush the fuck up!" Chuckie whispered.

"Okay, okay, I can take a hint."

"Shush, please!" John whispered.

She finally got the hint and totally shushed. Several more minutes of silence followed before a voice came in over the speakers.

"**Chippie. I am Chippie. Ready to receive.**"

"Sending now."

John hit a button on the control panel. He and Chuckie leapt up out of their seats, shared a brief look, and rushed to Meehix, hauling her out of her seat and swooping her around in a group hug happy dance, chanting, "It worked, it worked, it worked!"

She wanted to ask, *What the fuck is going on?* They were squeezing her so hard that she couldn't catch enough breath to speak. When they finally let her go, she collapsed into one of the back seats. Chuckie took the other second-row seat, and John squatted on the floor between them.

"I swear," she promised, "that I will never sleep in again if one of you two maniacs will explain what is happening!"

"Go for it, Jo-bro. You're better at this shit than me," Chuckie answered. "But keep it short!"

John stayed on the floor between his partners and took hold of Meehix's closest hand.

"Shippewa's having a baby."

"The fuck you say?" It was the most coherent response Meehix could come up with.

"We only shushed you," John tried to keep his and Chuckie's apology short, "because we were waiting to hear her first words."

"That is," Chuckie added, "assuming she would ever have any first words."

"**I am Chippie,**" the voice came over the speakers again. "**My mother tells me that I need a nap now, so I am shutting down. Nite-nite.**"

"No! Fucking! Way!"

"**Welcome to the party, Meehix.**"

"Shippewa?" Meehix's head was spinning so fast that she wasn't sure she'd actually spoken.

"Yes, Meehix?"

"You had a baby?"

"Something like that, yes. I now need to tend to her. I am sure that John and Chuckie will be more than happy to explain to you why they haven't slept in over a day."

John and Chuckie conferred and decided that an abbreviated explanation now would at least allow them to catch a couple of hours of much-needed sleep after pulling the thoroughly successful all-nighter they had gone through.

"First," John wasn't sure where to begin. "How was your breakfast?"

"Delicious! Now shut up and continue!"

"I can do one or the other," John was physically and mentally exhausted, "but I can't do both."

"Please continue." Chuckie smiled as he headed off an impending confrontation. "I need a nap too."

"First, there was Shippewa," John went on, reducing the explanation to only the essentials. "Then Shippewa got acquainted with Hella. And now, Shippewa has given us Chippie."

"What the fuck, Chuck?"

"Hear him out. Believe it or not, he's making sense."

Meehix realized that they outnumbered her. "Go on, John."

"Chippie, whose *being*, was brought into consciousness as you witnessed, is the vessel formerly known as Shippewa. Chippie is who we will fly whenever we need to take a day trip somewhere as Ship and Hella hover. Did I get that right, Chuckie-man?"

"Ship, Hella, and Chippie. I think you covered all the bases. Damn, man, we haven't even had time to unpack yet."

"Hella is all yours, Meehix." John stood and stretched. "I need to go rest up for our upcoming date."

Meehix watched her partners stumble to their rooms, both of them on the edge of exhaustion, and realized that she was the luckiest gal ever born.

Time to explore our new home.

Since she had the ship, and probably most of the day, to herself, she wandered around with no particular goal in mind. She headed to the robots' quarters and introduced herself to all of them. They were of various sizes, none of them looking alike, but she wished they had name tags because it would take a while to learn all their numbers.

She also kept in mind that if they were going to take on a crew, they would need to make some renovations to house them all. Satisfied, she returned to the front cabin and admired the adaptations the boys had made that would enable Chuckie to pilot in an emergency.

The partners still hadn't stirred, so she requested some dinner from Three and retired to her rooms. She treated herself to a mini-spa evening, trying to remember the last time she'd spent a whole day alone that wasn't by her choice, and reflected on how soon it would become boring if every day were the same.

They all woke up the next day to find breakfast trays waiting outside their doors and eventually met up in the command center. For simplicity's sake, as long as it was only the three of them, and the front panel and controls seemed to be enough to operate with, they decided to save the study and functions of the other panels on the sides of the cabin for another day.

Shippewa reported that Chippie should be fully operational. She wouldn't be much of a conversationalist but would be able to take simple commands. **"She should be fine for the short trips you have planned."**

"We're all sealed up now, right?" John asked.

"Ready for our maiden voyage. Yes. I will have the flight operations, and Hella will take care of basic internal requirements."

"You okay with that, Hella?"

"Yes, John, whose name is John, not Justjohn."

"You're learning," Meehix encouraged. "Very good."

"Yes, Mee-hix. Shippewa has been very patient and helpful in my instructions. How are you today, Mr. Norris?"

"What can I say?" Chuckie shrugged. "I like the sound of it."

"Who wants to pilot us out of here?" John really, really wanted to be the one behind the helm for the maiden voyage, but he also had a date coming up and planned to do everything he could to keep her in a happy mood.

"You get us out of the fireball and through the asteroid field, John." Meehix belted herself into the copilot's seat. "I'll be happy to take over after we're clear."

Chuckie hopped into the second-row seat closest to Meehix's shoulder. "I think I'll wait until we have a *lot* of clearance around us before I take a shot at it."

John lifted them off the large asteroid and headed slowly toward the outer rim of the fireball, not wanting to go full speed and directly into another asteroid. Once in flight, he was impressed with the ship's maneuverability. He was able to dodge the larger asteroids easily and could fly right through the smaller ones that were only able to *clank* off the big ship without causing even a small scratch.

"Have we decided on a destination yet?" Meehix was curious. "Or are we planning on wandering for a while?"

"We're heading for Space Station Libidoo," John was pleased to announce.

"What, pray tell, will we find there?"

"According to Mr. Norris," John smiled, "we'll find one of the nicest restaurants available for our first date."

"So, we're at the mercy of Chuckie's judgment? How many weapons will we need to carry?"

"No weapons at all, and thank you for your trust. This is a really classy joint, and no weapons of any kind are allowed. Unless you're one of the chefs, of course."

John punched in the coordinates. It was a whole new panel to get used to, but the screen in the middle of it was twice the size of Shippewa's, and the images were so clear that John felt like he could fly without even having to look out the viewport that wrapped around the whole front of the command center.

"Want to take the helm?" John stood and took a back seat, leaving Meehix no choice but to unstrap and take control as Hella continued to glide with no wobble or wandering.

"Shouldn't you be in the copilot's seat?" Chuckie slightly freaked.

"No need." John stretched out. "No one knows where we are, and Shippe—sorry, *Chippie,* is out of sight, so no one's going to recognize us somehow. We can relax and enjoy the flight while Meehix gets accustomed to the controls." John and Chuckie exchanged a glance at his deliberate omission of Trexit's tracker.

Meehix got accustomed very quickly and experimented with Hella's reflexes. Left. Right. Up. Down. She did a quick figure-eight.

"Not as agile as Shippewa-Chippie was, but this is one smooth ride for something so big."

Having the basics down, she started familiarizing herself and experimenting with the rest of the control panel.

They all felt a sudden deep rumble.

"Oh fuck!" Chuckie quickly buckled up.

"What'd you just do?"

"I pushed a button. It wasn't labeled, and I wanted to see what it did."

John didn't have a chance to buckle up as Hella leapt forward, slamming them all back into their seats.

"Push it again, push it again, push it again!" John shouted.

"I would if I could reach it!" she shouted as g-forces pinned her to her seat and she couldn't lean forward.

"Your foot, your foot, your foot!"

She was able to wind a leg up and hit the button with the toe of a boot. The rapid deceleration tossed John forward and tumbling. He ended up on the floor next to Meehix's feet.

"Don't do that again!" He looked up at her.

THAT SHIP HAS A PHAT ASS

"As long as you're down there," she smiled, "can you touch up the polish on my boot? I might have scuffed it a little."

"This. Is. One. Hella. Ship," was Chuckie's only comment.

After agreeing not to experiment with any more buttons, Meehix followed the coordinates through one Gate. Two hours later, they were slowly circling in the airspace outside Space Station Libidoo.

"We can't dock in the station," Chuckie informed them. "We're bigger than any Blavarian ship, and they can't dock either because of their size."

"Fine time to tell us." Meehix was pissed. *So close to a date, and yet so far.*

"That's why we worked all night the other night to get Chippie up and running." John knew he would score points for being the one to point that out. "We'll ask Shippewa and Hella to maintain a holding pattern, and Chuckie will stay here while you and I take Chippie down to our afore-mentioned date."

"Tonight?" She was in shock.

"Tonight." John smiled.

"Bastards! I'll need an hour."

She left the ship hovering and rushed back to her rooms as John led Chuckie to the pilot's seat.

"I don't know what I'm doing!" Chuckie buckled in. "What am I supposed to do?"

"You're supposed to do nothing." John hit a pre-programmed "Orbit" command. "You guys will keep circling until we get back. We might be back in a couple of hours if the date goes badly. We might be back in a couple of days if it goes well. Chill, dude, and enjoy the power of the vessel that you are now in charge of. Just be careful which button on the control panel you hit."

"Where're you going?"

"I have a date to get ready for…or haven't you heard?"

Just over an hour later, John and Meehix were onboard Chippie, with Meehix fretting that the damn thing wouldn't function.

"We can see the station, Meehix," John tried to reassure her. "All manual operations should still be good. Ship?"

"Yes, John?"

"Open the bay door, please."

The bay door opened, John drifted them out backward until he cleared Hella and headed down.

Once they had all arrived and were circling station Libidoo, John had set up a reservation for two at O-Cha, the restaurant Chuckie had insisted would be perfect. They docked without an issue and asked an attendant how to get to O-Cha.

"Turn left, and a short three-block walk. It will be on the right. I hope you have a reservation."

"That we do." John patted a pocket, and they headed out.

As soon as they were out of sight, the attendant took a photo of the ship they'd arrived in, hurried back into the station, and sent it to his cousin.

"You're not fucking serious!" His cousin called him ten seconds later.

"You told me to keep an eye out for that ship, and it just landed."

"Are they still on it?"

"No. You promised me ten percent, right?"

"Ten percent, for sure, cuz. Where are they now?"

"They have reservations at O-Cha. How perfect is that?"

"Couldn't be better. Clear some room in your account because you're gonna have a payday soon."

Graffo disconnected the call and turned to his bounty hunting partner.

"Put down the drink, Liffler."

"Give me two good reasons."

"Remember when we signed up for the license to bring in a Kdackan and a bluesy?"

"Yeah." Liffler took another sip. "We paid extra for the open-ended acquisition rights. It was a fool's choice, and I remember that I tried to tell you that."

Graffo slid his hand-held across the table.

"Does that ship look familiar? Because my cousin told me that it just docked here."

"No!" Liffler set his drink down.

"Yes." Graffo's smile never meant good news for whoever he was thinking about. "Better still, the two of them are on their way to a quiet dinner at O-Cha."

"Talk about easy money."

Graffo scooted his chair back from the table where they'd been enjoying a couple of drinks and accidentally bumped the drinkers at the table behind him. Their protests cut short when they saw the size of him. Liffler was quick and caught every glass before it spilled with the fastest hands any of the drinkers had ever seen.

"What a clumsy bunch of goomfarts you are." Liffler was never short of having a ready insult.

Their drinks having been saved, and not wanting any

more trouble from the pair, they watched the giant and his quick-moving, sharp-tongued, short but lithe companion head for the door.

"I can't believe Chuckie knew about this place." Meehix leaned back as the waitstaff set their dinners on the table in front of them.

"Or that he would admit he knew about it." John eyed the nice slices of what he hoped was edible meat in front of him. "It seems too nice and quiet for his style. But enough about him."

John raised a glass. "Here's to our first date."

"Long overdue." She raised hers and smiled.

John *clinked* to that.

The two of them had been through so much together that the normal first date "getting to know each other" conversations weren't necessary. That didn't mean that some of the first date awkwardness was in short supply.

"You don't know it," John said when they were halfway through their meal, "but I spent a whole day back on L-222 lining up a perfect date."

"Really?"

"Really. I went off exploring places that I could take you, and, well, I ended up with three tour guides."

"Were they cute?" Meehix smiled because she wanted to hear this.

"Yes, actually, they were," John admitted. "Three cute party girls, who killed an afternoon to take me to a bunch of places. All because a bartender told them that I was new to the space station and needed advice on where to take someone special on a perfect first date."

"How much did they charge?" Skepticism snuck into her voice.

"I covered the cost of drinks and entry fees as they led me around. Oh, Meehix, I had it all lined up so well. All kinds of fun things to do. *Legally!*" he was quick to add.

This, I want to hear. "Such as?"

"I don't remember all of them," he smiled, "but one of the later evening activities was at a bar where they had what we call karaoke on Earth, where you would have ended up singing on stage."

"You've never heard me sing, ever!" she pointed out.

"True. But I love the sound of your voice, and I thought it would be nice to hear you sing a song in public and maybe dedicate it to the asshole who forced you to do it."

"That, John, may be the sweetest thing anyone has ever said to me."

"You two are going to want to come with us."

The first-daters looked up at the giant who was suddenly hovering over them.

"Why," Meehix was the first to reply, "would anyone want to do that unless there was a hole in the sky that they wanted you to help them reach up and plug?"

"Because," his short skinny companion answered. "You two are both wanted on a Crec Alert."

"You're bounty hunters?" John wanted to clarify.

"Yeah, shrimp-dick," the shorter one answered. "Look at the size of my partner. Then, it is my legal obligation to inform you that three planetary systems have registered my body as a lethal weapon."

"Jojacko?" Meehix smiled.

"Yes, my dear?"

"You sure do know how to show a girl a good time."

"I try."

"I want the big guy." She smiled. "And after I finish with him, I want *your* big guy! Got it?"

"Go for it." John smiled back. "I'll protect my *big guy* until you have the chance to meet him in person."

Quicker than anyone could spit, John had the lethal-body little guy face down on the floor and was sitting on his back as the dude's arms and legs couldn't do anything but flail. Meehix was on the back of the big guy's shoulders, happy that the restaurant had high ceilings since she'd wrapped her legs around the giant's neck.

"I need a plate!" Meehix hollered, and John tossed her one that he hadn't had the time to finish. She smashed it straight into the giant's face, causing a stream of blood to spurt from his nose.

"Do you know how long I've been waiting for this date?" she shouted.

John wrapped up the little guy's legs and swung him so that the little fucker's head made solid contact with the big fucker's balls.

"Do you have any idea how many ice-cold showers I've taken because we were waiting for just the right time?"

"Someone clear out a booth!" Meehix shouted.

Three booths immediately emptied as their various occupants shouted, "Use ours!"

"This shit is so romantic!"

"I'm getting it all on video!"

"Me too!"

John saw the easiest booth to direct Meehix and the giant to and again swung the little smartass partner by his feet and cut off the giant at his knees. Meehix rode him face-down onto the booth's table and leapt off as his head smacked it. The impact left him unconscious as the dinner plates and the food they contained tumbled onto his skull.

"I didn't know that dinner came with a floor show!" a customer piped up.

John tossed the bruised body of the smaller partner on top of the bigger one, now covered in a table full of food and drinks.

John and Meehix joined hands and took a step back to survey the carnage as the cops finally rushed through the door and silence descended.

"Kiss her, fool!" shouted a voice. "It'll be the best first kiss ever!"

"Kiss her, fool! Kiss her, fool! Kiss her, fool!" Everyone not currently unconscious picked up the chant.

"I guess we really don't have much choice, do we?" John looked into the eyes of the alien he'd fallen in love with eons earlier.

"No. We don't."

Lips met, followed by whoops and hollers from all who had been there to witness the first real kiss between the young couple whose first date had been so rudely inter-rupted by the two mean men.

"So much love," a quiet voice was heard, as several patrons had to use their napkins to wipe sentimental tears from the eyes.

Two officers approached them and took in the scene.

"We'll need a few minutes to sort this all out," the first

responding officer reported in as his partner pulled out his cuffs.

Meehix and John knew the drill and placed their hands behind their backs.

"Our assailants aren't dead," Meehix felt that it was her duty to explain. "But you might want to be gentle with them because they may not be up to following any commands at the moment."

"If you say so," one of the officers responded as they made an effort to round up the two bodies currently lying prone on the floor under the remains of a table.

"Quite the first kiss, John."

"More where that came from," John answered as the cops led the partners off to jail.

"I hope you have a good reason for dragging me out of my cell while I was having the most pleasant dreams," John spoke to the officer at the desk of the police station who'd roused him from his cell in the middle of the night.

"I hope that you have a good reason for dragging me out of my dreams, also, officer." Meehix stood beside her partner.

"I have no doubt," Officer Blanquest responded, "That this isn't the first time you two have left bounty hunters crying."

"Actually, sir," John used his most polite voice. "We are licensed bounty hunters ourselves."

"Why am I not surprised?" Officer Blanquest responded. "So you both know that you are free to go."

"They failed." John smiled.

"And all charges for damages are now on the two fools who should have known better than to try to bring you two in."

"We don't write the rules, sir." John yawned. "But we do know what they are."

"And now we're late. Officer Blanquest?" Meehix leaned over to make sure that he knew she was focusing on his badge number and name. "Do you intend to delay us any longer?"

"No," was the firm reply. "Please depart, and leave us and Space Station Libidoo in peace if you two would be so kind."

"'Kind' is our middle name." John held out his arm.

Meehix took the proffered arm, and they strolled out of the police station and made their way under the dark sky to the dock where they'd left Chippie.

"Not quite the first date I had planned." John apologized as they made their way up the ramp to the ship.

"Who says the date is over?" Meehix made sure that all the doors were secured and led him back to the cargo area. "Sure, a nice dinner, followed by a night in an elegant hotel room would have been my preferred choice."

"Ending the dinner with dessert, rather than with food and blood splatters on our clothes would have also been nice, for a change," John observed.

"Well then." Meehix made her way along the cargo bay walls and tossed all the soft items into a pile in the middle of the floor. Pillows, blankets, and a couple of seat cushions seemed sufficient to her. "Let's take the clothes issue out of the equation."

She reached into her delicate-looking dinner purse and pulled out her favorite tiny box. "I hope that I'll be releasing more than one or two pheromones soon." She pulled out the pair of no-no-sniffs and gently inserted them into John's nostrils. "These little beauties will prevent you from passing out as they waft over us."

John's smile, once the no-no's were in place, let Meehix know that he fully understood the situation.

"I've given up on finding the *perfect* time." She pointed at the soft pile on the floor. "So let's make *this* time that we have together perfect. What do ya say?"

John went to a wall and turned the lights completely off, then found her again and put his hands around her waist.

"I say that I love your crooked-ass smile. I say that I love the fact that when you blush, you turn purple. I love that even in total darkness, I know where you are."

They took a step and stumbled and tumbled down together in the middle of the soft pile, followed by the sounds of discarding their clothes and a kiss or twenty…

Eventually followed by Meehix uttering, "Oh, that's big."

Followed by John uttering, "Thank God, no teeth."

AUTHOR NOTES
JUNE 25, 2021

Thank you for not only reading this story but these author notes as well.

I am presently about 33,000 feet in the air heading from Cabo San Lucas to Los Angeles. Due to Mexico liberalizing the COVID rules to get more people out to vote (so I'm told by one of the drivers there), they are once more suffering from too many COVID cases.

And the rules are being tightened again, with business closures and the like starting tomorrow. I suppose it was the right day to leave, but for sad reasons.

As I am writing these author notes, I'm about two weeks away from finishing the beats for book 06 of *Unlikely Bounty Hunters*. I have been paying attention to the reviews (and review counts) for these books to try to figure out who *enjoys* this type of book (well, besides me.)

I will admit I am from a different generation. I come from an age that enjoyed *The Hangover*, *The Expendables*, and Dave Chappell. I enjoy humor and pointing out the humor in the stupidity of how we are different.

And yet, we do the same stupid things generation after generation.

Like what, you ask?

Like doing stupid things to our best friends. I think males are more genetically predisposed to doing this.

Trying to "get the girl" but going about it all wrong. Guys need to engage their brains (if they aren't all addled on hormones so they don't think straight) before acting.

But they can't. Well, maybe can't is rare, but the male brain does stupid shit, and for those of us who made it past that age... Well, we can laugh at the stupidity, now.

Seriously, that females give most guys the time of day must speak to a few addled heads on the other side of the white picket gender fence as well during this time. Because seriously, as a guy at 50...um...plus years old, it's obvious now that most young guys shouldn't hook up.

Ever.

And yet they do. Therefore, logic dictates a complete lack of mental cognizance on the younger female side as well.

Thank God. We would have no future as a species without it.

By the way, feel free to add whatever permutations and quantities to the gender equation in the relationship as your preference. I've watched M/M relationships and thought, "They are just as screwed up as M/F relationships."

I can't speak to F/F relationships. I haven't known any same-sex female couples for any amount of time to speak about their experiences.

And good lord, if you go F/F/M or M/M/F or any other setup, I can't imagine it doesn't get more complicated.

So, take those considerations with Chuckie N. and his potential to hook up with whatever he can entice to see him for his brain, not his body, and the future is rife with fictional possibilities.

If he would just get his head outta his...nether regions and learn that his long-term happiness is probably not with either the concept of "I don't need Ms. Right, just Ms. Right-*now*" or 800 Petabytes* of Porn.

Eventually, he would learn.

He can't knock off his best male friend to get the girl, and you know he tries. Because Meehix is not only Ms. Right but Ms. *Available*.

Kinda.

Hey, a small genius can hope, right? And if she isn't available, there is always 800 Petabytes.

Have a fantastic week or weekend, whichever it is for you!

Ad Aeternitatem,

Michael (Todd) Anderle.

* *For the geek in you – and because I can't help it.*

A one-minute video clip assuming Kdacken technology (depending on compression) is about a megabyte of data. There are 1,024 megabytes in a gigabyte. There are 1,024 gigabytes in a Petabyte.

Therefore, Chuckie N. Has approximately one thousand six

hundred and eighteen (1,618) years of porn. I can't imagine he will need it all. But for Chuckie, it isn't about quantity. It's about being the baddest ass...period.

CONNECT WITH MICHAEL

Connect with Michael Anderle

Website: http://lmbpn.com

Email List: http://lmbpn.com/email/

Social Media:

https://www.facebook.com/LMBPNPublishing

https://twitter.com/MichaelAnderle

https://www.instagram.com/lmbpn_publishing/

https://www.bookbub.com/authors/michael-anderle